Chosen

Chosen

Lesley Glaister

**Tindal
Street
Press**

First published in May 2010
by Tindal Street Press Ltd
217 The Custard Factory, Gibb Street,
Birmingham, B9 4AA
www.tindalstreet.co.uk

2 4 6 8 10 9 7 5 3 1

A CIP catalogue reference for this book is available
from the British Library

ISBN: 978 1 906994 05 1

Typeset by Alma Books Ltd
Printed and bound in the UK by
CPI Mackays, Chatham ME5 8TD

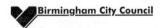

To Lawrence, Andy and Ginny with love

Chosen

DODIE

1

She stands on the dark front doorstep, shivering, listening to the sound of nothing happening inside. You can sense if there's someone in a house and there must be someone here – Stella never leaves the place. But that doesn't stop the awful feeling that there's no one here: no one who's breathing.

A weird red dress, Seth said. She should have taken more notice. He'd been round at her house after school one day last week – Wednesday? Thursday? He'd come through the door and dropped his school bag on the floor, as he often did, to scrounge something from the fridge – and to put off going home to Stella.

Crowing with delight, Jake had toddled over to Seth, to be swung, shrieking joyfully, into the air. Four-thirtyish, it must have been. That time when the day starts to collapse into a blur of mess and fretfulness, towards food and bed and bath and stories and at long, long last, quiet and a glass of wine.

So she hadn't paid much attention.

'But, will you babysit on Friday?' She definitely had asked that.

'I'll text you.' He'd grinned – and they both knew that meant yes. He loved to babysit, to get to eat pizza in front of the TV with a can of beer and his feet up on the coffee table – something Stella would never allow, not in a million years.

He'd put Jake down, gone to the fridge for milk. She'd watched his long knobbly fingers, clever fingers that could mend anything. He liked nothing better than to take a machine apart and put it back together.

And then he said: 'Mum's gone weird.'

'*Gone* weird!' Dodie said. 'And don't swig from the carton.'

With his sleeve, he wiped the milky moustache from his handsome face – well, potentially handsome, with his dark blue eyes, and humorous quirky mouth. 'Weirder than usual.' He burped sonorously. 'She's got this dress hanging in the hall. A red dress, like a *weird* red dress.'

'What's weird about it?' she asked, but at that moment Jake fell over and cracked his head on the table leg and then the phone rang for Rod and she had to go and get him out of his shed, and then . . . well it was all busy and hot and Seth had gone to lie on the floor and play trains with Jake, keeping him out from under her feet while she peeled the spuds.

And she'd forgotten about the dress, though in miniature it has been swaying somewhere at the back of her mind ever since: a red dress hanging in that cold bleak hall.

No one's going to open the door. The streetlamp shines a dappled light through the dripping branches of the laburnum on the wet pebbledash. She braces herself to go down the darker, dank side passage. The garden gate squeals, grating on its hinges. She stops and runs her finger inside one of the wrought iron twiddles, picking up a scratch of rust. *You'll get lockjaw*, Stella used to warn her – that lockjaw smell of swing chains, seesaws, seasick. She stands looking up at the back of the house, but there's no sign of life: just blank, black windows with the rain sluicing down.

She returns to the front doorstep, pressing her finger continuously on the bell and rat-tat-tatting with the fox-head doorknocker that used to scare her with its snarl. She opens the letter box, catching her finger in the sharp bristles behind it, angles her head down and calls, 'Mum, *Mum!*'

Seth had definitely said he'd text about the babysitting, but he didn't, and so she'd come round on Friday afternoon to find him. Rain gurgles and drips from the gutter – as it did on Friday – and a greenish mould spreads map-like from a leak in the drainpipe. Ask Rod to fix that, she thinks, though he wouldn't and she won't. Her stupid teeth are chattering. She will have to go back into that darkness, down the garden to the shed and get the key – but she puts off the moment, remembering how it went on Friday afternoon.

She'd stood here then, knocking and ringing and eventually giving up and trying round the back. But that time there had been a light in the downstairs window, and she'd seen the curtain twitch. 'Mum!' she'd called. 'I know you're in there.' Eventually the door had opened and Stella had stood hunched above her on the step.

'Going to let me in then?' Dodie said, and when Stella hesitated, 'What? You got a fancy man in there?'

Stella stepped back to allow her in. Dodie pushed down her hood and scrabbled her fingers through her hair. 'You look nice.' She took a closer look at her mother. For years Stella had crept about in a filthy dressing gown, but today she was tattily splendid in the weird red dress – which wasn't so weird, just ancient and ethnic of some sort – but weird, certainly, to see her so attired. Her hair, usually a mass of greasy rats' tails, was washed and fluffy and there was kohl smudged round her startling grey eyes.

Stella squeezed out a smile. She might have been dressed up but the kitchen was the same as ever: chilly, bleach scented, a trace of dope hanging in the air. As if checking for continuity, Dodie's eyes had ticked off the normal things: the tea cosy – a knitted cottage – derelict now; the potato masher with its split wooden handle; the giant scissors that could snip through bones. But there was also a carrot, half-chopped on a wooden board.

'Cooking?' Dodie said, surprised. Stella hadn't, to her knowledge, cooked for years.

'Soup,' Stella said. 'Thought I might.'

They stood in the tiny kitchen like actors in need of a prompt.

'You could offer me a cup of tea,' Dodie suggested and Stella turned – so thin that, from behind, the dress looked empty – to fill the kettle, before she led Dodie through into the dining room. On the table, as always, there was a puzzle, this time a view of Venice. It was almost completed, just a few jagged islands left to fill – a bit of sky, part of a façade, the curved prow of a gondola.

Dodie shivered and huddled into her jacket. 'Why don't you put the fire on?' The overhead light was a bleak 40 watts, flattening and ageing, seeming to drain everything it illuminated of light.

'Did you want anything in particular?' Stella asked.

'Actually I'm looking for Seth. He in?'

Stella went back into the kitchen, a fusty, patchouli smell coming off the old velvet as she passed. The one-handed clock showed it was gone five and Seth's schoolbag was on the floor, but if he was in he'd have come bounding downstairs by now.

'Seth told me about the dress. Why *are* you all dolled up, anyway?' Dodie said, studying the puzzle.

Stella returned with a mug of tea, centred it on a coaster on the table. She'd kept that table immaculate for years, an island of shine among the rest of the mean, dull furniture.

'He's out,' Stella said, avoiding her eyes.

'Out where?' Dodie said. 'Aren't you having one?'

Stella gnawed the corner of her thumbnail.

'Are you OK?' Dodie asked. She watched Stella frowning at the puzzle. Dodie spotted a piece, the gondolier's stockinged shin, and her fingers twitched. Half her childhood was spent here, like this, hunched over a puzzle, her reflection floating deep beneath her in the shine of the rosy wood.

'Mum, where is he? See, he's meant to be babysitting tonight but I can't get hold of him.' She took a sip of weak, bleachy tea.

'Not here to see *me* then?'

'That too, of course, Mum. Has he lost his phone or something?'

Stella ripped at her cuticle and a bead of blood appeared beside her thumbnail. She licked it off and Dodie looked away, watching her own hand pick up the piece and fit it in. *There.* Satisfaction at the snugness of the fit. The striped trousers distinctive; she immediately saw another bit.

'You know that if I thought you wanted to see me, I'd come more often.' She looked up at Stella but the face was closed, the winter-coloured eyes unreadable. There was a creak on the stairs and Dodie looked up at the ceiling.

'*Is* he here?'

'No.'

'What's that then?'

'The pipes?'

'Where is he?' Dodie insisted, but Stella only shrugged. No point trying to get round her if she wanted to be like that. Dodie went to the foot of the stairs, looked up, and called Seth's name – but there was no response, just cold gloom and she couldn't bear it. Besides, she had to get back and pick Jake up. She didn't have time for this.

Stella called her, and she went back into the dining room, irritated.

'What?'

'Help me.'

'*What,* Mum?'

Stella's eyes were wide, mouth opening on a half-formed word.

'*What?*'

'The puzzle,' she said. 'Only that. I want to get it finished.' Her fingers were trembling and she wound a strand of hair round one of her bitten finger-ends.

'I've got to go,' Dodie said. 'Tell Seth I'm expecting him at eight.' She kissed Stella's cheek, and felt the tension quivering through her.

'Dodie?' Stella said.

'I'll have to run for my bus. What?' Dodie opened the back door onto the rain, pulled up her hood and tucked her hair inside. Stella came to stand beside her on the step. '*What?*'

'I . . .' Stella extended her hand as if to touch Dodie, something that she hadn't done voluntarily for years.

'*What?*' Had the irritation shown in her voice? She looked at the rain glistening on Stella's outstretched palm. 'Come on, Mum, I'm getting soaked.'

'Oh, nothing.'

'Sure?'

Stella wiped her hand on her skirt and – sort of – smiled.

'I'm off, then,' Dodie said.

'Goodbye Dodie.'

'Bye Mum.'

That was Friday and this is Monday and she's still heard nothing from Seth. And he's always round at the weekend. Of course, she should have gone upstairs when she heard the noise; she shouldn't have let Stella fob her off like that, like always. She steps back to look at the rain streaming down the dark window-glass. She will have to get the key and go inside and find out what's wrong.

It's horrible going down the dark side of the house again, squeaking though the gate, stepping across the long soggy grass and snagging brambles to the shed, where the spare key should be hanging on a nail. The shed door creaks open on the smell of flower-pots and spiders and there are webs there, in the dark, where she must put her hand. From a neighbouring garden there's the half-hearted detonation of a firework going off, though Guy Fawkes was weeks ago. She presses her fists against her mouth before she can steel herself to feel about in the darkness. Her fingers tangle in a resistant softness before she finds the key, unhooks it from its nail and hurries round to the front of the house, grateful to be back in the wavery street-light. She scrubs her fingers fiercely against her jeans to rid them of the sticky sensation of cobwebs before she lifts the key and fits it in the lock.

2

She knows what she will see before she sees it. Once she's twisted the key, the door swings open and the streetlight illuminates in patches the bruisy velvet of the hanging dress. Her eyes flinch in their sockets, her fingers press against her lips. It's too dark inside to see properly. She reaches round to the switch, and in the sudden blare of light her eyes slide everywhere before she can make them rest on the central thing.

The rope is blue; over the head a brown paper bag; the fingers are curled and purple; the toes beneath the velvet hem are dusky. The bag looks comical with its poking corners, and a laugh like a curd of something sour catches in Dodie's throat. There's a strong smell of patchouli oil and a stain on the carpet. She shuts the door, turns her back to it, her hand going for her phone.

'Come,' she says to Rod, '*now*, and don't bring Jake.' And then rings off. She supposes she should call the police. Too late for an ambulance. There's something ludicrous and melodramatic about dialling 999. 'A body,' she says, giving the address. 'A suicide,' and her voice splinters on the word *mother*.

She slides down the door and crouches with her chin on her knees, arms clamped round her legs. Beside her is the old cow milk crate, its tail a pointer: *0 Pintas Today Milkman Please!*

Earlier in the day Rod told her he was leaving her. Timing, she thinks, the curd in her throat again, perfect timing. She'd rushed out to see Stella in order get out of there, to get away from him. If he hadn't said he was leaving, she'd have stayed at home and Stella would still be dangling undiscovered. Or Seth might have found her. Thank God, it hadn't been Seth. But his head teacher couldn't be right. 'Seth's gone to stay with your relatives in America,' he'd said when she rang him that morning. *America?* What relatives?

Rain patters on her hood and falls like interference against the light. Over the road a porch lamp glows cheery and innocent. It's not late, though it feels like midnight or past midnight or no time; it feels like no recognizable time at all. The police will be gearing up to investigate. Rod will be trying to find a babysitter.

'Let's have a drink,' Rod had said, once she'd done the dishes and Jake was in his cot – though he knew she was trying not to drink on Mondays or most Tuesdays.

'*America.*' Dodie had picked up a J-cloth and swatted half-heartedly at some crumbs on the high-chair tray. 'Why would he go to America? The head teacher said we had relatives there, but we *don't*, not that I know of.'

'Dodie?'

'And why didn't Mum say?'

Rod thumped his fist down on the table. '*Dodie.*'

'What?'

She knew what he was going to say, such a cliché she was embarrassed for him: 'We need to, you know, talk.' And then he glugged his beer with the relief of having said it.

She opened Jake's feeder-cup and watched the dregs of milk go down the drain.

He sat at the kitchen table then got up again. He finished the can and squashed it flat. The room was too small for him, too small for pacing about in.

'Christ, I need a smoke.' He opened the back door. Jake's plastic toys glowed in the rainy yard. The crusty old hydrangea heads glittered like disco balls in the spilled kitchen light. He stood just outside the door so the smoke, mingled with the rainy air, flowed inside.

'You might as well smoke in here,' she grumbled. Rod stood with his back to her, filling the doorway; a big man with broad shoulders. 'Go on then,' she said.

He cleared his throat. 'I think I met someone,' he said.

The tap dripped. The clock ticked. There was a streak of something like tomato ketchup on the door of the fridge. 'Think?'

'OK. I *have* met someone.' He turned and she stared. He looked just the same: thick sandy hair and eyebrows, blondish stubble, caramel eyes, shiftily refusing to meet her own. He sucked the last breath out of his fag and ground it out on the step, before coming back inside.

'What I'm trying to say is . . . Christ, let's have a proper drink.' He uncorked a bottle of Shiraz, splashed it into glasses and sat down at the tiny Formica table. There was just room for three, one each side and the high chair at the end. She sat opposite him and tried not to drink the wine.

'Why would he go to *America*?' she said. 'Why didn't he say anything?'

Rod reached across the table and took her hand. 'Forget Seth for a minute.' His leather sleeve got into something sticky and she was glad. She pulled her hand away.

'OK. Who is it?' she said.

'You don't know her,' he said, 'and nothing's happened and anyway, it's not that really. I mean it's not her. It's just that she, she's made me see . . .' He got out his plastic pouch of Drum and made a roll-up, his fingers trembling so that the tobacco spilled.

'See what?' She focused on the mole on his cheek that shifted up and down, just minutely, as he spoke.

'We hardly even knew each other when you got pregnant.'

'With your help.'

'And we never, like, made a real commitment, did we?' He licked his Rizla and rolled the paper tight. He finished his glass of wine and poured another.

'Didn't we?'

'Come on Dodie,' he said, 'you know how it was. I said I'd stick by you and I did and then you were ill, but now . . . It's not that I'm leaving you, I just need –'

'What about Jake?'

'– some headspace, you know? I'll always be here for Jake. I'm taking off.'

She bit the knuckle of her thumb. 'You'll always be here but you're taking off?'

'Got a flight to New Zealand.'

'You've *got* it?'

'It was a good deal. It was a now or never thing.'

She gave in and swigged her wine. 'When were you going to tell me?'

'Tonight. *Now*. I'm telling you.' He bared his teeth in an attempted smile. 'I'll only be gone a few weeks, a month. I promise. Three tops.'

'Three *months*?'

He shrugged. 'Round about.'

'So,' she said, 'you're leaving me. *Us*.'

'I just need to get my head together. You know I love Jake – and you.'

'When?'

'Coupla weeks.'

'Well, thanks for telling me.' There was a Le Creuset casserole dish on the shelf. She could easily have brained him. 'Is *she* going with you?' she asked.

'No! Shit, I shouldn't have mentioned that, it's just meeting her made me see I need a break, you know, time out.' He waved his long arms about. He was too big for her tiny terraced house; it had never fitted him.

She had to get out of there and she stood, shaking off his attempt to hold her. 'I'm going to make Stella tell me where Seth's gone,' she said, zipping up her jacket and cutting off his voice with a slam of the door.

There are more fireworks, a feeble celebration in the wet; she hears a laugh, catches a whiff of gunpowder. And Rod's taxi arrives, and behind it a police car. The blue light pulses over the wet privet hedge, making it surge and retreat like a wave.

When he sees the body, Rod begins to heave and goes to the downstairs toilet, which means dodging Stella's feet, which he misjudges, blundering against the legs and letting out a cry. The body rocks, the banister creaks. Dodie screws shut her eyes, sticks her fingers in her ears to block out the sounds of Rod retching and the faint rhythmic squeak of rope on banister.

A detective with a beige moustache takes an initial statement in the kitchen, and then leaves her with a policewoman, Donna, who makes tea. The carrot is still there on the chopping board, still half sliced.

'Did she live alone?' Donna asks. She has bubbly blonde curls and a face like a plastic dolly, way too pretty for her uniform.

Dodie hesitates. 'Yes. My brother used to live here, but he's in the States.' She's amazed how smoothly this comes out, as if it's normal and she's known it all the time. 'She's always been depressed. Sort of a bit ill. In the head.'

'Ah,' Donna says, cosily, 'a history of depression.'

Dodie hears the body being taken down. Rod comes back, face ashen. A guy takes her fingerprints, and Rod's, to rule them out. 'My brother's prints will be here as well,' she says. She tells Donna about Seth and the relatives in America.

'Address?' Donna says.

'I'd just popped round to get it from my mum.' *Popped*, she thinks, *popped*? She'd never say that, not in real life.

Donna gives her a curious look and jots busily. 'Empty nest syndrome?' she speculates.

'This her writing?' A policeman wearing maggot-coloured gloves holds the bag from Stella's head under Dodie's nose. *I die at my own hand and of my own free will. Stella M. Woods.* It's written on the bag, definitely in Stella's writing. 'Deceased two to three days,' he adds.

A police van comes to take the body away. 'Looks cut and dried to me,' Donna says. 'History of depression. Empty nest. Another cuppa? Shame there isn't any sugar.' Donna puts her cup down on the wood with no coaster; Stella would go mental. 'It's not up to me to speculate of course. There'll have to be an inquest.'

Dodie looks at the table. Stella's last puzzle – the sun glinting off the Grand Canal, the laugh of the handsome gondolier, the stripy stockings – is complete.

'I was here on Friday,' Dodie says. 'She was wearing the same dress.'

'How did she seem?'

'Weird,' Dodie says weakly.

'There you are then.'

'But she was . . .' she begins, *always weird* she nearly says, but it would seem disloyal. She starts to take apart the puzzle, then changes her mind, puts the pieces back one by one, there and there and there.

'You get home now,' Donna says. 'Get some sugar inside you. Or a stiff brandy.' She smiles and a dimple flickers in her cheek. 'Try and get some shut-eye.'

Rod takes her arm as they go out. A policeman drives them home. It's still raining and the wipers squeak a rhythm, *cut and dried, suicide, cut and dried, suicide*. 'You OK?' Rod says.

'I should have gone back,' she says. 'On Friday, she sort of reached out . . .'

'Don't go there.' Rod squeezes her knee as they round the corner.

The streets are all wet and glittering orange; the streetlights zizz past the windows like sparklers. In the house, Dodie runs straight up for a peek at Jake. Breathing, snug and warm and safe.

'What a little sweetheart,' the neighbour says, looking up from her knitting. 'Not a peep out of him, not a peep.' She finishes her row and squeaks her needles into the ball of yarn. 'I hope everything's all right?' Her nostrils lift, testing the air for gossip.

'Fine,' Dodie says firmly.

The neighbour waits, eyes sharpening behind her specs.

'We're shattered,' Rod says, and she takes the hint and leaves. 'Any time,' she says round the edge of the door. 'Little angel, up there, any time.'

'Thanks so much.' Dodie sinks down on a kitchen chair, elbows on the table. Rod's face is grey. A terrible shock for him too, of course, to see, actually to stumble into the corpse. That's an awful word. Not Stella any more, not a she or a her, but an it. A corpse in a velvet dress. Why would you start to cut up a carrot and then – but, *it*, despair, whatever, could strike as easily at that moment as at any other. It could strike you at any time. You could start chopping a carrot and then think, what for? What is the point of this? Your daughter could come round and then leave, leave you all alone with your half chopped carrot and –

'Coffee?' Rod suggests.

'This time of night?'

'Think we're going to sleep?' He flicks the kettle switch, tips the stale grounds out of the cafetière and into the sink.

'It's my fault.'

'Stop!' He holds up a hand almost as if he's about to strike her. 'She was depressed. She was ill. It was *nothing* to do with you. Say it.'

'It was nothing to do with me.'

Sometimes, she does love him despite –

She watches him spoon coffee, the bulk of him in her kitchen, the sexy shape of him. Will he still leave? The kettle clicks off. Rod fills the cafetière and fetches a bottle of Grouse and two mugs.

'Put some sugar in mine,' Dodie says, thinking of Donna's advice. Besides, it's nice with sugar. He stirs sugar into both and holds the bottle up.

'Why not?' It's like a treat, at nearly midnight. The strangest moments can become occasions. People do the strangest things. It can strike at the oddest moment or be calculated down to the last detail, is what the forensics man said. Halfway through a carrot is an odd moment all right, but he implied that he had seen odder.

'What if it wasn't suicide?' she says.

Rod sits down opposite her, hands cradled round his mug. '*What?* What are you saying? *Murder* you mean?'

Dodie takes a tiny sip. Sweet. Hot. Strong. 'Do you think they might think it's kind of suspicious that Seth's gone?'

He frowns at her. 'You're not saying you think *he's* got anything to do with it?'

She scalds her tongue on a slurp of coffee. 'Of course not!'

He shakes his head, exasperated.

'Seth would never hurt a fly,' she says.

'I *know*.' He adds more whisky to her coffee and his own. The alcohol and the hot coffee have pinked his face; his skin looks steamy.

'Of *course* it was suicide,' she says.

'I know.'

'How could you even think that about *Seth*? This is *Seth* we're talking about!'

'*You* mentioned him. Mind if I smoke inside? It's pissing down.'

Dodie stares at him and he eyeballs her right back. She runs upstairs to have another look at Jake, to shut his door and keep him safe from the smoke. He'll never remember Stella now. She bends to sniff his cheek, breathe in the soapiness of breath and skin. His eyelashes are such long, dark wings resting on the smooth roses of his cheeks. She nudges his shoulder and he wriggles and sighs. The sheet's a bit crumpled; she lowers the side of the cot to straighten it and his eyes snap open, stare at her blankly, bottom lip folding down.

'OK Jake,' she says, 'Mummy's here. *Hush little baby, don't say a word,*' she whisper-sings, '*Momma's gonna buy you a mockingbird.*' She watches till the thumb goes in and the lashes brush his cheeks again before she creeps out: stupid, guilty mother. To want to wake a sleeping child just because she needs comfort.

A mean niff of tobacco floats up the stairs. Inhaling, she goes down again, closes the door, feeling an urge herself. Exceptional circumstances.

'Roll me one?'

He raises one eyebrow and pulls out another Rizla. Dodie swallows the last of her coffee, squeezes a bit more from the cafetière. 'Anyway, *you've* felt like murdering Stella now and then,' Rod says. 'Anyone would.' He narrows his eyes and blows smoke in her face. They sit and sip and smoke. The fridge switches itself on with a panicky tremble. Stella is dead and Seth is missing and Rod is going away. The warmth of the whisky and the rush of the nicotine and caffeine send a flutter through her. None of it feels real at all. But Stella *is* really dead. Dusky toes under the velvet hem. Poor dead toes. Surely she should be crying? Did they think it suspicious that she didn't cry?

'I've got to let Seth know,' she says, standing then sitting down again with a bump, a rush of dizziness sweeping through her.

'Time for bed, Dodie,' Rod says.

'And *you* thinking it was him!' She tugs away as he tries to hold her. Tears splash down her face.

'Oh, don't be so fucking mental,' he snaps. He stomps off to the bathroom, leaving her there with the empty mugs and the spindly dog-ends in the saucer. She watches the tears land on the table. It's not like herself crying at all, it's like someone crying through her, or a natural phenomenon, like the rain.

3

It's a cold day. A cold day to be burnt on. Cold in the hall and the door sticks on the drift of post. Dodie stands and breathes: stale trapped breath, that faint cold whiff of bleach and incense. She forces herself to look at the place. Stella's head up there in the shadows, toes dangling right there, the creak of rope on wood. There's the stain on the carpet and fingerprint powder smudged on the banister but otherwise no sign that anything has happened. Breath held, she waits, to feel a presence, to feel something, fear or *anything*. But the atmosphere tells the truth. There's nothing. Only cold. The hall is just the same old hall. She scoops up the post and riffles through it. Nothing from Seth.

It's true that he is in the States; a card arrived the day after Stella died. A view of hills and forest from New York State. *Dear Dodie, Rod and Jake, it's great here. Don't worry, love Seth.* And that was it. Receiving it had shot relief like a drug through her veins. And then anger. How *dare* he do this to her? And then send such an insouciant card, *insouciant*, as if everything is normal, and no address even, no phone number? He's always told her everything before. When she gets hold of him . . . But at least, she tells herself, at least he is safe.

This is her house now. Rod reminded her of that. 'When I get back,' he said, 'we could move.'

'If I have you back,' she said. He'd lifted a corner of his mouth in acknowledgement of her puny joke. But could she bear to live here anyway, either with him or without him? She'd have to get the kitchen ripped right out and start again. The awful times she had in here, the awful drabness of the food.

Dodie fingers the softened edge of the old wooden draining board. She chucks the tannin-stained tea cosy in the bin and then pulls it out again, hangs it back on its hook beside the sink. Her heart chips like an ice pick at her ribs. In front of the sink the lino is worn to a dark smudge.

She smashed a plate here once. The plates were oatmeal-speckled and patterned with ears of wheat. Deliberately, she'd smashed one, and Stella, with a rare and sudden burst of vitality, had dragged her to the cellar door and shoved her so she tumbled halfway down the concrete stairs, banging her head on the wall and grazing her knee.

There'd been an airbrick letting in a drizzle of light and she sat on a box beneath it, waiting. She didn't shout or cry, just sat there throbbing with power, because this was the sort of thing you could report a parent for and maybe even get taken into care. That was her favourite fantasy: a normal foster-family with television and dogs and mess and other children. This was before Seth was born. After a while her eyes grew used to the darkness. Leaves had blown in from somewhere, and in the corner was a wicker dressmaker's dummy, draped in cobwebs. She kept her eyes away from that. *What if she never lets me out?* she thought, imagining her own skeleton sitting there for ever and evermore. She listened to the scraping clop of Stella's clogs up above and the creaking of the floorboards. It could have been hours – or maybe only minutes – before the bolt was shot open and Stella called out: 'Dodie?'

She limped up, exaggeratedly shivering and chattering her teeth. Stella mumbled an apology and Dodie felt her chest puff up like a pigeon's with the proud surprise of that – and Stella's eyes lingered, just for a second on her face, really looking at her, really seeming to see her, just for a moment, a moment that contained, maybe contained, a seed of love.

She looks at the scratches in the sink, the flaking paint on the window frame, the way the pattern has almost been rubbed off the Formica worktop. Maybe better to demolish the kitchen altogether. She could knock through to the dining room and make it like the dream foster-parent's kitchen, with an Aga, a huge pine table, children gathered round, laughing and squabbling, warm and cosy, warm, warm. Though she's got a jacket on and a scarf wound round her neck, she shivers. In the dining room she switches on the gas fire. It lights eagerly, with a woof of surprise. An immediate smell of burning dust, a flutter of blue turning to orange behind the silver bars.

The gondolier gleams up at her from the table and she makes to begin breaking up the puzzle – but how can she? A thin layer of dust has settled on the rosy wood of the table. How quickly it gathers. She slides her finger through it, makes a trail through Stella's skin cells. It *would* make sense to move in here. It's a nicer area, a bigger house, a proper garden – much better for Jake to grow up in than the cramped terrace that is her own. Seth could simply keep his old bedroom, when he comes back. *If.*

It does make every sort of sense. She looks out at the garden – you'd need a machete. She could get a sandpit for Jake, a climbing frame. Now the inquest is over Stella will be cremated. Dust and ashes. No suspicious circumstances. All, as the policewoman had said, cut and dried.

Dodie stands too close to the gas fire, the heat scorching her calves. At the inquest she'd learned that Stella had made several attempts before, the first when she was seventeen. *Seventeen.* Dodie never knew that. *Seventeen.* And she'd been sectioned after another attempt. The year was mentioned. It was the year that Dodie's father was killed in a car crash. She just remembers being looked after by Aunt Regina and her friend, Kathy, who had a smallholding in Scotland. Stella hardly told her anything about the past, even about her dad, except that he crashed a car and died and that Dodie was better off without him.

Averting her eyes from the banisters, Dodie runs upstairs to Seth's room. It's a musky, hormonal-smelling tip, drawers hanging open, clothes and books, dirty cups and socks and crisp bags tangled together on the floor. She stands breathing him in, remembering the way he'd loop his arm around her, kiss her on top of her head; recalling the croak in his newly broken voice. He'd been a titch for too long, got bullied for it, but he'd shot up suddenly last year, all that sudden growth of bone and muscle. She picks up a maths book and flicks through, noticing a series of red ticks and *Good work*, in a teacherish hand. He's left most of his stuff behind – which maybe means he hasn't gone for long.

Feeling like a trespasser, she opens the door into Stella's bedroom. On the dressing table: a sticky pot of kohl; a brush snarled grey with hairs; a bottle of sandalwood oil. At home she has Stella's ring, very thin and flat. Someone must have forced it from her finger in the mortuary. Dodie clutches her own ring finger. The ring fits her exactly, but she will not wear it. Sell it then? Never, no. The smell of Stella: dirty hair and something sour and greenish, like squashed stalks or the chilly scent of a flower shop. It hangs around in here. The bedspread is faded Indian. Dodie sits on the bed, opens the bedside cabinet. There's Seth's phone. Why did Stella take Seth's phone? She switches it on and reads her own texts, listens to her own anxious voice.

She stands up, catches sight of herself in the dressing table mirror, hunched, furtive, her dark hair dragged back into a sort of bun, a style suitable for a cremation. To get rid of the dragging lines, she forces a horrid smile. *Stop it. Do not be like, get like, Stella.* There were the months after Jake's birth when a thick grey cloud hung above her and within her, a dragging heaviness around her heart. And it had a taste: metallic, leaden, like a loosened filling. And sometimes there's an edge of that, or something reminds her and *no no no* she will not succumb to that.

The toot of a horn makes her jump. She lifts the net curtain; Rod's out there, engine running.

4

No one else in the crematorium. Dodie and Rod sit halfway back with Jake between them.

'Are we a full complement?' the official asks.

Jake begins 'The Wheels on the Bus' and the official raises his eyebrows, clearly expecting Dodie to hush him up but why should she? Who cares? The cheaply varnished coffin gleams, the tape of organ music crackles. The coffin looks too small and Dodie gets a vision of the legs, the poor, stiff toes, and she forces her mind away and onto Jake who fidgets and kicks his little trainers against the back of the chair in front. At last, the facile words are spoken, the Dralon curtains open and the coffin glides away.

'S'gone,' Jake says, pointing, and Dodie starts to laugh. She fights it at first, but it defeats her, the giggle building beneath her breastbone and growing into a yelp, a belly laugh, doubling her over, charging through her and up and out in awful blurts and gasps that turn to sobs and spurting tears. Part of her hovers above, detached and fascinated: *Hysterical*, she thinks, rather impressed; *I am literally hysterical.*

'OK. OK.' Rod puts his arm around her. 'It's all OK.' Dodie looks up. The Dralon has fallen back into its respectful folds. She looks down at her hands, the fingernails painted black this morning in honour of the occasion. Jake is staring at her, eyes round, one finger in his mouth, riveted.

The official comes forward with a box of tissues tastefully covered in Dralon. Everything makes her laugh now. Dralon will mean death for evermore.

It's time to leave. People are fidgeting about outside. *Next please*, Dodie thinks, and bleats again, hiding her ugly grin inside the tissues.

'Better out than in,' the official reassures Rod as he ushers them into the sunshine.

There's a park near the crematorium with swings and ducks and they stop the car. It's freakishly mild for late November. Their black clothes seem all wrong among the rusty tumble of the leaves. Dodie takes the pins from her hair and lets it fall, warm and friendly, to her shoulders.

They buy sandwiches and drinks from a kiosk, find a bench by the pond to sit and picnic among the greedy ducks. There are coots and moorhens as well as mallards and some pretty chestnut-coloured ducks with painted eyes.

'Dut, dut!' Jake shouts.

'What does a duck say?' Rod asks him.

'Quat, quat, quat.'

'Sorry about that,' Dodie says, calm now but bruised under her ribs by the exertion of emotion.

'Better out than in,' Rod says, and she laughs again and that makes Jake laugh. 'Quat! Quat!' he clowns, thinking he's the joke.

Dodie peels open her sandwich and takes a bite – chilly, tasteless, egg mayonnaise. She breaks a bit off for Jake to ram into his mouth.

'It's kind of worse –' Dodie watches a pigeon pecking at something on the edge of the pond, 'that there was no, you know, *love.*' Something shadowy happens to her heart when she says this but it's the truth, and truth is what you're supposed to tell, isn't it? Tell the truth and shame the devil. 'I mean if I'd loved her and she'd loved me at least . . . well, at least it would be a proper sort of mourning. A *normal* sort of mourning. Instead of . . . instead of . . . well, relief, I guess, but still it does hurt.' She screws her fist against her heart. 'It really, *really* hurts.'

'I think she *did* love you.'

Dodie gulps and shuts her eyes, picturing Stella's white hand reaching through the rain.

'People have funny ways . . . And you *did* love her,' Rod says. 'I know you did.'

'Did I?' Fallen leaves stick on the glossy surface of the pond as if enamelled there. '*Fuck!*' she says, suddenly.

'What?'

'Sorry, but I left the gas fire on. We'll have to go back.'

'Fut!' says Jake.

'At Stella's. I left the gas fire on!'

Rod pulls a face, looks at his watch, his eyes flickering away somewhere.

'Unless you've got plans?' Dodie says, an edge coming into her voice. 'Oh, I'm sorry if we're keeping you.'

'No sweat.' Rod pushes the buggy back towards the car. Dodie throws the rest of her sandwich to the ducks, watches the frenzied pecking, the floating flecks of greasy chopped-up egg white. Should you give eggs to birds? Isn't it like cannibalism?

'Anyway, where were you going?' Dodie asks, catching him up.

'To get my visa sorted,' he says. They walk in silence. The subject of his trip hasn't been raised since that night. A lad, thumbs hooked in the belt loops of his baggy trousers, zigzags his skateboard between them.

Rod unlocks the car. 'I can look in the shed,' he says, to change the subject. He's always longed to get in there, see if there are any tools.

'They'll be rusty.' Dodie struggles to force a wriggling Jake into his seat. 'Not been used since –' She gets the strap done up and climbs into the front seat. 'Well, since Dad was there, I guess.'

Dad. It seems so odd to say it; it makes her lurch inside. She does up her own seatbelt. Clunk click.

'I'm an orphan,' she says. 'Do you realize that?'

'Everyone is eventually,' Rod points out, 'and *that's* if everything goes to plan.'

'Cheerful. Anyway, it's all right for you, you've still got a mum. You ought to go and see her. *We* should. Even if . . . well, she's still Jake's granny.'

'Can you move your bag?' he says. She shifts it away from the gear stick and he starts the car.

'What a horrible word,' she says, gnawing at her nail, scratching through the black varnish. She picks a flake off her lip and flicks it away. '*Orphan*. Like *aw*ful, divo*r*ce, abo*r*tion.'

'Shut up.' Rod grimaces as he noses out of the car park and into the flow of traffic.

Torture, she thinks. She flips down the sun-visor and peers at herself in the mirror. *Corpse*. She's tear-smudged and flushed, hair all over the place. She runs her fingers through the dark tangles. 'Think I should get it cut?'

'No.'

'Let's go to Inverness – we could maybe get a cheap flight. Jake should get to know his only granny.'

Rod makes a vague noise in his throat and changes gear. Dodie looks out at the sunny streetful of windows, gardens. A trampoline taking up the whole of someone's front lawn. A dog trotting purposefully along.

'I wish Seth. . .' Her voice hollows out. 'I wish he was *here*.' Rod puts his hand out and squeezes her knee. 'If I could even get him on the phone. Fancy him not knowing about Mum.'

The sun is smeary through the dirty windscreen and she shuts her eyes. *Seth*. She longs for him in odd places, the spaces between her ribs and shoulder blades, the small of her back, are these where love is located? For years Seth was the love of her life – the focus. If it weren't for him, she sometimes wondered, where would she have learned to love? Where would he, if not for her? Precious little came from Stella, precious little of anything at all.

The first Dodie knew of Seth was more than sixteen years ago when she'd heard Stella vomiting. She'd crept to the bathroom door and called, 'Are you OK?' but there was no answer and the bathroom door stayed locked. A few months later she'd noticed, as Stella turned away from the sink, a new bulk round her middle. Nothing was ever said. And then one day when she returned from school, Aunt Regina and Kathy were there. It was a sunny afternoon and there were roses on the draining board and the incongruously friendly smell of baking cake.

'You've got a little brother!' Aunt Regina said. She was a frail old lady by then, about half the size of the big square Kathy, who never said much, but lurked threateningly in doorways.

'Can I see him?' Dodie asked, after she'd hugged Aunt Regina and been praised for having grown.

'Course you can.'

They'd gone upstairs where Stella lay back against her pillows, her face strained and sweaty-looking.

'Don't disturb him,' she said.

Dodie leant over the tiny tucked-up shape in the Moses basket. His head was fluffed with black and he had the most perfect little nose, very definite, and eyebrows like tiny rows of feather-stitching. As soon as she saw him she adored him. She wasn't like that even with Jake – some of Stella's darkness had got into her by then. But with Seth there was no complication; she'd been simply, immediately, swept away with love.

'Can I hold him?' she said.

'He *is* stirring,' Aunt Regina said. Stella shrugged and turned her face to the wall while Dodie picked him up and held him to her chest, breathing in the yeasty, newborn smell. And after that, she gave him all the love he needed. He would reach for Dodie before Stella and, rather than minding, this seemed to give Stella a grim sort of satisfaction. Though it made her too tired to work properly at school, Dodie would be the one to get up and change the nappies, give him his bottle; and even after she was sixteen and had left home, she'd made sure to take Seth out every weekend, to give him treats and fun.

Once, when Seth was about two, there'd been a rare flicker from Stella, a moment approaching closeness. Seth had said something sweet and funny and Stella had smiled and met her eyes. They'd been sipping tea on the back doorstep while Seth played with a toy tractor. It was almost companionable, almost normal, and Dodie had dared to ask Stella who Seth's father was, and instead of telling her to mind her own business, Stella muttered: 'No one you know. Besides he's dead.'

Dodie was almost afraid to breathe. It was like spotting a rare shy creature in a wood. Stella flicked her a glance, scared-looking – with those strange pale eyes. She'd wrapped her hair so tightly round her fingertip it had gone dark with trapped blood.

'How?' Dodie had whispered.

'Car crash.'

'When?'

Stella's face dragged down then, the thin lips bending like an iron bar, a fierce brightness skinning over her eyes. 'What's the use of raking it all up?' she'd said, and got up and gone inside. That was the closest they'd ever got to intimacy; the only time Stella came close to opening up to her. Dodie had almost been able to smell her grief for this mystery man – maybe American? – who must have snuck in during the night. Did he die immediately or did he live to see Seth? Had he ever visited? Sent money? Maybe he'd been married? Maybe, maybe, maybe.

A wave of pity for Stella threatens to swamp her: *two* men killed in accidents – no wonder she was so screwed up.

She opens her eyes as they round the corner into Lexicon Avenue, past the letterbox, past the laburnum. She blows her nose, looks round at Jake – fast asleep. Rod can switch off the fire, no need for her to go in there again. Not today. Enough today.

A huge glass of wine, soon as she gets home. And once Jake's in bed she will get systematically off her face. It you can't get legless the day your mother goes up in smoke . . .

'Hey!' Rod stops the car and switches off the engine. An estate agent's sign has appeared in the front garden. Bannerman's. FOR SALE.

'What?' she says. They sit dumbly, staring at the sign. 'It wasn't here this morning,' she says. 'We couldn't have missed it, could we?' She gets out of the car. Someone has chopped off some privet to make it possible to display the sign. The smell of severed twigs is bitter in the sunshine.

'Must be a mistake,' Rod says. 'Some wanker's put it in the wrong garden. I'll ring them.' He gets out his phone.

'I'll turn the fire off,' she says. She puts the key in the lock – but it won't work. She tries again. It *won't*. She holds the key up and squints at it. Definitely the right one. She frowns at the door. There are new scratches in the paint. She tries again.

'The lock's been changed,' she calls, but Rod is standing with his back to her beside the car, talking into his phone. She goes round the back, avoiding the pebbledash. The back door lock has been changed too. She looks through the window. Someone else has been in and turned the fire off. She folds down onto the back doorstep. Someone's been here since this morning and done this. The sun is hot. The jungly garden is prowled by feral cats; a pair of yellow eyes glare out between the stalks of a rampant bamboo.

Rod comes and stands looking down at her, scratching his head.

'There's no mistake,' he says. 'Someone's put it up for sale.'

'Who?'

'The lassie didn't know.' He sits down beside her and rolls himself a cigarette. He breathes in and then out on a plume of smoke. 'Said you need to speak to the lawyer. Mr Riddle.'

'But I don't know –'

'She gave me the number, you have to ring.'

'Better go, Jake might wake up,' she says, but they continue to sit there. She can see three cats now: young, ginger-striped, a half grown litter.

'When are you leaving?' She looks at her black knees. A spot of grease fallen from her sandwich, the usual smudges from Jake's fingers.

'Flight's Monday,' he says. There's a long silence into which a magpie interjects its rattle. 'Do you want me to change it?'

I want you not to go.

'I mean, will you be OK?' he says. He too is looking at his knees. He sucks at his cigarette and a slant of sunshine reveals the smoke as hazy yellow, carcinogenic.

'I'll have to be, won't I?'

'S'pose I *could* try the airline,' he says, grudgingly, 'see if I can put if off a couple *more* weeks, but it'll cost.' He stands up and grinds out his cigarette. 'Right,' he says, 'we'll go to Bannerman's now and get this sorted.'

He drives with a set jaw.

'Don't give them a bollocking,' she says. He flicks her a look. 'I mean, they're only doing their job.'

'Selling your fucking house from under you?'

'I wasn't in it,' she points out.

He speeds up as they approach a changing light. She flinches down in her seat, sees the tension in his knee, unfamiliar in suit trousers, the terrible charity shop suit he'd come back with so proudly: 'Only a tenner!' The trousers are too short, the lapels too big and there's an awful naff sort of shine to the fabric. But it's only for today.

'Are you really going?' she says, so quiet it could almost be a thought.

He scratches his ear, frowns, 'Dunno,' he says.

'Talk about it later?' she says. 'I'm getting rat-arsed when we get home.'

5

Dodie's head pounds with every step as she goes downstairs. When she woke earlier, groaning, Rod got up with Jake and, judging by the quiet, took him out – though didn't forget to set an alarm to screech at her from the landing before he left. He made an appointment for her to phone the solicitor as soon as they got home yesterday.

For nine a.m., the sadist. They should have stopped at one bottle; the evening's a blur, bathing Jake half-cut for the first time ever. Can't even remember eating – though there's a memory of Rod and a frying pan and, later, a hazy picture of the floor, Rod's hands on her hips, carpet burns this morning on her elbows and knees.

Mr Riddle has a gentle Geordie accent that almost lulls her to sleep. She sits on the kitchen floor, propped against the fridge, eyes squeezed shut to try and concentrate. She's never had a hangover quite like this one; not just her head but the entire kitchen is pulsing and the floor seems to be tilting towards her. Mr Riddle tells her that the house never belonged to Stella but was let at a nominal rent by a property holding company, and they have every right, now that their tenant is deceased, to sell it. Legally, Dodie hasn't got a leg to stand on.

She looks down at her legs, pale under the hem of her dressing gown. They need a shave. On her thigh is a scar, a pale and silvery crescent. Stella would never tell her how she got it. Every single lover has put his finger on it and spoken of the moon. Rod used to lick it – but not lately. She realizes she's sitting in something wet and sees Jake's cup leaking a stream of Ribena. The floor must really be tilting since it's flowing towards her. She shifts her bottom and shuts her eyes again.

Mr Riddle tells her that Stella left the contents of the house to herself and Seth.

'Don't think there's anything I want.' She pictures the dreary furniture – except the table; Rod will want that – the tedious curtains, the mountain of jigsaws.

'There's particular mention of a letter,' he continues, 'that upon her death, you should receive a letter. I believe – yes – that's been posted out already – you should get it today. And of course we'll arrange access to the house. You'll need to collect your property.'

Dodie thanks him, hangs up and sits blankly for a minute staring at her toes, then staggers up to look at the post. Among the junk are two actual letters, one in a solicitor's thick envelope, one airmail, which she rips open immediately.

Dear Dodie,
I'm sorry that I left so suddenly without saying goodbye.
Don't worry about me I am fine. I know you won't believe
it, but I have been chosen. Don't laugh. It's true. Will you
come and visit? Bring Jakey; it's cool here.

Yours in the Lord,
Seth

Dodie reads it standing up, then sits down and reads it again. *Yours in the Lord?* The letter had been printed out, but the signature is in Seth's familiar spidery scrawl. The paper is stamped with a logo, like a mask with tiny letters spelling SOUL-LIFE, and an address and phone number in New York State. She puts her head in her hands among a scatter of muesli. The door opens and Jake sings out, 'Mumma, mumma,' reaching from his buggy as Rod manoeuvres it into the kitchen. She unstraps him, lifts him up and rubs her face against his hair but he struggles to get down and play.

'So?' Rod says, dumping bread and milk onto the table. 'Did you ring?'

'My *head*.' Dodie puts her hand against her throbbing brow. The bread smells aggressively wholemeal. She moves away towards the sink where last night's plates are still submerged in greasy water along with a floating teabag and a fag end. Two empty wine bottles and the whisky nearly finished too.

'Read that.' She indicates Seth's letter, fills a mug from the tap and swigs it down.

Rod reads the letter and snorts.

'*Yours in the Lord?*' Dodie says. '*I have been Chosen?* That's not Seth is it? *Yours in the Lord*, for God's sake?'

'At least you know he's safe.' Rod flicks the kettle on. 'Coffee?'

Dodie winces. '*Safe?*'

'He's telling you he's OK.'

'But *chosen*? He never even went to Sunday school.'

'The lawyer?' Rod asks.

'Haven't you even *got* a hangover?' She swallows a couple of paracetamol that stick like boulders in her throat.

'A wee touch,' he admits, but he looks fine. Maddeningly fine. He drank just as much. More. 'What did he say?'

'It's not mine, the house. She rented it.'

He turns to stare at her. '*What?*'

'I don't care,' she says. 'I don't even want it.'

'How did you not know that?'

Dodie shrugs.

'You *don't want it*? Three hundred grand's worth of house?' He gives the biscuit tin a deafening rattle.

A surge of sick rises suddenly in Dodie's throat; she clamps her hand to her mouth and rushes upstairs, making it to the bathroom just in time. Tears spurt from her eyes as she vomits into the toilet, the paracetamol choking out again, not even dissolved. She sinks to her knees, beside a sodden nappy, a feeder cup on its side in a pool of juice.

Later, headache shrunken to manageable proportions, she goes out to the shed Rod calls his workshop. Jake's sitting on the floor, banging with a little hammer at a piece of splintery wood. He looks up and grins. He's got a cold and his face is shiny with snot; as he breathes a bubble inflates and deflates in one nostril.

'Bam, bam, bam,' he says.

'Are you sure that's safe?' Her fingers itch to remove the hammer, the dagger-sharp splinters. Rod sands the curve of the arm of a chair, a lovely sweeping line, pale wood. Ash or lime, she guesses. Those tiny pink fingers so near the banging hammer-head. Even a tiny splinter can poison the blood.

'He's OK.' Rod says, looking up. 'Feeling better?' He puts down his sandpaper, runs his finger over the smooth curve.

'Sorry about that,' she says. 'I'm going teetotal.'

He gleams at her ironically.

She groans, leans herself back against the workbench, eyeing Jake and the hammer. She reaches down and tries to wipe his nose, but he wriggles away from her and she gives up.

'So, did you ring the airline?'

He grins. 'Aye. Result,' he says. 'They've offered me a flight end of next week, only another fifty quid.'

'That's good,' she says,'because I'm going to see Seth.'

'*What*?'

'I just phoned. Didn't speak to him but I told them I was coming. I don't want to take Jake all that way, not with this cold. I'll be back before you go.'

'I'm staying here to support you and *you're* going away?' His voice rises. '*Christ* Dodie!'

'I can't not go and see Seth, can I?'

Rod's mouth sets in a stubborn line that means, yes, you certainly can.

Dodie picks up a chisel: fine, sharp-edged, easy to hurt yourself on. The glitter of the blade makes her shudder.

'All Stella's stuff is mine though, mine and Seth's. You can get your hands on the table,' she says. 'And anything in the shed.'

'I've just changed my fucking flight,' he says, 'to be with you. To be here for you.'

'You will be,' she says, 'you'll be here with Jake . . . for me.'

He reaches for his Rizlas. 'How much?'

'We can afford a cheap return. You've got the chair commission. What if it's a cult or something?'

'Christ's sake!' Rod suddenly slams his fist down on the workbench, scattering tobacco among the sawdust. 'You make such a fucking mountain out of every fucking molehill!'

She stares at him. Jake is staring too, open-mouthed, a clear trail of dribble running down his chin.

'*Molehill!*' she repeats, straining to keep her voice calm and pleasant. 'It's not a molehill! And it's OK for you to go gallivanting off but not for me? And I'm not even gallivanting,' she adds.

Rod picks up his sanding block and goes violently at the arm of the chair.

'I've got to at least *see* him.' Dodie pleads to Rod's back. 'He needs to know. I have to tell him about Stella, don't I? I'll go online for a cheap –'

Jake gives a sudden screech and drops the hammer, holding up his index finger wonderingly, eyes hugely round. Dodie scoops him up, sucks the finger into her mouth, kisses and kisses him. *See*. She shoots Rod a filthy look as she carries Jake away.

'Will you not mollycoddle him?' Rod snaps after her.

She turns in the doorway.

'*What?*'

'He's not even crying, for Christ's sake. Leave him be.'

Dodie holds Jake close, almost crooning into his hair, but he wriggles, he's seen his football. She sets him down and he staggers across, aims a kick, falls on his bottom and laughs. Her sweater is smeared with mucous. *Mollycoddle?*

Rod leans against the door frame of the shed.

'I've got to go.' She dabs at her front with a tissue. 'I won't be able to do anything till I know he's OK,' she says. 'You think I mollycoddle Seth as well?'

'You said it.'

'But he's got no one else, has he? If I don't look out for him who will?'

'Yeah, yeah,' Rod says. He goes back into the shed and slams the door.

Dodie catches Jake and takes him inside. She wipes his face and tries to show him how to blow his nose, but he can't get the idea at all. She gives him a cup of juice, sticks a DVD on and, once he's happily gawping, creeps away. In the kitchen her eyes snag on the other letter. She has a sudden fit of violent shivers, puts the kettle on and drapes a sweater of Rod's round her shoulders. She warms her hands on the belly of the kettle till it gets too hot, then, as if catching herself unawares, turns and tears open the solicitor's envelope, and the one inside addressed to Dodie in Stella's jerky hand:

Dear Dodie,

If you're reading this, I'm gone but this is something I want you to know. Even to write it is hard, as if my hand is trying to stop me. I'm sorry I was so horrid. I don't know why I was. I did love you but something would always come over me, like a force field or glass or something to stop me being nice. It was easier with Seth, a boy; that is something different. After you left home I did try with him. When you left I was glad. It made it easier for me to look after Seth without you watching in that critical way you have.

I have been horribly cold, I know.

Though I don't deserve it, please forgive me.

Stella.

Dodie reads it through twice then she turns to make herself a cup of Earl Grey. She puts two mugs out, but hangs one back on its hook. Let him make his own. Love is a tiny word with a taste like almonds and she holds it on her tongue.

6

The taxi stops outside a chain-link fence. It's a wide flat street with wide flat buildings separated by acres of lawn. There's no church or anything that looks the least bit like a church.

'End of the ride, lady,' the driver says. Dodie pays him, fumbling with the unfamiliar dollar bills. 'Have a good day.' It's mid-afternoon. He screeches his car into a three-point turn and swerves away. The sun is warm with an autumnal edge. Fall, she thinks, a fall edge – but that doesn't sound right. Sounds dangerous. Some things just don't translate. Once the engine noise has evaporated, there's silence. A black squirrel scrambles up the fence and leaps onto the branch of a tree. Blazing maple leaves.

The gate is made of the same toughened wire mesh as the fence. On the gatepost the small mask logo with

SOUL-LIFE in its mouth. OK. That's something. No handle on the gate, no way of opening it but there's a button with a speaker. She presses and waits. Nothing. No one comes. No one passes in the street. The other buildings all look flat and closed and far away. She scrunches her legs together. A long taxi ride on top of cups and cups of coffee – the waitress kept filling her up for free and her bladder is tight and tweaking. No bushes. It's all so open. What if she squatted down on the grass verge? She presses the button again, fidgeting urgently from foot to foot.

'*Hello?*' A crackly voice emerges from the speaker.

'It's Dodie,' she says, 'Seth's sister. I phoned and said I was coming.'

'*Hold on.*'

She holds on, resisting the urge to cross her legs. A stocky woman in a lilac dress comes scurrying across the expanse of grass, just as the gate glides open.

'Hello there,' she says, in an English accent. She's fiftyish with cropped grey hair, pink cheeks, a warm smile. She opens her arms in an embrace and Dodie stiffens. Relax, she tells herself, it's how they'll be, touchy-feely, Jesus loves you. The gate slides shut behind her with a judder and a squeak. The woman steps back, looks with odd intensity into Dodie's eyes. Hers are the colour of faded denim, surrounded by a comfortable mesh of lines. 'I'm Martha,' she says, a little breathlessly.

'Hi Martha,' Dodie says, stepping back. 'Sorry, but I'm bursting for the loo.'

Martha laughs. 'Easily remedied,' she says. 'Follow me.' As they go back across the grass she says, 'We thought you'd be bringing your little boy?'

'Decided not to,' Dodie says. 'He's got a cold.'

They stop by the door of a small extension to the main building. Martha punches a number into the keypad and they go inside. 'Bathroom through there,' Martha says. 'Take your time. Freshen up. I'll put the kettle on.'

Dodie only just makes it, gets her jeans down, sits and pees, sighing with the sweet relief. Arrangements of plastic flowers sit on the high window sill and on the cistern, and an artificial floral smell tickles her nose. She washes her hands and stares at herself in the mirror: a white face, dark shadows under her eyes – that Stella look again. She slaps a bit of colour into her cheeks, licks her teeth, scrabbles her fingers through her messy hair. In the hotel this morning she discovered her third white one and nipped it out. Is it normal to start going grey at thirty, or is it from all the shocks?

The little sitting room's decorated in an exaggeratedly homey style. The walls, carpet, curtains and upholstery add up to a flouncy floral hell. *Like your mum on acid,* she'll tell Rod. His mother's bungalow in Inverness is almost psychotically flounced, pelmeted and valanced – but much more tastefully than this. Dodie feels a stab of loyalty, even though she doesn't know her very well. Jake's only met his Scottish granny once. Once she gets home they'll put that right.

'Cup of tea?' Martha says.

Dodie sits on the sofa. The tea is set out on a tray with a milk jug, a sugar bowl, a cake tin. The cups are gold edged, chintzy.

'Pretty,' Dodie says, eyeing the tin. 'This isn't at all what I expected!'

'White? Sugar?'

'Just milk, thanks.'

Martha's hands are indoor hands, very smooth and white, almost pampered-looking. She makes a peculiar little humming sound under her breath as she pours the tea.

'Cake?'

'Please . . . but where's Seth?'

The smile falters. 'Ah, I'm afraid there's been a bit of a glitch.'

Dodie stares.

'He was called to another centre, across the state.'

'But –'

'I know,' Martha says. 'It's very unfortunate. He'll be back tomorrow.'

Dodie forces her voice to stay even. 'I did *say* I was coming.' She picks up her teacup, lets her hair fall and cloak her face.

'What a good sister,' Martha says, 'coming all this way.'

'I miss him.'

'And he misses you,' Martha says, 'and little Jake. I know he misses him.'

'He shouldn't have left then, should he?'

Grimacing sympathetically, Martha reaches out to stroke her leg. Dodie's muscles shrink from the touch.

'He'll be here tomorrow.'

'Where is he, anyway?'

'We have different centres,' Martha says. 'Now come on, this calls for cake.' She opens the tin to reveal a carrot cake, thickly covered with cream cheese icing. Despite everything, Dodie's mouth floods with saliva. She feels like a Pavlovian dog as she watches Martha cut a slice so huge it overlaps the dainty plate. Maybe it's true, they do eat more in America. But she has no objection. Not when it's cake like this, with a nubbly texture, little walnut flecks and the icing deep and sweet and toothsome. Martha nibbles at a smaller slice.

'OK now?' Martha beams. 'Not much that a slice of cake won't put right, is there?'

Dodie smiles, reluctantly cheered by the sweetness. They eat in silence and she licks the last of the icing from her fingers.

Martha opens her mouth to speak but stops when the door opens and a woman enters. She's about the same age as Martha, dressed identically but hectically pretty and thin.

'Welcome,' she says and leans down to hug Dodie.

'This is Hannah,' Martha says. Her voice has tightened. 'We're getting on quite well here thank you very much.'

Dodie catches a minute flicker in Hannah's eyes. Irritation?

'Cake?' Hannah frowns at Martha, whose face has stiffened and flushed. She's doing that humming thing again, a fixed smile on her face. Hannah switches on a smile for Dodie. 'Have a good trip?' Her teeth snaggle attractively at the front, giving her a slightly goofy look. She sounds Australian. 'Where's the nipper?'

'Jake? I left him with his dad.'

'Shame,' Hannah says, raising her eyebrows at Martha.

Why are they so bothered about Jake? 'Well, if Seth won't see me I'll go,' Dodie says, made uneasy by the staring of the two women and the tension that jangles the air between them. 'I'll come back tomorrow.' She puts down her plate.

Martha stands up and faces Hannah. She's a head shorter but twice as wide. 'Our Father needs you,' she says to Hannah, nodding towards the door. '*I* can manage here.'

Hannah raises her eyebrows, shrugs. 'See you soon,' she says to Dodie as she leaves the room.

Once the door has closed, Martha relaxes, smiles at Dodie almost conspiratorially – though why should she be expected to take sides in some unspecified dispute between strangers? The sugary cake has made her terribly sleepy and she blinks.

'Can you call me a taxi?'

'Why not stay?' Martha says.

'But all my stuff's at the hotel.'

'We can lend you everything you need. And what if Seth gets back tonight after all? What if he gets back expecting to see you?'

Dodie dabs her fingertip round her plate to pick up the last few crumbs. If she were alone she'd lick the plate. Frosting, in America they call it frosting. She sees Martha noticing her grass green fingernails. It's an expensive taxi journey and there's nothing in her luggage she can't do without for a night – and she *is* shattered. 'OK then,' she says. 'Thanks.' A great gaping yawn escapes her. 'Sorry.'

'You're jetlagged,' Martha says, 'poor baby.' *Baby?* 'What about forty winks?'

'They say it's best to stay awake till bedtime,' Dodie says, her throat hollowing with the effort of suppressing another yawn. 'To help the body clock adjust.'

Martha shrugs. 'If you're tired, you're tired.' She yawns herself, hand patting against her mouth to make a wa-wa-wa sound. 'Look, you've set me off now!'

'This is all very *normal*,' Dodie says. 'I mean – I, I didn't know what to expect –'

'We are quite normal really!' Martha's eyes twinkle in their nets; Dodie blinks, reminded of something, fishing for stars or something, part of a lullaby? Wink and Blink and a Nod . . . God, she's dropping off. How rude.

She half smothers another yawn, shakes the gathering sand from her head. 'It's weird though. I mean, Seth never showed any interest in God or anything before, not that he let on.'

'Not weird,' Martha says. 'It's people who are lost.'

Dodie bristles. 'He wasn't *lost*!'

Martha says nothing but Dodie can hear the hum again, just the faintest sound, not a tune, just a continuous note. It could get on your nerves.

'There's something I have to tell him.'

'About your mother?' Martha asks.

Dodie startles out of her tiredness. 'How do you know?'

'Well, the police –'

'So he *knows*? I gave them this number but I said I'd tell him.'

'He doesn't know how she died,' Martha reassures her. 'Something like that, best it comes from you.' She has one of those sympathetic faces that always look familiar: pleasant and unthreatening.

'Yes, I'll tell him,' she says. They sit in silence for a minute. 'But this is all so weird. His head teacher said he'd gone to a *relative* in America. No one would tell me anything when I rang.'

Martha chuckles. 'But you see we are *all* relatives here, relatives in the Lord.'

'Oh.' Dodie looks down at her fingernails. *Relatives in America*, she thinks, how stupid, how stupid of her to be so literal. 'But, it's just that Seth never would have done that, left like that, without at least telling *me*. We've always been like this.' She holds up two crossed fingers.

'People can be surprising,' Martha says. 'Don't fret. Look, why not put your feet up? I'll bring you an early dinner. Don't look so downhearted,' she adds. 'You *will* see Seth.'

'I'm just tired.'

'Got a photo of your little one?'

'Yeah.' Dodie picks up and rifles through her bag. 'Can I use your phone? I need to ring Rod and this' – she pulls her mobile out – 'won't work over here, some network problem thingy.'

'I'll bring you one, when I bring the dinner.'

Dodie switches on her mobile and opens her gallery. 'There.' Jake's grinning face snags at her heart. She tilts the screen so Martha can see. 'Here he is, with his first ice-cream – and that's Rod' – she hesitates – 'my boyfriend.' Seth is behind them in the picture, caught accidentally, unselfconsciously. Her three favourite humans in one tiny, lit-up square.

'Sweet.' Martha chuckles. 'Jake, I mean!' She stands up. 'Rest now.'

Dodie puts her finger on Jake's face. The tip of it obscures his whole head. What is he doing now? *Wink and Blink and a Nod one night*, it's a lullaby, maybe Aunt Regina sang it to her once, certainly not Stella, and she'll sing it to Jake if she can think of the words, *sailed out on wooden shoe, into a river of crystal light and into a sea of blue,* funny how it floats back, flows, when it's been dammed up for so long, *where are you going la la la la an old man asks the three . . .*

Dodie blinks. Her mouth is full of fur, her phone is by her feet, a lamp shines in a flowery corner.

'Better?' a voice says. 'Dinner won't be long.'

It's evening; she looks at her watch. A couple of hours have vanished.

'All OK,' Martha soothes. 'No rush. You take your time.'

Dodie scrubs at her eyes. 'I have to talk to Rod.'

'On the table.' Dodie turns to see the phone there. The tea things have been cleared and there are knives and forks set out; all that and she didn't hear a thing. Martha goes to the little stove; there's the clank of a spoon in a pan, a deliciously spicy savoury smell.

'I've just got to fetch some bread – if you want bread?'

'Please.'

She waits for Martha to leave and dials the home number, remembering the UK code. The phone rings. She pictures it on top of the fridge, pictures her kitchen with Stella's rosewood table crammed in so you can barely squeeze round it to get to the fridge – and already marked by a hot-cup ring. Stella would spin in her grave, if she were in a grave. Ashes. They've yet to scatter them. They're in the airing cupboard, safe under all the towels and sheets. Wait till Seth's back. Make a trip of it, a picnic, oh, shut up. The phone rings.

'It's me!' Dodie says, when she hears Rod's voice.

'Good timing, we've just got in.'

'Where've you been?'

'Out. So, where are you?'

'At the church, sort of, only it's not like a church, in what they call the parlour.' She lowers her voice. 'A sort of psychotically twee apartment for visitors.'

Rod grunts.

'Like your mum on acid,' she tries, hoping to amuse him, but there's a beat of silence.

'So,' he says. 'Seth?'

'Haven't seen him yet. Tomorrow.'

'Oh?'

'Jake?'

'He's right here. Still in his buggy. Jake, want to speak to Mummy? Say hello to Mummy.'

She feels in her belly the swoop of the phone down to Jake's ear. 'Jakey?'

She hears his breath. Shuts her eyes. Sees his puzzled face.

'Say hello to Mummy,' Rod says.

'Hello Jake,' Dodie says.

But he starts to cry. Rod comes on. 'That's foxed him,' he says, through the wails.

'Give him some juice and a fig roll,' Dodie says.

'It's lunchtime.'

'Give him banana on toast –'

'I know what to give him, thank you.'

'Sorry.' Her voice thins. 'Wish I was there.'

'I'd better sort him out.'

'I shouldn't have come.'

'Don't be daft; he's fine. Ring when you've seen Seth. OK?'

'OK.'

'Bye.'

And he's gone. She drops the phone and bunches over, arms wrapped round herself, round the twingeing of a phantom umbilicus. Thousands of miles away, Jake is crying for her and there's nothing she can do.

'All right?' Martha comes back in, a long crusty loaf under her arm. She inspects the pan. 'This is done.'

'Smells good.'

'Red pepper goulash,' Martha says. 'Wine?'

'Please.'

'Californian.' She pours two generous glasses of red. 'Cheers.' She raises her glass. 'Once again, welcome. And tuck in.'

'Cheers.' Dodie tucks her hair behind her ears and takes a sip of the wine; a bit sweet but still reviving. Reassured that at least they aren't teetotal, she forks up slivers of red in a sticky sauce: rich, earthy; tomatoes, paprika.

'Mmm,' she says. 'Where's everybody else?'

'We like to welcome guests in here – more of a personal touch.'

'But I'd like to see where Seth stays.'

'Tomorrow.'

'I need some water.' She starts to stand.

'No, no.' Martha is up and filling a glass from a fizzy bottle before Dodie can open her mouth to object. She hasn't been looked after like this since . . . well, ever. She swigs back half the glass.

'I don't even know how Seth came to be here,' she says.

Martha dabs her mouth on a napkin. 'I expect he ran into a Relative.'

'In Sheffield?'

Martha laughs. 'We get everywhere! I'm sure he'll fill you in tomorrow.' They eat and chat and Dodie finds her tongue running away with her – it must be the wine or the jet lag or Martha's kindly face – telling her all about Jake, how clever he is, so advanced for his age, so beautiful and funny. She tells her about Rod wanting to leave, about the shock of finding Stella's body. Martha leans forward as she listens to this, her eyes bright and curious. Dodie talks about Seth, how brilliant he is but how he used to get bullied at school, just for being outside the crowd, just for being himself. 'He hates football, drama's more his thing, he's really sweet and funny – well, you'll know that.' Dodie's voice cracks and she bites her knuckle.

'You'll see him tomorrow,' Martha says.

Dodie takes another forkful, chews, forces the food past the sudden blockage in her throat. Shame there's no TV or radio or music or anything, just the personal sounds of mastication and swallowing.

'Do *you* have children?' she asks Martha, to break the silence.

There's a minute flaring in Martha's eyes, then she withdraws a little and shakes her head.

'But you must have some family? Biological, I mean,' Dodie adds.

Martha nods.

'Do you see them?'

'Now and then.'

'But not much? God, I could never ever in a million years contemplate leaving Jake,' Dodie says. 'It's nearly killing me just leaving for a *week*. Seth is the only reason I'd ever leave him. Maybe I *should* have brought him with me. I was feeling kind of torn. Wish I had.' Has he stopped crying yet? How's his cold? She never even asked. Has he eaten his lunch? Is he napping? Or will Rod have him in the workshop with all the splintery wood, the dangerous tools?

'Oh, Seth,' she says, her voice beginning to slur. 'I just need to see that's he's all right then I'll go home.'

'Seth's fine.'

'I just need to *see* that. For myself.'

'Of course you do.' Martha puts her fork down and stands up. 'He's lucky to have a sister like you. Get off to bed now. God bless,' she says and, as Dodie passes on her way to the bathroom, she prints a kiss against her brow.

7

She floats up through a dream, rags and scrags of voices, the chink of cup against saucer – and Martha is standing beside the bed, smiling, holding out a cup of tea.

'How did you sleep?'

'Fine.' Dodie hauls herself up against the pillows, blinking away the cling of dreams. 'I haven't slept so deeply since . . . I don't know.' But then she frowns, remembering something. 'Was that other woman in here last night? Hannah?'

'No,' Martha says.

'I thought I woke up in the night and there she was, staring.'

'A dream,' Martha says. She puts the tea down and goes out of the room. Dodie lies staring at the ceiling, remembering the feeling of a face close to hers, the benign smell of breath. Her eyes had opened but in the dark she couldn't see. She'd put her hand up, and there had been nothing there. Maybe it was a dream, then? Though unlike any dream she's had before.

She sits up against the lavish pillows and sips her tea. Martha puts her head round the door. 'Just take your time now,' she says. 'We've got cereal and muffins.' There's a soft shine in her eyes, loving, almost like a mother – not *Stella* but a proper mother. It slams into Dodie anew each time she wakes that she has no mother now. Stella Marianne has gone. Up in smoke. This stranger, Martha, has already been nicer to her, kinder to her, than Stella ever was.

The tea is weak and barely warm, but at least it's wet. Dodie drinks it quickly, showers, dresses and brushes her hair. The muffin is amazing, warm, banana flavoured and studded with chunks of melting chocolate. You could never lose weight in a place like this. Can't ring home yet; they'll be asleep, Jake in his cot with the rosy light. He would love to taste a bit of muffin, cram his mouth full with his chubby fist. May as well have another; what's one extra muffin in a lifetime?

'You set?' Martha says.

The day is bright and cool and Dodie drinks in the fresh, faintly pine-scented air. The trees glow crimson and yellow gold.

'Beautiful day,' she says. 'Maybe Seth will take a walk with me, show me round.'

They stand for a moment soaking up the blue, watching sunlit birds fold shadows beneath their wings. They walk round to a door where Martha punches in a number and steps aside to let Dodie in. No chintzy flounces here. It's a bare entrance hall, wooden floor, white walls, monastic. They walk swiftly through a maze of identical corridors, plain white walls, white painted doors, no numbers or signs. Restful – but how would you ever find your way?

'It's very quiet,' Dodie whispers.

'The Brothers and Sisters are out at work, or in meditation.'

'People go out to work?'

'Of course!'

Reassured, Dodie follows her through a double door and down a short flight of steps. That second muffin sits like concrete in her stomach – definitely a mistake. At last Martha stops, presses a number into another keypad, opens the door. Dodie pushes eagerly inside, expecting Seth – but instead there are three strangers, all dressed in lilac, all with cropped hair.

'This is Dodie,' Martha says.

'Hi Dodie,' says a tall freckled young woman. 'Welcome to Soul-Life. I'm Rebecca.' Her accent is English too, her hair red and clumpy, wanting to curl if it was only long enough. 'This is Daniel.' She indicates an oriental-looking guy with blue-black hair that sticks up straight from his face as if he has his finger in a socket.

He nods his head at her and blinks. 'Welcome to The Church of Soul-Life.'

'Hi, I'm John.' A wiry, heavily-stubbled guy with a navy cross tattooed on his neck holds out a hand and wrings hers tightly. He grins, revealing a missing front tooth. 'We're here to greet you, make you feel at home.' His head is shaved to reveal the prehistoric-looking plates of his oddly shaped skull, but his accent is surprisingly soft and cultured – Southern maybe. He's older than the others and looks frail.

'Rebecca, John and Daniel will be your buddies for the rest of your stay. See you later.' Martha gives Dodie a nod and blinks at the others and they all blink back before she lets herself out.

'But what about Seth?' Dodie asks, but Martha has gone. 'I'm here to see Seth,' she explains to the other three. 'My brother.'

'Perhaps Martha's gone to get him?' Rebecca suggests, darting her eyes at John.

Dodie huffs and puffs with frustration. But what can she do? 'What's all the blinking in aid of?' she asks.

Rebecca's nose wrinkles as she smiles. Her eyes are gooseberry green with a clear brown fleck like a floating tea leaf in the left one. 'It's just part of what we do,' she says. 'You'll get used to it.'

'But I'm not staying.'

'No?' Rebecca smiles, head tilted.

'We're about to meditate,' John says. 'Care to join us?'

'Are we locked in?' Dodie goes to the door. 'I'm going to drag Seth out for a hike, it's beautiful out – have you been outside?'

'Martha will bring him, or fetch you,' Daniel says. He has a sharp chin, a small dimple in one cheek as he smiles at her. She feels like a dog waiting at the door.

'Have you seen him today?'

'Seth?' Rebecca asks. She frowns. 'No, actually I haven't seen him for a while.'

'Where is he then?'

Rebecca shrugs her shoulders. 'Different meditation group? Anyway, you might as well, like, join us while you wait.' Rebecca fetches two low wooden stools.

'How long have you lot been here?' Dodie asks.

'John's been here longest,' Rebecca says. There's a silence and Dodie catches an amused glance zipping between John and Daniel.

'So, where are you all from?'

'What matters is that we're *here*,' John says. 'See, Dodie, for us this is what is real. This' – he holds a finger up – 'instant. The past – irrelevant. Gone.' He slices off the past with his hand.

'No it hasn't.'

'You going to join us?' John has scars on the back of his hands, blurred self-inflicted tattoos on the back of his fingers. *They* haven't gone.

'Come on, Dodie,' Daniel says and flickers his dimple. 'It's a gas.'

Dodie sighs, shrugs, nods. Why not? She went to a meditation class as therapy after Jake's birth. It was supposed to help her out of the depression – even that word makes her shiver, the memory of the sky fallen and clinging like a dirty blanket.

'OK,' she says. 'But Seth?'

'Leave it to Martha,' Daniel says.

Rebecca shows Dodie how to kneel on the meditation stool, legs tucked beneath her. Surprisingly comfortable, though her boots feel hard and clumsy. The rest of them are wearing flat espadrilles in purple or grubby white.

'Meditated before?' Rebecca asks.

'A bit.'

'First relax,' John says, 'and sit. Just sit. Collect yourself. We call it collecting. Do not move. If you feel a sensation in your body, an itch, a pain, do not indulge it, watch it only and realize that's all it is. A brief, physical sensation. Look at it and let it go. And after a while, you'll hear the Wisdom.'

'Wisdom?'

John smiles and the darkness shows behind his missing tooth. *What were you?* she wonders: drug dealer? Hell's Angel? He's clean but has a deeply ingrained look of dissolution that can never be scrubbed out. He sits facing them and shuts his eyes, his face a knot of concentration.

Daniel's face is composed in a slight smile. He is beautiful, in the simple cleanness of the lines, the skin, the slick black eyebrows, and he's young, maybe not much older than Seth. Perhaps he knows Seth?

Rebecca nods at her and closes her eyes. Her lashes are fair, her eyebrows almost invisible, the first hints of lines at the corners of her eyes. There's a dint in her nose where she used to wear a stud and several in her ears. Dodie sighs and closes her own eyes. In the meditation class with a teacher talking her through the stages she'd been fine, safe in the breathing presence of others, but at home it never worked and she'd given up quickly, horrified by a glimpse of the churning chaos inside her head.

Now, she listens to the silence. Soon there'll be footsteps in the corridor and it will be Martha and Seth, or maybe Martha to take her to Seth and what will she say . . . Oh don't think about that now. Snuffly breathing from John; very, very faintly a bird outside, sounds like a blackbird, do they have the same sort of blackbirds here? She hears her own breath, feels the flow of it, in and out. Once she gets Seth out into the fresh autumn – fall – day, she'll tell him about Stella. (Will he be wearing lilac too? He'll need a coat.) How will he take it? Will he shed more tears than she did? Don't think about that now. *The Lost*, Martha told her, *have become the Chosen*. But Seth wasn't lost. Though she remembers the day, a few months ago now, when he barged into the kitchen and kicked the fridge.

'Hey!' she'd said. His face had been red, his breathing fast. 'Come on . . .' She'd gone to put her hand on his arm but he'd flinched away from her. And then she'd noticed that the redness on his face was bruising and that he'd been crying. That was when he admitted to her that he'd been being bullied, for years, by the same lads, the football team, who called him a poof and a ponce, tore up his physics notes, stole his PE kit . . . And then scolded by Stella when he got back without these things.

'Why didn't you tell her?' Dodie had asked, but of course she knew why he hadn't. What would have been the point? It would only have given Stella further confirmation of how awful life is, driven her deeper into her despair.

'Why didn't you tell *me,* then?'

He'd shrugged but she'd read something in his eyes that chilled her.

'*I* could have coped with it,' she'd said quietly. 'Seth, I'm not Stella, I'm not *like* Stella.'

'I know,' he'd said, 'but you've got enough on, like with Jake and that.'

'I'll go to the school, speak to the head.'

'You'll only make it worse.' And then he'd cried, great deep sobs in his newly-broken voice, face down on the kitchen table. And what could she do but hover and pat, make hot chocolate and soothing noises? She'd secretly rung the school and when, a week or so later, she'd asked him how things were he'd claimed that they'd got better – but maybe he was lying, trying not to worry her. Maybe he really did feel lost.

Breath in and out. In and out. Wall to wall pizza, she'll promise him, burgers till they come out of your ears. A swimming pool of chocolate if he wants. He can change schools, move into her attic. He doesn't need this lot. She will keep him safe.

Her foot is fizzing; surreptitiously she waggles her toes.

In and out. The sound like waves on a beach. In and out.

She realizes that John is humming, barely audibly; you have to strain to hear. She looks at Rebecca, at Daniel; their eyes are still closed and their faces are sharp, intense, almost eager as they each join in with their own humming, three different notes so that the sound is a chord vibrating on and on. One hum runs out, another overlaps and takes it over, sometimes three notes, sometimes two and sometimes silence. She feels the vibration in her chest and stomach.

After a time, she realizes that's it's gone quiet. She opens her eyes to find the three of them looking at her with maddeningly loving smiles. She bleats out a laugh. How long was that? She itches to look at her watch, but senses it is not the thing to do.

John puts out his hand and lets it rest on the crown of her head. 'That's fine,' he soothes. 'You were so still. Smooth.'

'You're a natural,' Rebecca says.

'Beautiful, Sister,' Daniel says.

'It was . . . nice,' she says. 'I actually feel quite peaceful – but what about the wisdom?'

Daniel chuckles. He is such a kid, just a few clear straggly hairs on his chin.

'Seth should be here soon,' Dodie says. 'What time do you have lunch?'

Rebecca tries to stifle a grin.

'Comfortable?' John says. 'Do you need to move?'

'A bit fidgety,' Dodie admits.

'Let's do the motions,' Rebecca says. 'We can show her the motions, John?'

'Cool,' says Daniel, jumping to his feet in one lithe movement.

Dodie stands, her knees creaking. She looks at the door, can't resist looking at her watch now. Two hours have gone. Two *hours*? 'I thought Martha was coming back.'

'She'll be here. And Seth,' Rebecca says. She stretches her arms above her head, limbering.

'He'd better bloody well show up.'

'Come on,' John says, 'follow.' The three of them fold over, hands dangling, fingertips almost brushing near the floor and then straighten and twist and move their arms and legs. Though John stops before the others and presses his fingers into his side, wincing. Dodie gives up trying to follow and watches. Rebecca has the body shape she'd choose if you could choose: long legs, flat stomach, good shoulders, small neat head. She and Daniel move in perfect unison. And stop, upright, hands folded prayer-like to their hearts, eyes closed.

'That's good,' Dodie says lamely, having another sneak at her watch.

'Sit,' John says, and they all sit back in silence for a few moments.

'It's completely weird that Seth's even here,' bursts out of her.

Rebecca puts her hand on Dodie's sleeve. 'It's not weird, she says, 'not weird at all.'

'It's simple,' Daniel says. 'He's been chosen.'

'Like you?'

'We are all chosen,' John says.

'Who by?'

'Our Lord.' His voice is fat with love.

'But *how*, I mean *who*?'

'Ours is not to reason why,' Daniel says, without a trace of irony.

'Yeah, I get that,' Dodie says, 'but I mean how exactly are you chosen?'

'We're, like, not encouraged to talk,' Rebecca says.

'Why?'

There is a moment of silence. Rebecca hums. John blinks. 'Sit down,' he says.

Rebecca and Daniel fold themselves down on the meditation stools.

'But look, I'm here to see Seth,' Dodie says, her voice too loud. 'I'm not here for any of this. I just want to see my brother and get out of here. And take him with me, preferably.'

'Hey Sister,' John says. 'Cool it. Sit down.'

'I'm not meditating any more,' she says. She goes to the door and rattles the handle, bangs on it. 'Martha!' she calls. 'Seth?'

The others close their eyes and start up the humming. She can feel it through the soles of her boots like a kind of swarming. She bangs at the door again and shouts but it feels futile, stupid, like a fly battering itself about inside a glass lampshade. There were always flies in the one in Stella's bathroom and the glass sphere always amplified their dying hum and they would take days and days to die. The bottom was a dark rubble of little bodies you looked up at from the bath, only tipped out when the light bulb was changed. The mystery was, how did they get in?

Dodie stands with her ear against the door, straining to hear footsteps. Surely Seth must be here by now? She needs to pee and have a drink and lunch and then a walk: is the sun still shining? To see Seth and get out of here. How can they bear it with no window? The rest of them are only human, they'll need a break before long. Coffee and a snack would do.

Time goes. She watches it roll off her watch and spool away into the air, into the hum. Her knees feel shaky with it. She gives in, just for now. There's nowhere to sit but the meditation stool anyway. She kneels and shuts her eyes, nothing else to do. The humming gets into you, the three notes, no – one, no – two, no – four now, and the fourth coming timidly from herself; she can hear a gap in the chord that must be filled and it lifts you up and sets you outside the everyday and the waiting and why not when there's nothing else to do?

And then Martha enters the room. She blinks and smiles at them all, nodding at Dodie as if pleased. Dodie gets up, looks past her – but there's no Seth.

'Where is he?' she asks, stumbling up, light-headed.

Martha doesn't answer immediately. The others gradually cease the humming, blink and grasp their own left thumbs. It's a kind of salute, she realizes.

'Eh?' she says. 'Where is he?'

Martha holds out a cordless phone. 'Here he is to speak to you.'

Dodie takes the phone, warm from Martha's hand. She walks towards the wall, turning her back on them all, hoping they'll take the hint and let her speak to her brother in private, but they don't leave. Martha says something to them and Rebecca laughs, a snort followed by a donkeyish bray.

Dodie sticks her other finger in her ear. 'Seth?'

'Hi Dode.' That familiar broken scrape in his voice, but oddly distorted, sort of muffled and warped.

'Where? Where are you?'

Silence.

'Speak to me, Seth,' she says. She rests her forehead against the cool plaster of the wall, shuts her eyes, trying to conjure up his face.

He says something too blurred to hear.

'What? Speak up.'

'You shouldn't have come.' It's a poor signal.

'You told me to come!'

She can just make out a female voice in the background.

Seth says, 'Why did you leave Jake?'

'How do *you* know that?'

Silence.

'I didn't want to disrupt him. He's got a cold.'

'Is he OK?'

'Just a cold. Look, I need to speak to you. Face to face.'

There's a hissing silence.

'Seth!' She can feel a smothered bristle of interest from the others in the room. Her eyelids bulge with tears. 'Seth? Don't do this to me.'

'Bye,' he says.

Sweat blooms in her armpits and on her palms. She swaps the phone to the other hand and wipes her hand on her jeans. 'I've come all this way to see you. Please.'

But the call is cut off.

'Seth,' she says, into the buzz. 'Seth!'

Martha eases the sweaty phone from her hand. 'He'll see you tomorrow,' she says.

She glares at Martha. 'But that's what you said last night.'

'Stay.' Rebecca looks to Martha. 'She can stay here with us? Can't she Martha? We'll take care of her. It'll be cool.' She grins at Dodie.

'No. I'm going back to the hotel,' she says. 'My stuff's there. I need to change. I suppose I'll come back tomorrow.'

'Of course. I'll call you a taxi,' Martha begins – then pauses. 'But maybe you *should* think of staying another night? Nearly a hundred bucks there and back?'

'And all the hassle,' John adds.

'Nicer if you stay,' Daniel says.

'Do,' Rebecca urges. 'I could do with a *girl* buddy.' She pulls a face at John and Daniel.

'Stay,' says John.

'It's even possible you *might* see Seth later today,' Martha says. 'And what a shame if you're not here. Imagine how disappointed he'll be.'

Dodie looks at them all. Rebecca has the sort of smile you'd need to be inoculated against, a little twitch of her freckled nose. She sighs. What else has she got to do? 'I suppose that makes sense. Can I use the phone again to tell Rod then?' she says. 'They'll be up now.'

Martha looks embarrassed. 'Actually, this phone only handles incoming calls.'

'Another one then?'

A bell rings dimly, somewhere far off in the building.

'Time to eat.' Martha smiles. 'I'm sure you'll be happy to join us, Dodie?'

8

Martha frees them from the room and John and Daniel hurry on, heads down, conversing quietly. Daniel flicks a look back at Dodie as they round a corner.

'You OK?' Rebecca says.

'Knackered. I just don't understand –'

Martha puts her finger to her lips.

'And I need to phone Rod,' Dodie says. But phone calls are not enough, not *tangible* enough, that thready disembodied voice, it only makes the missing worse. What she needs is Rod's arms round her, her arms round Jake. And Seth. Need, need, need. It's exhausting.

'Eat first,' Martha says. 'And after you've eaten you can speak to Rod. Then maybe you'd like to take instruction? The more you know, the more you'll understand. And understand Seth's decision to follow this path.'

'I was thinking more of a nap,' Dodie says. 'I'm just so tired.' She longs so much to be alone. 'I'll have a nap this afternoon, if you don't mind. Maybe you've got some magazines or something?'

Rebecca's pale eyebrows shoot up. 'Come on,' she says, tucking her hand into Dodie's arm.

'I need to pee,' Dodie says.

'I'll leave you,' Martha says, 'and see you later on, Dodie.'

'The phone?' Dodie calls after her, but Martha doesn't turn, just holds her hand up.

'Come on.' Rebecca takes Dodie to a long bathroom. On one side there's a row of washbasins, on the other lavatories – with no cubicles around them. A woman is sitting on one. Rebecca pulls down her trousers and does the same. Dodie accidentally glimpses a colourless puff of hair and looks away quickly. Her urge to urinate disappears. Rebecca finishes, wipes herself briskly with a wisp of paper. 'You get used to it,' she says. She runs her hands under a tap.

Three more women come in. The widdly sounds get to Dodie's bladder and, blushing, she goes as far away as possible, sits down and lets it out, gets up quick, flushes and washes her hands. No one takes any notice. Rebecca waits for her by the door.

'Why no cubicles?' Dodie says, when they're out in the corridor.

Rebecca shrugs. 'I know it seems weird at first, but when you think about it, why should there be?'

'For privacy?'

'We're not meant to, like, talk in the corridors,' Rebecca says. 'And there's *no* talking in here.'

She opens a door into a big dining room, a sea of lilac and lavender diners with bad haircuts, and an institutional soupy smell. Dodie follows Rebecca to a short queue by a hatch. She's the only person in here not in purple of some sort and conspicuous in her boots, jeans and sweater, long hair tangling down her back.

They sit at the end of a table of strangers, who glance curiously at Dodie, then return their concentration to their food. It's a bowl of soup, thin, with floating shreds of green, and white squares of tofu lurking at the bottom. There are water jugs and glasses on the table.

'Water?' Dodie asks, reaching for a glass. The others on the table look up sharply and Rebecca, wincing, puts her finger to her lips and shakes her head. *Oh for God's sake!* Dodie pours herself a glass. She eats the soup, very bland, and waits for Rebecca to finish so they can collect their next course – but there is no next course. They take the bowls to another hatch and pass them through.

'Is that it?' Dodie whispers.

What about the carrot cake and the wine? What about those luscious muffins? Maybe they get a better meal at night? John and Daniel are waiting outside the door, and Martha catches up with them all. 'Meditation now,' she says in a hushed voice.

'Oh, but I don't want to!' Dodie says.

Martha lifts her finger to her lips. 'Just twenty minutes or so.'

'I just wanted to chill this afternoon,' Dodie whispers.

'Hey, Dodie, there's no better way,' John says.

'Better than a nap,' Rebecca says. 'Honestly.'

'Scientifically proven,' Daniel adds.

'But I said I'd phone Rod,' Dodie says miserably.

'Later. You won't mind changing your clothes, first?' Martha says. 'Your different style of dress is distracting to the others and, besides, you must be hot? You'd feel more comfortable yourself, more at home with us.'

'Good jeans, though,' Rebecca says. Martha gives her a sharp look and a blush makes her freckles stand out almost green.

'Yeah, these are good aren't they? I think every person must have a best brand for their body shape. I'm a Levi's person –'

'*Hush!*' Martha's voice is a loud hiss and the echo of Dodie's words hang stupidly in the air. Rebecca won't meet her eyes. 'Rebecca, you come with us,' Martha says. She sends John and Daniel off to meditation and sets off at a great lick, round corners and along endless corridors of doors that look identical until eventually she opens one and they step into a lilac room filled with a sweet laundry smell and lined with hanging rails of clothes.

'Trousers or skirt?' Martha asks.

'Dunno. Trousers.' They look good on Rebecca with her long, slim legs. Martha selects a pair of floppy cotton trousers and holds them against Dodie to check the length, then finds her a T-shirt of a slightly paler lilac.

'Try them.' Martha says. The Australian woman, Hannah, puts her head round the door.

'Ha, there you are. He's asking for you,' she says to Martha. 'I'll take over here.'

Martha hesitates. She's breathless and rather pale.

'Where do I get changed?' Dodie asks.

'*Martha*. Our Father is waiting. Or would you rather I . . .'

'No, no.' Martha is clearly torn. 'See you later,' she says, blinking at Dodie and Rebecca, though not at Hannah, as she goes out.

'Going to try them on then?' Hannah says. Her eyes are still on the door Martha went out of, and there's a snarky little smile on her face.

'I don't particularly want to change,' Dodie says.

'You really *like* being a sore thumb?'

Dodie shrugs. It's not such a big deal, and she is hot. *All the things I do for you!* she'll say to Seth. She steps out of the jeans – should have taken the boots off first; she unzips and hops about ridiculously, while Hannah and Rebecca wait, looking at the floor. She puts on the loose, cool trousers, a little too long after all. Rebecca kneels to roll up the bottoms for her. Dodie peels off her sweater – her favourite, green cashmere – and hands it over. She pulls the capacious T-shirt down over her own vest. Of course there is no mirror. Wearing these pyjama-like clothes makes her sleepier than ever.

Hannah folds the old clothes and stores them on a shelf, alongside her boots.

'You forgot your watch.'

Dodie's hand clasps over it. 'I'd rather not, if you don't mind. It's just I always wear it.'

'Imagine if we all wore watches what it would be like here! All the time-junkying.' Hannah puts her hand out.

'What?'

'Ticking and bleeping and counting the minutes.'

Dodie looks to Rebecca for support, but doesn't get any. Hannah keeps her eyes on the watch until, sulkily, Dodie unbuckles the strap and hands it over.

'Keep it safe, though,' she says.

It was a present from Rod when she had Jake: a green strap, a wooden face with numbers he inlaid himself, a proper watch with tiny cogs, not digital. He made it secretly when she was still pregnant. He brought her home from hospital to a house filled with flowers, some bought, but mostly nicked from the Botanics: roses shedding petals, rusty dahlias and huge crunchy hydrangea heads. There was champagne on ice and a fridge full of all her favourite treats, cheeses and anchovies and a coffee cake he'd actually made himself. But the blanket was already descending by then, the sky squashing in on her like a collapsing tent and the baby in the car seat was a stranger, dangerous, with hard gums and a grotesquely pulsing head. She'd sipped champagne and strapped on the watch but the effort of smiling was a fight against gravity.

'Let's find you some slippers.' Rebecca chooses her a pair of espadrilles. 'These fit?'

Dodie sticks her feet in them. Now she feels properly ready for bed.

Hannah escorts them on yet another trek through featureless corridors. 'Enter silently and with respect,' she says. 'Follow Rebecca's lead.' The door opens into a larger room filled with a throbbing hum, it's like walking into a hive, but instead of bees, lilac people humming, the most powerfully undoing sound.

'Just copy me,' Rebecca whispers. She blinks and grasps her thumb, bows her head to a man inside the door, who's wearing a long white robe and a mask. Dodie snorts and glances at Rebecca, and receives a sharp green look. She presses her lips together and follows Rebecca to a stool in the back row. John and Daniel are both there. Daniel looks up, smiles his pretty smile, lowers his eyelids. The electric light illuminates the strange ridges of John's scalp and makes him look a ghastly colour, like parchment. He smiles as he hums – no it's not humming this time, but a kind of intense murmuring. In front of her a row of necks: black, brown, white; stubble from the cropped hair in every shade. The backs of ears have such a ridiculous and vulnerable look, such silly flaps.

Rebecca has started up the mumble now, but Dodie can't distinguish the words. *So sleepy.* No window in here, so you can't tell the time of day. Not enough lunch – and so late. Will they have a tea break; a slice of that nice cake? White ceiling, flat white light fitting. The chanting is actually quite soothing. Twenty minutes then, the time it takes to walk a mile, imagine walking from the park to the roundabout, that's about a mile. She closes her eyes. Does the bookie come before the dry cleaners? A car driving through a puddle sends up a sheet of water to soak her legs. *Stop it.* She breathes and watches and counts her breaths. Go with the flow, go with the flow; she watches the shapes behind her eyelids: clouds, and blurry light and a figure, shadowy, a broken puppet dangling in a hallway. *No.* Her eyes jolt open.

She studies the necks again, thick necks and thin necks. She closes her eyes. *Don't.* Seth. A prickle of frustration. *No.* Jake with his bright round eyes. *No.* She tries to be soothed and buoyed by the voices washing all around her, closing her eyes again. Breathe and breathe.

The sound is like water bubbling, all the individual voices merging into a continuous babble. She's on a bridge, water flowing underneath her, breathe in and out and in and out, water running over stones and rising and in the water Stella's face – *no!* She snaps her eyes open to all the lilac and hair and white and the distinct black dots of stubble on the back of someone's neck and nothing else to see so shut your eyes again, go with it, with the flow, and breathe and breathe.

The time goes slowly. The twenty minutes feel like hours. The sounds are petering out. She opens her eyes, blinks, feels like she's been asleep and dreaming something that has evaporated. Her mouth is dry. One foot is numb, she fidgets it and the blood returns just as a high, thin bell tingles in the air. Everyone raises their arms above their heads and stretches forward, foreheads to the ground, a groaning and cracking sound as their bodies move again. Dodie does the same, feeling a delicious popping in the muscles between her ribs.

They stand and do the movements: a stretch, a bend, a twist, like a speedy yoga class and she tries to keep up, copy the row in front of her and it's so nice to move after all the sitting still. She'd never learn it though, never learn to move in unison, and who wants to move in unison anyway?

'Cup of tea?' Rebecca whispers as they leave.

'God, *yes*,' Dodie whispers back. 'I'd kill for a cup. And then I really *must* phone. Rod'll be going spare.'

'Rod your husband?'

'Boyfriend. I *think*,' she says, tantalisingly, but Rebecca doesn't take the bait.

9

You'd keep fit here, all the hurrying through the corridors after the tiny lunch. John lets them into a poky room with two sofas and a low table. Daniel looks up at them over the rim of his mug. On the table there's a teapot, but no sign of any cake or even biscuits.

'What's with the masks?' Dodie says.

'The Masks have completed initial Process,' Daniel says. 'One day we get to wear them too.'

'But *why*? Why the hell would you want to wear a mask?'

John puts his finger to his lips. 'Sister, you are too loud,' he says.

Loud? Dodie opens her mouth again but nothing comes out.

'You understand in time,' Daniel says.

'Sit and have some tea.' Rebecca fills two mugs.

Dodie does sit on one of the sofas, kicks off the espadrilles and tucks her feet underneath her. 'So, how long have you been here?'

Rebecca hands Dodie her tea. 'Personal' – she seems to search for the word – '*chitchat* is, like, not encouraged.'

'Any activity that is a distraction from Soul Work is not encouraged,' John adds, then presses his hand to his stomach and winces. Dodie sips the tea, something herbal, greenish and a little bitter, not the Earl Grey she was hoping for.

'No biscuits?' she says.

'The Process requires a clearing out of mental . . .' John stops. 'Helps clear . . .' he says, 'the Process,' and then he stops again, droplets of sweat clouding his face. 'Pardon me.' He gets up, makes for the door. Daniel follows, puts himself under John's arm as a prop.

'Hope it's not the tea.' Dodie eyes her cup.

'Come, John,' Daniel says, supporting him while he takes two or three attempts to key in the right number – and then they are out.

Rebecca shakes her head. 'He's got something, I think. Like, you know, something really bad.'

'Poor John. But hey, how does he know the number to get out?'

'John is a big buddy – more advanced. Been here years.'

'How long have you been here?'

Rebecca wraps her hands round her mug of tea and looks round nervously. 'We're not meant to be alone, in a twosome,' she says.

'What?'

Rebecca sips her tea. Dodie copies her. Actually it's not bad; under the bitterness there's a hint of something sweet, liquorice maybe. 'Strange,' she says.

'A special balance of herbs,' Rebecca says. 'Helps concentrate the mind.'

'Like a drug?'

'Soothing.'

'What is it?'

Rebecca shrugs.

'I can't just hang around,' Dodie says. 'Rod'll be having kittens. Anyway, what's up between Martha and Hannah?'

Rebecca wrinkles her nose. 'Yeah, something. I dunno.'

'I mean, I thought it was meant to be all peace and love here.'

Rebecca puts her head on one side. 'Peace and love,' she echoes, thoughtfully. She stands up, sits again. 'Look Dodie, I think we should like, shut up and quietly wait. Just contemplate.'

'See, I've got too much to contemplate,' Dodie begins, 'it's driving me bonkers.' But Rebecca looks pointedly away. It would be an outrageous snub in any other circumstance, but Dodie senses sympathy. She considers leaving the tea; what if it *is* drugged? But she's thirsty. And Rebecca's on her second cup. 'I wonder what time it is?' she says. Nothing. 'Is this room bugged?' she asks. 'Is that why you won't talk to me?'

Rebecca gives a delicate snort.

'Why not then? How long have you been here? Eh? Eh?' She keeps saying it till Rebecca cracks and grins. She's not pretty but her face lights up outrageously when she smiles. She would be a laugh if you met her anywhere but here.

'Days like, lose their edges,' she explains.

'How come you're here?' Dodie says.

'OK.' Rebecca hunches forward and speaks quickly, keeping her eyes focused on her tea. 'Met this guy – this fisherman – at Manchester Piccadilly. He was selling flowers. I was, like, in a bad place and somehow, he scooped me up. He saved me.'

'A *fisherman*?'

'We call them our fishermen – and fisherwomen – they wait in like, airports, stations, places of transition,' Rebecca says, 'where people who need – people trying to, like, escape – often are.'

'The Lost?'

'Yup. The Lost shall become the Chosen.'

'Hmmm.' Dodie frowns. She gnaws the edge of her green nail, the colour disastrous against the lilac outfit. 'Who are the fishermen?' she asks.

'Us, the Chosen, once we've completed the Process. Once we're clear. I *so* want to be clear.'

'The Chosen,' Dodie says. '*I'm* not Chosen.' And nor does she want to be. 'So, what was up?' she asks. 'A bad place, you said.'

Rebecca drops her gaze and shakes her head. 'It was just . . .' She seems about to veer away from the question but then it snags her. 'This fisherman –' She looks nervously at the door. '– comes up and just, like, hands me this flower, a white carnation, just, like, an ordinary old bog-standard carnation but somehow it seems to glow. He tells me I'm chosen. Chosen. Ten minutes before I'd been about to throw myself under a train. *Chosen*, he says and just like that –'

'What *was* up?'

Rebecca sighs and puffs, reels off her troubles like a shopping list: 'Preggers, dumped, failed my exams, kicked out of college.' Her voice deepens as the memory takes hold. 'I lived with my Dad when I was a kid then he married some bitch and they had children of their own.' Her pupils flare. 'I had no one, *then*. I felt, like, nowhere. I had an abortion and then I was so, so, so, so sorry.' A choke comes to her voice. 'I wanted it you know, I didn't even know I wanted it till too late.' She begins to cry. 'My arms were empty.' She holds them out as if cradling a child. 'Then I just like went into a downward spin.'

Dodie goes to put her arm round Rebecca just as the door opens and Hannah walks in. She flicks a hostile look at Dodie as she goes to Rebecca.

'Sorry, sorry,' Rebecca sniffs. 'But John was taken ill and –'

'Your Brother must learn to be strong in the face of his symptoms.' Hannah takes a handkerchief from her pocket, puts a finger under Rebecca's chin and wipes her eyes.

'Blow,' she says and, like a baby, Rebecca blows her nose.

'There.'

Hannah takes Rebecca's hands and pulls her to her feet. 'Rebecca, Sister, look at me,' she says. Rebecca raises her eyes, the pale eyelashes spiky wet, and Hannah blinks into them. 'Let it go,' she whispers, 'let it go, let it go. Come on.'

They hum together, a wavering two-tone note that grows in strength until it breaks. Rebecca's chin rises, she blinks into Hannah's eyes and she smiles. 'Thank you, Sister.'

'This is why we don't encourage intimacy,' Hannah says. 'What's the point of getting yourself in a state about the past? Do you believe that? What is the past?'

'Nothing,' Rebecca says.

Satisfied, Hannah nods and lets Rebecca go. 'I'll get some more tea.'

'Is there anything to eat?' Dodie dares to ask.

Hannah frowns. The lines are deep as knife cuts between her eyebrows and beside her eyes. Her lips are thin and dry and bitten. '*Silence*. I won't be long.' She goes out with the teapot.

'*God!*' Dodie says, once Hannah's left the room, but Rebecca doesn't react. She looks straight ahead as if fascinated by the wall. 'It's not bad to feel things.' But Rebecca won't even look at her. 'You have to work things through. This place is crazy. *You're* crazy if you stick it.'

Rebecca blinks and mutters something.

'What?'

'You are a test.' Rebecca slits her eyes at Dodie. They don't even look like her own eyes any more. 'You've been sent to test me.'

Dodie goes to the door and thumps it. She tries jabbing any old numbers into the keypad but it won't open.

'How do I get out of here?' she demands.

But Rebecca only shakes her head. She shuts her eyes and does the infuriating hum till Hannah returns with another pot of tea, followed into the room by a tall white-robed man in a mask.

'*This* is Dodie,' Hannah says, as if she has been the topic of conversation.

'I'm off –' Dodie makes for the door but the Mask shuts it briskly with his foot.

'You can't *keep* me here.'

'Welcome,' the voice that comes from behind the mask is young, humorous, American. The mask is white and smooth, like half an eggshell, with two round eyeholes and a straight slit for the mouth.

'Ta,' Dodie says. Dodie takes a step away from his extended hand.

'Rebecca.' He rests his palm on top of her head. She closes her eyes and smiles.

'Now sit,' he says.

Dodie gives in for the moment and sits beside Rebecca as the Mask lowers himself onto the sofa opposite. Hannah stands beside the door, expression switched off.

'I'm only here to see my brother,' Dodie says.

'Sure.' It's peculiar to watch a blank mask speak; there's a little ring of dampness, condensation, round the mouth slit. 'But first, do you have any questions?' From within the eyeholes Dodie can just make out the glint of eyes. His fingers are long and tapered with blonde hairs on the backs.

'Obviously I have. When will I see Seth?'

The Mask chuckles. 'Only one person could answer you that. Another?'

'Are you stopping him seeing me? Are you brainwashing him?'

Hannah gives a strange growling laugh. 'How melodramatic! You've been watching too much TV.'

'Questions about Soul-Life, I meant?' the Mask says. 'How we began, maybe? See, Our Father here on Earth founded our little community, in the UK first of all, till the

Lord told him to move the operation here, to New York State. And boy, how we're grown since then. See, Dodie, in this big, bad, old world, wow, you only have to switch on the TV to see it's going down the john –'

'I'm not really that interested,' she cuts in. Hannah skewers her with a look. 'And what's with the mask, anyway?'

The Mask laughs. 'Straight to the heart of it, way to go, Dodie. See the mask –' he taps it, a thin hollow egg-shell sound, 'symbolises the desire to renounce individual personality.'

'But I don't see how a person can *possibly* lose their identity. I mean, how can you?'

'Correct,' the Mask says. 'Of course it is impossible. You got me there.'

Rebecca giggles.

'What is identity?' he says, and before Dodie can formulate an answer he's off again. 'Identity is made up of personality, self-image, attitude, memory, aspiration and appearance – yes?'

Dodie considers, nods. That seems about it.

Hannah comes forward, sits beside Dodie and takes one of her hands. 'Let's look at your identity, Dodie.' Dodie pulls her hand away. 'I see your nails are painted green.'

'So?'

'What does that say?'

'I dunno. That I like green?'

'I think it says you're a little unconventional: arty maybe?'

Dodie shrugs.

'Now, why do you need to display this to other people?'

'I don't *need* –'

'A little display. A little *posture*.'

'So?'

Hannah smiles but there's a sharpness in her eyes, a narrowing. 'It's just an example of the work you – anyone out there – must put into maintaining identity, the work of it, to work so hard to keep up, to keep up the identity; the work so hard, the effort so tremendous, the years, the years, the lifetime of effort to hold yourself separate. Green polish, the edges you construct, the way you hold yourself apart, the separation.'

Dodie forces a laugh. 'What a fuss about a bit of nail polish!' But her voice sounds phoney, nasal. 'Look at you!' she says, and feels Rebecca flinch beside her but she can't stop herself. 'You have your own hands and hair and mind and your voice and' – Oh God, the jeering voice pours out of her, can't stop now – 'you preach away to me but *you're* still *you*. And you,' she adds to the Mask.

Hannah smirks at the Mask. 'Finished?' she says to Dodie.

Dodie breathes and swallows, her heart hammers, her hands are wet; she looks at the green nails, how stupid they look, ten little exclamations: Look at me! I'm Me! I'm quirky! Arty!

'See, I wear the mask,' the Mask says, smoothly, soothingly, into the prickling silence, 'just for that, just to set myself free from the tyranny of expression, facial expression, and of inflicting that expression and the messages it sends – oh so many – witting and unwitting – that taint the words I say. *Of course* I can't get rid of all signs of human identity, you're not wrong, but I can minimise. The mask minimises – do you see? – the expressions of identity. Identity is the enemy of soul; that is the founding principle of Soul-Life. So thank you, Dodie, for your question.'

'I'm tired. I need to phone home. I want to see my brother and get out of here.' Dodie's voice has become tetchy and childish.

'You want to persuade your brother to give up his new found peace?'

'No.' Dodie stops, because, yes, of course, that is exactly what she wants. 'Well, it all depends. I just want to hear from him that he wants to be here, and if he *really* does, I'll leave him. Then I'll go home to Rod and Jake.'

'Jake, ah yes, your son.' The Mask is bowed for a moment, hesitating. 'And?'

'What?'

'What else do you want from life?'

Dodie shrugs. 'Ordinary things. Living. Enjoying life. Watching Jake grow up. Another baby. Travel maybe.' Dodie stops, it sounds thin, even to herself. 'I know it sounds trivial,' she says, 'but it's not when you're in it.'

'Exactly,' the Mask says, throwing out his arms triumphantly. 'That is the nature of the trap. You can't see it till you're out of it. Here you have a chance – wow Sister, think of it – you have a chance to see it from the outside in. You have a chance to escape.'

'But even if I wanted to, I could never leave Jake,' she says. 'Not in a million years. Not for anything.'

'What if Jake came here?' Hannah suggests.

'No! Rod would go ballistic. And no – *don't* even think of suggesting that he comes too.' She laughs at the idea.

The Mask stands up and holds out his hand. 'Great to meet you Sister.' He encloses her thumb in his palm and squeezes. Hannah opens the door and they all step out into the corridor. The Mask lopes off and turns a corner, out of sight.

'Before anything else, I want you to take instruction,' Hannah says, and holds her finger up to silence Dodie. 'It's what Seth wishes. Martha talked to him this morning. He said he'd see you later, *if* you take instruction. He needs you to understand where he's coming from.'

'I do understand.'

'Do you now?' Hannah's tone is mocking. 'Well, you need to understand better then, don't you? It's the only way.'

The way Hannah looks into her face, it's as if someone's rifling through her mind.

Dodie pulls her gaze away. 'What time is it?' she says. 'See, I must ring before Jake's bedtime.' *What if I screamed?* she wonders.

'After this.' Hannah keys in her code.

'But Martha said –'

'Martha's busy.'

'If you just let me phone, then I could relax. I do want to learn more,' she adds, 'it's just that –'

Rebecca goes in, but Hannah puts her hand on Dodie's arm. She pushes the door almost shut again, with her foot.

'All's fine at home, no worries.'

'What?'

'Rod phoned. Martha spoke to him.'

'*What?*'

'Shhh.' Hannah puts her finger to her lips.

'But why didn't you say? Why didn't she fetch me?'

'No need. He just wanted to know that you're OK. He said to tell you to take your time, enjoy the break. He's taking Jake to visit his mother – in Inverness, right?'

'Really?' Dodie stares at her. 'But he never visits his mum.'

Hannah raises her sharp shoulders in a shrug. 'That's what he said.'

'But *I* wanted to speak to him.'

'Anyway, you can relax now, can't you?'

'Not really.'

Hannah raises her sparse eyebrows. Dodie presses her fists to her eyes; she can't think straight. Her mind is so tired. She longs to sleep, to shut her eyes; maybe *then* she could think properly. If she sits down to meditate she'll probably fall asleep, and that wouldn't be bad, a rest from thinking just for a little while.

'If he rings again before I leave, *please* tell me.'

'Yes. Of course. Now, in you go.' Hannah gives her a little shove into the room and shuts the door behind her.

10

She recovers her balance in a roomful of kneeling people, all eyes closed, expressions rapt. A man with a mask stands at the front, speaking softly. This one sounds South African. He doesn't falter in his flow of words, but tilts his head, indicating that she should sit. John is there, looking very pale, and Daniel, both seated near the front. Dodie spots Rebecca at the back and settles down beside her on a kneeling stool.

Let the edges go, let go the edges.

Her heart scrambles against her ribs. Rod gone to his mum's? Well, that's good. When she gets back she'll go too, she'll go and stay in the little bungalow with its chilly view over the Moray Forth. Sometimes you can see dolphins, Jean said, the only time they visited her, when Dodie was about six months pregnant. They'd stood in a row at the window, a cup of tea apiece, gazing expectantly at the glassy grey surface of the water. If she could be there now, eating a scone with bramble jelly. A long growl comes from her stomach and she looks sideways at Rebecca, but she has her eyes clamped shut. Jake giggles when her tummy rumbles.

Let go the pain of edges, let go the immense effort of holding yourself separate.

She looks down at her stupid nails and winces, curls her fists to hide the green. She misses the green watch strap, can't prevent herself looking at her wrist. It's a nervous tic, tickless, hee-hee. What time is it? How adrift you feel if you don't know the time. If only there were windows so you could see the daylight or the dark. It can't be healthy; it's like living underground. Don't you need sunlight to make Vitamin A? Or is it D? *Let go the edges.* And time is full of edges, edges to the hours, edges to the minutes, edges to every second, what if there were no edges? Dizzying, the sudden expanse of time all washing loose. What is it, time?

Your separation is an illusion. Your separate self, illusory. All the soul pain of holding yourself so separate, let it go.

Is time a thing? Or is anything? *Let it go, let it go.* Her eyes want to shut, so sleepy. She tries to block the incantation from her mind but the rhythm is lulling, soothing, insistent, and despite herself, her mind seems to like it, wants to listen, to go with it. Think about Jake, the best thing, what? The day of his birth, the overwhelming pain of that separation, outrageous, nothing you could be prepared for, utter agony that afterwards seemed beautiful and pure, the wet head, sticky hair and furious screwed-up little face and how her heart came out of herself as he came out of her and has never been her own ever since.

The pain of owning. The pain of keeping the things you own, the pain of edges.

Tiny Jake in Rod's strong arms, the love flowing from his eyes for *her*. 'Thank you,' he said simply. 'Thank you for this.' And so he had a son, and then it all collapsed around her. Seth would come round, smelling of school, and sit in the dim beside her, but she couldn't even smile at him.

Let go the edges that separate you from the sea of soul. Let go the pain of edges.

Yes, OK then, she lets it go, just for now, just for this moment and she listens to the words and feels herself let go.

At some point the voice stops. And at some point it begins again, or perhaps it's a different voice, but what does it matter? They are all the same voice ultimately. It's hard sometimes to know if the words are still going on or if they are only reverberating in her memory. The pain of edges: something cries out within her, a creature trapped inside a shell, the pain of edges.

At some point they all rise, it's easy just to let herself be guided. They leave the room and walk as one body down the corridor, soft feet soft on the smooth floor. Someone hands her a toothbrush and they wash faces and clean their teeth and use the toilet and it means nothing and no one looks or cares and it's all so easy like that and now the idea of little secret rooms and the embarrassment of the toilet all her life seems ludicrous, funny, the lengths she'd go to so no one would ever hear her going, or smell her smells, and she finds herself giggling weakly as she sits on the toilet, light-hearted, light-headed, maybe it's the tea, but never mind, tired that's all, what time? It doesn't matter, just sleep, that's all that matters now, to sleep.

She notices a sound as she follows Rebecca and the others down a corridor and up some stairs where there's a window and it's light outside and the sound is birdsong. Morning then? The dormitory has maybe twenty beds, narrow and simple and lilac, the pillows white. There is a nightgown on the bed, everyone removes her clothes and Dodie climbs straight into bed. She sees the others on their knees muttering prayers, thumbs clasped and then

The waking bell comes what seems a minute later. One minute of stretching out and sleep. Of course it must have been longer than that. Everyone gets out of bed, so hard – another hour, another minute even – everyone yawning and stretching, and then the movements, she's the only one still in bed. She gets up and tries to join in, lifting her arms, moving her hands in time with them the best she can. She's dizzy when she stands, a flurry of white stars at the edges of her vision as if she might faint. There was no dinner, she realizes. Her stomach when she touches it is almost flat, the flattest it's been since before Jake – *Jake* – a sickening surge of longing now, yearning, a pain, a real pain, the real pain of separation. She hasn't thought about him for hours, for the longest ever, except for the constant thrumming of her missing, the umbilical ache and breastiness his existence causes in her. What time is it there? No idea even what time it is here.

They all remove their nightgowns and walk into the shower, one long shower, barely warm, bottles of gel scented with lavender, and entirely unselfconscious soaping of underarms, between the legs, between the buttocks, feet and arms and legs, gel rubbed into the hair, all the short crops so much easier than her own wet strands. A pile of towels white or lilac, nothing is their own, she sees, the clothes, the towels, the nightgowns, you just take the one you get and that's fine, all the different breasts and bellies, and patches of body hair. Many of the women are thin; Rebecca's ribs show and her hip bones jut. If Dodie stayed here she'd get like that, lose the last bit of her baby fat. Like a health spa without any of the pampering, think of it that way.

Morning now, she's got yesterday over and now she'll get to see Seth, hug him, shake him, get through to him. And phone home. Not home, phone Jean's. Or Rod on his mobile, but he's never got it with him. She scrubs the towel over her face and tries to conjure up his face, she knows the words for it – the caramel brown eyes, the wicked slanting dimples in his cheeks, the constant prickly stubble – but can't make a picture in her mind. Though as she dries between her legs she feels his face pressed there, a little squirm of longing, a secret shock.

She walks beside a young black woman as they hurry along a corridor, down a flight of stairs and round a corner. 'I'd never be able to find my way anywhere round here,' Dodie says. 'It must be huge.'

The woman grins. 'Yeah,' she says, 'it's pretty big. I'm Mary.'

'Dodie.'

Rebecca catches up with them.

'I wonder what's for breakfast,' Dodie says, despite the finger pressed to Rebecca's lips. She will not just obey every stupid rule. This isn't school. She isn't really part of it. It's funny using her voice again; she realizes she hadn't spoken since the long meditation last night, and how long ago that was she has no idea. They stop at a door and they issue not into the dining hall but another meditation room.

'I'm starving.' Alarmed, Dodie grabs Rebecca's arm. 'Aren't you?'

'Just a little meditation, Sister,' a voice says, and she jumps. It's another Mask. 'First thing on waking is a great time, the mind is most receptive.' It sounds like the first Mask. Are the Masks the same as the fishermen and fisherwomen? There's nothing she can do; even if she walked out she'd have no idea where to go. Grumpily, she kneels with the others. This is crazy. Her stomach flutters with emptiness. A diet is one thing but starvation quite another. Her head feels strangely empty too, and bad-tempered; low blood sugar always makes her crabby. Her hair drips and dampens the T-shirt on her shoulders, makes her itch.

Outside, Brothers and Sisters, bombs are exploding, people are starving, people are blowing each other to pieces in the name of the Lord, those people take the name of our Lord in vain, those perpetrators of evil are doing the devil's work, you, we, here, every one of us is chosen, chosen by the Lord God to rise above the evil, to defeat it with our purity and with our charity and chastity and with our love.

Chastity?

Outside, conditions are gathering for the end; as the world becomes corrupted with greed and ignorance, licentiousness with all aspects of evil. Even the planet itself rises up in protest and greater upheaval is on the way. You have been chosen to be apart, Brothers and Sisters, in our Lord, so let it go. Let the evil go.

'Let it go,' everyone says.

But they're not all evil, Dodie thinks, they are not, Seth's not and Rod's not and Jake's not and –

'Let it go.'

'Let it go.'

'Let it go.'

'Let it go.'

The chant swings back and forwards between the Mask and the rest and – even though she can feel the effect of what they say, the effect of those words on her which are beginning to have a physiological effect, a real sense of shedding of load – she will not join in, not be made to join in. The voices rise and become faster and faster so that there is no longer a distinction between the call and the response and it becomes a huge vibrating hum, loud enough to split the building open – and then suddenly it stops and the silence and the echo of the voices in it is a shock, like coming to a sudden edge and hardly being able to stop. She feels as if her legs are cycling frantically in empty air above an abyss.

Let it go, the voice says, soft now, *let it go, let go the pain of edges, give yourself a break and let it go.* At his words her hands loosen of their own accord, something in her stomach gives. OK, for now, just being here, just let it go; and it's a relief to give up the struggle just for this moment. *Let go the edges,* he says and it's almost frightening how easy it would be to utterly submit to this. She tightens her fists till her nails dig into her palms; these are her edges and she will not let go, the sharp blades in her palms must work as her reminder of who she is and that this isn't really her at all. Still. Let it – most of it – go.

11

And after a time a bell tingles in the air, like a taste of something thin and fine, and at last they go to the dining room. No pancakes or maple syrup or muffins, not even toast and jam but a thin porridge sweetened with fruit – not bad and quite filling. Dodie shovels it down quickly, looks up in the hope of more, but actually her stomach feels bloated with the sudden inrush of food. Her eyes want to close, her head to droop. She puts down her spoon and waits for Rebecca – who eats daintily, half a spoonful at a time – and her other companions: Mary, who raises her eyebrows and gives her a humorous grin across the table; Daniel, eating steadily, a secret smile dimpling his cheek; and John, whose skin is blotchy grey and yellow, lifting the spoon to his mouth as if it's a great weight.

A hand on her shoulder makes her start and Martha's warm breath comes close to her ear. 'Seth will speak to you now,' she says, and Dodie jumps up, jolting the table. 'Whoops, sorry,' she says. Martha hushes her. She clambers out over the bench. Martha nods from her bowl to the hatch and Dodie takes it, gives it to the poor pair of dishpan hands behind the hatch. Martha leads her to a tiny room with a couple of the low squashy sofas, one slit and leaking mustard-coloured foam.

'Sit down,' she says.

'Where is he?'

'Patience. Sit down.'

'Why didn't you fetch me when Rod rang?'

Martha touches her finger to her lips.

Dodie perches on the edge of the damaged sofa. Who damaged it, someone driven mad by all the rules, no, the *encouragements*? She runs her finger through her dryly tangling hair. No conditioner, no hairbrush: she must look a wreck; her fingernails are chipped to hell.

Martha sits down beside her. 'How are you today?'

'Fine.' She waits. 'So. Seth?'

'A moment first. How did you find the meditation?'

'OK, I suppose. Where is he then?'

Martha shakes her head smilingly and takes a phone from her pocket.

Dodie's stomach scrunches tight with disappointment. 'I thought you meant *see* him.'

'Seth?' Martha checks he's waiting and hands over the phone.

'Dodie,' Seth says. It's the bad line again.

She steadies her voice as she speaks. 'Where are you?'

She hears another voice. Hannah's? And then he says: 'Across the state.'

'What? Seth?'

'*Dodie*,' he says, as if he's only just clicked that it's her.

'Yeah, it's *me*.'

And at last she feels the old connection between them. 'Can you get over here? she asks. 'Or I'll come there. I need to talk to you.' Through a crackle of static she hears him breathe. She looks at Martha, puts her hand over the receiver. 'Do you mind?' she says, nodding at the door.

Rather to her surprise, Martha goes to the door. 'Tea?' she asks.

Dodie nods and waits till Martha's gone. 'Seth,' she says. 'I've come all this way. Stop pissing about. It's *me*, fuck it Seth. Remember Dodie? Remember *me*?'

This is not a place for swearing in, of course, but he's driven her to it, and anyway, the way he used to swear when out of Stella's earshot, the way he used to swear about Stella. And suddenly, in a big black whoosh comes the memory, the toes, the empty hands, the broken puppet head. She takes a deep steadying breath, stares at the stuffing bulging from the slit cushion. 'OK. You know Mum's dead?' Silence. Has he gone? 'Seth?'

She hears Hannah murmuring and then another surge of static.

'Seth? I need to tell you what happened,' she says. 'Face to face. Seth?'

No answer. There's a click and a hum then nothing. She

hurls the phone across the room and it cracks and comes apart, pieces of plastic spinning across the floor. Martha comes back in with two mugs on a tray. She sees the phone and tightens her lips, but says nothing.

'He's gone,' Dodie says.

Martha puts a mug of tea in front of her and sits down.

'He said he was across the state. I'll go there then.'

Martha shakes her head. 'Not possible.'

'I heard Hannah!'

'Hannah?' Martha looks startled. 'No, Hannah's here. Ah. . .' Her face lightens. 'That'll be Abigail – she's Australian. She does sound a bit like Hannah.'

Dodie stares at Martha's face, her eyes. Is there an insincere flicker. Is she lying? *Martha?*

'Or is he here? Is someone not letting him see me?'

'Don't be so silly, Dodie! Drink your tea.'

'Yeah, and drug myself!'

'Don't be silly. Only a little chamomile to soothe you.'

'Doesn't taste like chamomile. Are you lying to me?'

Dodie gets up and paces about. It's shocking, it actually hurts to feel these raw emotions when she's been so tranquil – a beastliness surging through her, animal, thick and meaty-tasting in her mouth. Martha doesn't say a word, just watches, until all the energy drains away and Dodie sits down again, slumps, head against her knees, brain swarming, fizzing with a threatened faint.

'Come on, Dodie,' Martha says after a few moments. 'Of course I'm not lying.' She breaks into Dodie's near slumber – it's strangely comfortable doubled over her knees like that, so tired, wrung out with disappointment and frustration, yet for a minute letting it all go.

'Sit up now,' Martha says, her voice motherly, and Dodie obeys, wobbly, fragile, a bubble that could, that might, break at any moment.

'Go on, drink your tea.'

'Maybe I should just go home,' Dodie says. 'I've done my best.' She takes a little sip of the tea, that pale herby taste. She's probably suffering from caffeine withdrawal.

'Seth will be so sad if you do,' Martha says, and it's as if she's reached right into Dodie's chest and squeezed her heart. She shuts her eyes, breathes through that sensation; it reminds her of breathing through a birth contraction. 'Don't give up on him,' Martha says, 'that's all I'm saying.'

Dodie studies the worn, pink face. 'Why do you care? Anyway, I thought separation from the biological family was –'

'I think he needs some sort of closure before –'

'*Closure!* I come all this way and . . .' Self-pity wheedles into her voice and she presses her lips together till she can control it. 'I need to phone Rod, talk it over with him, and if you say I can't, then I'll just leave now.'

'Drink your tea,' Martha says. Dodie picks it up and sips. It's getting familiar, the bitter overlaying the sweetness. It won't do her any harm. Maybe she should just walk out. But how? She'd need to be let out.

'Dodie.'

'What?'

'I, er . . . I spoke to Rod again.' Martha speaks cautiously.

'*What?*'

'You were asleep.'

'But *I* need to speak to him.'

Martha makes an apologetic face. 'You also need your sleep.'

'*God*, you said you'd get me next time. *Shit. Fuck.*' The swearing lets off the pressure of frustration but leaves the taint of something false and cheap hanging in the air. There is a long silence.

Martha makes unsticking sounds in her mouth as if she's trying to formulate the words before she speaks. 'Maybe. Look. Dodie, are you really hating this all so much? The community and the meditations?'

'I dunno,' Dodie says. 'Not *hate*. I just . . . I just never signed up for it.'

'No,' Martha smiles at her, almost shyly. 'But what about the meditation? What did you feel?'

Dodie sighs, drinks more tea, thinks. She won't admit how she's started to get the idea, understand what they mean about letting go. 'Anyway, you've changed the subject.'

'Just bear with me,' Martha says.

Dodie's eyes go to her wrist again, the lack of a watch makes her realize how often she checks the time, how ruled by it she is. What do they call it? Time-junkying.

'You see, you're getting glimpses. Starting to see past all the distractions.'

'So?' Dodie says.

'You're ready to change.'

'But what if I don't *want* to change?'

'Everything perfectly perfect in your life?'

'OK,' Dodie says, hating her own sulky tone. 'Was, anyway, before you got your hands on Seth.'

Martha gives Dodie a long level look, and the colour rises to her cheeks. 'Change is the one constant, Dodie; on that you can depend,' she says at last. 'Nothing stays the same.'

'Well I know *that*.' There's a tiny leaf floating in the greenish liquid of the tea. Dodie dips her fingertip in to try and fish it out.

'So. Your life has all been hunky-dory?'

'Of course not all hunky-dory, I told you . . . we had a pretty crap childhood. Mum was – but anyway, now she's dead.' She picks at the foam in the ripped sofa, pulling flecks of it out, rolling them into pellets between her finger and thumb.

'Better not do that,' Martha says gently. 'Go on.'

'And now my life is good, mostly good, as much as you could hope for. There's Rod. I love him. Though he – he's going off for a while, travelling.' Her voice cracks and she stops for a moment, steadies her lips round a sip of the tea. 'And Seth, of course. And Jake. He's my life now.'

'But you're upset?'

'Only because I miss them!'

'Dodie. Listen to me.' Martha rests her hand on Dodie's knee. 'Your need is too strong.'

'What?'

'You had an unhappy childhood.' Martha's voice sounds terribly sad, and Dodie flicks her a puzzled look.

'Why do *you* care?'

Martha removes her hand and Dodie edges away.

'And now you're clinging with all your might to the notion that you can mend that in a new family with Rod and Jake?'

'So?'

'Can you not see something wrong with that?'

'No.'

Martha sips her tea and hesitates before she speaks. 'Another approach would be to let it go.'

'What?'

'The misery.'

'I *am*, that's just what I *am* doing!'

Martha shakes her head. 'What you're doing is clinging to it, basing your life on it. Holding on to Seth and Rod and Jake – even more with Jake – as if they are lifebuoys in the sea, using them –'

'Not using!' Dodie gets up, goes to the door and though it's futile bangs on it till her fist gets sore, but Martha's voice goes on.

'Using them to rewrite the story of your life.'

'No.'

'What you yearn for, your happiness, is it not dependent on them?'

Dodie turns, rubbing her knuckles against her mouth. This logic is wrong, she knows it must be wrong but it sounds so right, her own thoughts and certainties struggle against Martha's words like birds trapped in handkerchiefs. 'But that's normal,' she insists.

'That doesn't mean it's right,' Martha says mildly, patting the seat beside her and waiting for Dodie to sit again.

But Dodie stands flexing and unflexing her fists. What's she going to do, punch Martha? This is ridiculous.

'It's OK,' Martha says. 'Ignore everything I've said. That's OK. You're leaving. Go out and live your life just as before. That's your privilege.'

'Don't worry. I will.'

'Fine.'

Silence.

Martha has folded her hands and seems almost to be in prayer. She clears her throat. 'As long as you know there's an alternative,' she says delicately, 'that's all. You could choose to get yourself sorted out. Then you could go back to them strong and whole.'

'You're making out I'm some kind of basket case!'

'No, no. Just good advice. But Rod did tell me you've been ill.'

Dodie breathes in sharply. 'He said that?' She sits down again, knees suddenly weak. She finishes her tea, cool now, and doesn't know what to do with her hands; scrapes a flake of nail polish into her mouth, picks it from her tooth.

Martha watches her all the time, sad love shining in her eyes. 'Want to speak to him?' she says.

Dodie looks up, startled. 'You mean now?'

Martha nods and takes a different phone from her pocket. Fingers trembling, Dodie tries home, she tries Rod's mobile, she tries his mother. No one answers. She leaves bleating messages on each answering service, then drops the phone and puts her head on her knees. Waves of frustration roll through her but, oddly, she finds she's a little detached from them; she can glimpse the separation between the emotion and herself. Maybe she *is* changing. Could it be that this is actually doing her good?

The door opens and Hannah comes in. She blinks and holds her thumb, but glares at Martha.

'Was someone banging on the door?' she says.

Martha frowns, her face darkening as if a shadow has fallen across it.

'Our Father needs you,' Hannah adds, shortly. 'Now.'

'I'll just finish here,' Martha says, a scrape of irritation in her voice. Again, there is a real bristle in the air. Dodie looks interestedly between them, notices the way they avoid each other's eyes, how prickly their body language is.

Martha turns her attention back to Dodie. 'You can leave if you want,' she says. Hannah makes as if to object, but Martha glares at her, and continues. 'But why not give yourself a few more days? And then you'll get to see Seth. Think of it as a holiday for your spirit. You've got a few days before you fly back?'

'What did Rod say anyway?' Dodie says.

Martha leans towards Dodie as if to speak confidentially, as if to shut Hannah out. 'Well, he thinks it might do you good to stay.'

'What?' Dodie feels the blood rise to her cheeks. 'Stay?'

'Not for life,' Hannah chips in drily. 'Just the rest of the week.'

'He didn't even want me to *come* in the first place – but then he did.' Dodie finishes lamely, remembering that it in the end it was his finger that pressed *Confirm* and finalized the purchase of the ticket.

'He said you needed a break,' Martha says.

'He said that?'

Martha nods. 'Let it go,' she says, and blinks into Dodie's eyes, and Dodie does let it all unravel. It all seems too complicated and exhausting and so very far away. At least, for this instant, and this instant is really all there is. She nods, half-shrugs.

'Good,' Hannah said, 'that's settled. Martha, you're letting Our Father down, keeping him waiting.'

'One moment.'

Dodie hears the gritting of Martha's teeth.

'Now *I'll* take you to your meditation,' Hannah says, holding out her hand.

12

She sits beside John, shuts her eyes and lets go, sinking into the words as if into a warm bath. Can't think straight any more anyway. The decision to stay is made and that's a relief, so hard to hold onto the resolve to do anything other than be swept along, soft and easy. It's wisdom, of course, it's obvious, *of course* it hurts to cling to things that will only ever be taken away, the only constant is change, and how restful that thought and how soothing. There are no decisions to be made, not today anyway, she can forget about leaving, just for now, forget about trying to think straight, and who wants to think straight anyway when the universe is made of curves?

Time goes on like that, loose and formless. But as she sits, something begins to happen in her chest, begins to stir and twitch, like a pupa ripe to hatch. It didn't click at the time, not consciously, because it wasn't thinkable, but in the dark recesses it has developed: what if Seth had something to do with Stella's death? What if he was there? What if he killed her and then fled? The guilt of it made him run, made him come here and now he won't see her, of course he won't because he knows that if she looks into his eyes she'll know. Her heart thumps and the nails serrate her palms and the words that come from the straight line of the mask are inaudible behind the thrumming beat of blood in her ears. *No.* But it does make sense. It makes a picture, the pieces falling into place with horrible ease.

That doesn't mean it's true.

Almost falling into place, but one piece is missing, a central piece: *Stella* told the school he was leaving; *Stella* wrote the suicide note. Maybe she needed to get him out of the way before she killed herself. Maybe . . . and the maybes start, multiplying like bacteria, maybe this and maybe that and maybe, maybe, maybe STOP.

Let go the edges, the voice is saying. *Let go the pain of edges. Let go those destructive thoughts, nothing out there matters, nothing that ever happened matters now.*

The voice coming from behind the mask is Caribbean this time, and warm as black treacle stirred in milk, like someone made for her once, sweet and dark to help her sleep – posset, is it? And surely that couldn't have been Stella.

Think of your dearest possession – now let it go.

She thinks. What? What is her dearest thing? Nothing much, well, the house of course.

Think of your dearest person – and now, in your imagination, have the courage to let them go.

NO. Jake. NO. Never.

She reaches for the pain of separation and it's there but fainter, her head a swirl of treacle, milk, water, words. And, hard to hold on to a single thought now, it's there but numbed into a faint umbilical thrum which she can tune into, up the volume, but she realizes with a little flash, she does have a choice, she *could* let go. People do do that; people actually do let go of children.

And some time passes, humming and finding the precise vibration to fit within the others, to lock in and block out all but the sweet sensation of space and blankness, the rising wordless chord that seems to lift you up and out until you are it. And there's another sleep that seems no more than a blinking, something else to eat, sweet porridge or savoury soup, it doesn't matter. More hurrying in the maze of white corridors. Even that, just following in the almost featureless passages, is restful, decisionless, another kind of letting go. Another meditation. A woman's voice this time behind the mask, Southern, maybe Texan. Something is trying to bother her but she tunes into the words and is carried away by them.

And, later – because even if there is no time there is still now and then and later – Martha takes her to a room to talk. Martha is like a mother to her here and it feels good to have a mother who is so warm, like being a child again, mothered properly this time, quietly bewildered at the ways of the grown-up world, but going along with it, and trusting. When she can let herself. Trusting. Trust is such a restful thing. She's never trusted anyone before and never even noticed the lack.

'And how are you now?' Martha says. They sit in the little room with the ripped sofa, mugs of tea before them. She's growing to crave that sweet and bitter taste.

'I'm fine,' Dodie says, 'I let go, like you said.'

'Not me, Dodie, *you*. It has to come from you.'

'S'pose.' Little pellets of foam on the floor where she rolled them before and she doesn't know how long before. Greedily, she sips the tea.

'What day is it?' She has to fight upwards to remember her purpose. 'Mustn't miss my flight.'

'We won't let you forget. We're all so pleased. And Seth is pleased. He'll see you soon.'

At the mention of Seth's name, a shark's fin rises; odd now to think he's the reason she's here. It's like her brain has come unravelled, a strangely nice sensation. 'I'll almost be sorry to go,' she says, and shivers, frowning.

'You don't *have* to go,' Martha says. She smiles at Dodie over the edge of her mug.

'Of course I do,' Dodie says. 'Jake –'

'Rod phoned again,' Martha says, putting down her mug.

'*What?*'

'He rang back after you left your messages. Everything's fine.' She smoothes her skirt over her knees; a small stain there, spilled soup maybe.

'But you should have told me!'

'I would have done, but actually it was Hannah who spoke to him and she deemed it wisest not to disturb you. Anyway, we did agree, didn't we? About how it upsets you to talk to him.'

'I never agreed anything!'

'Hush,' Martha says. 'Just *hush*.'

'I bet he loved that! I *never* agreed not to talk to him!' But the energy required for anger is just too tiring.

Martha kneels in front of Dodie, takes the mug from her hand, looks into her eyes. Dodie gazes into the pale cottony blue of Martha's irises and, as she blinks, Dodie's own eyelids feel heavy, drawn down into a matching blink. Martha begins to hum, a mid-note that begins softly and starts to bloom and when she has to stop to take a breath Dodie finds her own note, a tone higher, and the two of them vibrate like that and it's magical how calming it is, how it soothes. It's like something that holds you up and gets inside you all at once but then the flickery lights of faintness begin to play around the periphery of her vision, not good to get so worked up, not on an empty stomach, must have lost pounds, that's something anyway. The humming stops. The quiet is intense.

'He understood,' Martha says. She settles back on the sofa. 'He shares a concern with me.' She presses her lips together, formulating, it seems, a kind way to say what she has to say.

'What?' Dodie says.

'Now hold on to your calm. OK?'

'What?'

'He said he'd been concerned that you are too attached, smotheringly attached – his words – to Jake, and to Seth. You mollycoddle them. Don't allow them any room to breathe.'

'That's nonsense!' But the word *mollycoddle* zigzags through her like a bolt of lightning.

'Keep calm,' Martha reminds her. 'Now. Perhaps that was why Seth left? You still treat him as a baby when he's a young man, trying to grow up. Perhaps that's why he's ambivalent about seeing you?'

'No. That's not so. I don't believe that,' Dodie says, struggling to sound calm.

'Well, Rod thinks the separation is doing Jake good.'

'Rod would *never* say that!'

She shakes her head and the room swings from side to side, Martha's face swaying like a lantern. 'I don't believe you. I feel sick.'

She shuts her eyes. Inside, the furry light-blobs slide and blur. Martha goes to stand behind her, leans over, faint smell of lavender and sweat, and begins to massage her scalp with tiny delicate movements, so gentle and so subtle that it makes her want to cry. 'It's OK,' Martha whispers, 'let it go now, let it go.'

Her scalp rises to the touch of Martha's fingertips, her hair seems to lift and sway like underwater weeds. The calm of the hum returns and, in fact, Martha hums as her fingers move and Dodie sees behind her eyelids a picture of a woman, of herself, with Jake in her arms and Rod in the doorway of his shed, saying, 'Will you not mollycoddle him?' And she's clutching the child so desperately, because, why? Because he banged his finger and he isn't even hurt; *he* doesn't need to be hugged and he struggles to leave her arms. It's her need, not his. Is it true then that she smothers him? Mollycoddles him and Seth. Martha stops massaging and she feels a pang of loss.

'Rod says you've never really got back to your old self since the birth. Since your depression?'

Dodie stiffens.

'He says it runs in the family.'

Dodie turns slightly away and presses her own fingers hard into her scalp, scrubbing and scratching, rubbing out the soothing touch. 'It was nothing really, just a bit of post-natal . . .' But as she speaks the dark months are there: a taste like metal, the heaviness of the world closing in around her, the mean faces of the people in the streets and even the flowers and how, in the bath, the useless milk wound like sad smoke from her nipples and how could Rod tell anyone? Confide in Martha, this stranger, who he's never even met?

'Look at me,' Martha says, and she tries the blink again, but Dodie won't look into her eyes this time, or at her face.

'You can't make me. You can't make me stay. I'll go back to my hotel and wait for my flight there.'

'All right.'

Startled, Dodie looks up.

'You're right. We can't make you stay. This is not a jail. Maybe better if you do leave.'

Dodie stares at her knees, a lump forming in her throat, tears wobbling her vision. She feels an immensely cold space opening up around her. Martha, the mother, is letting her go. They sit there for a long time. She can hear a click as Martha swallows. The foam from the ripped chair is the colour of new baby poo; she remembers the sweet-sour smell. Sour was her blood then and her milk and now sourness trickles down her sides. How deep the pain. How will she have the strength to get up now and go?

'I can't remember about my ticket,' she says, weakly.

'We'll take care of that.'

They sit longer, no window to show the light, nothing to show the time and it seems there is no limit to it as far as Martha is concerned as it unspools loosely around them. Martha pours more tea but it's barely warm. Dodie drinks greedily. It does have an effect on her, restful and soothing.

'How do you feel now?' Martha says at last.

'I . . . I . . .' Dodie's voice quavers. She clears her throat. 'Weird.' She does a shivery laugh. 'Kind of – I don't know – lost or like I'm losing my marbles.'

'That's good Dodie, it feels strange, I know, but it's marvellous, it's your old identity moving back, letting you see past it.'

Dodie presses the heels of her hands into her eye sockets hard enough to hurt, to make red patches swim and jump. 'OK, I was depressed,' she swallows, 'but I got better. It *was* all . . . hunky-dory.'

'Truly?' Martha's eyes search hers until she has to hang her head. 'Rod's concerned that you won't go back to your teaching.'

'I only wanted to stay at home with Jake. Be a full-time mum. What's wrong with that?'

Martha says nothing.

'It *was* working,' Dodie insists, 'it *was*.'

'Look,' Martha says, 'look, why don't we make a deal? I'll take you to meditation, just one more, then you can eat, then we'll give Seth a last chance to see you and if you still want to leave after that I'll call you a cab. How's that?'

'Yes,' Dodie says, 'yes.' She feels a rush of relief. She can let go again, just for now, relax back into it, and her heart blooms when Martha smiles at her with such approving warmth.

'It's a deal,' Martha says.

Of course she wants to go home, but just a bit longer here; a little more of the calmness and the peace, and then Seth. The thought of seeing Seth is a little frightening now, a sharp edge in her mind. His eyes will tell her what he's done. Ludicrous to think her little brother . . . But she does just need to see his eyes, his face, his dear face and then home, to Jake, to hold her baby in her arms.

The Mask nods at her, and she goes to the back of the meditation room and kneels beside Rebecca, for one last time, and joins the humming. She can relax now; enjoy this last experience. She searches for the feeling of the warm bath but it's more of a choppy current now and it carries with it something insistent that bears down on her, something that refuses to be submerged or dodged, a rope, looping through the water, rearing out at her like an eel.

How easy it had seemed, what a treat and a relief to think of ending it. The image in her own mind had always been the rope: but *she* got better, *not* like Stella, she got better and she was filled with love, *not* like Stella, and is filled with love. Don't think of the blue rope and Stella doing it, the actual process of her doing it, of making the knot and climbing onto the banister and the moment of the drop, what went through her mind in the stretching seconds of that drop? And not to think about how close she once came to that herself. No one knows that, not even Rod, how very close she came.

The day was winter dark and never light and Jake cried and cried and his face was monstrous, his cries swallowing her down the red ridges of his throat and she knew she could shut him up for ever and she lifted the pillow – but then she stopped, she stopped and walked away. And then, then, shocked by what she'd thought of doing and to escape the cries that rasped through her mind and brain, she searched the house, and if a rope had been there ready she could have, would have done it, just to stop herself, to stop it, everything. But Rod came home and next thing was the hospital.

Emotions boil up around her, getting inside her, or maybe finding their way out of her, the rawness, the taste of depression, the smell of it, the terror of her own flesh and blood, her own child and his greedy mouth and hands, how could she feel that? Be that? She's a turmoil, a whirlpool, crazying the calm; where is that calm? The smooth water, the warm, where has it gone?

The way her heart is flailing she fears that she will drown, her breath won't come, she opens her eyes, her mouth to scream – but then it's over. It's calm.

The humming holds her up and she sees, feels an opening. There's light shining clearly between who she is and her experience, a clean space made of light. She gasps and almost laughs out loud at this sudden knowledge, glimpse, of wisdom is it? Yes it is. She presses her hands to her chest, waits for her heart at last to slow. So tired suddenly, but lovely tiredness. And of course it's easier after all, easier to acquiesce, like a child, to stop the frantic doggy-paddle against the flow, stop straining and float in it, allow the light of wisdom in, to let the edges go.

The bell to end meditation has tingled through the air. The Mask says, 'Now, I have good news.' They all look up, open and innocent as a roomful of babies. 'This evening,' he says, 'is the Festival of the Lamb. A very special occasion at Soul-Life, at which you will come face-to-face with Our Father.' He holds his thumb to his chest in the familiar gesture, and they all do the same. Dodie finds her own thumb clutched in her own hand, and even a smile, a flutter of excitement. She will have to stay for this.

13

One Mask offers little cakes off a tray; another offers paper cups of wine. Dodie takes one of each as she files through the door with a crush of others. The cake, in a fluted paper case, is iced and cherry-topped. The treats make people fluttery and childish. Dodie's mouth waters at the fresh spongy smell.

By the time she's inside and has found John, Rebecca and Daniel and squeezed among them at the back, the long, low-ceilinged hall is crammed. Candlelight glows from sconces on the walls – no, not real candles but electric simulacrums. There must be a couple of hundred people. A sea of white and lilac. She doesn't want to eat her cake yet, doesn't want it to be gone.

On a raised platform at the front, twelve Masks are lined up to face the audience. In the centre of the platform waits a kind of throne: empty, garlanded with white and lilac flowers. The atmosphere is giggly, restless with suppressed excitement. Dodie dips her lips into the warm white wine and strains her eyes for Seth. He must be here, surely. From the back it's hard to see; her eyes rest on dark heads, young men of his height, but it's too dim and packed. She studies the twelve figures on the stage. Seth could not be among them, of course not, could not in such a short time have become a Mask: but still she stares at one that stands beside the throne; it could be him, no it couldn't. The blank eyes stare out over the crowd. Even if it was Seth and he was looking, he wouldn't be able to see her, lost in a blur at the back. And on the other side of the throne is a Mask that looks like Hannah. Something about the stance – could it be Hannah? Hannah a Mask? But she has a name; she has an identity. She's Hannah.

'Is that Hannah?' Dodie whispers, but Rebecca lifts a finger to her lips. Dodie realizes she's eaten her cake without even noticing. And that is a bad habit, unmindful and fattening. She screws the paper into a ball, tempted to chew it for the last bit of sweetness. John hasn't touched his cake. Rebecca has eaten exactly half. Stop thinking about cake. She swallows the nippy wine and concentrates. The twelve blank Masks stare straight out. Different heights make an asymmetrical pattern, the row of eyeholes and mouth slits sipping and rising again, like some kind of dot-dash code.

Music begins, quiet at first and rising pompously. The fidgeting and whispering cease. A door at the rear of the platform opens and two Masks come through – Our Father and an attendant, the shape and size of Martha. Could *she* be a Mask?

A sigh goes up from the crowd and from somewhere a sob. One by one, clutching their thumbs, people drop to their knees. John lets himself down and Rebecca follows. Dodie leaves it a moment too long and so is the last one standing. The dark eyeholes of all the masks rest on her until she kneels.

'Our Father,' say the Masks.

'Our Father,' echoes the crowd.

Our Father stands at the front of the platform and raises his arms in a gesture of benediction.

'Our Father here on Earth,' chant the Masks and the crowd follows. 'Blessed be thy name.'

'Please be comfortable,' Our Father says. Dodie's startled by his accent – English, surely, with flat Northern vowels overlaid with an American twang and rather quavery, as if he is very old or ill. Everyone kneels. Dodie looks at Rebecca's fervent face and then at John's. He hasn't touched his cake.

'Do you want that?' Dodie whispers. He hands it over and she puts it in her mouth, mindful this time of the eggy vanilla taste and the sweet squelch of the neon cherry.

'It is too long since I last addressed you all,' Our Father begins. 'Since that time twelve new devotees have been chosen. Let us honour the newcomers. All of you who've arrived since our last ceremony, please stand.'

Dodie, Rebecca, Daniel, Mary and the other novices get to their feet. The kneeling crowd swivel to see them. Surely Seth should be among them? But he certainly is not.

'Welcome to the newly Chosen,' Our Father says. 'We honour you, we cherish you, we love you.'

Beside Dodie, John topples from his knees, head cracking on the floor, wine spilling.

'Our Brother is overcome by the power of the Lord's love,' Our Father says. 'Praise Him!'

'Praise Him!' echoes the crowd.

Dodie tries to help John up but Our Father says, 'Leave him be, and now, all of you, please kneel down.'

'Are you all right?' Dodie whispers, and John shifts a little, does the barest nod. Dodie pats his arm, looks at Rebecca, but she is absorbed in watching Our Father.

'Tonight is the Ceremony of the Lamb,' he says. 'But first we witness the sacrifices. Sister?' He indicates the attendant Mask – who surely is, *must* be, Martha – and she helps him – he must be very old and weak – to lower himself on the throne.

The Mask who might be Hannah steps forward. 'Peter,' she says, and yes it is Hannah's voice.

A tall guy stands and steps up on to the platform.

'What is your sacrifice?' Our Father asks.

'All my worldly goods,' he says. 'My company and my house. With no hesitation.'

'Your worldly goods will do you little good on judgment day,' Our Father says.

'Amen,' says everyone.

'But they will help us in our crusade to locate and educate the Chosen. Come close.' Peter kneels at Our Father's feet and receives a blessing. And then he rises, stumbles a little, as if overcome, and with both fists pressed to his heart, leaves the platform.

'Ladies,' Hannah says, and five young women stand and move up onto the stage.

'What is your sacrifice?' Our Father says.

'Ourselves,' Dodie thinks they say, and she looks to Rebecca but she is straining forward, a bright sheen in her eyes.

'We have no worldly goods to offer but we willingly give our bodies for Our Father.'

'Bless you,' Our Father says.

'Like prostitution?' Dodie whispers.

'Shh.'

Our Father blesses each of the women, and as they leave the stage, so much joy shines from their faces that it seems to brighten the dimness of the hall.

'We must honour the Chosen for their sacrifice. And each of you must search your heart and soul for what you will give. That which is dearest to you, will be best for your soul, and that which benefits Soul-Life is what is asked of you, and truly you will find it is no sacrifice for these are scales you must shed in your journey towards the Universal Soul.'

Our Father's voice is weakening. Dodie has to strain to hear.

'Amen,' makes a quiet ripple round the room in throaty, fervent whispers and it's almost quiet, only a cough here, a fidget there, as each contemplates what he or she will give. And Dodie looks down at the ground, littered now with paper cups and cake cases and crumbs, and knowing she has nothing more she will give, not her body, not her house, not her son, she feels a shiver of separation, a sliver peeling away between herself and the rest.

'Tonight is the Ceremony of the Lamb,' Our Father continues. 'The Lamb is a symbol of all that is meek and good.' He hesitates and the Mask that is Martha comes close to him, supports him, whispers in his ear before he continues: 'It is a symbol of the son of our Lord who sacrificed his own child for the good of mankind; the Lamb is a symbol of sacrifice itself.'

'Amen,' everyone intones, louder now. One of the Masks leaves the platform by the door and returns with a tiny newborn lamb in his arms. Another withdraws a long blade.

'The Blood of the Lamb is a benediction from our Lord in Heaven,' Our Father says, and he takes the creature tenderly in his arms. Against a steady background hum from the Masks, the lamb bleats and before Dodie can believe what is about to happen, it has happened and blood flows from the neck of the lamb into a bucket, audible above the hum, pumping out in a heavy splatter as the creature squirms, slackens, hangs empty across Our Father's crimsoned lap.

Dodie's hand flies to her mouth and she gags, eyes watering. She looks at Rebecca's expression, fixed and resolute. John still lies on the floor, eyes closed. But Daniel's eyes are bright, and his smile is joyful. The hum in the room rises, most people joining now in a multi-stranded crescendo, which, as Our Father lifts and holds out the little body as an offering, stops.

'To be washed in the Blood of the Lamb,' Our Father says, 'I invite you one and all.'

'Stand.' Hannah lifts her arms. And the pompous piped music rises again as the crowd stands, but not John. Dodie hunkers down beside him.

'John,' she says. She shakes him. '*John*.' But there is no response. 'Help me,' she says, and she and Rebecca pull John to his feet. Hannah has instructed everyone to file out past the platform. As they pass Our Father he dips a finger in the blood and daubs a cross on each forehead. There is a kind of glee about the whole occasion now as if this is a most outrageous treat, the giggliness returned. 'Bless you,' Our Father says to each.

'We need to get him out of here,' Dodie says.

'But he must be blessed,' Daniel says.

'But he's unconscious. He needs a doctor. We'll ask Martha.'

'Put him down while we wait,' Rebecca says. 'I don't think you're meant to stand unconscious people up.' They struggle John into the queue and allow him to slump down, head lowered between his knees. Dodie looks down at the shaved top of his head. Knotted white scars among the sandy stubble.

'Know what's up with him?' she whispers.

Rebecca shakes her head.

'It's the Lord's will,' Daniel says and Dodie feels more of herself peeling away from the fanatical shine in his eyes, the blandness of his face which might as well already be a mask.

Eventually, supporting John, they approach the platform. 'He's blacked out,' Dodie says. 'He really needs a doctor.'

'Bring him to Our Father,' Martha says.

Our Father's mask tilts towards the grey-faced man. The bucket is almost empty. He has to smear his finger round the sides to pick up enough blood to mark first John, then Daniel, then Rebecca, and finally Dodie with a cross. The blood is tacky and Our Father seems to linger with his finger, the eyeholes focused on her for too long. The iron tang of blood makes her want to gag again, that and the sick heaviness of John and the gullible shine of Daniel.

'Where shall we take him?' Rebecca asks.

Hannah steps down from the platform. She bends towards Our Father, holding her thumbs, and Dodie sees the shiny pink depression where the thumb joint was. A peculiar quailing sensation travels through her when she sees his thumbless hand, narrow, flipper-like, bloody from the lamb, and she finds herself clutching her own thumb close to her heart in the familiar gesture.

14

'Bring him this way.' Hannah walks away from them along the corridor. The elastic thread from the mask is tight round the back of her fairish-grey head. Manipulating John is like steering a drunk. There's some movement in his legs now, some life returning, and he staggers soggily between Dodie and Rebecca. Daniel has left them now and Dodie is glad, something like hate was growing in her for him, or for his ability to believe and follow. He glowed with a sort of holy smugness.

Hannah opens a door into a narrow room with beds and lockers like a hospital ward. One of the two lights fails to switch on – it's dismal and almost cold.

John has peed himself. They work off the wet trousers and put him into bed. His body is thin, the flesh waxy, the ribs and knobbles of spine showing yellow through the skin. His penis is a poor scrunched acorn lost in a drift of leaves. He lies flat and groans, flutters his eyes open for a moment. His breath is foul.

'He needs a doctor,' Dodie says.

'Water?' Rebecca asks him and he nods. There's water in a jug but it's dusty and half evaporated. She goes to the tap and freshens it, wets a cloth and wipes his face.

'Will you phone?' Dodie asks.

Hannah's mask holds still on her face. 'There's no medical intervention, don't you know that?'

'But this is really serious!'

'And Our Lord is really serious. If He wishes John to recover, then he will.'

'But he might –' Dodie begins, but can't say *die* in front of John.

'If it's God's will, our Brother will be released from the trials of life. He will let go, finally, the edges. He will be free.'

'We just let him go?' Dodie says. Hannah stares at her until she looks down. The blood crusts itchily on Dodie's brow, but she won't scratch, doesn't want lamb blood under her nails.

'You and Rebecca stay with him,' Hannah says. 'I'll be back in a moment. Rebecca: *remember*.' She blinks at Rebecca and leaves the room, locking the door behind her.

'Remember what?'

Rebecca concentrates on stroking John's cheek.

'What?' Dodie says. '*What?*'

Rebecca flashes a quick grin. 'Not to let you – Satan – get to me.'

'Satan,' Dodie says. 'Do you *really* believe in Satan?'

Rebecca frowns; she looks confused, a struggle going on behind her eyes.

John shifts and groans. He seems to be trying to say something, gathering himself for some effort.

'What is it?' Dodie says. 'What do you want?' He lifts his head but then it falls, his eyes roll back, the whites a frightening yolky colour.

'We should try and get a doctor,' Dodie says. 'Maybe someone here was a doctor?'

'No,' John says. His voice comes out with surprisingly strength.

'Are you sure?' Dodie asks.

'It's his choice,' Rebecca says. 'To come here. We all know there's no medical interference.'

'But –'

'God's will,' Rebecca says.

'It's God's will to let someone die when they might be saved?'

'It's a different meaning of saved.'

'If God didn't want there to be medicine, why did he let there be doctors?'

Rebecca won't meet her eyes; she's playing with John's fingers.

'Or are doctors and medicine Satan's work?'

Rebecca eyelids are veined like leaves. 'Remember, these doubts are good,' she says, and she still won't look up. 'It shows the new you is aware of Satan's tricks.' She says it like a recitation.

'I don't believe you believe –'

'Don't,' Rebecca says, sharply, a flutter of panic in her voice. 'Let me believe what I want to believe.'

'What you *want* to believe?'

A shadow moves across Rebecca's face. The blood has dried brown on her smooth white forehead; a flake fallen off and lodged in her pale eyebrow.

'What can we do, Brother, to make you feel better?' Rebecca leans over John, strokes the side of his face. He's so sweaty that the blood has smeared all over the place, ghastly red against the grey-yellow of his skin and eyes and lips and even his teeth, which seem coated in mouse fur when he gasps his mouth open for a rattly breath.

'I don't know if I can do this,' Dodie says, staring at the mess that is John. 'And that poor lamb.' She winces, remembering the heavy splattering of blood into bucket.

'The sacrifice is central,' Rebecca says.

'But why?'

'Don't,' Rebecca says. She blinks and hums, a high wavery mosquito.

Dodie sighs and grasps John's other hand. Runs her finger over the tattoos that mottle the back and crawl bruisily right up his arms under the fair curly hair.

'How did *you* come to be here?' she asks him, expecting no answer,

His breath is rattly and laboured but he has a smile on his face now. 'Chosen,' he gets out and then a sharp inhalation and, '*Man*.'

'What?'

'*Pain*.'

'Where?' Dodie says but he lays down his head and his eyes slide under his lids. 'Just rest,' she soothes, 'take it easy.'

'Let go,' Rebecca says, and the corners of his mouth lift. 'That's it, let it all go.' They sit and watch the breath struggle in and out of his bluish lips. His nostrils pinch open and shut with the effort.

'Will you do prostitution?' Dodie whispers.

Rebecca shrugs. 'Maybe.' She massages John's fingers, squeezing the tips between her own.

'I couldn't,' Dodie says. 'I just couldn't stand it.'

Rebecca gives a little shrug. 'We have to, like, do something. And there's teaching in it. That this body is nothing really, just a fleshmobile. Moving towards the loss of identity. It doesn't matter you see.'

But it sounds phoney, as if she's kidding herself.

'You know what, Rebecca, I *like* your identity,' Dodie says. 'If we were out of here we'd have a lot of fun.'

Rebecca flattens the corners of her mouth.

'Yeah,' Dodie says. 'Hannah's slipped up leaving us alone. I'll soon lead you astray.'

Rebecca loses her struggle with her expression and grins. There's a weak smile on John's face, or maybe a grimace.

'OK, John?' Rebecca says, but he doesn't answer. They sit for a moment, gazing at him.

'Don't you think . . .' Dodie picks her way carefully through the words. 'Don't you think it's kind of *exploit-ative*?'

Rebecca gives a scrape of her fantastic donkey laugh. 'Whores for Our Lord?' she says. 'That has a pretty good ring to it.'

Dodie stares at Rebecca, trying to read the smoothness of her face. The pale lashes are lowered, the sickly artificial light casts elderly shadows on her cheeks spinning her years into the future when the fair will be grey and the freshness will have faded. Dodie realizes she's been crushing John's hand in her own; she scrubs the brothy sweat on the leg of her trousers. She wets the cloth and wipes John's hands and squeezes a little water onto his dry lips.

'So, no sex among the Chosen but you can go and fuck any old pervert who's got a few dollars going spare?'

'Guess so,' Rebecca says evenly. 'But it must be a sacrifice. If it was nice it wouldn't be, would it?'

'It might be nice sometimes,' Dodie says. 'What if a gorgeous hunk walked in, would you turn him down?'

Rebecca guffaws again. 'Shut up!'

Dodie goes to speak but then she feels a shiver go up her arm as if something has travelled, evaporating, through her veins. The hand she holds has lost all tone. She and Rebecca feel it at the same instant and their eyes meet. He's gone. No question. The smeary lamb's blood on his brow looks almost fluorescent against his dead skin, sunken eyes, sickly smile. She lets his dead hand drop. A tattooed mermaid has her tail wrapped round his wrist. The hairs are crisp and light, the message not got through to them yet. The pupils are flared in the muddy hazel of his widened eyes. Rebecca swallows audibly. Tentatively, she puts her finger on the lids to press them down. Dodie gets a sudden shocking urge to giggle. She turns away and frowns at the wall, a dispenser of pocked blue paper towels. A Sprite can on a shelf. Her throat aches with the outrageous banality of death.

When she turns back, Rebecca has her head against John's chest. 'We let him die,' she murmurs.

'Yes,' Dodie comes close and looks. Rebecca's skin seems so buoyantly alive besides John's. Pale, but with a glitter in it. The blood is flaking off. Dodie scrubs at her own forehead with her sleeve. Washed in the Blood of the Lamb.

'It's what he wanted,' Rebecca whispers. She lifts her head from John's chest. Her lips are white. Her eyes pale and luminous green, the tea leaf fleck standing out as if in relief. She puts her hand to her mouth, looks round wildly and makes for a basin and vomits.

'I'm leaving.' Though Dodie's voice clogs, she will not cry. But she will leave. And she will make Seth come with her. This is not acceptable. 'Rebecca, we just let a man die.' She looks uneasily at John, not John, just the body of John.

Rebecca cups her hands for a slurp of water, wipes her mouth on one of the paper towels. 'I know but –'

'No buts,' Dodie says. 'Come with me.'

'Shh,' Rebecca hisses.

The door opens and Hannah comes in, maskless. Rebecca touches her lips with her finger, eyes hard on Dodie. Hannah glares at them both, grasps Rebecca by the upper arms and stares into her eyes. 'Dodie has been sent by Satan to try your faith,' she says. 'You must be strong. Let it go, Sister.' Rebecca's eyes close in a prolonged blink and together she and Hannah hum, a two-tone vibration that rattles Dodie's teeth.

Hannah leaves Rebecca and walks across to John. She picks up his wrist, feels for a pulse, drops it. The hand falls open on the sheet like a blown blossom. She sees the way Dodie and Rebecca stare at her, and turns back to the body. 'God bless you,' she says. She brushes a perfunctory kiss on his forehead and dabs her mouth.

'I'm leaving now,' Dodie says, suddenly absolutely clear and resolved. 'Just give me my stuff, and let me out. I'm sorry Rebecca,' she says. 'Come too?'

'So, Satan speaks,' Hannah says with a narrow smile. 'Come, Rebecca.'

'No,' Dodie shakes her head. 'Rebecca. It's not Satan. It's *me*.'

'Shut your ears, Sister,' Hannah says. 'Come.' She takes Rebecca's arm and yanks her out of the room. There is the click of the locking door.

Dodie stands exactly where she is. John's eyelids have lifted. A fly buzzes. How did it get in? It hums wearily around the light fitting and Dodie sees that there are other flies caught inside it, dead. There's no air in the room and she's forced to inhale the smell of vomit and the smell of death. It's only John, she tells herself. The air around her is thick but it seems to stir and ripple. Gooseflesh rises on her arms as she feels a sudden chill. She backs up against the wall, staring at the body. It's only John. It's only John. She likes him, liked him. A sort of growl comes from him and she screams, crouches, heart thundering against her thighs. Please God, please God, she finds herself saying, and even though she believes nothing she promises she will believe if only this could be over. She just has to get out of here then she'll leave. Somehow she'll get Seth and they'll run, sod the clothes, the watch, she'll find the police or the British Embassy or whatever and they'll run out in the pyjamas and run and run. And Jake, Jake, Jake, she will be home.

The door opens and Hannah stands framed. 'Scared?' she says.

'There was a noise,' Dodie says. She straightens up and flattens herself back against the wall.

'Wind in the guts,' Hannah says, 'or air in the lungs. He's gone. Can't hurt you.'

'I know.'

'It's not John you should be frightened of,' Hannah says. 'Satan has really got to you. How have you let him in?'

'I want Seth and I want to leave. Now. Don't try and fob me off or –'

'Don't you want to see Rod, and Jake?'

'*What?*'

'Rod and Jake.'

Dodie's mouth falls open. 'What do you mean?'

'They're here.'

'They're *here*?'

Hannah smiles smugly. 'Come along.' She grasps Dodie's arm and pulls her out into the corridor. The door bangs shut on John.

'But –' Dodie starts.

Hannah swings her round and holds her by the tops of her arms; she leans in, her eyes so close they seem to blur into one. 'Let it go,' she says, 'blink and hum, come on, with me, hum.' And they stand by the shut door and hum but even the hum will not drive away the turmoil of grief and anger and excitement and disbelief and Dodie's heart hammers painfully against the pitch of the humming and Hannah's hands are pincers on her arms.

15

Hannah takes her to the parlour. 'Wait there,' she says, and leaves Dodie alone in all the flounce and floral fakery, the sickly sweetness of air freshener. Feels like years since she was here. The fussy smell of material, pelmets, valances, silky flowers. Dodie paces, frowns. Jake? Rod? *Really?* Her heart hammers and the hum sticks in her head like interference and she can't make her mind go in a straight line and John is dead. She rubs her arm, shivery with the sensation of his life shimmying away, a wild man, dangerous once . . . but now he's dead.

Rod and Jake, Jake, is this some sort of trick? She looks down at the ridiculous lilac clothes and runs her fingers through her wildly tangled hair. She must look a sight. This is a trick, she's sure of it, don't get too excited, all the times they said Seth would see her. Maybe Seth isn't even here at all? What would Rod be doing *here*? What, what? Mind too jittery to think. Body too jittery to sit, she paces, paces, round the coffee table and the sofa into the room with the deep soft bed, round the coffee table where she ate the carrot cake, pacing, pacing.

She remembers the tiger when they took Jake to the zoo, much too young. He slept through most of the visit and she stood before the enclosure, the precious scrap of meat slumbering in his buggy, and watched the way the tiger paced, muscles rippling under the glossy stripes, tail swishing the dust, eyes focused on the distance continents away – and she'd felt small, had felt like nothing before his trapped magnificence. She snorts at the ludicrous comparison of herself and the tiger, but still she paces.

And then she hears a shred of a child's voice from the corridor, and the door opens on Rod with Jake in his arms. Rod fills the door, squared shoulders, brown eyes searching out her own and Jake shrinking back against him. Hannah pulls the door shut behind.

'Here we are,' she says, as if they are a gift for her to bestow, but Jake won't look at Dodie; won't look out from Rod's brown leather jacket that he's worn summer and winter ever since she met him. She knows the feel of that jacket, knows its waxy, animal smell when you bury your nose in it as Jake's doing now.

'Jake,' Dodie says. 'Jake, it's Mummy.' But he just screws his face against Rod.

'Hi,' she says to Rod, and he puts his head down for her to graze her lips against his stubbly cheek. The smell of him – outdoorsy, smoky, leathery – sets up such a turmoil inside her that she has to step backwards.

'Hi,' he says shortly. She tries to force a smile into his eyes but he jerks his eyes away.

'Sit down, I'll get some tea.' Hannah goes out, leaving them alone. Rod undoes Jake's hands from his jacket and puts him down but Jake clamps himself round his leg, face still hidden. He looks bigger; he has a new coat – puffy, silver – not what she'd choose, maybe Jeannie bought it for him, cold up in Inverness.

'Sit down,' is all she can think of to say. Her throat tightens. Jake will not even look at her. Give him time; give him time. Rod lowers himself on to the sofa and she sits beside him. Must not waste this time alone.

'God, it's really weird to see you here!' She tries to smile but her teeth are dry and her lip sticks grotesquely.

'Didn't have much choice, did I?' Rod glowers at his knees. 'Not putting off my trip any longer and Martha or, no, the other one, suggested I bring Jake and leave him here.'

'With me?'

'I *think* you're his mother.'

'Don't be like that.'

Rod raises one eyebrow at her.

'You're still going then?'

Though he still clings to Rod, Jake peeps at her – but when she smiles he turns his face away. Give him time. Let him come to you.

'What the fuck are you playing at?' Rod says.

His harshness is out of place; she'd forgotten that about him. He looks puffy, pouchy around the eyes. And he sounds stupid.

'I'm not *playing* at anything,' she says. 'I was about to leave. I'll take Jake home.'

'Poor little sod. Didn't take to intercontinental travel,' he says, looking at her properly for the first time, frowning at her clothes.

'I *know*,' she says, lifting a flap of lilac T-shirt.

He laughs and she laughs and the tension eases. His forefinger and middle finger are nicotine yellow; has he been smoking in the house, smoking around Jake? But then what can she say? Jake looks at her again, longer this time, allowing a meeting of the eyes.

'Hi Jakey,' she says.

He hides his face, then gives her another shy peep. Looks like his cold's better.

'What about Seth then?' Rod says.

'Haven't seen him.'

Rod's eyebrows shoot into a steeple; he starts to speak, then changes his mind, rubs his eyes. 'Christ almighty,' is all he says. His fingernails need cutting. There's a grubby plaster on his middle finger.

'I've tried to see him,' she says. 'And tried.'

'You can't have tried very hard.'

There's another silence. 'You finished your chairs?' she says.

'Martha said –' he starts.

'Oh yes, so you've been talking to Martha about me?' she breaks in. 'You told her about my . . . my bad time.'

'Thought she should know. Anyway, *you* wouldn't talk to me.'

'Not *wouldn't*, I –'

The door opens and Hannah comes in with a tray of mugs, a teapot and a plastic cup of juice.

'Does he like juice?' Hannah manoeuvres the door shut and puts the tray down on the table.

'Yeah,' Rod says, harshly, and Dodie holds back the objection that neat juice is bad for the teeth, that it's dangerous to put the hot teapot where Jake can reach it.

'Rod,' Dodie says, pleadingly, and she looks at him for a sign of love, for a sign he's pleased to see her – but he will only meet her eyes for brief scowling seconds.

Still anchored to Rod, and loudly sucking three fingers, Jake swivels his body so he can see her.

'Did you have fun at Granny's?' Dodie says. Her arms ache; her fingers itch with the need to touch him. Someone has cut his hair in a straight fringe above his eyes; he seems less a baby, more a little boy with that straight blue gaze that makes her heart flip.

'She likes to be called Grandma,' Rod says.

'Grandma,' Dodie says. 'Did you go and see Grandma?'

'Big fish!' Jake says, a wide bright grin bursting across his face so that she can see a new tooth.

She looks to Rod.

'A ride outside the Co-op,' he says. Jake lets go of Rod and edges towards Dodie and she holds her hands stiff on her lap. Don't reach for him, don't grab.

Hannah pours the tea – proper brown tea with milk. 'Are you going to stay for a bit?' she asks Rod.

'Big fish,' Jake says, he's talking to Dodie now; she could touch him if she wanted.

'No, my flight's tonight.' Rod takes the tea and blows on it, in so much of a rush he can't even wait for it to cool. 'Ta anyway.'

Now Jake is close, leaning himself against her leg, the soft weight of him in the puffy coat. He looks hot. 'Shall we take your coat off, Jake?' she says. He stares up at her and she quails at the pureness of his gaze. 'Mumma?' he says, and it's a question; he isn't sure, he doesn't even know her any more.

'Yes, Mumma!' she says, injecting bright into her voice.

He pats her knee one, two, three times, 'Mumma,' he says, satisfied.

She unzips the horrible silvery nylon. He's wearing dungarees she made from an old pair of jeans and a jumper that's miles too small; fancy bringing him all the way to America dressed like that! She dares now to lift him onto her lap, his back against her chest and she feels the flow, her love for this child is like electricity, her heart dances and plunges in the current. Her hands rest on the rise and fall of his round belly, and never will she be parted from him again, not until he's too grown up to want her and that is so far in the future she doesn't even need to think about it. She puts her nose into his hair, sniffs the warm, biscuity scent of his scalp – complicated by the smell of Rod's tobacco.

'I'll come to the airport with you. With Seth. Will you fetch Seth?' she asks Hannah. Surely she won't dare refuse with Rod here.

But Hannah ignores her. 'How was your journey?' she asks.

'Bit of a struggle,' Rod says, 'keeping *him* under control. And mad security at the airport.' He smiles for the first time. 'They looked in his nappy! Got more than they bargained for!'

'His nappy!' Dodie says, her hand treasuring one of Jake's.

Rod grins and shrugs. He sips his tea.

'Nice isn't it? The tea,' she says. God, so inane, all the things they should be saying, but how can they say them with Hannah here and even if she went out the constraint between them is mortifying, stultifying. He is supposed to be her love and there is nothing she can do to reach him. But Jake. As she tightens her arms round him, he struggles as if he wants to get down and she has to let him go – but instead of getting down he turns and wraps his legs and arms around her like a little bear, face pressed against her chest. He never did that before, he was never so clingy. Is this what she has done by leaving him?

'All right Jakey,' she says, 'Mummy's here.' She's stung by Rod's sarcastic look.

'So, will you fetch Seth now?' Rod says.

Dodie holds her breath, but Hannah opens her hands, helplessly. 'I don't know how to tell you this,' she says, 'but he's gone.'

'*Gone?*' Dodie and Rod say together.

'Decided it's not for him. There was some confusion. I think Martha might have told him you'd gone.'

'Why would she have said that?' Dodie has to take a deep breath against a sudden swimminess in her head. 'He's gone *home?*' she says. 'Back to the UK?'

'I reckon so.'

'I must go then. Now.'

Rod puffs out his breath and shakes his head at Dodie. All this for nothing then, says his expression, and Hannah's got her snarky face on.

'No, I don't believe you,' Dodie says. 'He *wouldn't*. He wouldn't do that would he Rod? He wouldn't hold out on me all this time and then go!'

Rod looks at her witheringly. 'Don't ask me.'

'But he wouldn't!'

'Well he has,' Hannah says, with a little shrug. 'It's Martha's fault.'

'Can I talk to Martha?'

'She's busy. She'd only tell you the same thing.' Hannah speaks to her but smiles at Rod, almost flirtatiously, almost deferentially. Because he's a man. He does seem very masculine here, out of kilter with the floral fussiness: wild, leathery, tobaccoey. There's a silence. Rod looks at Dodie again, shaking his head at her waste of time, her folly, the folly of the world.

'I'll be off then,' he says.

'No,' her voice comes out almost like a wail, but he stands anyway. 'Wait, I'll come with you.'

'Got a cab waiting, and . . .' There's an odd flicker in his eyes. She stares at him, not believing. Surely he hasn't got another woman with him?

'I'll take you out,' Hannah says.

Dodie tries to get up, but with the weight of Jake clamped around her she overbalances.

'See you,' Rod says. He leans over and briefly kisses her on the mouth.

'Have you . . .' she begins. 'Is there . . .'

'Bye Jake,' says Rod.

'Is it *her*?'

'Look after Littl'un,' he says.

'Wait.'

But Hannah opens the door, almost rushes him out. He lifts his hand in a kind of salute. 'See you,' he says.

'Keep in –' she says, and the door shuts, leaving her alone with Jake, '– touch.' She frowns at the door. Did she imagine that? Did she read too much into that hesitation? He wouldn't have someone else already. Would he? Or is she getting paranoid? If only Jake could talk properly, he would tell her. She sniffs his hair again, searching for a trace of perfume or other female smell. And *Seth*. Gone? But . . . her mind is exhausted, thoughts blowing round like rubbish at a blustery corner.

But at least if Seth has gone it means that she can leave.

Jake clambers down from her lap and goes to the door. And after all, he is what is important. She focuses on him. Her baby, real and live and *here*. His walking is steadier, he does look taller, chunkier, older. Can he really have grown so much in . . . how long? It's only been a couple of weeks. Hasn't it? 'Dadda?' he says.

'Daddy's gone,' she says. 'Gone,' she says again. Jake stands and stares at her, fingers in his mouth, the bib of his dungarees dark with dribble. Dodie smiles. 'Mummy's here though.' He continues to stare, his eyes so round and clear, reading, reading; she feels almost shy, shy of her own child's scrutiny. But Seth gone? And Martha telling him she'd gone and sending him away. She can't believe that of Martha. Martha was always on her side.

'Come and drink your juice,' she says. Jake stands beside her and she holds the cup against his mouth, and some of it spills, further wetting his clothes; he needs a bib, at home he always wears a bib, such a dribbler, but of course, Rod wouldn't think to put a bib on him. She can't think what to say. This is ridiculous.

'Incy Wincy Spider,' she begins, wiggling her fingers, 'climbed up the spout.' Jake laughs, knocks over the rest of the juice. Hannah comes back with Daniel. He blinks at her and smiles.

'Hi,' Dodie says.

'This is Jacob,' Hannah says.

'Just Jake,' Dodie says.

'Jake,' Daniel says. 'Hi there.'

'*When* did Seth go?' Dodie asks Hannah. 'Can I see Martha?'

Daniel flaps his hands at Jake but he hides his face against Dodie now and she puts her hand protectively on his silky head. She's mother again now, she's safety.

'I want to speak to Martha.'

'Sure,' Hannah says.

Daniel dimples and his eyes shine. The way he's looking at Hannah you'd think he was in love.

Dodie presses her face into Jake's hair. She's holding him too tight now; he starts to wriggle. Why are they both looking like that, both of them now, gazing so greedily at Jake?

'Can you call me a taxi?' she says. 'I need to change his nappy. I need to see Martha. No, I just need my clothes, my bag . . .'

She could maybe catch up with Rod at the airport, she thinks, if she goes now. Can Jake feel the punching of her heart?

'Take him,' Hannah says, and Daniel comes forward, arms outstretched.

'No!' Dodie tightens her arms.

'It's OK,' Hannah says, 'don't get hysterical. Daniel will get him cleaned up, give him his tea, while you get ready to go.'

'No. He's OK with me. I'll change him. Just bring me the stuff. Call me a taxi.'

'That's how it's going to be,' Hannah says.

'No it's not.' Despite herself, her voice rises. But must not scare Jake, must not. 'Can you fetch Martha?'

Hannah shakes her head. 'Martha is busy right now, and you're not thinking straight. Look at you. Jake needs changing, needs to be fed. Daniel will get him sorted while we get your things. You want to change, don't you? You need your tickets. You need your money.'

Dodie's arms tighten and Jake struggles to get away from her. 'It's OK, Jake,' she says, but her voice sounds anything but OK and she *is* frightening him.

'Look at the state you're in,' Hannah says. 'Let me take Jacob.'

'No.'

Hannah tries to lifts him from Dodie's arms and she holds on; but Hannah pulls hard and he starts to cry. She can't play tug-of-war with him. 'It's *Jake*,' she says weakly, letting go, but standing up, standing close.

'Mumma.' Jake kicks against Hannah's thighs with his little trainers, and reaches out for Dodie.

'Hey little fella,' Hannah says. 'He's leaking,' she adds and she's right, there's a reek of ammonia and a patch of wet-ness left on Dodie's trousers. He'll be getting nappy rash.

'Give him to me,' Dodie says, but Hannah hands him to Daniel, instead, and wipes her hands down her sides.

'Why don't I?' Dodie tries to take him from Daniel, but Hannah grabs her arms, holds them tight behind her back. 'Take him,' she says, and before Dodie can believe what's happening, Daniel has gone and the door's banged shut behind him. Jake's wail recedes along the corridor. Hannah lets her go and Dodie draws her hand back and punches her in the chest, first time in her life she's punched a person. Her fist striking ribs and the softness of a breast. Hannah gasps and shrinks away, arms crossed against her chest.

'Let me out!' Dodie screams. 'Help!' Her hands go to her mouth, gasps in the smell of Jake ghosting from her fingers, her breasts ache, her womb tightens, she breathes through the wave of panic. She bangs on the door and kicks. But nothing happens. Behind her she can hear Hannah breathing hard. Both of them are almost panting, like men, or bulls.

When she turns, Hannah's sitting on the sofa, hands protecting her chest. There's a ring of white round her mouth and she looks like she might cry. Dodie takes a deep breath in. Keep calm. This can't be happening.

'Just take me to Jake. Now. Please.' Her voice trembles below its even surface. 'Hannah, *please*.'

Hannah doesn't answer or move.

Dodie goes to the door again. 'Help!' she yells. 'Help!'

If Martha is near she will come. Someone must be able to hear her. Her heart is smashing itself against her ribs, the noise of it exploding through her head. She wonders if she's going to faint, or have a heart attack, the way her breath's gone ragged.

'Dodie,' Hannah says suddenly from too close behind her. Dodie whips round, ready to fight if she has to, ready to punch again, or kick, but Hannah steps back quickly and only says, 'I'm sorry.'

'Just let me out.'

'Fair dos,' Hannah says. She actually looks embarrassed. Ashamed. And so she should. What was it? A moment of madness? Martha will hear about it, you can't go round treating people like that, pushing people about, ripping their babies off them. Maybe she is insane?

'I'm sorry,' Hannah says again. 'Everything's so tense and . . .'

'Take me to my baby.'

'I will.'

Hannah opens the door and Dodie bursts out ahead of her, but there's no way of knowing which way Daniel took him.

'We'll get your clothes first, then we'll fetch Jake.'

'No, Jake first. Forget the clothes.' Dodie listens for Jake's cries but can hear nothing.

'I'm really sorry,' Hannah says. 'I shouldn't have done that.'

'I'll tell Martha.'

'Please don't.'

Dodie shoots Hannah a look. She doesn't look as contrite as she sounds. They are entering a new section of the building now, Dodie doesn't recognize these walls and they go down what is surely a different set of stairs, but you can't tell with all the white walls and doors, the same plain wooden floors.

'Here we are,' Hannah opens a door – and Dodie steps in, her arms already opening for her baby. But there's a hard shove between her shoulder blades; she stumbles to the floor and the door slams behind her. There's the sound of a locking mechanism – and then silence.

Her mouth dries and her heart shouts in her chest, knocks its fists so hard it hurts and quails away, screws itself into a corner of the cage of ribs. There's a bed, a toilet, a small basin with a tap. This is a cell.

STELLA AND ME

In 1974, when I was sixteen, and Stella thirteen, our mother died of drink. Dad was in Saudi with his brand new family. We nearly had to go and live in Peebles with Aunt Regina, but we convinced the social worker not to move us from our school. And after checking up on us a few times, and after several displays of stunning good behaviour, we were allowed to stay on in the house in Felixstowe, as long as Aunt Regina visited often – and as long as the Social Worker didn't catch us out.

In August, the day the O-level results came out, there was a party on the beach. I'd got six, with an A for English. So what? There was no one to tell. No one who cared. We'd gone round Cobbold Point, away from the tourists and the promenade, and built a bonfire in an old dinghy stuffed with tarry ropes and broken lobster pots. When the blaze got going it was a fierce and fabulous roar. We drank cider and smoked Player's No. 6 and some people smoked dope.

It wasn't dark enough for stars yet, and the sky was streaked with soaring orange cinders. Stella was meant to be at home but I saw her on the edges with her tragic friends. I ignored her. We always ignored each other in public.

It was mostly teenagers at the party but then some grown-up hippies came along, attracted, like shaggy old moths, to the blaze. I was sitting at the edge of the party, watching. Some guys were playing guitars and singing – while someone with bongos struggled to keep up. My friend, Marion, was dancing by the fire. She saw me looking and waved.

'Come and dance,' she called.

I pretended not to hear. I was raised above the party on a shingle bank, clutching my bottle of Merrydown. I felt detached. Out at sea were the lights of ships – one of them Radio Caroline. A hippy climbed up on the bank and sat down beside me. I didn't speak to him. The cold shingle was biting into my bottom and I'd been about to move – but I felt stuck when he arrived. I took a swig of cider and hugged my knees.

'Hi,' he said. He had long flat hair and his eyes were in hiding behind his little gold-rimmed specs. He lifted a long joint to his lips, breathed in, closed his eyes and held his breath. His nose was beaky between the flaps of his hair. He breathed out on an elegant lavender plume, then offered it to me. It was damp from his mouth and bits of tobacco tickled my lips. The smoke was sweetish and I held it in my lungs.

Stella was in the corner of my eye, pointing and laughing.

'What's your name?' the guy said.

'Melanie,' I told him.

'Far out,' he said.

A ship's hooter went; sea owl, I thought. Marion came back.

'Hi,' she said, giving me a beady look.

Smoke still held down, the guy said, 'Hi,' in a pent-up voice and passed her the joint before breathing out. She squatted down and held it expertly between finger and thumb.

'This is Marion,' I told him.

A woman came crunching gingerly up the shingle on her bare feet. She sat down and put her arm across the man's shoulder. The orange flames flashed off the lenses of his glasses.

'Hi Celia,' he said.

'You coming, Bruce?' She was wearing a thin paisley blouse and no bra. Her breasts were frighteningly adult, matronly even, and crying out for a control garment. I started to smile and the smile stretched across my face and right up into my ears. My face felt like grinning toffee.

'Where are you going?' Marion asked.

'Back to our pad,' the woman said.

'Want to come?' said Bruce.

'Yeah.' Marion sprang right up.

'Far out,' Bruce said but Celia was frowning.

'They're only kids,' she objected.

'We're *sixteen*,' Marion said.

Celia shrugged and got to her feet. She had dirty, broken toenails. I didn't want to go. All I wanted was my bed. Since Mum had died I'd lived as if someone was giving me instructions. Be home at midnight, was one of them. Stella stayed out till morning sometimes. I'd make her stop it when term started but for now I let her be.

I followed Bruce, Celia and Marion along the beach. Every time I took a step I heard the shingle rattling and shifting right down into the centre of the earth, and even when we'd left the fire behind I still had cinders flying in my eyes. We had to clamber over many breakwaters; it felt like hundreds more than usual. I got stuck on top of a high one, petrified of leaping onto the dark crunch of the beach. Bruce came back to lift me down, his hands big and tight on the soft of my waist.

I would have gone home, but by the time we arrived at the flat I needed to pee from all the cider, and didn't think I'd make it. The flat was above Freeman, Hardy and Willis in the High Street. You had to go round the back and up an iron staircase that juddered and clanged and gave off a sickly metal smell.

Inside, that smell gave way to a mixture of candle wax, joss sticks and cats. Sitar music was playing – Ananda Shankar, Bruce said. Marion was swaying along and watching Bruce greedily as he skinned up. I sat down and shot up again, shrieking – the sofa had shifted under me – and I realized

I'd sat on the legs of a sleeping person. He sat up grumpily and rubbed his eyes.

'Hey man,' he said.

'I'm so sorry,' I said. 'I didn't see you.'

'I'm so sorry,' Bruce mimicked. I flushed. The carpet was thick with cat hairs. The guy shifted his legs and patted the sofa beside him.

'Sit down,' he said.

'This is Melanie and Marion,' Bruce said.

'What's your name?' Marion asked.

'Bogart,' he said, and chucked out a laugh.

'Bogart?' With his long wavy hair and beard, he looked like Jesus or Cat Stevens, though rather cross and rumpled.

'As in, "Don't?"' Bruce said. I didn't get it. Bogart's eyes warmed as they looked at me, the irises round and brown as chocolate buttons.

Celia came through with a trayful of mugs and a huge teapot. As she leant to put the tray down I saw right down the front of her blouse between her hanging breasts to a loose roll of tummy. Her hair was a bit grey, I realized with a shock. It was the first time I'd socialized with a grey-haired person. I sat up a little straighter. I didn't want tea or to smoke any more but I didn't know how to get out. The sitar was playing 'Jumpin' Jack Flash', which made me nauseous.

'Tea?' Celia started splashing it into a selection of pottery mugs. The tea reflected shimmery patterns on the ceiling.

'I'm going,' I said, 'I'll be late.'

'For what? Her mum's dead,' Marion explained and I shot her a look.

'Your mum's dead?' Bogart leaned forward and looked at me intently and the way his eyes seemed to see right into me made me flinch. He put his hand out and touched my hair, pushed it away from my face and tucked a strand behind my ear. For some reason that made tears come. I stood up too quickly, stumbled and jolted the tray, spilling the tea.

'Come on,' I said to Marion, but she was lying back on a beanbag holding a spliff as if she'd been born to it. I was afraid I was going to throw up on the hairy carpet. The floor was tilting, I was sure. I thought of all the thousands of shoes in the shop below me, neat in their boxes, all in their pairs, and that made me lonely.

'I'll walk you,' Bogart said. 'I need to get some fags anyway.'

I looked helplessly at Marion but her eyes had gone into stars. Bogart staggered to his feet. I followed him down the stairs, clinging to the metal, not breathing till I got down and on to what I knew was solid ground, though it didn't feel particularly solid. To my surprise he took my hand.

'Where do you live?' he said.

I told him. His hand was soft and warm and dry.

'How old are you?' I asked.

'Thirty-two.'

'That's twice me.'

'Far out, man,' he said, and kissed me. I let him. I'd hardly been kissed before and never by an adult. We got to a cigarette machine outside a corner shop. He got his cigarettes then pressed me against the wall and kissed me again. A real snog, the beard grinding against my face. I was squashed between a drainpipe and the cigarette machine. His tongue went into my mouth like a warm eel and made me retch.

'I think you touched my uvula,' I said.

'Wow,' he said. 'Far out.'

'It's OK,' I said, 'it's just . . .' Only I didn't know just what. We were nearly at my house. He took my hand. What if a neighbour saw – but so what if they did? I was cut loose. There was nobody they could tell tales to about me any more. I felt very flat and in danger of folding up like a paper dolly with paper clothes, the sort you fix on with tabs. It wasn't even properly dark; the sky was a high light blue, only the ground and the houses were dark. Above the rooftops, the moon was a sickly grin.

'Here we are,' I said when we got to my house.

We stood outside for a moment. I didn't know what to do. In the end I said, 'Do you want a coffee or something?'

Having a stranger in the house made me see it differently. Stella had left her knickers bleaching in the sink so that's how it smelled. I put the kettle on. He suddenly came up behind me and I shrieked but he calmed me down as if I was a nervy horse, stroking and mumbling till I lay back against him.

'You're beautiful,' he said. The tap was dripping into the knickers with a very intricate sound. I was chilly and he was warm against my back. I yawned.

'We're going to be together, man,' he said.

'Are we?'

'Soon as I saw you.'

'But –' I said, and then stopped. The warmth of another body against mine was persuasive. And his eyes were melting brown. And he was so much older that I was inclined to believe him. And anyway, *anyway*, history has proved him right.

We ate all Stella's custard creams and then we went upstairs. My room was so babyish, with its single bed and posters of Cat Stevens, but he didn't seem to care. When he took off his clothes and his penis jumped out, I was shocked. I'd never seen a full-grown one before. It seemed like a joke or an exaggeration or a foodstuff of some kind. It didn't seem part of him at all with his ribs and the fine black hairs on his chest and then this swollen pointing sausage.

I changed into my pyjamas in the bathroom. We got into my bed. I was startled at myself that I should be so slaggish. But this wasn't a boy, it was a man and besides, nobody would know or care. Stella wouldn't be laughing at me any more when she found out.

He kissed me and touched me and I just let myself open up to him. He lay on top of me and when he pushed in it was a burning pain and not much pleasure, and then a mess.

Afterwards he smoked a cigarette. It was awkward and the mattress was tilting and I was trying to keep my bottom out of the sticky patch.

'When did your Mum die?' he asked.

'The end of May,' I said.

His breath stopped halfway through a puff. 'The end of *May*?' he said. 'May this year?'

'The thirtieth.' I said.

'Christ.' He sat up, scattering ash everywhere. 'Wow. Man. And what about your dad?'

'He lives in Saudi with his new family. He does send money.'

'So, you live alone?'

'With my sister.'

'Older?'

'No, she's thirteen.'

A series of unreadable expressions flickered across his face, and he got up and walked about the house. I put on my dressing gown and followed him. He went in all the rooms, just put his head round the door as if looking for something. I didn't like it when he peered into Mum's room or Stella's. I was shivering, with cold and strangeness. In the hall he put his arms round me and held me tight enough to stop the shivering. 'You poor little chick,' he said, stroking my back. I slumped against him. I needed to sleep.

'I'm going to bed,' I said. I went to wash and looked in the mirror on the bathroom cabinet. I thought, I've done it. What if I'm pregnant? I thought he'd get his clothes on and go home but when I got back into the bedroom he was in bed with his arms held out. I climbed back into his arms and clung.

'I knew that this was meant,' he said, 'soon as I saw you walk into that room.'

'But you didn't see me walk in. I sat on you!' I said. He didn't say anything to that, just stroked and murmured and eventually fell asleep. I slept hotly and uncomfortably, with my head against his booming chest.

†

Bogart never left except to fetch a rucksack full of stuff and his guitar. After a week of cramming into my room, he suggested we move into Mum's because of the bigger bed. At first I said no. Then I made him at least buy some new sheets but still, lying there with him on top of me, I'd always think of Mum.

He had a very windy stomach. Sometimes in the night I got out of the Mum-memories and the smell of farts and crawled into the innocent space of my own narrow bed. He was vegetarian and was always soaking chickpeas. Jars full of mung beans sprouted on the kitchen windowsill.

Stella didn't mind anything except us being in Mum's room. Although she was living in the house she was on a different planet. She hardly ate – sometimes I'd find half a biscuit in the tin, the broken end sucked soft by her need for something sweet. She grew fur on her arms and the slopes of her cheeks. Bogart worried about her weight and her obsession with cleaning, and did sometimes get her to eat the yogurt that he made in a vacuum flask. He talked about her as if she was a baby and even tried, when term started, to get her to go to bed at half past ten. We were in the kitchen and she was worrying at the grouting round the sink with a bleachy toothbrush.

'Who do you think you are?' she said.

He thought about that. It was just the sort of question he liked, even then. 'A mortal body animated by spirit –' he began but she cut him off.

'No, I mean who do you think you are to tell me what to do?'

I had my new timetable spread out on the table. Celia had come round. She laughed at the table mats with Constable's *Hay Wain* and I wanted to sock her in the mouth. I didn't like such big breasts in our kitchen, nor brushing so close to Bogart's face.

'You're a scrounger,' Stella told Bogart.

'Stell!' I said.

'You're like a hermit crab,' she said, 'scuttling into our house just because our mum is dead.' I was going to point out that that wasn't what hermit crabs did but she'd started to cry, the first time I'd seen her cry since Mum died. I went to hug her but Celia beat me to it and had her engulfed in her bosom.

Stella submitted for a minute then she pulled away. I followed her to her room. I hadn't been in it for weeks. It was neat and cold with the window open but still with a strange sweet smell. She was curled up in a little ball on the bed. I sat down beside her. She let me stroke her arm. I could feel the beat of blood through the skin.

'He makes a mess in the kitchen,' she said, 'and in the bog. What would Dad say, or Aunt Regina, or the Social Worker?'

'Probably freak out,' I agreed. Bogart started to play his guitar downstairs. I looked at Stella; surely she must at least enjoy his music?

'Do you want to go to Saudi?' I said. 'Or Peebles?'

She shook her head. 'Do you?'

I thought about it. Here I was, living almost like a married person with someone I hardly knew. In Saudi, maybe, I could go back to being a child again. I wanted someone to give me rules to break or follow. But then I imagined taking on a stepmother and two half-sisters. The only sister I wanted was Stella. I stayed beside her, listening to Bogart singing a song about a thin green candle, and to Stella breathing, until she fell asleep.

When I got back in the kitchen, Celia had gone and Bogart was frying onions. I stood watching him. From the back or the side he was good-looking enough, but you would only know his magic by looking into his eyes. He had this way of gazing at you that pierced your soul. Once he was looking at me, I could refuse him nothing: my own will shrugged its shoulders and slunk away. I suppose I loved him by then, though I didn't want to. I knew I should be telling him to leave; it wasn't fair on Stella. I was her big sister and it was up to me to care for her.

It was her fourteenth birthday on the first day of term, the most terrible day to have a birthday. And even if she wasn't going to eat it, I was going to make her a birthday cake.

'Do you mind, er, like going?' I said to Bogart.

He turned round to face me. I stared at the table but he put his finger under my chin and looked into my eyes. 'Going where, honey?' he said.

But I couldn't do it. I wriggled on the end of his finger. 'Going to get some cake stuff,' came out of my mouth. 'I want to make a cake for Stella.'

'A cake for *Stella*!' He laughed.

'You never know, she might have a bit.'

'I'll make it,' he said.

'No. *I* want to.'

'While you're at school, then you come home with Stella to a fresh-baked cake. Far out, eh?'

In the end I was grateful, the first day of term was busy and absorbing, getting different teachers and timetables for my new A-level subjects. I didn't mention Bogart to anyone else. The teachers and everyone were nice to me since I was bereaved. It felt so false. In my blazer pocket was a prescription for the pill, given very grudgingly by the doctor.

It was a melting golden afternoon when we came out of school. An ice-cream van was tinkling Brahms' Lullaby and Marion was waiting for me. She wanted me to come to hers, but I had to go to the chemist and get my pills.

'Mum says you should come to tea, both of you,' Marion said. 'She doesn't think it right you living on your own. You could come once a week.'

'Tell your mum we're fine,' I said, and I think she was relieved. I watched her walk off down the road, satchel bumping against her hip.

Bogart's cake was not the pink and white confection of my imagination – it was dark brown and shaped like a brick. I'd bought and blown up a few balloons and wrapped presents – a velvet smock and a copy of *Bonjour Tristesse*, which I'd read carefully, so I didn't mark the pages. Bogart gave her *Siddhartha* and I felt jealous. He'd never given me a present – but then it hadn't been my birthday yet. Dad sent her a cheque, and Aunt Regina a nightie.

'There's something else. A present for us all,' Bogart said.

'Where?' Stella asked.

'You'll have to wait till Saturday.'

'What?' I said.

He tapped the side of his nose and grinned.

I put a night light on top of the cake and we sang Happy Birthday. A balloon fell off the lampshade and popped on the candle flame, making Bogart say, 'Holy shit.' Stella did look pleased with our effortful celebrations. She even smiled at Bogart before she took the bread knife to the cake and sawed three slices. It was amazing to see her eat. She just took a bite as if this was quite an everyday thing to do. When she saw me staring she said, 'What?'

'Nothing.' I took a bite myself. It was made with molasses and wholemeal stuff, quite dry and hard to chew. Why did Stella eat it? To be polite? Or was she starting to get better? Would she have got better? She opened her presents and held the smock against her; it was maroon, beaded, bought from the Indian shop on the seafront.

Bogart rolled a joint and made a pot of tea. I was petrified the police or the social worker would burst in, but why should they? My new timetable was in my satchel and my first homework: read *A Passage to India*. I wanted something plain to eat, something with mashed potato and then to do my homework and go to bed early.

Stella, to my amazement, continued picking at the cake, cramming crumbs in her mouth and giggling. She reached for the joint and Bogart let her.

'Hey,' I said.

'It's my birthday,' Stella said, just as he was saying, 'It's her birthday,' their voices sliding into a collision that they found funny. Suddenly I needed to throw up. I got to the bathroom in time and stayed there for ages, my cheek on the seat of the toilet, which thanks to Stella was spotless. I put my lips around the end of the tap and drank water, swilling it round my mouth. I looked in the mirror at my cheeks, white where they were usually pink, and at the shadows under my eyes.

Downstairs, Stella was puffing away and nibbling at the cake. Bogart had his feet – bare and yellow-soled – up on the table.

I looked in the cupboard. 'Shall we have spaghetti?' I said. Stella put the joint in a saucer and Bogart quickly snatched it up and filled his lungs. Stella got up and stared past me. Her widened eyes looked pink and rabbity.

'What?' I said. 'I know *you* don't want spaghetti.'

She pointed towards the door.

'What?

Her lips had gone white. Her pointing finger shook. 'Mum,' she mouthed.

'Woah there,' Bogart said. 'Take it easy.'

'No,' she said, 'no, can't you see her?' Her mouth tried to form a smile, a smile for Mum.

Bogart frowned at me as if there was something I could do.

'Let's watch telly,' I said.

'She's gone,' she said. She closed her eyes and swayed and then she opened them and started to giggle.

'You monkey,' Bogart said. 'She was having us on.'

'She *was* there,' Stella insisted, 'but she was wearing, I don't know . . .'

'Telly,' I said, and steered her into the sitting room. I turned it on and it was *The Clangers*, Granny Clanger knitting tinsel out of frost. When Mother Clanger came on, fussing about and making Small and Tiny go into the warm cave, Stella started to cry.

'They're just puppets,' I said, but I was fighting against the urge myself, the sweet whistling creature was nothing like our mother, of course, who, even if she was still alive, would probably be sneaking vodka into her tea.

A smell of burning curry powder drifted from the kitchen and my mouth filled with the taste of sick.

'Don't cry,' I said, 'it's your birthday.'

'It *was* Mum,' she said. 'I wouldn't lie about a thing like that.'

'OK.' I patted her arm. I had to do my homework and get changed and put the washing on. There were LPs all over the floor and little bits of torn-up cardboard. Bogart wouldn't let the others come round, except sometimes Celia and Bruce, but he never let them stay over. He was a funny mixture of looking after us and then filling us with drugs and screwing me every night.

I think it started then, with Stella. Her illness, I mean. Bogart told me later that he'd put Red Leb in the cake and she ate so much, and then smoked – but then she was already turning into a mixed-up kid without his help.

†

On Saturday Bogart got up early and brought me a cup of tea. I sat up against the pillows and he pulled the curtains back so I could see the window of the house opposite, curtains still drawn, which is what Mum must have looked at in the morning too.

'What are we doing then?' I said. It was already a hot day and the dust whirled about in the air. Stella never cleaned in Mum's room and there were cobwebs in the corners full of colourless trapped flies.

'Out,' he said. He had a mysterious gleam about him. I watched his olive skin disappear into his clothes. He leant forward to kiss me before he left the room and his breath was sour and smoky. I managed to get Stella up and we all – even Stella – ate Rice Krispies before we set out. It was a golden melting September day, hot but threaded with a ripple of the chill that would be coming soon. We walked along the prom to the point and then carried on along the beach, climbing over the breakwaters and jumping down onto the shingle. The holidaymakers had all gone and there was only the occasional dog-walker, and someone fishing from the beach. When we reached the golf course, Bogart stopped.

He took something from his wallet, a little strip of paper with bumps like cap-gun caps, and he tore it in three. He put one on his tongue and told us to do the same.

'What is it?'

'Acid,' he said. 'It's time for your first trip.'

'What will it do?'

'Blow your little mind,' he sang.

'Stell?' I said, but she had already taken hers and was grinning.

Bogart took me by the shoulders and looked into my eyes: 'Honey?' he said and when he called me that it made me glow in the place where my ribs divide.

I swallowed the tab. We carried on walking towards the ferry. Nothing was happening and I was relieved. We took the ferry across to Bawdsey. The old ferry-man took our money happily enough, but eyed us suspiciously – especially Bogart – as he puttered us across the estuary. The patterns on the water were amazing; I was getting lost in the swirl of ripples and the flat shiny bits and it was taking on the pattern of paisley. We stepped out of the boat and walked round the steep shingly banks. The sea was rougher here and there was a deep grumbling sound where the shingle shifted in the waves.

'OK Stell?' I said, and when she looked at me I saw her eyes were turning in her head and I had to look away quick to stop my own eyes disappearing.

Bogart flopped down on his back. Stella crouched and I lay beside them. Words had turned to lizards in my mouth and they didn't want to move, only the tails were uncomfortable around my teeth. I didn't want to bite them off, although lizards can grow new tails, but still.

'Man,' Bogart said, 'far out, eh?' He was smiling at the sky and I felt tremendous love for him and the sky and everything. The clouds were lined up in a grid and that seemed obvious. Stella was humming something, I don't know what. The two people I loved were there and the sun shone and the sky was orderly and the shingly growling seemed contented, as if the earth was purring. Something opened up, or fell away, like blinkers and it felt so right, so perfect, so beautiful. The world came together like a properly-done sum. The lizards leapt out in a stream and the way I talked made them dance and Bogart and Stella smiled at me and kept on smiling till

I had to look away again in case the smiles would split their heads right open.

And then there was a roaring in the sky. It wasn't gradual, but suddenly there, and a flapping shadow over us.

'Shit man,' Bogart said, 'what a bummer.' It roared and scrabbled at the air like a gigantic metal budgie and it hung above us, blotting out the sun. Bogart put his arm around my shoulders and I put mine round Stella's. I couldn't bear to look at the tons of metal just above us – it could have dropped at any moment and flattened us to nothing – but Stella had her face tilted up and open like a fairground flower with the great big grin and the revolving eyes.

'Mum's dead,' I said suddenly, out of nowhere, and her face swung round and the smile was gone and the helicopter chopped and chopped like it was chopping the sky up and ruining the order and the harmony.

'Mummy,' Stella said, and suddenly got up and began to run up the shingle bank, but I followed and Bogart followed after me and it was like a sliding mountain of brown and grey and the words it said under our feet were in another language and then I was up and there was the flat expanse of mud with water shining in such intricate rivulets, like feathers, like paisley again, all the world opening out into a great big paisley shawl. Stella was running and running along the path that rose above the mud and I saw her nearly knock down a small child on a bike as she ran past. I couldn't run any more. I tried but the air was too syrupy to get into my lungs.

Bogart came panting up behind me. His skin was beady with sweat. 'Shit,' he said, shading his eyes to try and see her.

'She went that way,' I said. We walked because we couldn't run. In my stomach was a bulldog clip, which I realized was the hard tension I felt about Stella. We stopped to watch a heron and it was so perfect and perfectly strange, the way it jutted its head and the secret knowing in its eyes.

I don't know how long it was till we found Stella. We'd gone way past the places where it was safe and easy to walk.

She was up to her knees in the mud. A man with a fishing rod was sitting by her. She'd been right in, you could see, her loons were stuck to her and the beautiful velvet smock was stained and clotted. Her face and hands and the tips of her hair were green and brown and flaking.

'Is she yours?' the fisherman said.

He was a wolf in everything but the fur. I could see the barb on the end of his hook and, in a plastic bag, a writhing knot of worms.

'She's my sister,' Bogart said. 'Come on Stella.' He put his hand down for her to take.

'Sister?' she said.

'Come on Stella,' I said. 'She *is* my sister,' I explained to the wolf, but I couldn't take my eyes off the poor worms.

'Is she defective?' he said. 'She was face down. If I hadn't come along –'

'Stella!' Bogart scolded.

We stood there, Stella growing out of the mud and the worms trying and trying to tell me something. 'Well, I'll leave you to it,' the fisherwolf said at last and he stomped off, his rod shimmering and quietly whooping through the air.

Bogart and I sat on the bank and Stella stood there for ages – I don't know how long – but I remember it started to get cold and I got a fierce thirst.

Eventually Bogart pulled Stella out of the mud and it was like uprooting a small tree. She came out with a squelching plop and the mud sighed back into the space she'd left.

We got home and tried to eat but the food all seemed alive. Stella kept calling out to me in the night and in the end I went and squashed into her single bed with her. She was talking and I was scared that her mind really had been blown and would never come back to true.

Stella calmed down as the sun came up. The birds started their racket and the pale curtains whitened and just as a blackbird had finished off a solo, she said she wanted to die. There was no point in living only to die in the end anyway. She couldn't be bothered to go through it all. When she was a tree in the mud she could see the futility of it all. Learning in order to take exams in order to work in order to eat in order to live in order to die. And reproduction was even worse since you were setting someone else off on the same futile cycle.

'What about ... the smell of honeysuckle? Or Cat Stevens? Or love?'

She gave an almost elderly laugh. 'Illusions,' she said, 'just to fool us that there is a point.'

'But . . .' I started, but there was no use arguing; her voice had that flat sound that will not be lifted. And what she said couldn't be contradicted; her train of thought was a snake eating its own tail.

†

Dad came back just before Christmas. Because he gave us warning there was time for Bogart to clear out. Aunt Regina came too, with a man, Derek, who she'd met at Esperanto. She'd put the pugs in kennels, which made me think he was a good influence. He was kind and beardy and we liked him. Dad brought us presents and we had an early pretend Christmas since, of course, he had to be back with his new children for the actual day.

Aunt Regina brought bath oil and a thousand-piece jigsaw of Mount Everest, for us to share. She'd gone vegetarian in line with Derek. She moulded a sort of roadkill turkey shape out of Sosmix, and we had crackers and home-brewed beer. Dad spent most of his time on the phone to Saudi. I don't think he really saw us at all – except as an obligation. He patted us and complained that Stella was too thin, and mended a gutter before he left.

'Ring me any time, night or day,' he said, pressing a fiver into each of our hands. 'I'm still your father.'

We stood side by side to be kissed. I was aching for Bogart. I hadn't known how much I loved him till he wasn't there. He was my new family and his love was making me a new person. It was fascinating to be inside the old one as the changes happened, like a conscious chrysalis. Aunt Regina and Derek stayed on for an extra day and it was Derek, who was a teacher in a Steiner school, who said he thought Stella was depressed.

Before they left, we tipped the jigsaw puzzle out on the coffee table and all sat round, cosily, doing the edges. Derek thought jigsaws were therapeutic and had a routine – edges first, working strategically towards the centre. They left as soon as the border was completed. I lost interest once they'd driven off, but Stella loved it. As soon as they'd gone I phoned Bogart, who was staying with Celia and Bruce. It was the day before Christmas Eve and Celia was having a party.

'Come,' he said.

'I can't leave Stella. Can't you just come home?' I hesitated and I sensed him hesitating too, noticing that I'd said *home*.

He gentled his voice. 'Later, honey,' he promised. I went to bed naked, which he preferred to any of my nightwear, and lay in wait. But he didn't come back and I fell asleep. I woke when the luminous figures on the clock showed four o'clock. I put on my dressing gown and went downstairs. The room was burning hot from the electric fire and Stella was still hunched over the puzzle. She looked up at me with dazed and ragged eyes.

'Let's not take drugs any more,' I said, sitting beside her on the sofa. She nodded and slotted a piece in. The mountain was beautiful, shining and surrounded by a silvery veil of blown-off snow. She wasn't following Derek's method though and it was the sky that was missing.

'There's so much blue,' I said, picking up a piece and hovering my hand around where I thought it might go. She made a funny throaty little sound.

'I'll look after you,' I said. 'Maybe you should go to the doctor?'

She took the piece out of my fingers and fitted it in.

'Bogart will look after me and I'll look after you,' I said. It made me feel better to say that. She gave me a curious look, curious in both senses. 'Everyone needs someone to look after them,' I said, defensively. She was only fourteen and looking at me as if I was a fool.

'Who is Bogart?' she said. 'Do you even know his real name?'

'What does it matter?' I said.

'He should pay us rent,' she said.

I picked up another piece. That had never occurred to me. I made us hot milk with a spoonful of black treacle. She sipped a little of hers. 'It's Christmas Eve,' I realized, and the thought was like a hook in the stomach because we'd had our lame sort of celebration already and all that was left was like an empty box.

'Go to bed,' I said.

'I want to finish it.'

'Please Stell,' I said.

To my surprise she got up and I could hear the bones in her knees and neck snapping as she got out of the hunched position.

'Night night,' she said in a lonely voice.

Back in Mum's bedroom I put on the light and my transistor. I thought of the blinking lights of Radio Caroline out on the night-time sea; it felt comforting that it was there. 'Mouldy Old Dough' was playing and I hummed along to it as I continued my secret knitting. I liked the clickety-click of the needles. It had to be ready for tomorrow.

†

Bogart came back at lunchtime. He was a mixture of stoned and drunk and gave me a deep, peculiar-tasting kiss.

'Happy Christmas,' he said. 'We're going to Celia's for lunch tomorrow. It's far out, she's got all the trimmings, brandy butter, you name it.'

'I don't think Stella'll come,' I said.

'We'll drag her,' he said. He flopped down on the sofa and started rolling a joint, dropping specks of tobacco all over the nearly-finished puzzle.

'Make us a pot of tea, honey,' he said. He put the telly on and *White Christmas* was showing. The house wasn't Christmassy, except for a few cards. There was a tinsel tree in a box under the stairs but I couldn't bring myself to get it out.

I put the teapot on a tray on the floor. Bogart had his feet on the table now and a corner of the puzzle had slid off and broken.

'Careful,' I said, quite strictly. It was the nearest I'd come to telling him off. He quirked his eyebrows as he blew out smoke and offered me the joint, but I declined. Stella was still asleep so I brought my knitting down and sat with him, trying not to breathe in smoke as I half watched the film. The phone rang and it was Marion. She'd got really into drugs and hanging round at Celia's and I hadn't seen her since breaking up from school. She came round with a bottle of ginger wine and I did have some of that. I finished off Stella's present and wrapped it before she came down.

Stella gave me my present – a puzzle ring – and I gave her mine: Mother Clanger. I was pleased with the way she'd come out, ears perked up with pipe cleaners and shiny black buttons for the eyes. Stella's face went soft when she saw it and she snuggled it against her neck. Bogart laughed in a fond way, shaking his head at the two of us.

'I keep forgetting you're such baby chicks,' he said.

His present to me was patchouli oil and joss sticks with a starry holder; and for Stella a little wooden elephant, carved out of sandalwood. He'd wrapped them up in newspaper.

†

On the morning of Boxing Day I woke with the most terrible pain in my side. It was such agony; I couldn't believe it was true. I'd never been in agony before. It was the wrong side for appendicitis, the only thing I could think that it could be. It was so bad I had to stay in bed. Bogart brought tea up and Stella came in to see what was up with me. I couldn't drink the tea; the pain was making me feel sick. It was like a knife digging in and twisting.

'Probably period pains,' Bogart said, which made me realize I hadn't had a period for ages. I'd lost track of when I should and when I shouldn't take the pill so I just took it every day. Except when I forgot. Bogart still wanted me to go to Celia's with him, but I was too ill so he went off alone. Stella stayed behind with me. I did manage to crawl downstairs and we watched TV. She broke up the puzzle and started it again, darting worried looks at me between fitting in the pieces.

After a while I stopped being able to talk or even think. The pain got too big to fit inside me and oozed out, filling all the room, squashing the lampshade against the ceiling. I was cold and sweating. I had to be sick and Stella fetched me a bowl because I couldn't move. She held my hair back while I vomited. I felt a bit better for a while and then the pain came roaring in like a high-speed train.

'Mum's here,' Stella said, looking at the empty doorway. 'She says I have to phone an ambulance.'

I looked where she was looking. Everything was cloudy and in the cloudiness Mum might have been there. I couldn't say for sure if she wasn't or if she was.

'Shall I?' Stella said.

I opened my mouth to speak but all that came out was dribble.

Stella dialed 999 and soon I was carried away by paramedics whose voices came from inside a tunnel, saying, 'Good girl, Melanie, there's a girl.' Stella came with me in the ambulance and next thing I knew I was waking up.

'Melanie,' someone was saying and it felt like a long strip of bacon was being ripped out of my throat. 'Cough for me, there's a girl,' and I coughed and opened my eyes to see a long plastic tube slithering away. I was wheeled into a ward all decorated with cards and streamers, and Stella waiting for me with a bleached face and huge eyes and at that moment she reminded me of someone from a charity appeal.

A doctor came and explained to me that I'd had an ectopic pregnancy. It was caused by a bad infection in my fallopian tubes, which was sexually transmitted. I'd had one tube removed and it was likely that the other was badly blocked and scarred. I also had a malformation of the womb, so all in all, it didn't look as if I'd ever have a baby.

That didn't matter to me then.

'Do you know where you might have contracted the infection?' the doctor asked.

I nodded.

'Well, the *gentleman*' – she leaned on the word – 'will need treatment. Could you ask him to phone this number?' She gave me a card.

'Is it the clap?' I asked, and her face twitched before she shook her head.

'Nothing so dramatic,' she said. 'It's a tedious and rather common infection, which is largely symptomless in men but does have this occasional unfortunate effect in women. But' – she lay her hand comfortingly on my arm – 'due to the shape of your uterus it's unlikely you could ever have achieved a normal conception, anyway, so look on the bright side, at least you know.'

I was in hospital for three days. Carol singers came and I got sick and tired of mince pies by the end of it. Marion visited a lot, and Stella every day, but Bogart never once.

When I told Marion about the infection she went white. 'What?' she said. 'Caught from Bogart?'

'I don't know where *he* got it from,' I said. Of course I didn't, he'd had fifteen years of screwing around before I even knew him.

'I'll never be able to have a baby,' I said. 'Not that I want one.'

'Because of that? Shit!' She got up and looked round wildly and I realized at once, with a horrible cold slump of the heart, what was the matter.

'You?' I said.

She went from white to red and tears came into her eyes. 'I'm sorry,' she said, and then it all came spilling out. It had been the night of the party when Bogart hadn't come home. She'd slept not only with him but with another guy, she didn't even know his name. It had been that kind of party, everyone all loved up, she said, hands going everywhere, at one point she had the two of them going at her at once. I listened with an understanding snippet of a smile pinned on my face. I knew Bogart didn't believe in fidelity or any of that bourgeois crap, but still I never thought he'd sleep with Marion.

'You'd better get some antibiotics,' I said. 'I need to sleep now.' And I slammed my eyelids down like shutters.

'Sorry,' she whispered. I heard her hesitate, then watched through my lashes as she bolted off towards a nurse.

When I got home there were flowers everywhere, stiff white chrysanthemums and a ragged red poinsettia in a pot.

'I'm so sorry, honey,' Bogart said, and hugged me tight against his jumper.

'Have you been to the clinic?' I asked, extricating myself.

'I've got an appointment,' he said. 'I'm so sorry, I didn't know.' He looked pale and his eyes were strangely wide.

I thought about asking him to go, but then I thought of Stella's idea and asked him for rent instead. He shrugged. 'OK,' he said. And then he said, 'I've bought us some rubber johnnies.'

'I'm moving back into my own room,' I said. 'I'm not even allowed to have sex for six weeks.'

He started objecting but I went up the stairs and crawled into my single bed. The bed was against the radiator and it was toasty warm. The kind brown eyes of Cat Stevens looked down at me. Stella brought me up a cup of tea but the milk was old and had gone into blobs and I couldn't touch it.

'Bogart's just a lodger now,' I said.

She shrugged.

'I'll never be able to have a baby,' I said.

'Do you want one?'

I shrugged.

She sat on the bed. 'I know I said life's not worth anything,' she said, 'but I'm really glad *you* didn't die.'

'Did you think I was going to?' The thought pulled me up to sitting by my hair. It had never occurred to me.

'You nearly did.' We sat in silence for a few moments while I let that sink in, and tightly we squeezed each other's hands.

†

Once I'd stopped letting him screw me, Bogart spent much more time away from the house. He did sometimes give us ten pounds out of his dole for rent. He slept in Mum's room, and I slept in mine. I kept my eyes averted when he looked at me. Months went past and I worked hard at school. I forgave Marion and we were friends again but she had a new circle of older and dangerous friends and I didn't see her much. Stella and I stayed in together and watched telly, with Stella clutching Mother Clanger to her neck, or Stella did puzzles while I knitted – I was doing Bogart a Tibetan hat – and then we discovered the spirits.

It was a friend of Marion's who showed us how to arrange Scrabble letters on a tray and put an upturned glass in the centre. We did it as a game, but when it was just Stella and me it stopped feeling anything like play. We'd light candles and sit on the floor either side of the coffee table. It was always Stella who knew the time to start. We'd each rest a finger on the wine glass and, in a specially hollow voice, she would say, 'Is anybody there?' Usually the start was wobbly, the glass sliding and hesitating towards the letters Y – E – S. The first time I thought that Stella was pushing, but sometimes, once it got going, we both stopped touching the glass and still it moved.

'Who are you?' was the next question. The first one was called Ralph. We asked him if knew our Mum and he said, N – O. We asked him what it was like on the other side and he said, O – K. We asked him how long he'd been dead and he said, U – N – C – E – R – T – A – I – N. I thought we could have a more interesting conversation at the bus stop.

But it wasn't always like that. A person called H – U – R – S – A said, Y – O – U – R – M – O – T – H – E – R – I – S – B – E – S – I – D – E – M – E. There was a long gap while Stella and I locked eyes, silently daring each other to continue, until the glass quaked under our fingers, as if impatient. 'Why doesn't she speak to us?' I asked. R – I – N – G – R – E – G – I, was the answer and that spooked us because Mum sometimes used to call Aunt Regina that. 'Why?' asked Stella. D – O – C – T – O – R, came the answer, and then the glass began to spin and tilt; R – E – G – I – D – O – C – T –O – R it said.

'Is she ill?' I asked, but it just repeated the words faster and faster until our fingers couldn't keep up and the glass spun right off the table. Stella shrieked, jumped up, upsetting the tray, and went for the light. There was a weird cold thickness in the room. You could feel the presence.

'Go!' I shouted. 'Go back!' I flapped my arms and I could feel it there like silk tangling about them, and then my arms were free and it was gone and we could breathe.

Holding hands we went into the kitchen. I poured milk into a pan. Everything looked frightening, even the toaster with its snarl of burnt crumbs, even the cottage-shaped tea cosy, the windows like gone-out eyes.

'Let's not do it any more,' I said.

'But it was Mum.' Stella's voice was tiny.

'Shall we ring Aunt Regina?' I said.

Stella nodded and the milk hissed in a frothy tongue over the edge of the pan.

We stood together in the hall with the gloomy stairs looming above us.

Derek answered. 'Everything all right with you girls?'

'We're fine,' I said, filling my voice with brightness.

'Stella eating?'

'Yes,' I said, and it was true she'd settled into eating a

little bit more and she was actually sipping at her milk and treacle as I spoke.

'Funny thing, I was going to ring you tomorrow. We thought we'd come down for Easter. How does that sound?'

'Fine,' I said. 'Lovely. Yes, do come.'

'How's the weather?' he said. 'Can't make up its mind here.'

'Same here,' I said. 'Can I speak to Auntie?'

'She's taken herself out, this evening.'

'Where?'

'Rushcraft. I'll get her to phone you later shall I?'

'Or tomorrow,' I said. 'How is she?'

'Blooming,' he said. 'Quite the spring in her step. I'll get her to call you back, shall I?'

'Sounds like she's all right,' I said to Stella after I hung up. 'Maybe the . . . Hursa . . . is wrong.'

'Maybe,' she said, 'but still.'

I lay awake in my bed and even Cat Stevens looked spooky, the way he kept his eyes on my face. I closed mine but I was still aware of the gigantic face. I got up, took him down, rolled him up and shoved him under the bed. I kept the door open for the light and so I could hear Bogart come in. I listened to my transistor quietly. *Desperado* was playing, which I found hard to listen to, the voice so desolate. And then I heard Bogart. He was humming when he went into the bathroom. I waited till he'd gone to bed before I crept in.

'Hi ho,' he said. 'This is a turn up.' I snuggled into his arms and it felt so safe to be hugged tightly against living skin and flesh and warmth.

'We back on then?' he said.

'If you want,' I said.

'Shall I use a johnny?'

I sighed. It wasn't really sex I wanted, but warmth, but it was hard to get the one without the other. I saw that it was one of those deals you have to make in life and so I made it.

†

Stella was disgruntled that I was back with Bogart.

'If you get pregnant again you might die,' she reminded me.

'I can't get pregnant,' I said, 'and anyway he's using rubbers.'

'I know,' she said. 'I saw one floating in the toilet.'

'Sorry.'

'I'll tell Aunt Regina,' she said, but I knew she never would.

Bogart had told me that his father was a rich banker – wanker, he said, the son of an Earl. He'd grown up in Derbyshire in a huge place near Sheffield and gone to Eton. His mum had died when he was six, and he'd spent his holidays riding and boating and visiting cousins in Devon. He was the only child and would eventually inherit the family fortune, he said, which is one reason why he didn't work.

'Why do you get the social screw then?' I asked. The brown envelopes, addressed to Mr A. Robertson, had begun to arrive soon after he moved in. 'Can't your Dad send you money?'

'Dad and I . . .' his face hardened. 'We don't speak. Bastard. I won't ask for a penny from him, won't give him the satisfaction. No, I'll wait, me, I'll wait till he's gone then I'll be quids in. You should see the place, Mel, we can have a commune – Celia, Bruce, Marion, Stella – and we can have a barrel-load of kids all rolling about under the apple trees.'

He would often paint this picture of how the future would be. It made him more exciting, sexier, that he was rich and posh and that he was a rebel too. His Dad had expected him to follow him into the bank. 'Can you imagine me in a collar and tie?' he'd say, and mime being hanged.

'Can we go and have a look?' I said.

But he refused.

'Just from the gate?'

But he shook his head. 'I'm not setting foot within a mile of the place,' he said, 'not till he's six foot under.'

At night I'd sometimes get Bogart to tell me stories of his childhood. His cousins Hugh and Perry and their ponies, the adventures they'd have boating out to islands with a tent. It reminded me sometimes of *Swallows and Amazons*, sometimes of the Famous Five. After making love and feeling so falsely adult it was comforting to snuggle childishly under his arm and fall asleep listening to his tales.

†

Bogart went on Good Friday and I opened the doors and windows to let out the smell of smoke. It was a breezy spring day with sweetness flying in the air and I noticed that the daffodils in the garden had bothered to come up, even though nobody cared. We'd done nothing in the garden since Mum died.

Derek's first words when he and Aunt Regina arrived were, 'I'll get the mower onto that,' nodding at the waving, dandelion-starred lawn. They brought eggs from their own hens, and Easter eggs too that Aunt Regina had made herself in fancy moulds. It felt normal in a comforting way, though not normal at all for us, for Stella to be out in the garden helping Derek with the weeding while Aunt Regina and I made a simnel cake. She gave me the ingredients for the marzipan and I watched her as she creamed butter and sugar, the muscles glimmering through the fat at the top of her arms.

'How are you coping with your grief?' she asked, pausing with the sieve in the air to give me a meaningful look while a fine veil of flour floated down.

'Fine,' I said.

'Has Dad been in touch much?'

I lied and said yes. He was still sending money but he hardly ever rang us.

'And how are *you*?' I said.

'Fine,' she said, 'maybe a wee bit' – she tapped the sieve on the bowl edge and started to fold in the flour with a lovely scooping action of her wrist – 'out of sorts. My age,' she explained.

'Seen the doctor?'

She shook her head. 'That looks gorgeous.' She smiled at the ball of marzipan. 'Could you zest me those lemons now? No need for any doctor. It's just the change.'

'But you could still . . .'

'Oh, I'll soldier on.'

Derek came into the kitchen, bits of grass snarled up in his curly grey beard, and to my horror he patted Aunt Regina on her bottom. Stella pulled a face at me from behind him and I stifled a giggle in my lemony hand.

'I had a really strange dream last night,' I said. 'I dreamt Mum came into my room.' I looked at Stella. 'And she said to tell you' – I pointed at Aunt Regina – 'that you should go and see the doctor.'

'I wonder why she didn't come and see me?' Aunt Regina said. She sounded quite put out.

'Well, I dreamt the Prime Minister turned out to be a dog,' Derek said, and guffawed into the sink.

When they left on Easter Monday afternoon, Derek slipped us each a pound and said how welcome we'd be to visit, and to ring in an emergency any time of night or day. I hugged Aunt Regina tight as she made me promise to make Stella eat.

'I will,' I promised, 'if you do what Mum said and go to the doctor's.'

'You wee fusspot!' She shook her head. 'I will, if you promise to look after yourself.'

'Promises, promises,' Derek said. 'Can I have a go? Will you two promise' – he smiled between Stella and me – 'to laugh at least once a day?'

'We'll try,' I said.

We stood and waved as they drove away, then I went in to phone up Bogart and tell him to come back home.

†

It was at Bawdsey on a mellow trip one hot afternoon that Bogart first met Jesus. The mud was drying on my calves into itchy lettering, a kind of script; I don't know what the language was. Somehow, I must have gone off the path, searching maybe, or just enjoying the warm suck of the mud. I found Bogart sitting cross-legged in the long grass, his face a blaze of bliss. He pointed to the sky and said, 'He came to me.'

I sat down beside him, and examined my legs. 'What language is this?' I said.

He only glanced. 'He bade me wait,' he said.

'Who?'

'Our Lord. Melanie.' He turned to me and his eyes had gone golden as a lion's. 'I have seen the light. I have seen Jesus. And he has bade me wait.'

'For what?'

'Don't know,' he admitted. We waited there for the rest of the afternoon. The thing about the acid was the way it stretched the surface and changed the way I saw things. One time I felt like an animal, my sense of smell sharp as a dog's and I snuffled and wagged along the street, feeling a tail, real as my hand, feeling the blood pound in my veins and the air go in and out of me of its own accord. I knew then for absolute certain that our physical bodies are pets for our souls, and we must look after them as kindly as we would tend a pet, and that not only did we have souls but so did rabbits and snails and trees and all the babies that never got to be.

I wandered off and played for a while with a black dog, chasing and laughing (and the dog was laughing) and then it started to wear off, which leaves you with a strange emptiness, as if the elastic that holds your mind together has lost its snap. I found Bogart again and he hadn't moved a muscle. A frown in the sky had obscured the sun and the hairs on my arms hissed and swayed.

I got hold of his hand and tried to pull him up, but he seemed to have grown into the ground.

'I've got to wait,' he repeated.

'I've got to go,' I said. But it was another age and the sun had oozed its yellow juice between the stones before I could get him to budge.

'What did he say again?' I said.

'To wait.'

'Yeah,' I said, 'but that could be for days or weeks. He probably means wait for another sign or something.'

He looked at me, eyes spinning in opposite directions. And then he stood, tottered unsteadily for a minute. 'Fucking foot's gone to sleep,' he said, stamping so that the ground shook.

The sign, when it came, was on the anniversary of Mum's death. Neither Stella nor I referred to the date, but Aunt Regina phoned and made us acknowledge it. She said that she and Derek would be coming to see us for a week and to keep strong and had we kept our promises, because she'd kept hers.

'You went to the doctor?' I said, bracing myself. 'What did he say?'

'There's nothing amiss,' she said, 'but we've become friends. Kindred spirits.'

'Good,' I said.

'Or soulmates,' she continued. 'Between you and me, Derek is finding it all rather trying. Nose out of joint sort of thing.'

'Anyway, you'll be coming to see us,' I said. She gave me the likely date and I wrote it on my hand.

That evening, for the first time in months, we had a seance. It was in the hope of attracting Mum, of course, or someone who'd act as go-between. Bogart was in the garden snoozing on a deckchair. The Bible lay on the table; he'd taken to searching it for clues. Since Jesus first spoke to him he'd been waiting for another sign, searching the sky, the television and the post, taking regular doses of acid to keep his mind open – but to no avail.

Stella arranged the Scrabble letters while I lit the candles. I'd cried earlier, privately, and then I'd removed a school picture of me from a frame and, by trimming the edges off, got a picture of Mum in there. I sat her on the table by the letters and polished the special glass with a silky petticoat.

'Is anyone there?' said Stella and we waited, and, as usual, at first there was nothing.

'Is anyone there?' Stella repeated, and at last, the glass began to tremble.

'What's your name?' I asked.

The glass hesitated and seemed to change its mind several times, before eventually it went to H.

'Maybe Hursa?' Stella whispered.

'Is our mother with you?' I asked.

The glass began to move more certainly now. C – A – L – L – A – L – A – N, it spelled.

'Alan?' Stella said. 'Who's Alan? We don't know an Alan,' she told Hursa. C – A – L – L – A – L – A – N it said again, and, whatever we asked, that's all it would spell.

I was getting bored. 'Shall we give it up?' I said, talking to Stella, not the spirit.

At that moment Bogart came in. He opened the door and stood in the doorway.

'Piss off,' Stella said.

'What you doing?'

'Communing with the spirits,' I said, frostily. He came in and watched. I could feel the shape of him in the doorway behind me and I waited for him to start teasing, but he just said, 'Go on then.'

'Nothing's happening,' Stella said. 'It just keeps saying Call Alan.'

He was silent for a moment, then: 'What did you say?'

'Call Alan,' I said. 'It's getting on my wick.'

'Christ,' he breathed. 'Jesus Christ.'

'What?' Stella and I said together.

'That's me,' he said.

We stared at him in the flickering light. '*Alan?*' I said. Of course Bogart wasn't his real name and early on I'd plagued him to know it, and the letters that came to the house said Mr A. Robertson, but I'd forgotten lately, he was just Bogart to me. My arm was aching from holding it in position over the glass.

'Can I?' Bogart said.

'I don't know if you can join in part way through,' I said. I didn't want him there; this was something that Stella and I did together, and really by now it was about the only thing. But he knelt down by the table and put his finger on top of mine, on top of Stella's, on the glass.

'Alan is here,' I said, and Stella and I pulled a face at each other and she started to giggle. Nothing happened.

'Are you still there?' I said. 'You said call Alan and we've called an Alan. Is he the right one?' My tone had gone facetious, which I thought would kill the mood. But the glass began to move again.

'Fucking hell,' Bogart whispered. 'Are you doing that?'

'Shhh,' Stella and I hissed as the glass tremulously spelled out, H – E – R – O – N –H – E – R – O – N – H – E – R – O – N.

'What?' we said together. And when we asked what it meant it just spelled the same thing again and then started onto a nonsense jumble of letters till it flew off the table and the seance was over. I switched on the light and Bogart stood, his forehead furrowed, staring at the letters until Stella tipped them back into their drawstring bag.

'That's it,' he said.

'What?'

'The sign.'

'Yes?' Stella pulled a face at me.

'Heron,' he said. 'I have to find a heron.'

'Or three herons?' Stella said. She switched on *Crackerjack* and went back to her puzzle.

I followed Bogart out into the garden. He stood with his head tilted back, staring up at the navy blue sky. 'Looking for herons?' I teased.

'He spake unto me,' he said.

'I don't see why you have to say it like that,' I said.

'Herons,' he said. 'There are herons at Bawdsey. Remember?'

'Better go back there then.'

†

Every day after that, Bogart took acid and went to Bawdsey. Term ended and I lay in bed till ten or eleven and so did Stella, but as promptly as if he was going off to work in his dad's bank, Bogart would be up and out early in the morning. He'd walk to the ferry and get the first boat there and the last one back in the evening. I don't know what the ferryman thought.

He'd taken to praying and would spend hours on his knees before a shrine he'd made on Mum's dressing table. There was a picture of a crucified Jesus and one of a heron torn from my *Observer Book of British Birds*. He lit a candle and joss sticks and put a fresh flower there every day, at the very least a dandelion.

He took me by the shoulders one night – we hadn't been having sex much since his visions began. I would snuggle up to him, and wrap my legs round him, but his head was usually too full of Jesus to be interested.

But on this night, he said: 'The Lord wishes me to beget a son.'

'But –'

He put his finger to my lips and made me look into his eyes. 'If the Lord wishes, then it shall be so.'

Since my operation, I'd been on the pill to make absolutely sure I should not conceive, as it would be so dangerous to my health. I had an appointment for sterilization in a month's time. The consultant thought it was the safest and best thing for me to do, and remembering the pain and how I'd nearly died, I went along with it. 'Dispense with all that nonsense for good and all,' was how he put it. I thought it would be better than being on the pill for all my life. I hadn't told Bogart, or anybody except Stella about the sterilization. It sounded so hygienically final, that word, about as far from sexy or desirable as you could get.

Bogart took my pills from the drawer in the bedside cabinet, popped them out of their circular blisters and flushed them down the lavatory. His eyes had a new blank shine in them as if he was seeing an idea in front of him and not a person.

'Do you still love me?' I said. He hadn't said so for ages.

He kissed my forehead and I had to take it that that meant yes. We made love and despite everything there was an extra kind of excitement in it for me, not being on the pill, the danger of it. Did I believe Bogart when he said the Lord had spoken to him? Did I really think that I would have a son? Looking back, I see myself as a little goose imprinted with him. The way goslings will follow the first thing they see when they have hatched, even a fox or a ferret or a football.

'Tell me about when you were a boy,' I said, snuggling under his musky armpit.

He said nothing.

'About your cousins,' I prompted. I touched his skin with the tip of my tongue to taste the salt.

He sighed. 'What do you want to know?'

'Just a story.'

'A bedtime story,' he said. 'Such a kid.'

I pulled away from him and sat up. 'It's never bothered you before.'

He turned to me. It wasn't quite dark and I could see the shine of his eyes. 'I wish you were older,' he said.

His voice sounded so flat, not like his voice at all.

'Sod off then,' I said, 'and *find* someone older.'

'I can't,' he said. 'You are the one.'

'Am I?'

'Jesus has confirmed it,' he said. 'With you I must beget a son. We must fornicate for that purpose.'

'Fornicate?' I repeated, my voice gone weirdly shrill. '*Fornicate?*'

Bogart did a long patronizing sigh. 'Lie down,' he said.

I sat ramrod straight. I wanted to get up and go to my own little bed but he wrestled me down and put his arms round me to hold me there.

†

Stella came to visit me in hospital. I was only in one night. I told Bogart it was a school trip. How could I tell him I was going to be sterile? Stella came rushing in at the start of visiting and chucked a Caramac and a yellow rosebud on the bed. Her eyes were huge and luminous and she had a pimple on her chin. She had her hand jammed against her side like she had a stitch and was panting.

'What's up?' I said.

She perched on the edge of the bed struggling her hands anxiously together. The ends of her fingers were blunt and ragged where she chewed and chewed.

'*What?*' I said.

'Aunt Regina's here,' she hissed when she'd got her breath back.

My eyes darted round the ward. '*Here?*'

She nodded and talked fast and low, and I went cold as I listened. 'They turned up. Marion's mum told the school about Bogart and they rang Aunt Regina and she got here last night and caught Bogart and me smoking and chucked him out, I mean literally chucked, you should have seen it, Derek got hold of his arm and pushed him out of the door and Aunt Regina threw everything she could find of his out of the window, and said she'd call the police if he hadn't skedaddled in two minutes flat.'

We stared at each other. 'Bogart,' I said. My wound twanged and jangled. Stella opened her mouth but before she could get another word out, Aunt Regina, Derek and a woman in a kaftan arrived and stood in a row looking down at me.

'Huh-hmm,' Derek said.

Aunt Regina shook her head. 'Deary me,' she said. 'Deary, deary me.'

I looked at the woman in the kaftan. 'Kathy,' Aunt Regina said. 'My new friend Kathy.'

I saw a cloud cross Derek's face and guessed that this was the doctor and soulmate.

'Hi,' I said. She had a toby jug look, with jutting chin and wilderness eyebrows. She stuck out a broad hand for me to shake.

'How do?'

'Wonderful,' I said.

'You're coming home with us,' Aunt Regina said. 'All packed. Dad knows and agrees.'

'House on the market, pronto.'

'No!' I said.

'It's all arranged,' Aunt Regina said.

'But school –'

'There's a school in Peebles. All arranged.'

'But – but –' I looked at Stella but she had her thumb jammed in her mouth. I could see the bulge of Mother Clanger in her cardigan sleeve.

Derek inserted himself between Aunt Regina and Kathy. 'We went to see the headmaster.'

'God.'

'Questionable whether you'll get your A levels – altered behaviour, a falling-off of friendships, and of Stella, apparently' – Stella's head hunched further into her chest – 'they've seen neither hide nor hair this half term.'

'Stell?' I said, but she wouldn't look at me. 'I didn't know that,' I said weakly. Kathy gave me a broad and cheery grin quite at odds with the topic of conversation.

Aunt Regina folded her arms. 'The truant officer called to be confronted by a long-haired beatnik –'

A puff of laugh came out of me at that word.

'And the parasite has –'

'Parasite!' I said. 'He's not, he's –'

'Don't get het up,' Derek said. 'Sterilization!' he added. 'You should have consulted us. I'll be having words with the authorities about this.'

'It's *my* body. *I* decided.'

'This just goes to prove you are not capable of looking after yourselves.'

'We are,' Stella whined.

'He even pays rent,' I said. 'Bogart –'

'*Bogart*? *Bogart*!' Aunt Regina shrieked. Spit flew out of her mouth and landed on the edge of my blanket. The whole ward was riveted. She realized this and lowered her voice. 'In any case, it's all arranged,' she said.

'I love him!'

'Love!' she squawked.

'They do love each other,' Stella added, helpfully.

Derek got hold of Aunt Regina's arm and it seemed to deflate her.

'Love,' she muttered, and they all shook their heads in identical gestures of despair.

†

I didn't see Bogart for a year. Moving to a new country and a new school when you're seventeen, freshly sterilized and pining for your lover is hard – particularly when you find yourself in the sticks, knee-deep in goats and chickens, and in the middle of a tetchy middle-aged ménage à trois.

School was all right. I got by. I made friends but no one special. Sometimes a boy would ask me out, and once or twice I even went, but they *were* boys, not men, and my heart was still too full of Bogart. After him, how could I fancy a skinny youth?

I had no address for Bogart, no way of getting in touch. I wrote to Marion and asked her to find it for me. She said he'd gone off travelling and she didn't know where. I thought about running away to try and find him – he'd be in Morocco I guessed, he'd often talked about going there. But then he might be in India. How ever would I find him? And anyway, I couldn't leave Stella.

We each had a tiny room in the loft. You had to go up a ladder and, to get into my side, squeeze round the hot water tank. There was a skylight that I forced open and if I stood on my bed I could stick my head out. This I would do, night after night, all that first long summer, sniffing the air like a caged animal, watching the stars, hearing the owls and the screeches of savagery from the hen coop. In the summer we sweltered, in the winter we shivered under piles of patchwork and Kathy's home-cured goatskins, that turned out, we discovered during a plague of flies, to be not quite cured enough.

Three years later I went to teacher-training college on the outskirts of London. Aunt Regina was disappointed that I chose to go so far away, but I needed to, I needed distance. And I thought Stella was old enough by then to cope without me there.

I found it a thrill to live just a bus ride from the Embankment or Regent's Park, to be able to browse in the British Museum or the Tate, or to swan through Harrods with a bored and snobbish expression on my face. I bought black lipstick from Biba; had my hair cut at Vidal Sassoon. There was an IRA bomb scare one day in Oxford Street and I was caught up in the fantastic rush, the stampede to get out of Debenhams. I watched it on the news that night, back in my hall of residence.

On the last Saturday before the end of term, I went up town to do my Christmas shopping. I'd spent all day trudging about and was standing in Piccadilly Circus gazing at the decorations when I heard a person preaching. He had his back to me. There were a couple of people standing beside him, giving leaflets to anyone who would take one. They all wore long flowing robes. The guy was saying, 'Wait and listen for just one moment. Just one moment is enough to save your life and save your soul.' And he was saying it in Bogart's voice.

The rush of love went up from the wet pavement through the soles of my boots, whooshed through my body and out into the drizzly light. It was strong enough to stop my heart. Because I'd halted so abruptly, a man bumped into me and swore but I didn't care. I stood still and became an island that the crowd flowed round. I moved closer to Bogart and his fellows and became one with them.

I kept my eyes on the side of his head where his curls were beaded wet and his nose was reddened with the cold. A current snaked from me, from my heart to his, a golden snake of light. And he felt it, and turned. He'd been speaking but when he saw me he stopped. Our eyes met and I went straight into his outstretched arms and it might be a cliché but it's true, that it felt like coming home. The lipsticks and the records and the lesson plans; the posters, the discos, the whole flimsy construction of my life rattled to the ground around me. There was only love and there was only Bogart.

He was living in a squat in Tooting Bec with thirteen other people. This was the foundation of the movement, before we even called it a church. It was the Soul-Life commune and it was bursting full. The community was spreading the word and raising funds to buy the house, which had been scheduled for demolition. Through a miracle – the discovery that the portico was of art-historical interest – the demolition order was lifted. Such, it seemed, was the power of prayer.

Bogart called himself Adam now, since he was the first, the founder, of the Soul-Life Community. Something in him had changed. The magic, always in his eyes, had got into his voice, giving it a new resonance (at least a resonance I didn't remember), and into his demeanour. There was a kind of light around him, and people were attracted to that light as if it was something they needed to see by.

All his followers had taken biblical names. Isaac and Hannah had been with him in the street that day, but I'd scarcely registered them. There were not supposed to be any partnerships in the commune. There were dormitories for each sex, sleeping bags and carry-mats in every corner. Everyone wore black socks and pants so they could all be washed together, and in the morning you just helped yourself to any from the sock and undie mountains on the landing.

Because he was prey to frequent visions, Bogart – Adam – slept alone. He had a single room with a tiny balcony, just wide enough to stand on, and when you did and craned your neck you could see a pub and a small triangle of the common. The walls were covered in pictures of herons:

postcards, pages torn from books, a couple of paintings. He slept on an airbed with a slow leak that had to be re-pumped with a foot pump every night.

'This is my bride in Jesus,' Adam told the people that first night. 'And we will call her Martha.'

I would have liked a prettier name. The Bible is full of lovely names, but with all the eyes – interested, jealous, suspicious even – on me, I couldn't object.

We sat down to share a meal of curried chickpeas with yogurt and chapattis.

'We've heard about you,' Hannah told me. She was a thin and pretty Australian, with a pointed nose and teeth that crossed foxily.

'What did he say about me?' I asked her.

'He was waiting for the Lord to bring you back to him,' she muttered.

'And he did,' I said proudly, but privately doubtful. Was it really the Lord who'd made me move to London? Was it really the Lord who'd carried my feet towards where Adam was preaching?

'Believe in miracles and they happen,' Adam said, tuning in to our conversation. He had a chapatti crumb caught in his beard and, as I leant forward to pick it off, I caught the narrow look that Hannah gave me.

'Always?' I said.

'If it's the Lord's will.'

'But how do you know if it's the Lord's will?'

'If it happens.'

'But –'

'Martha will be staying here,' he said firmly, and loudly enough to count as an announcement, 'and as my wife, she will share my room.'

I said nothing more and didn't dare to look at Hannah again. It was Saturday and it didn't matter if I stayed away from halls that night. But there were only two more days of term and then I was set to go home. On Wednesday Derek was driving all the way to fetch me.

After the meal the women cleared the table and washed

up while the men chatted, making plans for raising funds. I'd begun stacking plates but Adam put his hand on my wrist.

'Go and bathe,' he said, 'there are robes in the airing cupboard.' Hannah's hair flew out in zigzags as she flounced off to the kitchen. I went up the stairs. You could tell that this was once a rich person's house; the banister was a gracious curve of shiny wood held up with ornamental ironwork, acorns and corn sheaves and dormice that some idiot had painted over with a thick white gloss.

Upstairs smelled of damp. The bathroom had a sloping floor and the bath was scribbled with curling hairs. There were orange knobs of fungus pressing out from behind the toilet and shimmering green patches on the walls. When I turned on the tap, though, the water was hot. There was a ferocious roar from the boiler and the water thundered from the calcified mouths of the taps, filling the room with steam. Hannah told me later that Isaac – a skinny guy with white eyelashes – had worked for the gas board and had illegally connected us to the mains.

I was in a peculiar detached daze, as if I was stoned, but there had been no drugs, nor even anything to drink with the meal. I stared at my face in the toothpaste-splattered mirror above the basin and wondered about fate or miracle or coincidence. If I hadn't gone down that street at that time, I'd have been back at college by now, in the canteen stuffing myself with crispy pancakes, chips and gypsy tart – my Saturday treat. I'd probably be getting ready to go to the Christmas party in the Student Union. My patchwork maxi-dress was waiting in the wardrobe. Parties made me nervous, but still I might have gone. What if I had? I might have been kissed by someone under the mistletoe that night. I might have met a budding teacher and stayed on to become one myself. And then what?

I stood shivering as steam rose from the bath and clouded the mirror till I disappeared, knowing, as you rarely do, that this was a moment of choice, a hinge point in my life. I could have gone downstairs, slipped out of the door and into a different future. I did consider it. I thought about the dress poised for the evening, the mistletoe, the buffet and the disco. As I stripped and lowered myself into the hairy water, I imagined swigging beer and trying to dance to 'Bohemian Rhapsody'. There was a third year called Wayne who fancied me.

The bath was so big I had to press my elbows against the sides in order not to drown and I lay there, braced, imagining a kiss from Wayne, imagining taking him back to my room – but it was no good. Now that I'd seen Bo – Adam – again, there was only him for me. I was a goner.

†

There was no curtain in the heron room, but Adam had put night lights on the windowsill and the flames reflecting against the glass seemed cosily to exclude the night. I stumbled into the room in the too-long gown I'd found hanging among others, all in shades of lavender and lilac. This was the colour of spirituality, Adam told me, and the 'girls' had dyed them. Before we made love we knelt and prayed.

'Thank you Lord for delivering my true love, my wife in your eyes, back to my arms. Forgive me for doubting that you would do so in your infinite wisdom. Now she is grown-up and ready to serve you through her service to me. Oh Lord, we make love blessed in the sacred joy of your love. Amen.'

And then we did make beautiful and familiar love on his funky-smelling sleeping bag. He was just the same, and his fingers found me out in just the same old way. 'Maybe this time my son will be conceived,' he said, and he splayed his palm over my belly. That was when I should have told him I'd been sterilized – but it was a moment I didn't want to ruin. If I'd told him that there was no possibility of a child, then what? The choice to deceive him was made, out of cowardice, out of tiredness, and couldn't be unmade. I began to shiver. He re-pumped the airbed and we squashed together into the sleeping bag. He started talking about tomorrow and I told him I had to go back.

He just laughed.

'It's the end of term,' I explained, 'and then –'

'Forget it. This is your calling: me, us, Soul-Life.'

'But –'

He put his finger on my lips, and replaced it with his mouth. I was too tired to argue. I could feel myself slipping into a drowse. I'd explain to him in the morning. I'd tell him I needed to be in Peebles for Christmas but that I'd be back. I'd tell him I wanted to finish my teacher training, but I could come to him every weekend. But I never did. It must sound pathetic that I said none of these things and in fact didn't go back, even to collect my books and clothes. It was the Lord's will, you see. Or at least it was Adam's, which was much the same thing to me.

When Derek came to fetch me on the following Wednesday, I wasn't there. I was unaware of the fuss that ensued until I saw myself in a newsagent's window. It was nearly a week later. I'd gone out into the streets with Adam, Isaac and Hannah to spread the word and sell some Christmas pompom decorations we women had made. It was the first time I'd been outside since I'd arrived. The sky was high and white and tiny grey snowflakes shimmied about in the air. People gave us such looks as we paraded along in our lavender robes and woolly hats, and I had to keep in the proud giggliness I felt, to be a part of something like this, and such an important part.

I'd been meaning to ring home but there was no phone in the house and I hadn't been out. It was thoughtless and heartless and a failure of imagination not to realize how anxious Aunt Regina, Derek, and especially Stella, would be. I'd kept telling Adam that I must go out and ring, but because of the intensity with which he – and my own feelings – engulfed me, I lost track of the days. When, passing a newsagent, I saw a picture of me, taken from a school photo, my silly grinning face under the headline – NO CLUES ON VANISHED STUDENT – I stopped as if I'd hit a bollard. The others sailed on ahead, but missed me eventually and came back. We all stood and looked at my grainy face.

Adam went in to buy the paper. He handed it to me,

and with the snow skittering off the print I read about my disappearance. A quiet and somewhat naïve student, who kept herself to herself, was how I was described. Aunt Regina was quoted as saying it was uncharacteristic behaviour and they were out of their minds with worry. Anyone with any information as to my whereabouts should contact the police. *Naïve?* I thought. We all trooped to a phone box. Adam gave me a 10p piece and they waited outside while I rang. I shut my eyes and imagined the goatskin rug on the hall floor and the dusty black of the telephone on the bottom stair. I prayed that Stella would pick up but it was Aunt Regina who answered in a tight, high voice.

'It's me,' I said.

There was a silence before she shrieked: 'It's her!'

'I'm really sorry,' I said. 'I should have rung.' I could hear a commotion taking place as they all crammed into the tiny hall.

'Where are you?'

'I've kind of joined a religion,' I said.

'She's joined a religion,' she relayed.

'What denomination?' I heard Kathy ask.

'Let me handle this,' Derek said, and then his voice came loud down the receiver. 'Has this got anything to do with that beatnik?'

I shut my eyes and flinched. 'If you mean Bogart, yes.'

'What did I say?' he said to the others, and to me: 'Where are you?'

'Tooting Bec.'

'Address?'

'It's Cooper Road,' I said.

'Number?' He was barking the questions like a sergeant major. 'Pen,' he ordered. He would be pinching his fingers together and twitching his hand around. *Why the devil can't we keep a pen beside the phone*, he was always saying, and in fact I'd tied one to the banister once but someone had taken it down to use the string.

I put my head out of the box. 'What number do we live at?'

'Sixty,' Hannah said, before Adam could stop her. I shut the door again. There were cartoon faces scratched on the thick plastic glass and the smell of pee was somehow comforting.

'Can I speak to Stella?' I asked.

'We'll set off immediately,' he said. 'Eight hours should do it.'

'Just a quick word,' I said, and I don't know if he would have fetched her but the pips went and there was the buzz of an empty line. I opened the door again. 'Can I have another 10p?' I said, but Adam dragged me out. He was furious. I'd never seen him like that before.

'Great,' he said. 'Now the pigs'll be round.'

'So?' I said. 'We haven't done anything wrong.'

He looked at me.

'She's right,' Isaac said.

'I'm nineteen,' I reminded him. 'I'm a free agent.'

Adam's face relaxed. He stood for a moment, thinking, opening and closing his fists. 'Phone the pigs,' he said at last, fishing in his robe for another coin.

By the time I got through to the right department, Derek had already talked to the detective in charge of the investigation. All I got was a telling off for being so inconsiderate and I took it meekly, saying, *sorry, sorry, sorry,* looking down at the wet that had soaked into the bottom of my robe. I was lucky not to be charged for wasting police time. I could feel my communal knickers drooping between my legs as I apologized.

Isaac and Hannah went off with the bags of pompoms while Adam and I returned to Tooting to get ready for my family. We tidied up the kitchen, and Bethel made some biscuits. We sat in his room cross-legged on his sleeping bag, face-to-face. He held my hands. It was so cold I couldn't stop shivering but he thought it was nerves.

'Be strong in the Lord,' he kept saying. 'They will try to take you back, but you won't go with them because you belong here with me. The Lord, in his grace, allowed them to have you back until you were ready, until you were mature. Now you are an adult and you can go wherever you want to go, be with whomsoever you choose to be with. And you have chosen me.'

'I know,' I said.

'You have chosen the Lord.' He smiled and cupped my cheeks in his hands. 'They will try to persuade you. This is the Devil's work. Remember, Martha, that he is wily and his sleeve is full of tricks.'

'I'll be OK,' I said. My teeth were chattering. He went down to fetch tea and came back with a hot water bottle. He wrapped me in a blanket with the bottle. His beard was soft against my forehead as he kissed me.

'You're my wife,' he said.

'But I'm not,' I said. 'Not really. They won't see it like that.'

I felt steamy in the wrapping, like a baking pie. Adam picked up his guitar and twanged about a bit before he settled into a long rambling song about miracles and herons. The chorus went:

You seem to be a bird
With feathers and a beak
You seem to be absurd
You seem a little freaky
But though you cannot speak
You bring the word
You bring the word
You bring the word.

It was catchy and from my blanket nest I joined in. He sang with his eyes closed and a spiritual smile flickering at the corners of his lips, then stopped abruptly and put the guitar down. 'Thank you!' he said, looking at the ceiling.

'What?'

'Stay put.'

I could hear him galloping downstairs. I snuggled into the blanket, the hot water bottle burning the skin of my belly. I couldn't believe they would be coming all the way to London. Derek thought nothing of driving thousands of miles; it was one of the things Aunt Regina loved about him. No sooner did she say she wanted to go somewhere than he was revving up the engine. He'd be driving now, peering forward like a tortoise from its shell. Aunt Regina would be beside him and in the back, maybe Kathy (though I hoped not) taking up three-quarters of the seat, probably handing out her sickening goats'-milk toffees, and Stella would be crammed into her tiny quarter, screwed up in a knot of arms and legs.

It was nearly dark and a street lamp slanted through the struts of the balcony and the window frame, making a complicated grid of shadows on the wall and floor. Some of the herons were trapped in shadow cages. A Salvation Army band started up, a few honks and squeals before launching into 'Once in Royal David's City'. I wriggled towards the window in the sleeping bag to look out – they were on the corner outside the pub. There was a tree in the pub window. The scene looked like a corny Christmas card; you only needed to sprinkle on a bit of glitter.

Hannah, Bethel and Kezia came into the room, all giggly and fluttery. They pulled me out of the sleeping bag. 'Oi!' I said.

'Who's getting married?' Kezia was a plump and rosy American with a hairy face, a bit older than the rest.

'Married?'

'So that your family can be there,' Bethel explained. 'Adam's in the downstairs bog, shaving!'

'No!' I said. 'But I love his beard!'

Hannah had begun to brush my hair, which was damply snarled, and I yelped like a child. 'Stand still,' she said. 'We have to try and make you beautiful.'

'No one asked *me*,' I said.

Bethel went out and returned with a clean gown, a bit smaller and at least, I noticed gratefully, warmer looking than the polyester thing I'd been wearing.

'No flowers,' Kezia grumbled.

'And anyway, we can't get married just like that,' I said. 'There are legal papers and stuff.'

'Got any make-up?' Hannah was pulling harder at my

hair than she needed to. She began to pin sections of it painfully against my scalp.

'I came with nothing,' I said, aware of the biblical ring.

'Get mine,' Kezia said, and Bethel fetched a filthy zip-up pouch, leaking patchouli oil. She outlined my eyes in kohl, and filled my lips in deep maroon.

'It won't be a real wedding,' I said, when she let me have my mouth back.

'Better?' Kezia asked Hannah, who frowned at me before saying, 'Best we can do.'

'We need flowers,' Kezia said again. Then she laughed. 'Hang on, people.' She hurried out.

'Let's try a bit more blusher,' Hannah muttered. 'I never thought Adam would.'

'He said,' Bethel explained to me, 'that Jesus told him we shouldn't get into couples. It's too individual.'

'That's a contradiction in terms,' I said. Hannah was dabbing at my cheeks. I could see in the mirror she was making me look clownish.

'It's different for Adam,' Hannah said, an edge of sarcasm in her voice. '*Jesus* chose a wife for him.'

'I think that's enough.' I ducked away from her red-smeared finger.

†

Kezia came bounding back in with someone's Christmas wreath. 'A good cause,' she said. With a pair of nail scissors she snipped a couple of red plastic roses out of it. 'I could make a table decoration,' she said, removing some holly and a few gold-sprayed fir cones. 'Think they'll notice?' She held up the denuded wreath. It actually looked better, from a minimalist point of view. She went to sneak it back.

The doorbell rang and I heard it being answered and Derek saying, 'Where is she?' I looked in the mirror and there I was, all dolled up, and that was the right expression given the way my face seemed to have been drawn on.

'Melanie?' Aunt Regina called up the stairs. I went to the top and looked down. Her face was tilted up at me, soft in the lamplight, beautifully withered.

'Come here.' She held out her arms and I ran down the stairs and into them. She smelled goatish and powdery and she let out a little sob as she hugged me.

Derek stood shaking his head. 'What's this get-up?' he said, looking me up and down.

Stella was standing in the shadow. 'Stell,' I said, and hugged her. She felt insubstantial in my arms; thin, yes, but more than that. It was as if some essence within her had ceased to exist, or maybe it had never been there in the first place.

'Have you really got religion then?' she said in my ear.

At that moment I didn't know. It wasn't about religion; it was about Adam. A beardless stranger came into the hall, and I saw that it was him.

'Alan,' Derek said.

'Adam now,' I said.

'I thought he called himself Bogart?' Aunt Regina said.

Adam radiated patience at their folly. 'What's in a name?' he said, smiling beatifically at them.

'In which case, I'll address you as Alan,' Derek said.

Adam shrugged. 'No problem,' he said, but I caught his twitch of irritation.

'Will someone explain to me what this pantomime is all about?'

'We're getting married,' I said.

'Married!' Stella said. 'What, *now*?'

Derek choked.

'Married?' Aunt Regina said. She and Derek exchanged looks. 'We'd like a word with Melanie,' Aunt Regina said. 'In private if you don't mind.'

'You won't change my mind,' I said, and Adam beamed approval at me.

'Can we get out of this perishing hall?' Derek said.

We went into the sitting room, softly lit with many candles. The fire was crackling and Kezia had made a decoration out of holly, fir cones and the filched roses. It looked cosy and festive, though there was smoke leaking out of a crack in the chimney breast.

'I want to talk to Stell.' I took her hand and led her up to the bedroom. 'How are you?' I said.

'Fine.'

'How's school?' These were not the questions I wanted to ask or that she wanted to answer. She made a throaty non-committal noise.

'Where's Kathy?' I said.

'She stayed home so there was room in the car – in case.' Her eyes met mine and she raised her eyebrows quizzically. 'She's going to cook the fatted calf,' she said. 'Well, kid actually.'

'Do *you* want me to come back?' I said.

'Up to you.' We could hear raised voices down below.

'They were arguing in the car,' Stella said. 'Nearly all the way from Peebles. Married, Mel!' she added, narrowing her eyes at me. 'Are you sure?'

'It's not real anyway,' I said, 'I mean there's no vicar or council thingy or anything.'

Stella frowned. 'Why bother then?'

To keep Adam happy was a possible answer, but I didn't give it.

'If it *was* a real wedding, would you?' Stella asked.

To my own surprise, I nodded.

'Well then,' she said. 'You know what I think?'

I shook my head.

'You two were made for each other.'

'Really?'

'Seeing you together . . .' She waved her hand and smiled.

'He makes me feel safe,' I said. 'You know that Cat Stevens song that says, *You know how I love you honey*? Well I always, *always* wanted someone to call me honey, Cat Stevens ideally . . .' We both giggled. 'But Bog –, I mean Adam, he does call me that and he does make me feel loved and he makes me feel . . .' I hesitated, 'important.' For some reason that word closed my throat up for a moment and I had to strain not to cry and ruin the make-up.

'Are you coming down so we can get this farce over with and get back on the road?' Derek called up the stairs.

'You're on then,' Stella said.

I felt so close to her. I think it was the best conversation we ever had. There was one more question that I had to ask her. 'You don't still want to die, do you?'

She smiled and shrugged. 'Can't think of any reason for living.'

'But you said you were happy.'

'I am.'

Adam opened the door. 'Come on you two.'

I grabbed hold of Stella's twig-like arm. 'We're still talking,' I said, but she pulled herself away.

'Can I be bridesmaid?' she said. She was wearing a red velvet dress under her coat, quite suitable for a winter wedding.

The room was crammed. The ceremony was brief and to the point.

'Do you take this woman, Melanie Anna Woods, hereafter to be known as Martha, to be your wife in the eyes of our Lord Jesus Christ?' Isaac said.

'I do.' Adam's hands were warm as they grasped mine. I looked up into his face and I did wish he hadn't shaved his beard off; it showed that he had a weak chin. But still, it was his beautiful melting brown eyes that mattered, that flowed with love, and that held mine as Isaac asked the reverse question of me.

'I do,' I said. To my surprise, Adam put a ring on my finger, thin and silver with a turquoise stone. I found out afterwards that he'd borrowed it from Hannah.

'You may kiss the bride,' Isaac said, and we did kiss, though it made me blush with Derek and Aunt Regina watching.

'Where's the champagne?' Aunt Regina said.

'We're teetotal,' Kezia told her.

'If that doesn't cap it all!' said Derek.

'We have a ginger cup,' Kezia said. 'Come through into the kitchen.'

The table was spread with a huge bowl of hummus, bits of carrot and chunky home-baked biscuits. Bethel ladled the hot gingery drink into mugs.

'Ten minutes,' Derek said.

'You're surely not driving straight back to Scotland?' I said. 'That's mad!'

'Mad?' Derek spluttered. 'Did you hear that, Regina! Do you hear what the pot is calling the kettle?'

'Now, now,' Aunt Regina said.

I tried to sneak off with Stella again, but Aunt Regina got hold of my arm. 'Congratulations,' she said, and kissed me on the cheek. 'Take no notice,' she added, meaning of Derek's grumpiness. 'And we'll break the journey at Birmingham – Derek has family there. I hope you'll be very happy.' I don't know what it cost her to say that, and sound as if she meant it too.

'Thanks,' is all I could think of to say.

She sipped her drink. 'And you can always come home if you change your mind. Mmm, this is rather good, very festive; you'll have to get me the recipe.' She pressed her lips together and looked at me with over-bright eyes. 'I didn't approve of your friendship with –' she couldn't decide what to call him. 'But you're older now and if you still think you love him –'

'Not *think*, do.'

'– after all this time, then good luck to you. Will you bring him home for Christmas?'

'Maybe. Aunt Regina, I'm worried about Stella.'

'I've got my eye on her,' she said.

Derek came over and glowered at me, and then suddenly grabbed me hard and pressed his lips against my hair. 'Good luck, you silly, silly goose,' he said. Startled, I glanced at Aunt Regina who was giving me a *see, he loves you really* look. I gave him a hard and meaningful squeeze around the waist.

†

After Aunt Regina, Derek and Stella had driven away, I went into the bathroom to let out a few tears. This is not how you should feel on your wedding day, I know, and it wasn't from any doubt about Adam, but I couldn't help thinking about the poor kid roasting in the Rayburn and how jolly it would have been at home, with pea-pod wine or Derek's farty home brew. But I'd made my choice and it was the right choice. I got over that wave of sadness as you always do. Learn to let it wash over you and let it go, that's what I advise. Life is full of losses – and all rehearsals for the big one in the end.

Adam continued to get his messages from Jesus, always heralded by herons, which meant he had to spend a lot of time on Romney marshes, the nearest reliable habitat, and the Soul-Life Community grew larger. Jesus told Adam he must accumulate money in order to spread the word, and gave him a new method that brought in so much more than selling pompoms, fudge or flowers. The main work was not savoury and I was shocked at first and hardly believed that Jesus could have come up with it. But you see, you can do anything, however bad, if you believe the ultimate cause is good. When I objected, Adam said that Jesus sees into your heart and understands your intentions.

It went like this, and we called it fishing. Bethel, Kezia, Hannah and I (and the other women whom we recruited) would go out with the leaflets, preaching and asking for donations. Usually, of course, people ignored us, skirted round us or crossed the road. Sometimes we'd hook a person and get them to take a leaflet and put some money in our collecting boxes. And the women's particular job was to be bait for likely-looking men, to behave in a flirtatious and deferential manner towards these potential catches. Surprisingly often, we persuaded one to come back for a cup of tea and a further chat, and many of those who did ended up in the boudoir, as we jokingly called the basement room of the second squat: a damp place bedecked in Indian bedspreads with joss sticks constantly burning to hide the smell of the three paraffin heaters it needed before it was bearably warm. The money from the sex was handsome, but handsomer still was the money from the blackmail. Because, of course, many of the fish were married, or had other reasons not to want their activity known.

I did not personally take part in the sex, because I was Adam's wife, but I was good at the hooking and the reeling in. It was a sort of sport.

While the deed was occurring, one of us would take the wallet and – not steal – but remove any interesting documents, have a look, jot the necessary information down and then replace them. And, from behind one of the draped bedspreads, a photograph would be taken. Abel set up a darkroom and developed the shots. And, a few days later, the fish would get a letter, enclosing the evidence, and the blackmail would begin. We didn't ask for extortionate amounts, but we did require a monthly commitment to the Soul-Life Community. It would show up as such on his bank statement and if questioned he could pass it off as a charitable donation and make himself look good. So where was the harm in that?

Not every fish would pay up, of course, and there were threats of the law, but because of the evidence of their fornication they'd drop them if we did. You can't win them all, of course, but we became adept at recognising which types were most likely to succumb and to pay up. It amazed me how successful this ploy was, and after a year the bank balance was burgeoning and a new member, an ex-accountant, Obadiah, began to work full-time on the books. Members of the community couldn't own money or property independently – everything was donated to the cause – and Obadiah began to invest in the stock market, for which, it turned out, he had a talent.

Once there was enough money to buy a property, we did so, and the skilled members did the renovations. By the beginning of the 1980s, when house prices were starting to go wild, the Soul-Life Community had amassed a small fortune all in the name of the Lord. Adam was happy and so I was too. He loved me. He really did. What I'm about to describe might make you doubt it, but I don't. He was led by his visions, by Jesus manifested in the herons, and I can't blame him, even though I did then.

†

It was September, nearly two years later. I can remember the day so clearly. Memory prints especially brightly on momentous days. The morning had been soft and grey. I'd woken with a niggling pain in my groin and found that my period had started. It was a few days late and Adam had been confident that this time the miracle had happened. The secret of my sterilization was like a bit of grit caught up in my heart, scratching at every beat.

I was sitting in the kitchen with a cup of tea while Hannah and Bethel loaded the washing machine with towels. As Adam's wife I wasn't expected to do as much of the domestic work – at least that was his view, not shared by my Sisters, particularly not by Hannah. Usually I did pitch in anyway, but not that day. Bethel and Hannah were singing one of Adam's songs and I had my eyes shut, trying to be soothed by their voices and the heat of my mug of tea.

When the phone rang it made me jump. Hannah shot me a look, so I got up to answer.

'Is that Melanie?' Derek asked.

'Yeah. *Martha*.'

'Stella's in hospital, she's tried to . . .'

'No!' I said, loudly, to cut him off, as if that would stop it being true. I wanted to drop the phone and stick my fingers in my ears. I wanted not to hear any more, not to let it in.

'She's all right,' he said. 'We found her in time.'

'How . . . ?'

'She tried to hang herself,' he said, 'in the barn. Kathy found her.' His voice, which had been sounding quite stern and normal, cracked at that point and I could hear him swallowing. 'She's in hospital,' he said, 'just for overnight observation and then she'll be transferred to the psychiatric unit.'

'Psychiatric?' I said.

'Regina's with her now. I've just got back.'

'I'll come, shall I?' I said.

'Ring me with your ETA at Edinburgh Waverley.'

I put the phone down and turned round. Hannah was transferring raisins from a huge paper sack into jars. Bethel was kneeling with her head in the fridge. Kezia came into the kitchen laughing about something.

'What's up?' she said, noticing my expression.

'My sister's in hospital,' I said. 'I've got to go.'

'Oh, sweetheart,' Kezia said.

I stared at the row of jam jars packed with wizened raisins. There was a butter bean on the table and a hair clip and a plate with a blackened toast crust.

'She tried to kill herself,' I said.

'Wow,' Hannah said. 'That little Stella?'

'Heavy,' Bethel said.

'C'mere.' Kezia smothered me in a squashy hug. I submitted for a moment then pulled myself free.

'What can we do to help?' Bethel said.

'They're putting her in a loony bin,' I said, 'but she isn't mad.'

'Well . . .' Hannah crinkled her blonde brows.

'It'll be for her own good,' Kezia said.

'But, see, she's always wanted to do it. She hadn't gone mad. She just can't see the point in living.'

'Maybe that *is* mad?' Bethel said.

I frowned at her and stood in the middle of the kitchen, flexing and unflexing my hands. *Was* it mad? It hadn't sounded mad at all when Stella had said it, rather – dangerously – sane.

'We'll pray for her,' Kezia said.

There was no point trying to explain. I had to go. Adam was still out so I had to leave without seeing him. Obadiah gave me a lift to King's Cross and paid for a ticket to Edinburgh and said he'd ring Derek to say when I'd be arriving.

When I got off the train five hours later, Derek was waiting. He looked so much older – his skin almost the same grey as his bushy beard and hair. We hugged and he took me to the car and we set off without saying a word. Then he reached over and patted my leg.

'Good to see you,' he said gruffly.

'How is she?'

'Just herself,' he said, giving me a slidey, puzzled look.

'Yeah,' I said.

'Could you not have worn a different get-up?' he asked.

'I don't have any other clothes,' I said, looking down at my lilac skirt. 'Anyway, what does it matter?'

He said nothing but his expression hinted at a wealth of reasons why it might. We didn't speak any more till we got to the hospital. I saw Aunt Regina first, hands fisted against her chest as she leant over the bed, and then Kathy, who was doing something immense in macramé. And then I focused on my sister. Her face looked puffy and ill but when she saw me, she smiled her old smile.

'Mel,' she said, and I didn't correct her, just grabbed her hands and kissed her. Aunt Regina scrabbled and fussed at me and Kathy gave me her broad grin. I'd never seen her look the slightest bit perturbed and she didn't now.

'Could I be alone with Mel for a bit?' Stella asked. Her voice had a painful husky catch to it and I saw then the purple bruising like a choker of love bites around her throat. She saw me look and her hand flew up to cover it.

'Cup of tea, Regi,' Kathy said. She draped her macramé over the end of the bed and led Aunt Regina away.

'God, Stella,' I said.

'It's a hammock!' She chuckled hoarsely and nodded towards the macramé.

'*Stella.*' I took her hand and squeezed.

'I think it would have worked,' she whispered, 'only it wasn't quick like I thought. I think I started to die.'

I didn't know what to say. I sat on the bed holding her hand and though I tried to keep them in, some tears did run down my face.

'Don't,' she said.

'Why now?' I said.

'You don't need me any more,' she said.

'I do, I always will.'

'That's not fair.' She looked at me fiercely. 'You don't. When I die, yeah, you'll be sad.' Her own eyes watered with the strain of speaking and of swallowing. 'But you'll get over it. You've got Bogart.'

'Adam.'

'You've got Jesus or whatever.'

'But I still need *you* to be alive,' I said. 'And Aunt Regina and Derek would be devastated. Can't you see how . . .' I struggled for a moment, 'how *selfish* this is? You might not want your life but other people want you to have it.'

She shook her head and I caught an almost compassionate look in her eyes. 'They didn't want you to marry Bogart,' she reminded me, 'but you still did it. Was that selfish? Now I want to die. It feels like the right time.'

I was trying to think what Adam would say. 'Only God can decide if it's the right time.'

'I don't believe in God but,' – she reached for her glass of water and sucked a little through her straw, wincing as it went down – 'if I *did* believe, maybe I would say that God said it *was* the right time.'

'That's rubbish,' I said. 'Did you know they're putting you in the loony bin?'

She shook her head and her cheeks stained with an angry flush. 'They are not. Listen,' her fingers twisted round mine until I thought they'd break, 'will you promise me something?'

'Anything,' I said.

'Do you promise that you'll promise?'

'Yes.'

'Cross your heart?'

I nodded.

'Swear on your life? On Bogart's life?'

'Yes,' I said, though she was beginning to make me nervous. 'What?'

'That you'll help me. When the time comes. That you'll help me do it.'

'No!' I snatched my hand away. I stood up. '*No*, Stella.'

'You just promised,' she pointed out. 'You swore on your life. You can't take it back.' I couldn't look at her. Mother Clanger was sitting on her locker. I picked her up.

'Aunt Regina brought her in for me.' Stella gave a painful scrap of laugh. 'She said, "I've brought you your precious rag-rat!"'

I made myself smile.

Stella half closed her eyes. 'I'm so tired,' she said. 'Mind if I. . .'

'I'll just sit here,' I said.

As she slept, I sat and watched the minute movements of her nostrils as the precious breath flowed in and out and the promise hung darkly round my heart.

†

I stayed with Aunt Regina, Derek and Kathy for three more days and I witnessed the awful battle to persuade Stella that she needed psychiatric treatment, and the eventual decision to section her. I saw her sedated, a floppy doll-version of herself who looked out with flat eyes, like bad paintings of her own with all the spark missed out. I talked to Adam on the phone and he said that he'd come and see her in a few days' time and take me home. The sound of his voice made me hollow out with longing and I knew I couldn't wait a few days. I'd go back early and surprise him and then we could travel back together to visit Stella.

I just couldn't feel at home at Wood End any more. I'd gone back to wearing my old clothes and even to eating meat and having a glass of Derek's beer but it seemed different. It wasn't just me that had changed. The balance of power had shifted. Now it was Aunt Regina and Kathy on top, with poor Derek underneath them, being either ignored or used. They let him drive them around and walk the pugs and cook for them, but they didn't include him in conversations. Kathy had only ever grudgingly acknowledged him but now Aunt Regina was nearly as bad. I went out of my way to address remarks particularly to Derek, and helped him wash up and fold the washing, while Kathy and Aunt Regina were upstairs practicing massage.

On my last night at Wood End, Aunt Regina climbed the ladder to my room. They'd begun to use it as a glory hole so I'd had to clear a path to uncover my bed.

'Can I come in?' she said, putting her foot through a lampshade as she scrambled towards me. 'We'd have tidied up,' she apologized, 'but, well with, you know . . .'

I shrugged. I felt grumpy and childish in a way I hadn't since Adam, since I'd become a married woman.

'Look,' I said. 'I'm sorry I haven't kept in touch very well, but . . .' But how could I put into words the space that had opened up between us? It was as if I was looking at a tiny version of her across an abyss.

'Well, the main thing is, it's lovely to see you now,' she said. We were quiet for a moment. There were piles of my old school books and papers in the corners. I could see the red corner of a geography project that I'd sweated over for months.

'You can chuck all that away,' I said.

'One day we'll have a clear-out,' Aunt Regina said. And then, 'Are you happy?'

'I am,' I said. 'Are you?'

'Cloud nine, dear.'

'Why are you so horrible to Derek?' I dared.

She recoiled. 'I'm not! What nonsense! The silly fool, what's he been saying?'

'Nothing. I'm not blind. You shut him out, you and Kathy.'

She frowned, plucking at the goatskin on my bed. She had chequers on her forehead and the spray of lines at the corners of her eyes had spread to meet the brackets round her mouth.

'He's a good man, Derek is; he's lovely,' I said.

'You don't have to live with him day in, day out.'

'I *did*,' I pointed out. 'He's so kind.'

There was a bird hopping about on the roof, the claws scritch-scratching on the tiles.

'Things change.' She looked up at me, her eyes naked. 'Feelings change.'

'Don't you love him any more?' My voice had fogged up.

'Love changes too,' she said and now a skin seemed to close over her eyes. She became businesslike, rubbing her hands together. 'Now then. Let's talk about what we're going to do about Stella.'

'What *can* we do?' I said.

'Well, I for one intend to visit her every day.'

'We can't do anything to change how she feels inside.'

'We can try to make her happier.'

'But she's not unhappy. That's the thing. She just doesn't want to live.'

She snorted. 'She just needs something to live *for*, that's all. A boyfriend. Or a hobby.'

I laughed, and I knew that Stella would laugh too when I told her that all she needed was a hobby.

'I know that sounds feeble,' Aunt Regina said, 'but everyone needs something. Kathy's got her goats; Derek his Esperanto . . .'

'*You* used to like Esperanto.' I pointed out.

'You've got your cult – and Bogart,' she said.

'Adam. And it's not a cult.'

'Adam then.'

'So. What have you got?' I said, and her eyes skidded away.

'There's Poochy and Princess, and –'

'And *Kathy*?' I suggested, and she blushed a deep, unbecoming crimson.

I stared. The bird above us squawked. 'Aunt Regina,' I said, 'have you become a lesbian?'

She didn't say no. You could hear the wings of the bird as it took off. There was a gleam of sweat in the grain of her wrinkles.

'I should mind my own business,' I said into the long silence.

'So you should,' Aunt Regina said. She got up, though the ceiling wasn't high enough to allow her to quite straighten up and she stood hunched.

'I'm going back tomorrow,' I said.

'Oh Melanie. Don't go yet. Stella needs you.'

'I'll see her tomorrow,' I said, 'and I'll come back with Adam at the weekend.'

'All that way? To stay here?'

'Don't know,' I said. 'I'll phone.'

†

After we'd visited the doped-up Stella, Derek drove me to the station. I couldn't bear to see Stella like that, dimmed and diminished. I couldn't bear the sickly smell of the hospital or the loony-looking people. Stella was not one of them; there was nothing wrong with her. She was completely sane.

The sunshine showed up the last few gingery strands among the grey in Derek's beard. He peered forward through his little glasses and I felt an intense flood of love for him.

'Thanks Derek,' I said.

'No trouble.'

'No I mean, thank you for being kind to Stella and me over all the years.'

He coughed and spluttered and fussed about with the gears.

'Are you OK?' I said. 'I mean you and Aunt Regina.'

He snorted away the ridiculous question, signalled right and negotiated us round a roundabout. Someone blurted a horn at him and I saw him shoot a look into the driving mirror.

'Road hog,' I said, supportively.

We drove along in silence for a while.

'It just seems –' I started.

'Well, what with the stresses and strains and so forth,' he broke in.

'Kathy seems to have taken over,' I said, and he flinched.

'She's a very capable woman,' he said.

'But it must be hard, living as a threesome?'

He put the radio on until we got to the station.

†

I hadn't said exactly when I'd be back. If I'd rung from the station, someone would have come to pick me up, and all would have been different. But it was a lovely day. I was out in the world, and still wearing what Derek referred to as my 'civvies': jeans and a corduroy jacket. I felt like a different person striding about in town. I had the fiver that Derek had insisted on pressing into my hand when we'd said goodbye. I decided to get the bus part of the way and then walk.

I bought myself a strawberry Mivi and licked at it as I dawdled across the Common, procrastinating about going home. I watched a couple of golden retrievers playing: chasing and leaping and rolling with such joy it almost made me weep. I sat on the grass for an hour or more, just watching all the people and other creatures, listening to the huge buzz of city noise, traffic and voices, the jangling of an ice-cream van and the high speckling sparks of birdsong. Within the Soul-Life Community, the implicit attitude was that those outside were lesser beings. We alone were the Chosen. We were special – and I felt especially special to be Adam's wife – and it made us regard outsiders with pity or even a mild form of contempt. But on that day my heart was full of love for everyone, chosen or not, and especially filled with a flood of love and longing for Adam.

†

I went into the house. The kitchen was empty. I made a peanut butter and honey sandwich and poured myself a glass of cloudy apple juice. I planned to sit outside in the sunshine to enjoy my snack – but first I went upstairs to change my clothes. I picked a robe, some pants and socks and went to the room I shared with Adam. I opened the door and for a second didn't understand what I was seeing: his long back, his buttocks going up and down.

Hannah saw me. She lay there, flushed and smiling, jerking underneath his movements. He caught the direction of her gaze and turned his head to see me. He stopped and rolled off and I saw the moment when his long cock withdrew shining from the redness between her legs. I've never forgotten that picture, though I've longed to.

'Martha,' Adam said. 'Would you give us a moment?'

I shut the door but continued to stand there, quite stunned.

I could hear their voices through the door but not what they said. And then I heard Hannah laughing. I went downstairs and dropped my sandwich in the compost bin. My face felt hot and I could feel the pulse in my ears. The sun shone bright on the scarlet flowers of the runner beans but was cut off in shadow before it reached the kitchen window. I tried to pray for guidance but I wasn't in a mood to listen, even if Jesus had bothered to reply. Eventually Hannah came into the kitchen. Her hair was wrapped in a towel.

'He's waiting for you,' she said. I waited for her to say something else, but she only began to grate a beetroot.

I went up and into the room. He'd opened the window but still there was the wrong smell of someone else's sex.

'I'm sorry you saw that,' he said.

'You're sorry I *saw* it?'

'You're my wife in the eyes of the Lord,' he said. 'You know that nothing will ever change that?'

I saw Hannah's anklet on the floor. It was a silver chain with a small cross that dangled just above her instep. I'd always admired it.

'Mere fornication with the other Sisters . . .'

'Plural?'

'. . . makes no difference. I am full of the love and the spirit of our Lord Jesus Christ.'

'You are full of bullshit,' I said quietly.

He shook his head at me and the patient loving look in his eyes reminded me of Stella's when I'd said I wanted her to live. As if they were both way above me in some hierarchy of understanding.

'How did you find Stella?' he said.

'I went to Ward Ten and there she was.'

He raised one eyebrow.

'So have you been fornicating with *all* the other Sisters?' I said.

He shook his head. 'Hannah and I have always had a special bond. A special connection in the Lord. She was the first Sister in the community, you know that.'

'Why didn't you marry *her* then?'

'Because our Lord, in His wisdom, told me to marry you.' And he began to tell me the story that I'd heard many times before about how Hannah (called Elaine then) had approached him as he sat on the river bank watching a heron and how she had never doubted that the Lord spoke to him, not for a moment. And how *she* would never call the word of Jesus bullshit, which was incidentally blasphemy, but he understood my confusion and would let it pass. He tried to draw me down beside him on the mattress, half deflated by their activity, but I wouldn't be drawn.

'I'm going to have a shower,' I said, but I didn't. I went to see Obadiah in the box room that had become his study. He wasn't there and I went in. I knew where the cash was kept and I took it. I didn't count it, just stuffed it into my shoulder bag. I was still wearing my civvies. I walked out of that place and stood on the Common for a while. The Common was the same and the sun was still shining but instead of the joy and birdsong and love of all mankind, now there was swearing and sirens, dog shit, and a poor old man alone and quaking on a bench.

†

I spent the journey to Edinburgh with my face pressed against the window. I was crying and the tears smeared dirt from the glass onto my face. But by the time I'd changed in Newcastle I'd pulled myself together. I washed my face in the station Ladies' and sat in the cubicle counting my money. Three hundred and eleven pounds. I bought a cup of coffee and a cheese sandwich to take on the next train. The coffee splashed on my lap on the jolty journey and the bread was pappy, the cheese bland and greasy inside it. But I wouldn't let them make me lose my appetite.

I was glued to the window as we got to Berwick-upon-Tweed, where the bridges laced together the two halves of the town and the estuary was flecked with swans. The sun was setting and the clouds were like clusters of soft apricots. The train was crowded and a guy with a terrier got on.

'Do you mind?' he said, indicating the seat.

I shook my head and pressed myself closer to the window. We were passing a caravan site and I saw a woman framed in the door of her caravan, smoking, and just in that glimpse of her I caught such an immense sense of bleakness that it set me off again. I tried to cry silently and not to let the guy see, but maybe the smell of my tears was fascinating to the dog or something. It began snuffling about at my knees and stood up with its front paws on my seat.

'Stig,' the guy said. 'Down, boy.'

'It's OK,' I snuffled. I wiped my eyes on the sleeve of my T-shirt and turned. The dog had wiry brown hair and it was looking at me intently, head cocked on one side. It licked my hand, relishing, it seemed, the salt taste of my tears.

The guy was thin and fair and twitchy. 'You OK?' he said.

I nodded and sniffed, horribly embarrassed by the snot and with no tissue to blow my nose.

'Toffee?' he said, and drew a crumpled paper bag from his jacket pocket. I took a bit and stuck it in my mouth.

'Me mam made it,' he said between squelchy chews. 'Never leave home without her giving us a bag of toffees.'

'It's lovely,' I said.

'Hanky?' he said. The pockets of his jacket seemed to be packed with all sorts, and he brought out a tissue for me, crumpled but clean. I blew my nose and wiped my face.

'Where you off to?' he said.

'Edinburgh.'

'Why are you going there?'

I sniffed and smiled. 'You're pretty nosy.'

'That's me, man.' He grinned proudly.

'Is he named after the book?' I said. The dog had settled his head on my knee now, looking up at me with pleading eyes.

'Aye,' he said, 'Stig of the Dump, aye. Me mate's dad found a litter of puppies on the tip, like.'

'I remember it from school,' I said.

'Me too, man,' he said. 'I loved that book.'

And that was Greg from Gateshead. He took me to a squat in Edinburgh, where I met a whole new circle of Godless friends. I didn't go back to Peebles after all, but stayed in the city, got a job in a café on the Royal Mile, saved up and went travelling with a guy called Bill – we were together for a while, but we split up in India. I got a job teaching English to women on a literacy project and stayed on in Calcutta. I kept my heart in a cage and never rang home but I did send postcards to Stella and the others at Wood End so that they wouldn't worry.

After two years I returned. I'd been ill with dysentery. I missed Cheddar cheese and marmalade and proper tea with milk. I missed Stella. I even missed the winter. So I decided it was time to return to Wood End. When I rang from London to say I was about to get the Edinburgh train, Aunt Regina sounded overjoyed.

'Kathy, kill the fatted calf,' I heard her call, and the faint reply, 'Will do.'

'We'll meet you at the station,' she said, and it warmed me to hear such love. Before I could ask more, the pips went. I had no more change, so quickly garbled out the time I'd be arriving. It was February and shivery-cold and gloomy. Flying into London had meant flying down from a clear turquoise and orange-streaked sky into a cloudy lens clamped over the entire UK. But I didn't care. All I needed was to sit by the range in the Wood End kitchen and drink hot tea and be at home again. After so long in flip-flops it would be a novelty to wear a pair of socks. And, of course, I was longing to see Stella. I felt in my bones that she was better, though of course I couldn't know that. I believed that the promise to help her kill herself was null and void now. She hadn't recovered from her suicide attempt when she'd made me make it. I'd seen enough dead bodies in India just lying by the road or floating in the river to know there's nothing special or romantic about death; it's banal and dirty and it stinks. I'd tell Stella that and maybe even take her to India to see for herself; maybe that would cure her of her death wish.

To my astonishment it was Aunt Regina who drew up outside the station.

'You're so thin,' she said, peering at me through a new and startling pair of green-rimmed glasses. 'So brown.'

'And *you're* driving!'

'Passed my test before Christmas,' she said. I hoiked my rucksack into the boot and climbed in beside her. She'd had her hair cut in a proper lesbian style. It was sugary white now and made her look younger. 'We'll have to feed you up,' she said. She squeezed my knee through my filthy trousers. 'Goodness me, you're nothing but a bag of bones.'

'Ta very much,' I said. She drove in hesitant jerks down the middle of the road and though I'd grown accustomed to traffic chaos in Calcutta, I had to look down at my lap and force myself not to flinch and shriek at every oncoming vehicle.

'How's Stella,' I asked.

'Whoops,' she said, as someone hooted and she lost the gear. 'People are so impatient aren't they? Mind if I concentrate?'

'Go right ahead,' I said. The car leapt forward.

'I'm not normally this bad,' she said. I shut my eyes until we'd got out of the city and onto quieter roads.

A saucepan was rattling its lid when I went in, but the kitchen was empty – except for Princess, the one remaining Pug. There was a smell of roasting kid. Aunt Regina was trying to get the car into the garage and didn't want me to watch, so I'd gone in on my own. I went to the bottom of the stairs and called, 'Hello! Hi there! Don't all rush to say hello!'

Aunt Regina came into the kitchen, just as Kathy came thundering down the stairs.

'Melanie!' Kathy hugged me. She'd been washing her hair and it stuck up in wet tufts. 'You're so thin,' she spoke over my head. 'My God, Reg, she'll take some feeding up.'

'Just what I said.'

'So,' I said, distentangling myself, 'where's Stella? Where's Derek?'

'We forget you've been so out of touch,' Kathy said.

'Derek has moved on,' Aunt Regina said.

'What?'

Kathy rattled some frozen broad beans into a pan and it sounded like rifle fire.

'A year past. We've got an address if you want to keep in touch. I believe Stella does.'

I sat down, legs gone weak with the disappointment.

'What happened?'

'It was after Stella left.'

'Where's *she* gone?'

'He said, "Now those girls have flown the nest I'm superfluous to requirements." Of course I told him that was nonsense,' Regina added quickly, avoiding my eyes, 'but once he'd got the notion in his head . . .'

'Upped and off,' Kathy finished. She put the goat on the table. The thick roasty smell made me feel sick. I'd eaten almost nothing but plain rice for the past few weeks; anything else sent my bowels into a panic.

I swallowed the bile that rose into my throat. 'And Stella?' I said. I saw a look pass between Aunt Regina and Kathy. 'What?' I said. '*What?*'

I started to go dizzy then, humming and buzzing gathering in my ears and blotting out my vision. I put my head down on the table and let the feeling of dizziness roll over me.

'Barley sugar,' Kathy said. 'Quick Reg, she's blacking out.'

'No I'm not.' I sat up and the fuzziness drained out of my head and I could see straight again. 'I'll have a glass of water though,' I said, and in their eagerness to get it, they collided at the sink.

'Where is she then?' I said. I was quite clear-headed now. 'Did you tell her I was coming?'

'I left a message,' Aunt Regina said, putting the water down. 'Sure you wouldn't rather a cup of tea? Or a glass of pea-pod? I expect she'll ring this evening. Has the phone rung?' she asked Kathy.

'I've had my head in the bath,' Kathy said. I could hear the broad beans roiling to a boil. She began to carve the meat and I had to look away.

'Where is she then?'

'Set the table, Reg?' Kathy said.

'London,' Aunt Regina said. The table mats, that looked like they'd been knitted from string, were new, but the knives and forks, with their stained bone handles, were so familiar they made my stomach hurt.

'What's she doing? Has she got a job?'

'Shall we open a bottle?' she said.

'Aunt Regina!' I said.

'It's rather awkward,' she said.

'What?'

'I don't want your homecoming to be ruined.'

'*What?*' I shrieked.

'After you'd gone, Bo – Adam – came down in search of you, of course.'

'Did he?'

'And he went to see Stella, in order to find out if you'd said anything to her, anything about your whereabouts. She was – well, you know what a pickle she was in at the time. He talked to her, he stayed with us for a while and really, Melanie, he was marvellous, it was a new insight into him: off to the hospital like clockwork every day and he quite pulled her round. Of course there was a lot of religious claptrap, but we were at our wits' end – if it worked we didn't question it. And to cut a long story short . . .'

My hands encircled the cold water glass. 'What?' I said.

'She went back with him and joined the, what's it?'

'Soul-Life Community,' Kathy said, with mocking emphasis, slapping a wad of meat onto my plate. 'Do open the wine,' she added.

'That's OK,' I said, 'that's not so terrible.'

Kathy gave Aunt Regina a significant look. 'Oh, get out from under my feet you stupid dog,' she said, and there was a yelp from beneath the table. 'Wine?'

Aunt Regina busied herself with the corkscrew.

'What aren't you telling me?' I said.

'Let's enjoy this feast,' Aunt Regina said.

But the hefty slab of meat, the mountain of potato, the greasy wash of gravy and the beans were impossible for me to touch. I did swallow a little of the sharp green wine.

'Please tell me,' I said.

They exchanged glances again, then Aunt Regina sighed, got up and went to the dresser. She took out a yellow Kodak envelope. She pulled a photo from the wallet and put it down beside my plate.

And that is when I first saw you, Dodie. You were in Stella's arms, and behind you both stood Adam. I picked it up and looked at it and put it down. I got up from the table and went upstairs to the bathroom to be sick. I climbed the ladder to my room, which had been hastily cleared, lay down on my dusty bed and stayed there. Sometimes I heard the phone ring, and sometimes Aunt Regina came up with a cup of tea and a piece of toast. Sometimes I took a sip or two or a nibble of crust. For several days I stayed there sweating and shivering in turn, till Aunt Regina sent Kathy up the ladder. She wanted me to go to hospital but I refused. She prescribed antibiotics and the fever went, leaving me in a weak but strangely blank and cheerful state of mind.

One day I woke up and Stella was sitting at the end of my bed. It took me several blinks before I could believe she was really there.

'Do you want me to go?' she said.

I squinted at her. The sun was shining through the skylight and sparking off her. She looked the same, though not quite as thin, and with more colour; more gloss and thickness to her hair.

'I'm sorry,' she said.

'Have you really had a baby?' I asked.

'Do you hate me?'

'Where's Adam?' I said.

'I bought you some flowers, freesias, shall I bring them up? Aunt Regina wants you to get up so she can do your sheets. You could have a bath. It does honk in here.'

'Ta,' I said. 'What's her name?'

'Baptized Dorcas,' she said, 'but I call her Dodie.'

'Adam called her Dorcas?' I guessed. 'Where on earth did that name come from?'

'Need you ask?'

'Jesus?'

She snorted and from downstairs there came a thin bleat of sound.

'Get up and you can see her,' Stella said. She went down the ladder. I rolled out of my sheets and followed her down, my legs like string. I visited the bathroom and saw my thin face printed with crumple marks. I was yellow from the faded suntan and the sickness. I splashed my face, brushed my teeth and went down in my pyjamas.

Stella was feeding you with a bottle. Her blonde hair fell down in a curtain and your little hand was tangled up in it. I could see at once that you should have been mine.

Of course, I didn't say that. I simply sat at the kitchen table and watched as Stella fed you. Aunt Regina watched me nervously. She gave me a hot elderberry drink and went up to run my bath and change my sheets. There is something lovely about familiarity – it makes a warmth grow in the heart – and *you* were so familiar. Stella sat you up and rubbed your back to make you burp. Your eyes were the blue of bottle glass and they looked straight at me, skewering my soul.

'I'd let you hold her, but . . .'

'When I've had my bath?' I said. I knew I smelled. I hadn't had a proper wash since I don't know when. Not even since I got back from India. My hair was greasily matted together, practically in dreadlocks.

'Do you think you're contagious?' she said.

I shook my head. I knew in my bones I could never be bad for you.

Aunt Regina called me to say my bath was ready. 'Please don't go,' I said to Stella.

'Of course I won't!' She smiled. 'I'd like to stay for a few days – if that's all right with you?'

'Of course it's all right.'

'Mel,' Stella said, as I left the kitchen, 'I can't *believe* you're not angry.'

But I wasn't angry. Not at that moment. I was over-whelmed. I was undone by love but I wasn't angry. In the bath I looked at my shrunken body. Stella and I had changed places. Where I had been the big sister, the one who was in charge, now I was weak and lost and she was the grown-up and sensible one; she was the mother I would never be. My hip bones stuck out like jug handles and my breasts were empty. Stella was heavier and for the first time she had proper breasts. Why didn't she feed you with them? I wondered. I would never have fed you with a bottle.

I tried to wash my hair but couldn't get my fingers through it. When I got out of the bath I hacked out the lumpy tangles with a pair of nail scissors. I didn't want to scare you with the odd way I looked. I put on the clean pyjamas Aunt Regina had laid out for me and I called her in to cut the rest of my hair short. She took me into the kitchen where you were sleeping in your carrycot on the table, and took her dressmaking shears to me.

'Where's Stell?' I said.

'She's having a nap. This little tinker kept her up half the night.' She nodded towards the carrycot. 'I'm very impressed, Mel,' she said carefully, 'with how mature you're being. Stella was petrified you'd never speak to her again.'

I didn't say anything.

'In the old days,' she told me, 'when someone was sick they'd often have their hair cut off. Long hair was thought to sap the strength.'

When she'd finished I rubbed my fingers through the wet spikes of my hair – she'd cut it short as a boy's – and then I studied you, your perfectly familiar face that made so much sense to me. I put out my finger to touch your corona of downy hair, just the soft black of soot.

'Isn't she exquisite?' Aunt Regina whispered.

I stroked your cheek. 'Of course she is,' I said.

†

Next day I got up and dressed for the first time. I found clothes I hadn't seen or thought of for years: a pair of velvet jeans, a long, belted cardigan. Everything was too big – but the way Aunt Regina was about to feed me up, it wouldn't stay that way for long.

It was early March and for the first time it felt like spring. After lunch, Stella and I sat in the garden. I had a blanket over my knees, but I didn't need it; the sun was warm on my hair, such a shy and polite sun compared with the blaring show-off in India. There were primroses on the lawn and the birds sang sweetly in the green-flecked beech hedge. You lay in your carrycot waving your arms and legs about. You were dressed in an outfit knitted by Aunt Regina in horrible lemon wool. I'd been telling Stella about my time in Edinburgh, how I loved the city and how, when I was better, I might move back.

'What will you do?' she said.

'Dunno. Waitressing, maybe?'

Aunt Regina came out with tea and biscuits. 'Not too cold?' she said. 'Make her come in, Stella, the minute she shivers, won't you? Not too tired? Don't let her tire herself out.'

'I'm fine,' I said, a little sharply and she grimaced humorously at Stella and went back inside.

'Have a biscuit,' I said to Stella, but she shook her head.

'Need to get my figure back,' she said.

'You look much better like that.'

She pulled a face and lifted up her jumper to show me the slack tummy flesh where you had stretched her out of shape.

'Why aren't you breastfeeding?' I said.

She shuddered. 'I couldn't,' she said. 'It's much too personal.'

I wanted to laugh at that. Too personal! If you'd been mine I would have fed you from my breasts for years. Everyone knows that mother's milk is the best thing for a baby. Too personal! But I did feel pleased about that; I don't pretend to be a saint. She might be a mother but she was not as good a mother as I'd have been.

'I'd like to see Adam,' I said.

She stared at me, her eyes pearly pale in the sunshine. 'Would you?'

I nodded. 'Don't forget I *am* his wife,' I said, and I let that last word sound neutral, with no trace of bitterness at all.

'But it wasn't a legal ceremony,' she said. 'It wasn't real.'

'Real in the eyes of the Lord.'

'I bet you've slept with loads of people since . . .'

'So has he,' I pointed out.

You woke then and she picked you up and held you against her shoulder. I put out my finger for your little fingers to clutch at – and oh, you clutched so tightly!

'She's strong,' I said. 'Before I go back to Edinburgh, or wherever, maybe I should come back with you?'

'Back?' Stella said.

'To London.'

'I . . .' I could hear a click as she swallowed. 'Adam's dad died,' she said.

'Oh?' I said. 'So? Is he cut up about it?' I got a flash of memory, the frowsty comfort of curling against his shoulder while he told me stories about the great house he was set to inherit. 'But they didn't get on, did they?'

'I'm going to stay at his place,' she said. 'Me and Dodie.'

'Not Adam?'

'He'll be in London.'

'Why don't you stay with him then?'

She lifted you from her shoulder and scrubbed at a bit of milky dribble on her shirt.

'Let me,' I said, 'then you can drink your tea.'

She hesitated for a moment before she put you in my arms, and, with the slight but solid weight of you, the heat of you through the ugly lemon suit, I was overcome. I couldn't speak for a moment. You lay and looked up at me, perfectly calm and full of recognition.

'Do you want her to call you Aunt Melanie or just Mel?' Stella said. She stretched her legs out and flopped back in her seat, staring up at the sky.

'Don't mind,' I said. 'So, *why* aren't you?'

'See . . .' she took a sip of her tea. 'When I was . . . well after . . .'

'When you were in the loony bin?'

She snorted. 'That's when Adam came to see me. He wanted to know where you were. If you'd only told me, he might have come after you . . .' She left me to work out the implications of that. And yes, maybe he would have followed me, found me. Maybe everything would have been different. But the point is, it wasn't.

'But then Dodie wouldn't be here,' I said. Your lashes were fluttering sleepily and your fingers were splayed, relaxed, perfect; poised as if about to conduct a symphony.

'And he talked to me about Jesus being a reason for living, him giving his life and all that and, well, somehow or other, Mel, he talked me out of wanting to die.' A sparrow was hopping about looking for crumbs but my hands were busy holding you, and Stella was looking fiercely into her tea as she spoke. I breathed out quietly with the relief of being absolved of the awful promise.

'But I don't like living communally,' she went on. 'I don't like there being so many people I don't know and wearing other people's knickers and everyone interfering all the time and Hannah hating me and, anyway, I don't really believe in it.' Her look dared me to challenge her. 'He's always having visions and stuff and it's always Jesus telling him to do exactly what he wants to do anyway.'

It was very hard not to laugh when she said that. It was a thought I'd never allowed myself to have. 'Is he still sleeping with Hannah?' I said.

'Probably. Who cares? Anyway, now his dad's died and he wants someone to go and live in the house so I'm moving there. It kills about a million birds with one stone – somewhere for me to live, somewhere for him to come and see Dodie, someone to caretake the house.'

We could hear the scrunch of Kathy's car coming up the gravel drive. Princess, who'd been asleep on the lawn, hauled herself stiffly to her feet and trotted round the front to meet her. You squirmed in your sleep, a smile flickering on and off your face. Your lips mimed sucking for a moment and then you were still again, the warm and precious weight of you secure in my arms.

'I'll take her and you can drink your tea,' Stella said, but I held on to you and let my tea grow cold.

'Do you –' I swallowed. Such a humiliating question to have to ask. 'Do you love him?'

She frowned. She was only eighteen but she already had deep vertical lines between her eyebrows.

'It's just' – she tore at the edge of her thumbnail with her teeth – 'he was part of growing up and he did give me a reason to live, but now' – her eyes went to you – 'now I have another reason to live. Do *you* still?'

'Love him?'

'Yeah.'

'Yes,' I said, and my voice took on a beautiful simplicity. 'I'll always love him.'

'Even though you ran away.'

'I still feel married to him. I want to see him.' And saying it made it true, made it urgent.

'Why don't you come to his dad's house with me?' Stella said, a rare ripple of animation in her voice. 'Oh *do* come,

Mel. We could live together with Dodie, maybe we could both get part-time jobs or something and share the childcare. And then' – she hesitated – 'you'd get to see Adam when he comes to visit.'

'I might,' I said. I was starting to feel tired and shivery but I didn't want to let go of you. Princess came trotting round, grinning doggily. The thing I don't like about pugs is not their screwed-up faces but the way their tails curl up and give you such a good view of their bum-holes. It was like a brown rosette flexing and winking at me as she begged Stella for a biscuit and I had to look away.

Aunt Regina and Kathy came round the back with another tray of tea and some steaming scones.

'We've come to join you,' Kathy boomed.

'Good day at the surgery?' Stella said.

'Sterling.'

'Let me take the wee poppet,' Aunt Regina said and scooped you out of my arms. I shivered at the sudden emptiness. Of course I would come and live with you, there was no question about it.

†

Obadiah came to fetch us and drive us to Sheffield – to Adam's father's house. It was a warm day, the sun slanting through the windscreen of the van and I nodded off, wedged between Obadiah and Stella with you on her lap. I was still convalescing and needing to take little snoozes during the day, particularly as I was often up with you in the night.

'Here we are,' Stella said, and the van stopped and I opened my eyes. We were in an ordinary street of 1930s semis.

'This isn't it,' I said.

Stella flapped the envelope with directions in my face. 'Thirty-three Lexicon Avenue,' she said.

'Aye,' agreed Obadiah. 'It is.'

'But Adam said it was a mansion with acres of land.'

'Adam says a lot of things.' Stella gave me an infuriating look.

We climbed out of the van and stood in the yellow light filtering through a laburnum tree. There was a gigantically overgrown privet hedge and we had to push through its fronds to get through the gate. It was a white house with a bay window. A fox doorknocker snarled from the door. On the step was a quaint little milk crate with a cow whose tail swivelled to indicate to the milkman the number of bottles to leave. You loved to play with it as a child. Do you remember how once we ended up with eight pints after you'd been fiddling with the tail?

You are such a liar, Adam, I thought. Still, it *was* a big house for two young women and a baby, with its four bedrooms and long garden, its steep gloomy staircase and wonky plumbing – you had to learn a special way to pull the chain in the downstairs toilet. Obadiah unloaded our paltry store of belongings into the fusty, tobacco- and trousery-smelling hall.

'Any chance of a cuppa before I head back?' Obadiah said. We searched the dispiriting kitchen and, of course, there was no tea. Someone had been in and cleared out the fridge and cupboards. The sink was deep and cracked and stained and there were cobwebs strung between the taps. The cupboards were full of chipped plates and dented saucepans: everything we'd actually need, though all terribly depressing.

I put the kettle on the stove and, while Obadiah drove Stella to find a shop, I carried you into the garden. It was long, narrow and overgrown, with tulips fighting through the grass. I put my foot in a pond I didn't even see and stumbled, nearly dropped you – but saved myself, saved you. The garden was full of birdsong and the hum of insects, full of sunshine and life. It was beautiful, and so wild. At its bottom were some fruit trees – a plum, a pear and an apple I later learned – and I held your face near the blossom so you could inhale the sweetness.

Stella called me, her voice a little frantic. 'Mel? Mel?' And I carried you back through the long grass. The kettle was whistling and they'd bought tea, crumpets, butter, jam and baby formula. We sat in the dining room at the beautiful table under the window. We'd pulled layers of oilcloth off it and discovered the tabletop was a wonderful swirl of glossy wood. Obadiah said it was rosewood, and would be worth a bomb. He thought it was probably antique. It was the only piece of furniture in the entire house that we actually liked. Everything else was fusty or fussy or old-fashioned or just plain dismal.

I tried to make it an occasion, putting the milk in a jug and finding a set of table mats to protect the wood.

'To us here, then,' I said, raising my chipped cup to Stella.

'Cheers,' Obadiah said. He had a horrible habit of blowing across the top of his tea, slurping while it was still too hot, then smacking his lips and saying, 'Ah!' At Soul-Life I'd always tried to avoid being around him when he drank tea for this reason – the petty rage it stirred up in me was disturbing. Otherwise I liked him; he was slow and deliberate, about as unmercurial as a person could be. He was the oldest member of Soul-Life, a safe and stable person, fatherly.

'Are these the only cups?' Stella said. She was still uneasy around food and didn't like to be seen to eat or to be in the company of others while they ate. She was regarding my butter-slathered crumpet almost with fear.

'It's all right, Stell,' I said.

There was a long pause filled with the sound of Obadiah munching and slurping. 'Oh, by the way,' he said to me, 'you've been forgiven.'

'What?' I watched a trail of jammy grease crawl into the thicket of his beard.

'Your theft. The cash. The three hundred and eleven pounds,' he said.

I laughed. 'I can't believe you knew the exact amount!'

'Of course.' He looked offended.

'Sorry,' I said, 'that's why you're an accountant.'

He took another explicit gulp of tea. 'Anyway, you've been forgiven. Adam said to tell you to forget it.'

That was the first direct message I'd had from Adam since I'd left him over two years ago. *Forget it.*

'Tell him I already had,' I said.

†

We began to settle. Adam sent enough money for us to live on. I started looking for a job, but soon Stella stopped eating and starting scrubbing and soaking everything in bleach again. I forced her to go to the doctor and he gave her pills that made her sluggish and dull. It wasn't practical for me to go out to work with you and Stella to care for. It was a golden time, a golden summer. Each day I took you for a walk. I showed you the world. At night when you woke, I woke with you. There was such a special sympathy between us that I would sometimes be there beside your cot before you even whimpered.

†

After a few weeks, Adam came to Lexicon Avenue. There was no warning. You were sleeping in your carrycot in the garden. Stella was also asleep, in a deckchair beside you, and I was trying to cut a bit of grass with a rusty old mower, to give us more room to sprawl. I was hot and sweaty in my cut-off jeans and vest. I'd put weight back on – not too much, about right I'd say – and my skin, which had gone sallow over the winter, was getting brown. I'd stopped pushing the mower and was wiping my hand across my forehead, pushing the sweat up into my hair, when I saw Adam. It gave me such a shock that I shrieked and woke both you and Stella.

His hair was past his shoulder blades and his beard was long. He was wearing a white grandad shirt, open at the neck, over faded jeans and leather flip-flops. There were beads around his neck and as soon as I saw him I felt a sort of upward smack in my stomach. Poor Adam! He didn't know which one of us to greet first and he dealt with the moment by going straight to the carrycot and leaning down at you.

'She's changed!' he said.

'We've all changed,' I said. Our eyes met piercingly and I swallowed and smiled, saying in my smile that I forgave him everything. He came close and held me against his chest. Home is not so much a place as a feeling. When I smelled him and heard the beat of his heart against my cheek, I knew that for sure.

I went inside to fetch glasses of water for us all, and to avoid seeing how he greeted Stella. Quickly I washed, sprayed on a bit of deodorant and brushed my hair. I went out with the water and Adam was sitting cross-legged on the grass with you on his lap. There was no conversation going on between Adam and Stella and for that I was glad.

He stayed one night. We all prayed together. He'd been given a method of meditation by the Lord, a long wordless prayer where you let your mind dissolve into the oneness of the universe and if any thoughts came you blocked them with a hum. We developed this method further: each person had their own pitch, a pitch that worked to block – well I need not tell you this. It's a most soothing and nourishing method of prayer, though on this occasion you woke and cried and I had to get up and walk you round the garden till you were quiet. And afterwards, Adam and I ate omelettes while Stella took something to her room. It was awkward. Neither Stella nor I knew what would happen when it came to bedtime. If he'd chosen to sleep with Stella I don't know what I would have done.

After you'd been fed and bathed – by Adam – and settled in your cot, Adam came into the dining room where Stella was doing a puzzle and I was reading, or trying to. I looked up and smiled at him.

'Leila?' he said. (Leila was the name given to Stella at Soul-Life.) My heart shrivelled and my breath stuck as he looked at her, his eyes so soft and dark and bright.

'*Stella*,' she said, refusing to meet his eyes. And then she looked at me. 'I am disenchanted, Mel,' she said, much more loudly than necessary. 'You can have him if you want.'

She was like that, sometimes, my sister, your mother, who I did love – but this was pure spite, and that word, *disenchanted*, she must have stayed up all night thinking that one up; it wasn't the kind of word she'd ever use: *disenchanted*! She knew that Adam would choose me over her, you see, and didn't want me to have that satisfaction, she had to spoil it; she had to be seen to be giving him back to me. And why didn't she say it before, while we were on our own? No, she had to do it in front of Adam.

But Adam rescued me to some extent. 'I was about to ask to speak to you alone in order to tell you that I still consider Martha my wife. She is the true wife of my soul, despite all that has passed. Martha?' He put out his hand to me and I got up and took it. My hand was trembling and I was surprised to find that his was shaking too. So strange to be called that name again; I felt myself take on a slightly different shape. Stella said nothing. She fitted a piece into her puzzle, but as we were leaving the room she gave me a gruesome smile.

I led the way into my room. 'Funny. This was mine when I was a kid,' he said. He pointed out the place on the door frame where his height had been marked as he grew up. We sat side by side on the bed. All the things that had happened in the past couple of years ached between us. I didn't know what to say or even what I felt except for the most overwhelming love, the sort they call unconditional and that you only have for your own child, it says in the textbooks. But the textbooks are wrong in this case, because even though I knew he was a liar and even though I wasn't sure how genuine all his advice from Jesus was, and even though I'd actually seen him screwing Hannah, and even though he'd done the same with my little sister, I still loved him. Could you get more unconditional than that?

He stood up from the bed and went to the window.

'This is not how you described the house,' I said to his back.

'Bedtime stories,' he said. 'Didn't you like them?'

'I did, but –'

'But nothing. I told you stories you would enjoy.'

'It was lies.'

'*Stories*, Martha.' He turned and knelt down in front of me. 'You're angry,' he said. 'The baby –'

'I love the baby,' I said, and my voice was fierce and choked. 'I look after her, you know; Stella's too ill and doped.'

'I know you love her,' he said. 'I knew you would.'

'I wish she was mine,' I said, and bit my lip hard.

He smiled, but sadly. 'Listen. Will you listen to me?'

'Of course.'

He got up from his knees and lay down on the bed. 'Come.'

I lay down with him on the narrow bed, our faces just inches apart, and the heat of his body beat a pulse in the air, which my own pulse joined with as he spoke. He described his early conversations with Stella, his frustration with her negativity and the breakthrough when he got her to believe in Jesus and to believe in life. He'd gone back to Soul-Life, he said, in the hope that I would have returned or contacted him there since I hadn't let them know at Wood End where I was.

'And there I had a dream,' he said, 'and in the dream Jesus spoke to me.'

'Don't you even need herons any more?' I said.

He flattened his lips and was silent for a moment. 'Jesus told me I must have a child.'

'But –'

'He told me you would come back to me but that until you did I must take Stella – Leila – into Soul-Life and that she must bear me a child.'

'Why did you give her a prettier name than mine?' I asked.

'It was not my wish to be with her. I've never seen her in that way. I don't find her –' He paused. 'I'm not attracted to her.'

The throb that surrounded us was becoming deafening and my heart was thudding and my blood was beating in my ears.

'And what did she say when you told her that?'

'I think she was glad to get away from home.'

I forced myself to look him in the eye as I asked, 'And what was it like, screwing my sister?'

His eyes were sad as he looked back, the pupils dilating madly. I didn't expect him to answer, but: 'She's not happy in her physical being,' he said. 'However . . .'

'However, you did the deed. How *could* you?' My voice warped and so did my face and I stuck my head against his shoulder to stop him seeing the ugliness. I was helpless to stop the tears and the sobbing that ripped though me and as he held and soothed me I was furious that he, who had caused me so much pain, should be the one to comfort me, and yet I couldn't bear him to take his arms away.

'You're my wife in the eyes of the Lord, and in my heart,' he said. 'You, Martha; you.'

'But what about the others? What about Hannah? I can't forget what I saw. I wish I could.'

'Find the hum,' he said, 'and block it out.'

'I can't bear that you –'

'If it hurts you so much, and if you will come back with me, then I will stop it. I will make that sacrifice for you.'

'Will you?' I said, 'will you really?'

'I will. I need you.' He kept saying that and stroking my back. I could smell his sweat and my own tears that had soaked the pillow and the shoulder of his shirt. He kissed me and our mouths were wet and salt with tears and feelings that flared through me, through both of us, and made us fuse into one hot animal – and we yelled, we both yelled, at the passion, it was like a detonation.

'It's never like that with anyone else,' he said, when we'd got our breath back. 'Oh Martha, I want *you* to bear me a son.'

'But what if I can't?'

He was quiet for a moment, and then: 'Martha, Stella told me you about your operation,' he said. I hid my face against his chest. Of course she would tell him, of course she would. My skin was burning.

'You lied to me,' he said softly.

'Not lied –'

'Lied by omission.' I could feel the puffs of breath his words made in my hair.

'I thought you wouldn't love me.'

'How little faith in me you have,' he said.

I counted twenty of his heartbeats before I dared to look up. Love was flowing from his eyes.

'I won't ever be able to have a baby,' I said.

He smiled, bent down his head and licked away my tears. 'Jesus has said it will be so,' he said. And he rocked me in his arms, his hairy thighs tangled round my smooth ones, the stickiness itching on my skin and his voice soothing in my ear, his heartbeat thrumming the rhythm for mine to join with. I couldn't believe his faith in miracles. But they do happen sometimes, they do, and maybe this one would. I had to be open to the possibility that it could.

Adam went to sleep, his mouth loosening and drool spilling from the corner. I studied his face in the dying light: so beautiful, so right, so mine. I heard the very beginnings of your waking from the little room beside mine. I never let you cry for long, didn't want Stella disturbed. I wriggled out from under Adam's leg, put his shirt on and crept out into the hall – but Stella was already up and on her way to pick you up.

'There was no need to make such a song and dance about it,' she hissed. 'You woke Dodie.'

'Did we?'

'I've just put her back down.'

'I didn't hear.' I was shocked. You began to squall. 'I'll get her,' I said, 'you need to sleep.'

'You honk of sex,' she said. 'I'm not having you touching her like that.'

'I'll wash, then I'll take her.'

She didn't answer, but stomped into your room. I heard her pick you up, your crying stop for a moment and then begin in regular bursts like someone trying to start a moped. It made me hurt to hear you cry like that and I knew it was for me. You'd grown used to *me* in the night, not cross, doped-up Stella who never had a comfortable way of holding you. I had a quick wash and crept into my room – where Adam was making the little pocking noises in his sleep that I'd forgotten. I removed his shirt and put on my own nightie and dressing gown.

Stella was sitting on the sofa downstairs and your too-hot bottle was waiting on the table while she struggled to keep you quiet. She held you as if you were made of wood and in response you made yourself stiff against her shoulder.

'You go to bed, Stella,' I said. 'Let me.'

She got up and shoved you into my arms.

'Remember she's *mine*,' she said.

'I know.'

She went upstairs and I heard the door of her room slam shut. I carried you over my shoulder, singing into your ear and you chomped angrily at your fist until I'd cooled the bottle under the tap. We sat down on the sofa together and you were so hungry that you gulped and choked at first, before you settled into a rhythmic suck.

'Hey,' Adam said, 'my two best girls.' He was naked but for a towel around his waist. I gazed down at his long narrow feet. They had black hairs on top and on each of the toes except the smallest. I could hold both your tiny feet in one hand and feel the petal quality of soles that have not yet been walked on.

'I can't come with you,' I said. 'I want to, but I can't. How can I leave Stella? She can't look after the baby on her own.'

'Bring her, then,' he said. He sat down on the sofa beside me and put his hand on your round tummy. 'Bring Dorcas with you.'

'Stella would never . . . and anyway . . .' I trailed off. We both knew that you were Stella's only reason for living. 'I could try and persuade her to come back to London with us,' I said.

'No,' Adam said, with surprising vehemence.

'Why?'

'She's not good there. Not a good influence.'

'Not a good influence?' I asked.

You finished your bottle then and I sat you up to burp. We both laughed at the mature, manly tenor of the belch.

'You're a natural,' he said.

'But you can come and see us? Often?'

'We'll sort it somehow,' he said. 'I'll pray for guidance.'

You needed to be changed, but still you drowsed heavily against my chest. He put his arm round me as I was holding you and we sat there for hours in perfect harmony while Stella slept upstairs and while the starry sky wheeled past the window and paled into dawn.

†

Adam left early in the morning, before Stella was awake, and I went back to bed alone. The bed smelled of him now and I luxuriated in the frowsty sheets and pillows, burying my nose and sniffing and sniffing until I fell asleep. I woke late. It was hot again. I could hear birds and your voice too. For once, Stella was up before me and out in the garden.

I leaned out of the open window and looked down. She was wearing her dressing gown, her pale hair hanging greasy and dull. She was hunched over and so thin you could see her ribs and the knobbles of her spine even through the material. I thought that if a person saw her this way they'd think she was thirty at least. She was smoking, even though she had you on her knee. I hated it when she did that. Sometimes I'd pick you up and find your fluffy hair smelled of smoke, or was speckled with flakes of ash.

I showered and went down. Stella was still outside and you were lying on the ground now, kicking your legs and fretting. I scooped you up.

'Hi Stell,' I said cautiously. 'You're up early. For you.'

'I'm the mother,' she said.

'I know that. I'm just trying to help.'

She looked at me and blew out smoke and then her face softened just a bit.

'Yeah,' she said, 'but I've been taking advantage . . .'

'No, I like it.'

'I need to do more myself. She'll grow up thinking you're her mum at this rate.'

'You can't help being ill,' I said. You were happily playing in my arms, snatching at my nose and mouth, even gnawing my chin, as if it was a teething ring. 'Adam told me you told him about my operation.'

She wound a strand of hair tight round her finger and blew out a puff of smoke.

'It's OK, he doesn't care,' I said. 'I'll get her bottle shall I? She needs changing.'

'I'll do it.' She ground her fag out with her clog and took you from my arms.

It was hard but I had to let her take you over. She wasn't good at it. She didn't have the softness or the love in her – well, you above anyone know that. Adam was right that she wasn't happy in her body. She'd hold you in the wrong position and my fingers would itch to take you myself and to show her how, but I resisted. Of course, it was partly to punish me for getting back with Adam that she developed a sudden interest in you. I understood and took a step back. Though I think she was already beginning to develop her agoraphobia, she did take you out to the park sometimes – and it was on one of these outings that she met Ross.

She didn't tell me straight away. She began to go out more and I was pleased by this sign of recovery. I noticed after a while that she'd started paying attention to her appearance again. She washed her hair and got me to trim the ends. She put violet kohl round her beautiful pearl-grey eyes.

And one day she asked me to babysit in the evening.

'Babysit?' I said. It seemed such a demeaning word. We were together always and never went out in the evenings. That seems strange when I write it now, two young women, a bit of money (Adam was quite generous). Why didn't we go out? Why didn't I, as Stella put it, get a life? The three of us huddled together in that house, as if protecting ourselves from something. When Adam came he was included, of course. And Aunt Regina and Kathy visited us sometimes, had a go at the garden and stocked the fridge with home-grown greens and goats' cheese. Otherwise it felt as if we were under siege – but there was no siege, just you to nurse, and Stella's condition.

'Sure,' I said. 'Where are you going?'

She smiled mysteriously. 'Just somewhere.' Before she went out she had a bath and brushed her hair till it shone like platinum. She looked young again and nearly beautiful. After your bath and feed, I lay with you on my bed, watching you grow drowsy, and it made me drowsy too and I fell asleep to be woken hours later by movement in the kitchen.

I tiptoed you to your cot. It wasn't long before the smell of dope, along with the sound of the Eurthymics, drifted up the stairs. *I'm never gonna cry again.* I managed to restrain myself from going down, and after a while they came upstairs. I heard a male peeing, that heavy horsy sound so unlike a female piddle. And then I heard much more than I wanted through the bedroom wall. At first I thought Adam was wrong about Stella – she didn't sound frigid to me – but then I understood. This was payback for the noises Adam and I had made. But while we'd been so abandoned that we hadn't given noise a thought, hers was a calculated performance.

In the morning, when I carried you downstairs for your bottle, there was a stranger making tea in the kitchen, dressed only in his underpants. I wasn't startled; I'd heard him moving around, but he nearly dropped the kettle in his fright. He was tall, with a skinny caved-in torso, feathered hair and eye-liner – smudged from his night-time exertions.

'I'm Stella's sister,' I said, 'and this is her baby.'

He opened his mouth but nothing came out, and then Stella came floating in wearing her nightie, with a love-bite on her neck and stars in her own smudgy eyes.

'This is Ross,' she said and put her arm round his naked waist.

Later she told me that he had a pierced foreskin and that she loved him. She told me he was the first person she had ever loved. 'The first person, or the first man?' I asked, and she had to think before she said, 'Well after my family, I mean.'

It wasn't long before Ross had moved in, and I was glad for Stella. He was a good guy. But when Adam found out he was not pleased. He liked to be the only man, I think, with us like three females marooned on an island, desperate for his visits. At least, I was desperate for them. But now there was another man around and music all the time, music Adam didn't like – Bowie, The Pretenders, The Police – but I persuaded him to let Ross stay. It makes her well, I pointed out, like nothing ever has, not even Dodie. He had to see the sense in that.

Stella had her hair cut like Ross's and was more animated than she'd ever been before, precariously happy; I say precarious because there was something hectic about the way she'd laugh and flit about and dance on the lawn in her nightie – or once, in nothing.

It didn't take long, three months at the most, before Stella announced that she was pregnant again. She had the smuggest expression in the world, when she told me. I knew Adam wouldn't like it and I didn't dare tell him. There was always a buffalo feeling in the air whenever both men were around and they avoided each other when they could.

In the winter of 1981, I began visiting Adam at Soul-Life again. It was hard to tear myself away from you and very strange to be back. It was quite different: Adam and the core members – Obadiah, Isaac, Hannah, Kezia and others – had moved to a much more plush house in Islington. There were four houses now, all linked, and close to a hundred members. By now, the community had been formalized into The Church of Soul-Life. There were other elders apart from Adam and, though it was all democratic and co-operative, there was a tacit acknowledgment that Adam was supreme.

He was, after all, the one with the direct line to Jesus. He'd achieved guru status, and I felt more honoured than ever to be his wife. The more people who believed absolutely in his visions and dreams – and these were not stupid people, some were highly educated – the more I tried to convince myself they must be true. Or at least that there was sense in believing them.

†

The next time Adam visited the house was in March, by which time Stella was six months pregnant – and on her small frame there was no hiding it. She was stronger in pregnancy; more vivid in her hair and skin and body. She was queen bee in the house and Ross and I became her drones. She had less time for you and I took over again, like an unpaid nanny – but not unpaid, I was paid in love by you. Ross did youth work and was out in the afternoons and evenings and we settled into a smooth routine.

Adam arrived with no warning, as usual, and it happened that Ross was in. He and Stella were eating cheesy baked potatoes (when she was pregnant, Stella overcame her aversion for food) and I was upstairs bathing you. I heard the door and I felt the tremble in the air, the slight shifting of the power and balance. I heard the voices in the kitchen and then Adam came bounding up the stairs two at a time, and into the bathroom.

'Why didn't you tell me she was up the fucking spout?' he said.

I just stared. I wanted to cover your little ears. I'd never heard him speak like that before. You were sitting up, plump and pink, your wet tummy gleaming.

'Dada,' you said. It was your first word. I don't know if it was Adam you were trying to say, or if it was daddy.

He fell to his knees. 'Sorry,' he said to me, and turned his attention to you, 'Hey little chickadee,' he said, and you splashed and kicked excitedly.

'I thought it was up to Stella to tell you,' I said.

He closed his eyes and hummed, getting his feelings under control. 'When's it due?' he said eventually.

'Middle of June,' I said. 'Dodie will be eighteen months by then.' Adam lifted you out of the bath and snuggled you into a towel. Once you were dressed in your sleepsuit, you waddled about. He hadn't seen you walk and was enchanted. 'I've missed so much,' he said.

Adam came more often after that. He and you and I would go for walks like a family. We were a family. Me and Adam, Stella and Ross: or like two rival families with you as the wobbly little bridge between us. And there was the new member growing in Stella's womb. Secretly, I hoped that when that baby was born she would be so taken up with it she'd let Adam have you. I hoped and wished and prayed. Ross might be happier with just his own child and I could move out, take you to Soul-Life, which is what Adam wanted too. So we all waited through a long warm spring and early summer for the birth.

Adam came in June, on the date the baby was due. Three days later he was still there. I didn't understand why he wanted to be around for the birth of this baby. It wasn't his business – and I could see Ross felt the same. They managed mostly to be in different rooms and, since the weather was so hot, Adam spent much of his time in the garden.

Ross had been about to go to work on the twenty-first of June, and had just joked, 'Keep your legs crossed till I get back,' when Stella hauled herself up out of her chair and there was a sudden heavy splatter on the kitchen floor. Her hand went between her legs and Ross sat down with a bump. 'Shit, is this it?'

It was about seven in the evening. Adam was in the garden drinking wine while I cooked fish fingers for us to have with salad. You were in your pyjamas, thin blue ones I remember, with a pattern of ducks.

'Juice,' you remarked. The waters had splashed one of your pyjama legs.

Not expecting Adam to be there, we had already made a plan for the birth: Ross would take Stella to hospital in a taxi – he had no car – and I'd stay behind and care for you. But Stella panicked and grabbed my hand. 'I want Mel with me,' she said. 'I want my sister.'

'But what about Dodie?' I said.

'Bring her. Please Mel, please?' She was bent double, holding onto the kitchen table. Ross was put out, I could see.

'Shall I?' I asked him. I was excited by the idea, and moved that Stella wanted me. We are sisters, after all, I thought; we are sisters. And birth is exciting. My new niece or nephew was nearly here. I'd not even thought of being at the birth.

'If she wants you,' Ross said, shrugging.

'Adam can stay with Dodie,' I said. The fish fingers were burning and I switched off the gas.

Stella started to say something, but had another contraction, began to puff and pant, and then to cry. 'It's not right,' she said. 'It doesn't feel right.'

'OK, Baby.' Ross pulled himself together and got up to rub her back.

I scooped you up and carried you out into the garden to tell Adam. He stood up and knocked his wine over. He was excited too, I could see. It would have reminded him, I suppose, of your birth. Maybe, it was that memory that made him want to be involved. You shrieked with joy as he lifted you over his shoulder and carried you back into the kitchen. Ross was phoning a taxi.

'Leave it; I'll take you,' Adam said, jingling his car keys.

Stella had straightened up but she was grey in the face, her hands cradling the weight of her swollen belly. 'Just get me there,' she said.

'OK,' I said, thinking fast. 'You drive us, Adam, and then bring Dodie home.' I didn't like to think of him driving with you in the car, but he could strap you in, I thought, and it was an emergency, you could almost have called it that. I didn't realize how much he'd had to drink. None of us did. We should have stuck with the taxi plan. Or even called an ambulance. But we did what we thought was best and that is all that anyone can do. That's what I told myself afterwards over and over and over again.

I got the bag we'd packed for Stella with her nightie, sanitary towels, even a puzzle in case the labour was long, and Ross and I each took an arm and supported her out to the car. She had a contraction as she got one leg in the car, and was stuck there, moaning and panting. I saw a trickle of fluid, pink-tinged, trickling down the inside of her leg.

Once she could move again, she squeezed herself in behind the front passenger seat. I sat beside her, you on my lap. You kicked your little legs about, shouting, 'Car!' delighted by the unheard-of treat of a bedtime ride.

'It doesn't feel right,' Stella said again. 'It doesn't feel like last time.'

'It'll be OK,' I said. 'I expect it's different every time.'

'You didn't like it much last time,' Adam remarked, and Ross threw him a look of loathing.

I took Stella's hand and it was cold and wet. She began to shiver, though it was boiling hot inside the car, which had been sitting in the sun with the windows shut all day. The plastic leather seat stuck to the back of my thighs.

Ross was in the front passenger seat and had to twist round awkwardly to see Stella.

'OK Baby?' he said. 'Soon be there. Remember to breathe. Want some music on?'

'No,' Adam said. 'No sounds.' He was driving jerkily, grinding the gears, and he didn't stop at the Give Way sign at the end of the road. There was nothing coming, luckily.

'Adam,' I said, 'take it easy.'

'Easy!' he laughed. 'Don't worry. Jesus is driving this car.'

'No he's not, mate: you are,' Ross said. Over his shoulder, he shot me a worried look.

'Ow,' Stella said, 'another one coming.'

'Mum, mum, mum,' you said, and it was all I could do not to cry out as we lurched round a corner and Stella gripped my hand so hard I thought my fingers would break.

'Maybe you should stop, mate,' Ross said. I could hear the controlled panic in his voice. I turned you round, Dodie, so you were facing me and pressed my hands against your back.

'No,' Stella moaned, 'just get me there.'

We were on the dual carriageway now, passing the university, not far to the hospital and, though he was drunk, I don't believe what happened next was entirely Adam's fault. I saw it all with utter clarity. Adam was changing lanes when another car, a white estate, shot suddenly out of a junction, so Adam veered back into the outside lane and into a blue plumber's van. I say it wasn't his fault, but if he hadn't been drunk, if his reactions had been quicker . . . well, no one can ever know. Our car was smashed between the others. Most of the impact came on the passenger side from the white car.

I can remember the sudden frostiness of the windscreen as it crazed and then the dazzling clarity as the glass fell away. There was the silver glint of an aeroplane high up in the blue. I can remember silence as if the world had stopped and then a painful chunter as it started off again. Someone, somewhere screamed. There was a stench of metal mashed with flesh, plastic, faeces, blood. A blur of blonde on the white car's bonnet. Ross's bum on the dashboard, his head invisible. I remember your hot body in my hands, alive, like me, almost unharmed.

Stella was unconscious and at first I thought that she was dead. Adam had his head in his hands against the steering wheel; his thumb was hanging by a thread of skin, but there was very little blood. I stared at the dangling digit, amazed by that. We were near the hospital and help came quickly. You had a gash on your thigh from the seat belt buckle and I had whiplash. They treated us and sent us home.

Stella's right leg was broken and she lost her baby girl. It had been a breech and already in distress before the accident. They said she might have lost her anyway.

Ross was declared dead at the scene.

Adam escaped unscathed, except for his thumb. A surgeon tried to save it, but later it was amputated.

Adam said it was a miracle that he, Dodie and I had survived. It proved God's purpose. But what about Ross? I said, or the poor blonde girl whose skull was smashed?

What was God doing there? And what about Stella's baby and her mind? Her leg may have healed, but her sanity was gone. She spent the next two years in hospital and Adam nearer three in prison.

On your back the bruises from my fingers, where I'd held you so tight against my breast, were like shadowy wings; it took weeks for them to fade. And your leg healed with a pretty scar, like a sickle moon.

Oh, Dodie, you really were mine then, for two whole years. Often Aunt Regina and Kathy came to stay, and sometimes we went for a holiday to Peebles where you toddled about with Princess and where Kathy milked a nanny goat straight into your beaker. I took you to visit Stella who wouldn't even look at you for months. Once I took you to visit Adam in prison, but all you did was scream and kick.

Stella was discharged two years later. At first I was glad, of course, glad for her, and I welcomed her home to Lexicon Avenue but she wouldn't have it. She wouldn't have my welcome and she wouldn't have me. No sooner was she back than she told me to get out. She blamed me, when I was simply not to blame. There was no rational way to frame it like that – but then she wasn't being rational. I don't think she ever was again. I offered to take you away but she said no. You were frightened by her inconsistency. Sometimes she was intense and sometimes blank. Sometimes she squeezed you half to death and sometimes ignored you.

I phoned Aunt Regina in a panic and she came to help. It was plain Stella would never manage you and the house alone. Aunt Regina took you and Stella back to Wood End and I was left to take care of the house. Adam was still in jail. I was alone. I didn't even feel I could visit Peebles without upsetting Stella, though I did try. I did try to see you. I longed for you. I knew you'd be unhappy to be snatched so suddenly away from me; we had built up such a bond. I was afraid that you would be disturbed, damaged even. Aunt Regina worried too, but said it would be better if I stayed away to keep Stella calm and to minimise your confusion.

Though Stella refused to see me any more, Adam said he lived for my visits. But I could hardly stand to see him looking so grey and diminished. The guilt and shock of life in jail, where he wasn't special any more and his preaching gained him only ridicule, made him doubt everything. It even made him doubt the signs, the fact that he was chosen. He took the blame for the accident and felt it deeply, grieving for the child that wasn't even his. It was Satan who'd got into him, he said. Satan who'd made him drink all afternoon, Satan not Jesus who'd driven the car that day. Maybe the herons were coincidence? Maybe he was nothing but deluded? His light had gone out. And even his eyes had lost their power: they were normal, mortal eyes; bloodshot, bleary. Nothing happened when they looked into mine; they stirred nothing but pity.

I needed to get away, right away. I needed to escape from the house that was booby-trapped with reminders of you; it almost drove me mad. I tidied away your toys and then I got them out again. I walked round with one of your little vests in my bag to sniff at. I could feel myself sliding down; the sides were slippery, I could have let go, but instead I took to walking. Walking my way up and out, walking my mind into a soothing rhythm, walking my way through the soles of my shoes. I walked for miles every day in every sort of weather, keeping my eyes away from parks and swings and pushchairs and then, one day on my way home, I paused by the Post Office and saw an advert in the window.

Family house wanted urgently to rent. I rang the number and a man came round to see the house. He was an Iranian doctor working in Britain and wanting to bring his family over. I let it to him right away.

†

'Don't go and leave me,' Adam pleaded when I told him of my plans. But what could he do about it, stuck in prison? I thought a clean break would be better for us both. I went back to Calcutta. There were people I still knew there.

Away from it all, I was able to slip back to a previous life, a previous self, could sometimes forget the grief, forget Adam even, for hours at a time. I returned to my old job teaching English, rented a room and began a relationship with a young sitar player, Ravi: gorgeous, skinny, funny and young. Well, my own age, but after Adam that did seem sweetly young.

There were always lots of little children playing in the streets; at first I couldn't bear to look at them but then I softened. There was a pair, a boy and girl, twins I think, who took to hanging around my door. I taught them nursery rhymes and songs: 'The Spider and the Fly' and 'There's a Hole in my Bucket'. Playing with them soothed the pain of losing you and after all I knew you were safe; you were with your mother. For both your sakes I had to let you go.

I could have stayed in India forever. I thought of staying – until I got a letter from Adam with his release date. He needed me, he said, and I found I had to go. Ravi was lovely but he wasn't Adam. The soul connection wasn't there. When we made love it was good but I didn't feel as if I was plugged into the mains like I did with Adam – or rather, like the mains were plugged into me. I said goodbye to Ravi with regret, but there was no heartbreak on either side. That relationship had been a balm, a treat, *fun* – a word foreign to Adam since he'd found Jesus – but it was like a shallow-rooted plant, easy to pull up. The roots of my love for Adam were as deep as those of an old oak tree and entwined round my guts, my liver, my heart.

On the day of Adam's release, I went to meet him at the prison gates. I hadn't seen him for more than a year. I was shocked and disappointed. His hair was grey and thinning, he'd lost one of his incisors and put on weight. He was badly shaved and had a pale, puffy look as he stood blinking in the autumn sun. I had to keep my eyes away from the shiny red scoop in the side of his hand where his thumb should have been.

'Honey,' he said, and he hugged me tight and I had to hold my breath against the poor sourness of him. Actually, he wasn't poor; there was still money left in the Soul-Life account, and rent coming in from Lexicon Avenue. But we didn't go back to London right away. He wanted to be near the sea, somewhere wild and beautiful. We caught the train to Oban and got the ferry to Mull. We stayed in a cottage by the water. He took it for granted that I was still his wife and expected us to make love but at first I couldn't bear him to touch me, not with his deformed hand, not at all.

'Not yet,' I said. I told him about Ravi and I did have a pang remembering that perfect hard young body. In those first few days, I thought about going back. On the first night we drank a bottle of Jura between us and Adam told me the things that had happened to him in prison and you do not want to know them. Just imagine the worst and you'll get off lightly. I told him where you were, of course, and cried all over him because you were Stella's, not mine, and I had no right to have you.

He asked me to forgive him for the accident. I was the only one on earth whose forgiveness mattered, he said; the only one whose love could wash him clean.

The sun shone, his skin lost its pallor, his beard grew back. He swam every morning, though the water was too cold for me. We bought him new clothes in Tobermory and, eating chips on a bench and sharing a bottle of cider, it started up inside me again. Something he said, I can't even remember what it was, but it made me laugh and our eyes met in the old way, conspiratorial, us against the world. He was getting himself back and I got him back too. I took his bad hand and ran my fingers over the awful dark and puckered place and it just felt soft and warm. It was nothing to be frightened of. It was only him. And I forgave him.

We couldn't wait to get back to the cottage. We found a secluded, sunny slope and made love among some sheep, who didn't even blink.

One morning I woke up late, reached sleepily out for him, but he'd gone. I went back to sleep for a while then got up, bleary and hungover, and made some toast and sat in my pyjamas on the step eating it, watching birds and a red admiral butterfly on a buddleia bush by the back door. The horizon was made of hills and a blue line of sea. I could smell seaweed baking in the sun.

I got dressed and walked down to the beach to find Adam. He was sitting cross-legged on a rock. His eyes were closed and his lips moving. I lay on my belly and stared into a rock pool. The ginger weed swayed in the invisible water and a magenta sea anemone wriggled its tentacles. The reflections of gulls flicked by as if they were down there in the depths. There were colourless crabs scuttling on the sand, and hanging in the water like a feather, a tiny swaying fish. It was a whole miniature world with business going on as usual – until I moved and my shadow startled the fish and the crabs away.

Adam didn't stir for hours and I didn't want to disturb him. I went for a walk along the beach and then returned to the house to eat a hunk of bread and cheese and doze on a deck chair on the lawn. When I woke up, Adam was sitting on the step with a cup of tea. His eyes were blazing with incredible light and I've never seen such a joyous smile.

'There was a heron.' A ripple of laughter came out with his voice.

'Naturally,' I said. I sat beside him and licked the sunny saltiness of his skin.

'It was Jesus and we spoke and spoke and the messages, it's incredible, everything is clear now, everything is different. We have to go to America,' he said.

'Why America?' I said, though I didn't mind. This was exciting. 'Where in America?'

'New York City to begin with,' he said. 'We must go back to London now. I must reveal the new wisdom that the Lord has bestowed upon me, we must act on it immediately, move the operation to America . . .' He went on and on and I listened and made more tea. My heart sank at the biblical language and I had to fight against the little voice niggling in my head. It had grown from the bad seed Stella had planted there, a voice that mocked and told me he was deluded, mad even, and power-mad too. Why should Jesus choose *him*, out of all the people in the world?

We returned to London and he was welcomed like a hero, like a martyr. He told lies, or rather sculpted the truth. This was hard for me to take and sat inside me like a lump of undigested food. Of course they knew about the accident – Obadiah and Hannah had visited him in prison – but his account of how it occurred, presenting him in a heroic light, wasn't true. He lost his thumb rescuing Stella from the wreckage, he said. When, later, I criticized him for this, he explained that he too hated lying, but he'd had to make that sacrifice for the sake of Soul-Life. We mustn't let there be any doubt in the Brethren's mind about him, about Adam as Our Father. It was all for the sake of the Church, and moreover it was Jesus' instruction. And later, you know, I think he believed the story himself, as anyone might come to believe a lie that's endlessly repeated.

As he preached, in the days that followed, I had trouble hearing him past the interference of another voice. And it was a snake's voice, and I had to squash it down, not succumb to cynicism. That is Satan's most pernicious power, because cynicism flourishes most strongly in clever people and these are the people who lead the world. Cynicism is a cheap cleverness that undermines belief and makes faith a laughing stock. As I sought to immerse myself in the teachings this became clear to me and I understood why Adam had sent Stella away from Soul-Life. Stella was a cynic. She was dangerous.

'Should Stella be allowed to influence Dodie then?' I asked. If we could have got you back then, my happiness would have been complete, but Adam said we had to let you go and that one day you'd reject Stella's influence and turn to us, to Soul-Life, of your own accord.

†

Soul-Life flourished in New York, as Adam had said it would. He was inspired by the accident into a new conviction: Ross and that little girl weren't lost at all, he claimed, but liberated from the iniquity of identity to become part of the Universal Soul. His guilt was therefore washed away and he symbolised this regularly in the Festival of the Lamb. I hated the cruelty of the sacrifice but did find solace in the belief behind it. It took me back to thinking of my ectopic pregnancy, which had meant nothing to my child-self, only pain and blood. But maybe that child-who-never-was had a soul and was part of the Universal Soul now. That thought was a comfort.

Through all the good – the golden – years of Soul-Life, about a decade of them, before trouble began to brew, Adam still believed that I would have his son. Of course, I didn't conceive, hardly expected to, but it did mean that we continued to make love – and we were always good at that. One day in bed I noticed a swelling in one of his testicles. The swelling grew, became a lump and a distortion, began to cause an aching in his groin. I begged him to see a doctor of course, but he was steadfast in his refusal. 'If God wishes me to have the disease, so be it,' he said, 'and if he wishes me to die, so be it.'

'But why are there doctors?' I said. 'Surely that's evidence that God wishes people to be able to heal each other?'

This was an argument that angered him from other people, and I'd never dared to voice it before, but he gazed at me softly, sorrow rather than anger in his eyes.

'What matters the individual, Martha?' he said. 'The kind of medicine that saves a single life, all it does is glorify the individual. In fact it doesn't matter when we die.'

'If I died?' I said.

'When,' he reminded me gently, and then sighed and stroked my hair. 'If you die first I'll be sad, of course, on a human level, but I shall rejoice that your soul has joined the Universal Soul, and will welcome my own death when we shall mingle again. But before I die, I must have a son. Jesus has told me my son is the chosen messenger.'

'It's not going to happen,' I said.

'I had a dream,' he said. 'In which Stella handed me a son.'

'*No*,' I said immediately, shocked that he could even think it. 'Surely even *you* cannot expect that!'

He looked offended by my emphasis, but didn't rise to it. 'It is not my will, it is the Lord's,' he said.

Every argument I ventured only seemed to strengthen his resolve. And if Adam believed it was the Lord's will, then it would be done.

†

It was the first time we'd been back to the UK in more than ten years, and oh, how dismal and cramped it seemed. We stepped off the aeroplane into freezing January drizzle and I had no sense of homecoming, or belonging. You didn't know it but I saw you on that visit. We'd hired a car and parked in Lexicon Avenue outside the house, debating how to approach Stella with our request. How strange it was to be there again in that suburban street. It was late afternoon, the sky bulging with charcoal clouds, the streetlights casting a sickly wash over the wetness. We sat in the car under the dripping black laburnum. And then you came along the road. I gripped Adam's arm.

'It's Dodie.'

You walked with your head down, a bag of books over your shoulder. I knew it was you the instant I saw you. Your step was like Stella's, quick and light, despite the heavy bag, as if you only skimmed the ground. Your long black hair was glistening in the rain. You were in school uniform but with a gothic twist: dark eye make-up, black tights. I caught a glimpse of black nail polish – but your cheeks were fresh and pink. I saw your breath float in the air and my own breath caught in my chest. You were still you. I felt like I'd been punched. You pushed open the gate and paused, before you went off down the side of the house.

Neither of us had the spirit or the energy to go in right away. Adam drove us to a hotel in town where we slept. We had room service for our dinner and watched television. Neither of us had seen it since arriving in America and it was a shocking intrusion into our heads, the blaring sound and speed of the skipping images, the brightness, the colour and the pernicious messages that pour from it and into the brain, anaesthetize the senses against anything more subtle. I had to agree with Adam about that. We turned it off and Adam prayed for help and guidance.

Next morning – you would have been at school – we drove back to Lexicon Avenue. Again we parked the car under the laburnum. The rusty squeal of the gate was just the same. The smell of rust and privet engulfed me in such a flood of memory that I had to lean on the wall to steady myself. We rang the bell and waited on the front doorstep, but there was no reply. We went round to the back door. I tried the handle but it was locked. We knocked. The curtain moved aside in the dining room, and Stella peered round it. She froze as she recognized us and let the curtain fall. We had to hammer on the door before, eventually, we heard the key turn in the lock.

She was wearing an old dressing gown that I remembered from years back, and her hair hung down in curtains. It was thinner, with a few threads of grey and when we got inside I saw the lines on her face. She was only thirty-three but looked so much older, raddled and pickled with sourness and smoke.

'Have you come to keep your promise?' was the first thing she said.

'Stella,' I said, 'it's been so long.' I tried to embrace her but she was like a bunch of twigs and I didn't dare to squeeze too hard in case she broke. She didn't return my embrace. The kitchen was over-scrubbed and chilly, reeking, as always, of bleach.

'I've missed you,' I said.

She pulled a face and stepped away.

'What about a cup of tea?' I said.

She turned and put the kettle on. 'What do you want?'

'Just to visit, to see you, to hear how Dodie is.'

Adam was standing looking at his feet and I tried to sound normal, cheerful, to inject a bit of warmth into the place, if only with my voice.

He wanted me to ask her: sister to sister. I'd only agreed because I knew she'd say no to this charade. She'd laugh in my face. And I'd comfort Adam in his disappointment. We'd return to Soul-Life and wait for a new dream to tell us how to proceed. What else could we do? We could hardly force her.

Stella poured the tea and carried it through into the dining room where a puzzle – the Mona Lisa – had been started on the rosewood table. The table was polished to a deep and layered gleam. I looked down at it, beyond my reflection, and it did seem as if you could travel miles down there into a warm and rosy world.

There was no sign that a teenager lived here. Everything was immaculate and just as it had been fifteen years before, only more worn from all the scrubbing. The only thing of beauty was the table – and Stella still, when she turned her head or when in a certain light a little shock of loveliness spilled out between the lines. I'd grown heavy, my hair hacked off in its institutional cut. I'd seen in the hotel mirror how middle-aged I looked, though I too was only in my thirties.

'The Lord has sent us here for a purpose,' Adam said.

'So much for small talk.' Stella cackled. There was a silence, then: 'You're not getting your hands on Dodie,' she said, narrowing her eyes.

'Your sister will speak to you, while I . . . perhaps I'll step out into the garden,' Adam said.

'He looks like shit,' Stella remarked. And then, after a long awkward silence, 'Well?' And when I didn't answer, she snorted. 'I suppose he had a dream?'

'How *is* Dodie?' I said.

'She's strong,' she said. 'She's doing well at school. She's *normal*,' she added, a trace of pride in her voice.

'I'd love to see her,' I said.

She shook her head. 'She's forgotten all about you.'

'What?'

'You're never mentioned.'

'Not even by Aunt Regina?'

'No. We stopped mentioning you when you went off and left her,' she said. 'Aunt Regina thought it best.'

'I didn't leave her! I only went away because you wouldn't let me see her!' I couldn't believe that Stella thought that. Did she really think it? I felt sick.

Smiling to herself, Stella picked up a piece of chin and fitted it in the puzzle. 'So. Tell me about the dream, then.'

I told her what Adam claimed Jesus wanted from her and she stared. Her mouth opened and closed and nothing came out at first, and then a splintered laugh.

'You're asking me to fuck that old git?'

'I knew you'd say no,' I said.

'He killed my last baby, now he wants me to have another?'

'It's not *about* that,' I said, and couldn't prevent myself from adding: 'She might have died anyway.'

She made a tiny gasping sound. 'But not *Ross*.' Her eyes were huge, the pupils flared.

'Oh, Stell. You still miss him?'

She shook her head in disbelief, then, frowning, rolled herself a spliff. She inhaled and blew out smoke, head on one side. She offered it to me, but I shook my head.

She smirked. 'All right then,' she said, at last.

I stared at her. '*What?*'

'If he pays me enough,' she said.

'No.'

She licked her lips, breathed in smoke, took a sip of tea, wiped her mouth on her sleeve before she breathed it out again. 'Ah,' she said, 'I get it. I'm meant to refuse?'

Adam came into the room at that moment. 'The answer's yes,' she said, before I could intervene. 'And it's the middle of the month. So come on.' She stubbed out her spliff and stood up. 'You can get on with the puzzle,' she said to me. 'Unless you want to watch?'

†

We flew back to New York a week later. There had been several opportunities for conception. I couldn't speak to, or even look at Adam, certainly not touch him. It wasn't till we were back among the Brethren that my repulsion began to fade. It was only sex, after all. I was dubious that it would work, but Adam had complete faith that Stella had conceived. He'd written her a contract, saying that on proof of pregnancy he would double the allowance he paid her every month, and that if she bore him a son he would give her twenty thousand pounds when she handed him over. I thought that even if she did conceive, she might refuse to give us the child. And what if it was a girl? Of course, I pointed these things out to Adam but he looked at me in that way he had, as if I was naïve. His faith that it would all work out was absolute. He asked Stella to write as soon as she knew. And special prayers were made at Soul-Life for a son for Adam.

Adam's plan was that as soon as we knew for sure that his son was on the way, *I* would pretend to be pregnant. What was the need for the deception, you might wonder? I didn't like it myself, but Adam said it would be difficult to explain to the Brothers and Sisters how another woman had come to bear his child, especially since sexual continence was a Soul-Life requirement. The miracle of the conception after all these years would be a source of rejoicing, an injection of energy, something that, since Adam had been unwell, had seeped away.

There was no word from Stella for over a month. Naturally, I thought it hadn't worked and I admit I was relieved. Not that I didn't crave a child in my arms again. Adam spent his days in prayer, puzzled by the lack of news, niggling away at Jesus, I'm sure – but there was no sign, no heron, not even a significant dream.

And then one day the letter arrived. He breathed out as he read it, then fell to his knees in prayer. The baby was due on the eighth of October. Adam had Obadiah seek legal advice. Adoption and surrogacy papers were drawn up. To my surprise, Stella signed and returned everything that Adam sent her.

And Adam recovered. Perhaps it was the glad tidings, or perhaps – I wondered then – it hadn't been cancer after all, but an infection that had, of its own accord, eventually cleared up. Naturally, Adam pronounced it a miracle. The lump didn't go away but it got no bigger and he felt fine, though we were no longer intimate, and this I missed. The last semen that he shed he shed in Stella. I tried not to dwell on that. And I argued against the end of sex. How could God mind us expressing our love in the beautiful, physical way? But Adam was decided. Now the son was on his way there was no longer any need for fornication.

†

Stella wrote to us monthly with news of her progress. The pregnancy was normal; the scans confirmed the due date of the birth. In late September, Adam and I flew to the UK and returned to the same hotel. It was a relief to drop my padding; there was no need for pretence away from Soul-Life. I phoned Stella. She told us not to come to the house. She didn't want to see us. She would keep to the bargain only if we stayed away.

We visited the lawyer Obadiah had found us, the only one he could find prepared to do this work – and he was uncomfortable with the situation. His name was Colin and he was beige all over – hair, skin, eyes and even teeth. 'It's most irregular,' he said, riffling through the papers and frowning. 'I've never dealt with a case like this.'

'Yet it's perfectly legal,' Adam insisted. 'I am the child's father and our surrogate is in full agreement.'

Colin grimaced and sucked spit through his teeth. 'I've yet to be convinced of that,' he said.

There was nothing for us to do but wait. We phoned Stella each morning but didn't know what else to do with ourselves besides meditation and prayer. Adam was waiting for guidance and had taken to sitting by the lake in the park, hoping to see a heron. The tension between us was intolerable and we sniped at each other for the first time ever. While he was seeking herons, I shopped for baby things, just enough to see us through till we got home: a packet of newborn nappies, some Babygros, a Moses basket, bottle and infant formula.

The baby was late. A week after the due date I dared to mention this to Stella.

'It's in God's hands,' she said, which I knew was aimed at riling me.

'We need to see you,' I said.

'I told you no.'

'But how do we even know you're really pregnant?' I said. Adam darted me a startled look. 'Maybe you've been stringing us along.'

I heard her breath suck in.

'Just let us see you.' I softened my voice. 'I'd like to see you, you *are* still my sister.'

'All right then,' she said, 'but not while Dodie's home. I don't want her seeing you. I don't want her tainted by this.'

'Tainted!' I said. '*Tainted!*'

She waited for me to quieten down, and told us when to come. Adam and I sat in the car waiting to see you leave. You came out of the gate and I held my breath. I soaked you up with my eyes in those few seconds. Your messy black hair tumbled right down to your slim, black-clad waist, and even though it looked as if you'd tried to whiten your cheeks, they were still rosy, and your eyes, under their glossy black brows, were that strong deep blue. You looked like Stella, yes, but stronger, more vital and vivid. We both watched you walk along the street with your special graceful gait.

'Beautiful,' I said. I looked at Adam and his face was illegible, but there was an extra brightness to his eyes. And then he closed them and shut me out. We got out of the car and went round to the back of the house. We knocked and, after checking us through the window, Stella came to the door.

She was almost unrecognisably spherical. It wasn't just the pregnancy but all of her; the calves showing under the dressing gown were like fat white skittles.

'Can I?' Adam raised his hand. He wanted to touch her belly, to touch through her fat, his son. She held onto the door jamb and came down one step. She looked away, and flinched as Adam put his hand on the mound stretched under her dressing gown.

'Satisfied?' she said.

'Well you certainly are up the spout!' I said, trying to lighten the atmosphere. 'It's lovely to see you, Stell.' I reached forward to hug her but was chilled by the look in her eyes. She gave a mirthless laugh.

'Likewise,' she said. 'I'll let you know when it's born.' And then she hauled herself back up the step and shut the door.

Three days later we got the call. Stella had given birth to a son, 7lb 7oz, at 6.30 a.m. Although it was expected, the news hit me like a thud between the ribs, leaving me winded. Adam sank immediately to his knees and I knelt too and watched through my eyelashes the tears of joy that trickled down his face.

†

Colin's BMW was already parked outside the house when we arrived – and there was also a muddy Land Rover, which I guessed was Aunt Regina's. She shouldn't have been there. That wasn't the arrangement. She shouldn't have been involved.

Adam was trembling. I took his hand and my thumb sank into the soft depression where his should be. Colin got out of his car. 'Let me reiterate that I'm not entirely comfortable with this,' he said. 'I'll need to see the mother and make sure she's clear in her intention.'

'Naturally,' Adam said. We went through the squeaky gate to the front door. The cardboard carton from a cot mobile was squashed up against the wall. I saw Adam register it, and Colin too. Aunt Regina opened the door. Despite the fact that she shouldn't be there, I felt a sudden gust of fondness and hugged her hard. 'Melanie,' she said. She held me away from her to take a proper look. 'Don't you look lovely?' she said kindly. My hair was speckled with grey, and I was overweight, and in Soul-Life, as you know, we don't pluck our chins or eyebrows or use make-up. Lovely was not the word for how I looked. We hugged again.

She'd shrunk a little but seemed otherwise unchanged. Her glasses had rainbow frames and she was wearing a V-necked vest that showed the brown leathery creases on her chest. 'Adam,' Aunt Regina nodded unsmilingly at him. 'And?' She looked at Colin.

'Our lawyer,' Adam said.

Aunt Regina sighed. 'You'd best come in,' she said.

We all went through into the dining room. Kathy was standing with her hands on her hips, glaring. Her eyebrows were white now, and more wirily wild than ever.

'Is Dodie here?' I asked.

'She's at school,' Aunt Regina said. 'Can we have a moment, dear?'

'Can I see Stella and the baby?'

'That's just it,' Aunt Regina said, 'I'm afraid she doesn't want to see you.'

'She told us to send you packing,' added Kathy.

'She can't do that,' Adam said. In my bag was the suit I was to take Seth home in. I saw a bottle sterilizer on the draining board. 'Can she?' He turned to Colin, who was hovering on the threshold looking uncomfortable.

'She can,' he said.

'But she signed papers.'

'Papers mean diddly-squat when it comes to a situation like this.'

'To try and buy your sister's child!' Aunt Regina gave me a look of outraged disappointment. 'You should be ashamed of yourself.'

'It's not *like* that,' I said, although I shrank inside. 'It was always going to be ours. Adam's I mean. He *is* the father.'

'The less said about the ways and means the better,' Kathy said darkly.

'Ho hum, well I'll be on my way,' Colin said. 'You'll get my bill.' The door banged shut behind him. Adam pushed past Aunt Regina and up the stairs. I ran after him. Stella had been asleep but she woke when we came in. The baby was in a carrycot beside her on the bed. Stella's face was ashen and her greasy hair tied back. She gave a tired, triumphant smile.

'Well done, Stell,' I said.

'You're not having him,' she said. 'I've changed my mind.'

Our eyes met for a moment and then she blinked. 'Just go away,' she said.

'All right,' I said.

Adam started and looked at me. 'Martha? We can't leave without our son.'

'We can,' I said, just as Stella was saying, '*My* son.'

He looked at me. I'd not seen him look so helpless since I met him at the prison gates. His mouth hung open and his hands dangled empty at his sides. 'Can we see the baby?' I asked Stella. 'Before we leave?' Aunt Regina and Kathy had come upstairs by then.

'All right, dear?' Aunt Regina said to Stella. 'Do you want them to go?'

That word *them* stung like a wasp.

'Come on,' Kathy said, 'off, out. Sling your hook.'

I blessed her for saying that because it woke Stella's contrary streak. 'They can see him if they want,' she said.

'Sure, dear?'

Stella nodded and Aunt Regina reached across her for the Moses basket. Kathy was lurking around the doorway, flexing her fists and scowling like a bouncer.

'Adam *is* his father,' Stella said, a flick of enjoyment in her voice.

The baby was asleep. He was lying on his side and wearing a cotton hat. All we could see was a wisp of sooty hair, a closed eyelid, a tiny nose and lips like a crumpled moth.

'Seth,' Adam said, and reached out gently and touched his cheek.

'Can I hold him?' I asked.

'Shame to wake him,' Aunt Regina said.

'I might *not* call him Seth,' Stella said.

'But we *agreed*.' Adam said.

Stella gave a little shrug. 'I might have changed my mind.'

'What do you want to call him then?' I asked.

'Bogart,' she said, narrowing her eyes. 'Or Bogbaby.'

'How nice,' I said.

A corner of her lip lifted in the ghost of a smile. 'Well, anyway, you can go now,' she said. 'I need some sleep.'

I took Adam's hand. He was staring down at Seth. 'Come on,' I said, and tugged him away.

'Oh, and you can keep your twenty thousand pounds,' Stella said, and I felt Aunt Regina's disgust ripple after us down the stairs and out.

†

We went back to the hotel and prayed. It was a gloomy room with olive walls and dark green drapes. A print of a carp added to the underwater atmosphere. I couldn't actually pray but I knelt with Adam. I could see our reflection in the mirror on the wardrobe door. It looked like a painting: two people in the green gloom, praying. My eyes met my own eyes and it was like electricity. I got a raw, shocking glimpse through a gap that had opened in my own life of how lost I was. What was I doing? No wonder Aunt Regina had looked at me the way she did.

I watched the mirror-Adam: head bowed, forehead furrowed, lips moving. The damaged hand clasped in the other. In his beard there was a blob of jam left over from breakfast when we had been nervous and jubilant that this would be the day he would get his son.

We kept phoning till they stopped answering. We tried to visit, but each time Kathy came to the door and wouldn't let us in. On the third morning after our disappointment, I woke to find Adam on his knees under the print of the carp. He sensed that I'd woken, opened his eyes and smiled.

'It's all right,' he said. He got up and sat on the bed, and took my hand. 'I had a dream.'

I shut my eyes against the jeering chorus that set off inside me. I pressed my lips together.

He waited till I looked at him. 'The child must stay with Stella till he's sixteen.'

'*Jesus* told you this?'

He gave me an irritated look and withdrew his hand. I'd not meant my voice to come with a serrated edge.

'I saw the boy waving to his mother and coming, with his arms open, to me.'

'How did you know he was sixteen?'

'I knew. And in the dream I felt blessed.'

'OK,' I said. His eyes were on me, willing me to look at him and to smile, but I couldn't. The dream was convenient, just as Stella said. It was expedient. Eventually I met his eyes and smiled. 'OK,' I sighed. I looked at the pile of baby things I'd bought from Mothercare. 'We might as well take that stuff back.'

'No, we'll give it to Stella,' he said. 'We'll go in peace, bearing our gifts and let her know we relinquish our claim.'

'For now.'

'No need to mention that,' he said.

I phoned to leave this message, and was surprised that Stella answered.

'Oh good,' I said, 'I thought you weren't picking up.'

'Reflex.'

'Who is it?' I heard Kathy booming.

'You're not having him,' Stella said.

'We're going back to the States,' I said. 'He's your baby and you should keep him.'

'Thanks very much.'

'We've got some presents for you, shall we bring them round?'

'Give it to me.' It was Aunt Regina. 'Melanie,' she said, in a voice of strained patience, 'what do you want now?'

'We've decided to go home,' I said. 'It was wrong of us, it was all wrong, I see that now. You were right. I'm ashamed.'

Adam was glaring at me, and I turned so that I couldn't see him. I stared at the carp instead. The light was reflecting off the darkly varnished surface.

'We're flying back tonight but we've got all this baby stuff we bought. Can we drop it round?'

'You can leave it in the garden. It's not raining.'

'Could I see Stella?' I said.

'What are you up to?'

'Nothing, honestly, just, I'd like to say goodbye.'

The receiver was muffled for a moment and I could hear them arguing. Aunt Regina came back on the line. 'You can come in for five minutes before Dodie gets back from school. Just you. We won't have that man in the house.'

Adam didn't like it, of course, but consented to wait in the car while I unloaded the baby things. When I rapped the fox doorknocker, Aunt Regina opened the door immediately.

'Stella's in the sitting room,' she said.

'Auntie?' I put my hand on her arm. If only she'd smiled at me.

'The clock is ticking,' Kathy said, looming up behind her and tapping her watch.

I went through. There was no sign of the baby in there except for a changing mat on the floor. Stella was curled up in an armchair. Her towelling dressing gown was freshly washed and smelled of Persil. Her hair was clean for once and buttery fair in the sunshine that slanted through the window and caught the ends of her long pale lashes, making clear water of her eyes.

'I suppose you want to see him?' she said.

'That's not why I'm here.'

'Kathy said you were up to some trick. She was all for calling the police.'

'No tricks. Stella, did you plan this all along?' I said. 'To keep him?'

She shrugged.

'Well, I'm glad you're keeping him,' I said, and I found I really meant it. 'You're his mother.' She studied my face to gauge my seriousness. 'You know what Adam's like, I sort of get drawn in.'

'Yeah, blame Adam.'

'No, I don't mean that.'

'You know what you are,' Stella said, 'you're Adam's puppet.'

'I am not!' I realized I could hear someone creaking outside the door, ear to the wood no doubt.

'Anyway, what do you want?' Stella said.

'Just to say goodbye,' I told her. 'We're going back.'

'Bye then,' Stella said. She put her thumb to her mouth and bit savagely at her cuticle.

'If you ever need any help, or you want me to come and stay or anything . . .' I said.

She wound a strand of hair tighter and tighter round one of her fingers till the end bulged dark with blood.

'Sorry, Stell,' I said in a small voice.

She shrugged. I got up and stood. I wanted to kiss her or hug her or something but there was a sort of force field around her that I dared not enter.

'Remember what you promised me?' she said, and darted me a look.

I nodded and my heart beat thickly with the memory of it. I thought she'd forgotten. 'But you've got a new baby –'

'Not yet,' she said quietly. 'Now, just go.'

I stood looking down at the top of her head. The door opened and Aunt Regina beckoned me out. I looked back at Stella, who hadn't moved, hoping for a smile, but she was frowning at her knees.

'Bye,' I said, and followed Aunt Regina out into the hall.

'You can have a look at Seth if you like,' she said. She was regarding me in a kind but wary way. Seth was in his carrycot in the dining room, awake, lying on his back. He had a funny round little head and his black hair spiralled upwards like a puff of smoke. His eyes were that indeterminate hazy blue that could turn any shade.

'Do you think she'll be OK this time?' I said. 'I mean, what if she gets ill like with Dodie?'

'We're here,' Aunt Regina said. 'You don't need to worry. Now you'd better go.'

'Aunt Regina?' I began.

'We all make choices,' she said firmly. 'And you have made yours.'

'Auntie –' I tried again, but Kathy loomed between us, looking significantly at her watch.

I felt like a stupid fish, my mouth opening and shutting. I thought of the glossy carp, I couldn't formulate what I wanted to say and I could feel clouds gathering inside me. 'I'll go then,' was all I said, and I let myself be propelled towards the door. I looked back at Aunt Regina but she had turned her face away.

†

We arrived back at Soul-Life with no child and I was clearly no longer pregnant. Adam had an explanation. We wanted the child brought up in England, in secret safety in case of trouble. Even back then, there were grumbling problems within Soul-Life – families trying to get their children back, internal disagreements about protocol, financial complications – and our prolonged absence had exacerbated these. Soul-Life's golden age was over, but while Adam remained strong, we kept it under control. His vision kept it under control.

I went along with the story. I didn't want despair to bring back Adam's disease. It's an interesting word: dis–ease. I wanted him to be easy again in his dreams and visions and beliefs. For that he needed absolute faith in me. I saw that. I knew that. I was his rock. It had never been so clear before.

The first time we'd met, when I sat on him – though he has it that he saw me walk across the room – I thought I needed someone and I thought that it was him. But every day after we got back from our futile trip, a few more flakes of illusion fell away and left my vision clearer. The strength had been within me all along. If we hadn't met I would've been all right. Maybe even Stella would've been all right. How could I allow that thought and not go mad?

'We all make choices,' Aunt Regina said. And she was right. And I couldn't unmake my choice. This was the path I'd chosen, and now Adam needed all my strength. Through a lawyer, Stella negotiated extortionate child support until Seth was sixteen, when Adam could take over his upbringing. Who knew if she'd stick to it when the time came? There was nothing we could do except wait. For once, even Adam had doubts. My role was to reassure him. But the stronger I seemed on the outside, the more I broke apart inside. I had to admit to myself that I didn't believe in Adam's visions. I believed he *had* the visions but I stopped trying to believe they were any more than delusions. But what delusions that could persuade so many!

I considered leaving. If I could have left in the few months after our return, then maybe I would have done so, though leaving Adam would have torn my heart out. One day, in a fit of despair, I went into the office while Obadiah was out and phoned Aunt Regina.

'I want to come home,' I said. 'I'm so sorry.'

'Best stay away, dear,' she said. (She *did* say dear, and I treasured that tiny crumb of comfort.) 'Stella's on a reasonably even keel and we don't want that upset.' We talked on for a little while. She told me about Kathy's arthritic knee, a glut of pears, the birth of another kid. I had nothing to contribute. Nothing about Adam or Soul-Life would have interested her.

'Best not ring again,' Aunt Regina said, when our conversation had run aground. 'Best let things be.' Her voice sounded kind but then it vanished into the click and hum of all the miles between us. I thought of running, then. I thought of returning to India. I could live as I had before, in cheap and grubby anonymity. My mind began to fold and shrink against itself; memories disappearing into creases. Shuttering of light and stuttering of meaning. I think that I was ill, maybe like Stella was ill. It had never happened before but now my mind reached the edge of a slippery slope and I slid into the darkness. I was put into a room alone.

Every day Adam came and held my hand and talked and talked and pulled me back as surely as a fisherman. He reeled me in again. We prayed and meditated. He thought it was the disappointment of not having the child with me. Perhaps there was some of that. Adam was right that I suffered from the lack or loss of a baby in my arms, but it was more than that. It was a loss of faith, not just in God and Adam and his visions, but in myself and the way I'd chosen to live my life – and that is worse.

And then Adam's disease returned. He became so ill we all thought that he would die. From somewhere I found the strength to nurse and meditate and pray with him. Hannah and Obadiah took more responsibility for how things were, how the money was, the bad press Soul-Life had begun to generate. As if there was something dangerous going on within our walls, when all it was was love. Even if it *was* deluded, it did no harm.

While Adam suffered his relapse I became the fisherwoman and my hand in his hand the line that reeled him in. You see the human love we gave each other? Beyond all else, despite all else, there was a solid mortal love between us. From that time my soul was split. I lived the life, the soul life, and no one lived it more thoroughly than me, but I lived it with a voice up on my shoulder, a parrot with Stella's face perching there and making a mockery of everything I said and did. You can't imagine the pain of that. To live without integrity is the greatest burden a soul can ever bear. But I bore it. What else could I do? Out of love for Adam I bore it for another fifteen years.

And, to my relief and amazement, Adam recovered once more. This was the power of his belief. There *was* power in it, you see. *Real* power can come out of delusion. He never entirely regained his former health – he was weaker and the times he revealed himself to the Brethren became fewer. Where once there'd been a meeting every week now there was scarcely one a month, but it was enough. Perhaps the scarcity increased the intensity of joy among the throng when he did speak, and he did so with a renewed fervour since he'd emerged from the illness to a series of new visions and visitations.

Crows replaced herons, and our place flocked with the horrid creatures, so he would sit outside and wait and almost always one would come to him. And he dreamed one night of a man without a face. The dream haunted him, it had the atmosphere of something vital, he said, and he prayed and fasted and meditated until it came to him. To be faceless is to symbolise the destructive futility of personality, of individuality, which is the enemy of the very oneness which must be our goal. That is when the idea of the masks occurred to him.

For a while every recruit wore a mask and relinquished possession of a name – but this proved impractical and there were a few months of chaos until Jesus spake again. The masks were only for those who had proved their worthiness, who had shed their worldly personalities through the clarification process. And then they would only be worn for ceremonial and teaching purposes and to maintain a distance between the truly absorbed Soul-Life members and those still to be tested in their resolve and their belief.

Once I said to Adam, 'What is the end of all of this?' We were sitting in our own white room. It was after celebration and sacrifice. I'd bathed the blood from his hands and washed his feet, as he loved me to do. And I didn't mind that. I loved him as a mother loves a child by then, that is how I reconciled my lack of belief in what he said, with the storm of tenderness I felt in his proximity. I cut his toenails and rubbed hand cream into the rough skin on his heels. I was used to waiting for him to formulate his reply but he was only looking at me.

'What are you asking?' he said.

'There are millions, maybe billions, of dollars in the bank accounts. You have hundreds of devotees.'

He nodded.

'But what . . .' I paused. I didn't want to anger him, nor did I want to say anything to rock his own belief, since that was all that held him together – that and my love. 'What's the point of it?' I dared myself to ask.

'That is the question of a child,' he said coldly, 'and do not pretend to me, Martha, that you are so naïve.'

I swallowed. 'What's at the heart of it?' I persisted. 'For *what* are the Chosen chosen?'

'Eternal life,' he said.

'I know, but –'

He began tiredly to preach at me and it was all words I'd heard before. The parrot was cackling as he spoke and it was saying, '*Nothing*, there's nothing at the heart of it,' and that voice was louder to me then than Adam's voice. And when it shut up I heard silence ringing like a tongueless bell.

'Yes,' I said, to force words into that silence. 'Oh yes, you're right, Adam, of course you are. Forgive me. It must be Satan trying to work into a chink.'

'I'm glad you spoke your doubts,' he said. 'Of course Satan will try his luck every now and then even with one so devoted as you, my love. You must be his greatest challenge.' And he stroked my hair as I lay my head against his knee and my heart wanted to scream out with the tragedy of his belief in me, and how easily he could be deceived.

†

Five years after Seth's birth, Stella wrote to tell me that Aunt Regina had died. She'd had a stroke and had lived for six months with Kathy nursing her and then, just as she'd seemed to be recovering, she'd had another massive stroke. When I heard this news, the weakness came into my mind again, and it was some months before I was better. I prayed for belief as strong as Adam's to help me deal with Aunt Regina's death, and to deal with the fact that now we never could be reconciled. There was a chasm in my poor fake soul that could never be mended.

†

It was November last year, Seth's sixteenth year, when I phoned Stella. Adam was there with me. He was very ill. Too ill, I thought, to wait till the following October and Seth's birthday. The disease had come creeping back. He said nothing of it until I happened to sees him undressed one night, saw how thin his limbs had become and how lumpy and distorted his abdomen.

'Please let us see a doctor,' I said, though I knew this would anger him.

'Why can't you understand that this is the will of God?' he said and, before I could reply: '*Hannah* understands.'

I stiffened. 'What?'

'I must live till my son is here,' he said, 'until my son has received the wisdom, and then I will be pleased to join the Universal Soul.'

'Please don't talk like that,' I said.

He sighed and shook his head, put on his night robe and got stiffly into bed. I lay down with him, feeling his dear body in my arms. His breath was foul, as it had been for a long time, but I didn't care: it was his breath and it was precious. His heart was still beating strongly. I put my ear against his chest to listen. I couldn't believe that such a strong heart would ever stop.

'We'll pray again,' I said. 'You have the will to live and we have the will to keep you alive.'

He was silent for a moment and then he said something he'd never said before, not in all the time I'd known him: 'I'm tired. I'm tired. I've had enough.'

'If you die, I might as well die too,' I said, though as I spoke the words, something pugilistic sprang up inside me, fists clenched. No, I was not ready.

'You must look after Seth. You've been my rock,' he said. 'It's not your time and you must carry on.'

We lay and stroked each other, taking such comfort as we could. His hand stroked my skin from shoulder blade to buttock over and over and I sighed with the pleasure of it.

'Adam,' I said into the darkness, 'if I am to carry on, I need guidance. I understand the process of clarification and the holy work and the investing of money, the fishing, all of that, but I don't feel I have an overview . . . do you see what I mean? I don't know' – I hardly dared to say it again – 'I don't know what's at the centre of it all. I don't know the point, the end point. Without you it will be a light going out . . .'

'Shhh.' He put a finger to my lips. 'My son will show you the way. He is the next step. Have faith, Martha. All will be revealed.'

Passing the buck, sniped the Stella-parrot.

We lay quietly then, and I listened until his breath had deepened into sleep and he began to snore gently, the sound of a boy sawing balsa wood, soft and soporific to my ears. I turned away from him and lay huddled round my lonely, secret, lack of faith.

When he went, I would go too: that became clear to me then. I would leave Soul-Life. I took to spending time in the admin block – Obadiah's territory and where, unfortunately, Hannah took to hanging around too. She didn't like it when I came in; she made that obvious. But when she wasn't there, I got Obadiah to teach me about computers, to use a laptop, to understand something of the way the finance worked – though it was too vast and confusing an operation for me to understand more than the tiniest bit.

Adam and I went together to the admin block when we deemed it time to phone Stella. He sat in a chair, listening, his good hand squeezing and kneading the maimed one as it always did when he was nervous.

'It's almost time, Stella,' I said.

'He's not sixteen.'

'It's his sixteenth year.'

She was quiet for a long time. I was almost certain she'd laugh her head off at us for believing she'd stick to her agreement. Or else she'd make us wait till next October, till the actual birthday. I could hear the brittle catch in her breath and even the ticking of the clock over the dining room fire. 'All right,' she said. 'Come and fetch him.'

I was surprised enough to hold the phone away for a moment and stare at the scattered holes of the mouthpiece. 'Are you sure?' I said, but she'd put the phone down.

Adam had never doubted it, he told me, although I'd seen and smelled the anxiety in him these last few weeks.

'What if it's a trick?' I said. 'Like last time? What if she's taunting us?'

He shook his head at me, a glaze of sadness in his eyes.

✝

Adam was hardly well enough to travel. I said he didn't need to come with me, but he was determined. We bought first-class tickets in order for him to be more comfortable: two outward, three back. Stella had given us the information we needed to organize a visa for Seth. I still could not believe her co-operation.

This time we said nothing about our mission to the community – except to Obadiah, Hannah and Isaac. We booked into the same hotel as before, but it had changed hands and the swimming-carp room that had once been so cool and gloomy green had been jazzed up with red wallpaper and pictures of hot air balloons. The bath had a jacuzzi feature, which proved wonderfully soothing for Adam's aching body.

Once we were settled, I rang Stella again. 'You can come and get Seth tomorrow,' she said.

I still did not trust her. 'What if he doesn't want to come?' I asked.

'He'll come.' She gave a parched little laugh. 'He hates school, gets himself bullied. I said, "How'd you like to go and stay with some relatives in America for a bit, and if you like it, you can finish school there?" He jumped at the idea. I phoned his school and said he was transferring.'

'No trouble?' I said.

'The Head tried to interfere of course, but there's nothing they can do.'

'So you're happy about this?' I asked, pulling a disbelieving face at Adam who was lying awkwardly back against a pile of scarlet fun-fur cushions, beside which his skin was ghastly lemon.

'Tomorrow, five o'clock,' she said.

'What about Seth? You mean he'll just drop everything and come?'

'"Beam me up Scotty," were his exact words.'

'But his friends, school. . .'

'He's miserable at school and I'm not making it any better.'

'Oh *Stell*,' I said, in a rush of fondness.

'Five o'clock,' she repeated.

'Is there any chance we could see Dodie?' I dared to ask.

She laughed and rang off. I put the receiver down and watched the sweat on it evaporate.

'Surely she won't let it be this easy?' I said, but Adam only did his holy smile and closed his eyes.

On Friday we went to the house. It was a dark afternoon, everything gloomy and dripping. I knocked and we waited, Adam leaning against the wall. Stella came to the door in her old red velvet dress. Her hair was clean and brushed. If it wasn't for the age in her face she could've been a hippy chick again.

'Mel,' she said, 'Adam, do come in. What years it's been!' I guessed she was projecting her voice for Seth's benefit.

I clasped her hand, leaned to kiss her cheek and felt her stiffen as my lips touched her skin. 'Come on in,' she said again. She didn't acknowledge Adam. She led us into the dining room. On the table was a near-completed jigsaw puzzle, a view of Venice.

There was a school bag on the floor and I looked around for Seth. 'Where is he?' I asked.

'Upstairs, packing,' she said. 'Cup of tea?'

'Please.' Adam looked done in. 'Sit down,' I said. 'Mind if we put the fire on, Stell?'

She gave a shrug and went to make the tea. The one-handed clock still ticked away, the other hand like a dead insect at the bottom. Adam sat on an upright chair, elbows on the table, head supported in cupped hands. The space where his thumb should be was deep and withered, powdery and bluish. He looked old and threadbare, the scalp showing through his thinning hair. When Stella came back into the room I saw her glance at him and flicker with satisfaction. My heart was hectoring away inside me.

There was a rumble of feet on the stairs and Seth was suddenly in the room. I couldn't help but gasp – and Stella smirked to see it – because he was so much like Adam – so like Bogart had been: tall, dark-haired but with your startling blue-glass eyes.

'Mum, have you seen my phone?' he said, and then: 'Hi.' He flicked back his hair and darted curious looks at Adam and me.

'This is your uncle and aunt,' Stella said, 'who are kindly taking you back to the States with them.'

Seth gave us both a shy smile and extended his hand.

'But I need to tell Dodie first,' he said. 'I'm meant to be going round.'

'I'll tell her,' Stella said.

'You can ring her later,' I said.

'But I've lost my phone.'

'I'll tell her,' Stella said again.

'Tell her I'll email, soon as I get there. I'll have another look for it.' He went thundering back upstairs to continue his search.

'He's lost his phone?' I said.

Stella shrugged and wouldn't meet my eyes. 'There's his bag.' She pointed to a scruffy rucksack. 'Passport and stuff in the pocket. Adam can take Seth straight away, but I want . . .' – and now she did look at me – 'I want *you* to stay with me for a bit.'

'Of *course*,' I said.

I worried for Adam since he wasn't strong, and called a taxi to save him driving. Seth was plugged into a music player, head nodding to some inaudible sounds.

When Adam and Seth had gone, Stella rolled herself a joint and we went into the sitting room. She kicked off her clogs and curled up with her legs beneath her, puffing and narrowing her eyes against the smoke. The grey-blonde hair that straggled either side of her face was faintly yellowed. There was a long pause while we waited to see who would speak first. Her lips made papery sounds as she smoked, and with every inhalation I expected her to say something, but in the end it was me who spoke first.

'Why did you say yes?'

She smiled mysteriously at me through the smoke. Another silence.

'Why didn't you tell me when Aunt Regina was ill?' I tried.

She blew out a long thoughtful plume of smoke. 'That was years ago! You're not still hanging onto that?' She grinned to herself. 'Why don't you *let it go*?' She said this last bit in an exaggerated Soul-Life voice, and then reverted to her normal one to tell me that Aunt Regina had asked her not to let me know. 'She didn't want to see you. I wonder why?' She began ripping at her fingernails with her teeth.

I looked down at the flattened tufts of the carpet. 'What does Dodie know about me?' I asked.

Stella spat out a fragment of nail. 'She doesn't remember you at all.' Her lips crinkled till they resembled the gills of a mushroom. 'All she knows is what I told her.'

'What?' I said, 'What did you tell her?'

'That you tried to steal her from me when I was ill, that's all. And that's the truth. And then, when I was better and you realized you couldn't keep her, you walked right out of her life.'

I swallowed hard. 'You've warped it,' I said, when I could speak evenly. 'I was only trying to help.'

'You were trying to steal her.'

Our eyes locked for a second. I was first to look away. The pattern on the carpet had faded. I remembered the roses as pink but now they'd gone to the grey and beige of food stains. I ran my finger round a furry petal.

'How often do you see her?' I said.

'Who?'

'*Dodie.* Do you know where she is?'

'She could be dead for all I know.'

'*Stella!*' I said, and she did flinch then and flush, and busy herself rolling a joint. Once she'd lit up and taken a puff, she tucked a hank of hair behind her ear.

'She'd run a mile rather than speak to you, anyway,' she said. 'Keep away from her. Keep Adam away from her.'

'But you're letting us take Seth.'

'He's a boy, a man, he'll be OK.'

'*She'd* be OK with us too.'

'Don't be stupid. She's grown up now. She's got her own life. What would she want with you?'

She made a wet sound. I couldn't believe it, but a single tear rolled down her cheek. When I made a move towards her she started, spikily, and I withdrew.

'Stell?' I said.

She stubbed out her fag and blinked slowly so that I could see the green veins on her eyelids. 'Why did I never show her any love?' she said. Her voice was tight, as if it was squeezing out past a massive obstacle. She hugged her knees against her chest and was quiet for so long I thought she'd stopped, but then she looked up and her eyes met mine for a wincing second. 'Sometimes when she was small, you know, four or five or six, I'd look at her sleeping and be so overwhelmed with something – love, was it? – that I was petrified.' She was speaking urgently now. 'And I'd think *tomorrow* I'll be loving, *tomorrow* I'll say nice things – but then, tomorrow, there she'd be, bright as a button – and I would be so cold. And sometimes I think I actually hated her. I don't know why.' She bit her thumb. 'It seemed so bloody easy for *you* to love her. And I hated *you* for that.'

I didn't dare reply and we sat in silence for a while. The phone rang and sent electric sparkles through me, but Stella didn't even look up.

'It was a bit easier with Seth,' she continued. Her face was pressed against her knees now and I could barely make out her words. 'I'm not saying I was a good mother but I could smile at him. You know? I went through the motions with him. Sort of. But it was *Dodie* I loved the best. *Why* couldn't I show it? What's *wrong* with me?' It came out as a plea, but I failed her. I had no idea what I could say that wouldn't make it worse.

She scrubbed her face childishly with her fists, her mood abruptly changed. 'It was fun at first at Wood End, wasn't it?' she said. 'Remember Derek?'

'Course I do.'

She struck a match and breathed in smoke before she spoke again. 'Shame Aunt Regina went off with Kathy.' She lay her head back and watched the smoke that matched the silvery grey of her eyes as it uncoiled towards the ceiling.

'He was so nice. I wish I'd kept in touch with him,' I said.

'*I* did,' she said, and gave me a lazy smile. 'Oh yes, he moved to not far from here.'

'Why didn't you tell me?'

She shrugged, held a breath of smoke in and let it slowly out. 'I guess I just wanted something for myself. You got Adam.'

'But you had the children!' I didn't mean my voice to go so shrill but really, it was outrageous that she should think like that. 'You had the kids, the house, you had Aunt Regina loving you right till the end!'

'Your choice,' she said.

'Adam was mine first anyway,' I said, hating the spite that had crept into my voice. 'And you didn't want him.'

'Too right,' she said. 'He's a sad deluded old pisspot and you're welcome.'

I found my note and hummed until I was calm enough to let this pass. When I opened my eyes again, she was regarding me with her head tilted to one side. The coolness of her scrutiny made me squirm.

'Do you have to do that stupid hum?' she said.

'Derek . . .' I said. 'You said he lived near here. Tell me about Derek.'

She made me wait till she'd inhaled and exhaled again. The whites of her eyes had gone pink. 'He used to visit now and then. He married someone, but she died. Then he died.' I was just absorbing this heartless summary of a life, when she added, casually, 'He was shocked that you tried to buy my baby, of course.' She crossed her legs and smoothed the red velvet tent between her knees.

Thought-stopping can be achieved almost as effectively by imaginary humming as by real humming if the imagination is strong enough and if the pitch is right. Some days, some weeks, some months I'd hummed aloud or silently almost all my waking hours.

'Derek blamed Bogart,' she went on. 'He thought you were a brainwashed little goose. Said he was disappointed in you. Thought there was more to you than that.' She left a moment for the sting of that to take effect, then: '*Bogart!*' she said. 'Did you ever think about that name? Aunt Regina thought he must really fancy himself, calling himself after Humphrey. I told her it wasn't that, it was about bogarting a joint and she thought I meant a leg of lamb!' She giggled, sounding almost like her old self, or like the self she could have been.

'Bog-Art,' she added, 'graffiti in a toilet. Suits him.' She started to really giggle in that infuriating stoned way – infuriating if you're not also stoned. The giggling brought a hectic colour to her cheeks. Her teeth were awfully stained with all the tea she drank and the constant smoke and there was one missing at the side.

'*Why* did you do it, Stell?' I said, when she'd stopped. '*Why* did you agree to have Seth?'

That started her off again. 'You should have seen your face when I said yes!'

I opened my mouth to speak and realized the smoke was getting to me; the air was thick with it. 'But surely that's not *why* you said yes,' I said, carefully.

'It was to start with. I couldn't resist it!'

The phone rang again but neither of us moved. I guessed that it was Adam back at the hotel. Or it could have been anyone. It could have been someone selling windows. Or maybe, Dodie, maybe it was you.

'I said yes for a joke,' she said. 'And then I thought, well, why not? You know, in my whole stupid life the only time I ever felt well, *normal*, was when I was pregnant. And it was a reason to keep on.'

'What do you mean?'

'Keep alive. *Obviously*.'

She began to gnaw her fingers and I looked away. Neither of us spoke for ages. And then she got up and went through to the dining room, sat down and began to do her puzzle. I followed her and watched her thin stained fingers busying about with the pieces.

'Are you pleased with your life?' she said suddenly. A gondolier was growing under her fingers, and an intricate pattern of ripples on water. 'What you've done with your precious life?' She turned in her chair and looked up at me. 'What *have* you done with it?' she said. 'What's your greatest achievement?'

I flinched as she hit my tenderest spot. I opened my mouth to ask, 'What's yours?' but she would say the children, and I couldn't bear that.

'Loving Adam,' I said, instead. 'Really *loving*.' It felt like a mean thing to say.

She widened her eyes at me. Water, silver, smoke, they saw right through me. 'Shall we have some soup?' she said. I was surprised; cooking was the last thing she ever did. 'It's a special day,' she said defensively. I followed her into the kitchen and watched the inexpert, almost childish way she cut slices from a carrot.

'I should really go,' I said. 'Adam will be wondering.'

She turned from her chopping. The knife was a small sharp one with a black handle. She stuck the end of it in her finger and a bead of blood rose and swelled and spilled.

'Stella, *don't*.'

'Did you really think I'd let Seth go, just like that?'

'He's gone,' I said.

'I still have his passport.'

'But Stella –'

'*I* have it.' She licked the blood off her finger and wiped it on her skirt.

'Is this one of your stupid tricks?'

She held the knife by its blade and offered me the handle. 'Remember your promise?' she said. I took the knife, only to protect her from the blade. 'Don't pretend you don't know what I mean.'

The Kitchen Devil glinted in my hand. And then the doorbell rang. Stella froze, and I did, too. We waited for a moment, holding our breath, and then there was a banging on the back door. Stella peered out of the window.

'It's Dodie,' she said. 'Go upstairs.'

'You said you didn't see her anymore –'

'Go! She'd run a mile if she knew it was you.'

'But –'

'Go.'

If I hadn't, she wouldn't have opened the door to you that day. I put the knife down on the chopping board and went upstairs. From the landing I strained my ears to try and catch the conversation, but it was no good. Stella's room smelt of patchouli and, lurking beneath it, something sour as cat's pee, though there never was any cat that I knew of. I went into the room that was yours: empty of any trace of you, but full of memories. I *would* go down and see you, I thought, I *would*, what could she do?

'Seth?' you called up the stairs. 'Seth?'

I froze until you went back into the dining room and the door clicked shut. I went down then. I was standing in the hall, ready to walk in, practising what to say. *I'm your Aunt Melanie*. Or Aunt Martha, would that be more honest? Or just Martha? Or, *I'm Stella's sister*. And then I heard the back door open. You'd only stayed two minutes. I ran upstairs again and caught a glimpse of you in the light from the kitchen door, dark hair and shrugging shoulders in the rain, one snatch of Stella's outstretched hand, and then you turned your back on her and went out through the gate.

I started down the stairs, to open the front door and catch you – but Stella was there.

'*Don't.*' She clutched my sleeve. 'Please, Mel, *please.* Leave her be.'

'But –'

'*Don't. Please.* I need to talk to you. *Please.*'

And so, Dodie, I let you go.

'Help me,' Stella said, and I flinched, heart plummeting, but she only meant help her finish the puzzle. We sat and put in the last few pieces. The sunny world it showed, full of light and vistas and reflections, mocked the dismal atmosphere in the room. Our breath condensed on the cold shine of the perfect table. Once the puzzle was finished, Stella stood and looked at it, nodding with satisfaction, as if something, at least, was complete.

'Come upstairs,' she said.

'What about the soup?' I was worrying about Adam, how on earth he would be getting on with Seth.

'I'm not hungry now,' Stella said.

We went back up the stairs and into her room. I sat down beside her on the rumpled Indian bedspread. It was the one that Adam had bought to replace the gruesome pink candlewick when we'd first moved in there. Her fingers trembled as she pulled a ragged thing out from under her pillow. It took me a moment to recognize Mother Clanger. Her tail had gone and she was squashed from so much squeezing, but her expression was still there. Stella sat with the toy against her neck, twizzling a finger in her hair. 'Remember when you made me this?'

She put Mother Clanger in my hand. The black button eyes looked up at me, filled with chips of reflected light. I could see the square cut-up shape of the window in them: so, so tiny.

Stella had curled her arms round her knees. 'When you made me that you were my saviour and my sister.'

'*Saviour?*'

'Remember the seances and everything after Mum?'

'You used to see her.'

'It was only pretend.'

'Was it?' I stared at her until she looked down.

'Not sure now,' she admitted. 'Anyway, you looked after me.'

'No I didn't.'

'Did.'

'Didn't.'

'Did.'

'Didn't.'

We smiled at each other, a real smile for once, at the echo of our childish squabbling.

'But . . . remember what you promised when I was in hospital?' she said. Mother Clanger's eyes were bright and blank. 'When you made me that –' she nodded at the toy. 'It was the kindest thing ever. I think it was the kindest thing anyone ever did for me in my life.'

'No,' I said. 'Aunt Regina was always kind. *Much* kinder than me.'

'But it came naturally to her, so it was different.'

I stared.

'Anyway, when I told you I wanted to die, you were maybe right to say no – then. I was young. I could have been wrong. But I wasn't wrong, Mel; I've never wanted anything more than to die. Bringing up the children – it was like something I had to do before I went. And having Seth – well, maybe I said yes to put off the moment. Maybe that was the real reason. But now Dodie's all grown up with her own life. You're taking Seth away. And there's not even Aunt Regina or Derek to be upset.'

My mouth had gone dry. 'But there's *me*,' I said. 'There's your kids.'

She let this go.

'Stella, you've still got years ahead, you could . . .' I tried to think of things that she could do, but she smiled and shook her head.

'Don't bother, Mel. You want Seth's passport; you keep your promise.'

'No.'

'You'll never get him out of the country without it.'

'I don't care that much.'

'But Adam does.' She paused. 'You will look after Seth, won't you?'

'Of course I will.'

Stella was perfectly composed; she was perfectly clear and determined, Dodie; it's important you believe that. She opened a drawer, took out a pair of pop socks and rolled them onto her feet and up her shins. 'If you ever had any love for me, you'll keep your promise.' She held my eyes until I had to look away. I could see the two of us in the dressing table mirror, my hair cropped, hers long; my face wide, hers narrow; her eyes, huge and grey, mine eyes small and blue; every feature different but there was still something the same about us, I saw for the first time ever; something that showed that we were sisters.

'If you want to kill yourself, why do you need me?' I asked. My voice was husky and I cleared my throat. 'Why don't you just get on and do it?'

'Because I don't want to be alone and you're my only person.'

A bird thudded against the window and Stella and I both let out a shriek. I got up, opened the window, and leaned out to see a blackbird flapping about on its side on the grass. 'I think it's broken its wing,' I said. But then it righted itself, hopped about and flew up into the laburnum, swaddled in its puffed-up feathers.

'What if it doesn't work?' she said. 'I'm scared of that, Mel. Of hanging there. I do want it to be quick. I need you to make sure it's quick.'

I sat down again. The mattress was trembling.

'If I helped you,' I said, and my voice came scraping out, 'then it might look like murder. I might end up in jail.' I stared at her face to try and read whether this was her intention, but she was grave and organized and I don't believe that was her plan.

'We can clean all the door handles and everything you've touched so there are no fingerprints,' she said. From the way she spoke it was obvious she had this all planned out to the last detail. 'And scrub the teacups. Then you can wear rubber gloves and take them with you. My fingerprints will be all over everything. I'll write a note, all Bony Fido.' The corners of her mouth went up, acknowledging the joke – it was what Derek had called one of Aunt Regina's pugs. 'They'll believe it, with my history of depression and that. You wait till you know it's worked and then you can take Seth's passport – I'll tell you where it is just before – and then you just go. You can be out of the country before I'm found.'

We sat for a moment and then I was moving close to her and putting my arms around her. She was brittle and thin and smelled of shampoo and the old musky, incense-scented velvet. Even though we were two middle-aged women, she was still my little sister and I held her tight.

'Do you really want it?' I said.

'It's *all* I want. It's time.'

We sat and rocked for a while.

'I would love to have seen Dodie.' I couldn't help saying that, but she pulled out of my arms and stood up. I could see her struggling for a moment, emotions flocking across her face, and then she caught sight of herself in the mirror, laughed and did a clumsy twirl. 'I've been saving this dress for years.' She smoothed the velvet against her thighs. 'I wore it to your wedding, remember?'

I nodded.

'It's lasted very well,' she said. 'Only a little moth hole here and there.'

She sent me down to begin the task of cleaning the banister, the door handles, the cups, and came down with her hair brushed, reeking of fresh patchouli. I wore her yellow rubber gloves and she worked with bare hands. All the time we were cleaning, in such a strange companionable silence, I didn't think that it would really happen. I didn't think I could really stand by and let her do it.

She wrote a note on the paper bag she planned to put over her head so I didn't have to see her dead or dying face.

I was thinking I'd wait till she told me where Seth's passport was and then stop her. She had a rope tied ready in a knot. How did she know what kind of knot to tie? It was brand new blue polypropylene. Where did she get it? How long had she had it? I finished cleaning the bathroom and when I came out she was on the landing with the rope around her neck.

'Now,' she said. She was trembling so hard her teeth were chattering.

'No.' I backed away from her intensity. A rank animal smell was coming through the patchouli.

'Please. You're the only person I can ask. You don't have to do a thing. Please just make sure I've gone before you leave.' She squeezed my hands; hers were shaking and cold, yet wet with sweat. 'Be brave Mel,' she said, 'it's what I want.' She got up on to the banister, balanced herself against the wall and put the bag over her head. I watched how her toes bent to cling onto the wood, an instinctive reaction as her body fought to save itself. I grabbed hold of her ankle but she kicked back with such a force I was knocked to the floor.

'In my sock,' were the last words she said, and then she dropped with a great creak of wood and a scream from her mouth or my own and a brutal scrunching crack. I crouched on the landing floor with my hands over my eyes and my fingers over my ears. I stayed there for minutes, I don't know how many. I could hear water running and a faint squeak from the rope but nothing else. I stood up and walked down the stairs. My shoulder was numb where she'd kicked me. The watery sound was urine. I still had the rubber gloves on and they were full of sweat. I reached up. She'd not told a lie. The passport and Seth's birth certificate were tucked into one of her pop socks and they were warm and wet. It took me a few goes to have the nerve to hold her swinging body still and take them out.

It had definitely worked.

I went out of the back door still in the rubber gloves and got into the car and drove away. Someone might have seen me, I don't know. I drove all over the place and stopped by the park. I went into the Ladies' and was sick and then I went back to the hotel.

Adam was really too ill to move, but for once I put my own needs first. I moved our seats onto the next flight to Kennedy airport and off we went. At the airport I was terrified each time I saw a policeman and, of course, due to the current state of security, it was swarming with them. I was sick in the airport Ladies', and again on the plane. I was too shocked to cry. I couldn't look after Adam the way I liked to. Seth stayed plugged into his electronic world and Adam in his trance of exhausted pain.

†

Seth wasn't nursed into Soul-Life as you were, Dodie. There was no parlour, no gentle introduction – and no warning about what he was about to be plunged into. Neither Adam nor I were in a state to talk to him on the flight or on arrival. I withdrew. I could think of nothing but Stella. I learned, later, that Seth had become distressed on arrival at Soul-Life and it had been necessary to medicate him to prevent harm to himself or others. I should have stayed with him: maybe then he'd have been all right. But once we were back I was almost paralyzed. I couldn't speak for days, not even to Adam. I couldn't even hum. Or cry. And the pain in my chest came clamping back as if someone was taking my heart in their fist and squeezing.

And in the time that I was incapacitated, Hannah took Seth over – and it was she who nursed Adam, too. If it couldn't be me, he would have no one else. For a time, I didn't care, but as soon as my strength began to return I went back to Adam's room, our room, to find Hannah there.

You should have seen her smile. I wouldn't rise to her. I said nothing. Adam was lying back against the pillows, fidgety and troubled.

'I want to see my son,' he said. 'Bring Seth to me.'

'I've explained to Adam that he has a cold,' Hannah said. 'He's infectious.'

Adam sighed, his old hands fretting each other. 'Martha?'

'She's right,' I said, though I wouldn't look at her. 'We can't have you catching a cold, can we?'

He seemed to accept this, though he wasn't happy. And he said to me, his voice petulant, '*Hannah's* been keeping me abreast of Soul-Life business. She tells me there are problems.'

Hannah smirked over her shoulder at me as she left the room. I took a deep breath and gritted my teeth. Yes, the IRS were demanding access to the accounts; and yes, some families had started actions to reclaim their children, but I'd been deliberately keeping all this from Adam in what must surely be his last days. What was the sense of agitating him now? I didn't want him going to his death thinking Soul-Life was in collapse.

'It's nothing,' I said. 'Just details. Obadiah's dealing with everything.' I took his hand and soothed it in my own. 'Nothing for you to worry about. Sleep now, or would you like some tea?'

'Hannah is bringing me tea.'

He began to mumble the story I hated, about how she was the first of his followers and how very faithful she had always been to him. I couldn't stand to hear it and thought-hummed to try and block his words.

She came in with mugs on a tray, two mugs only – and I don't think the second one was meant for me. My impulse was to get out of there and scream but I only smiled at her and said, 'That's very kind, Hannah, thank you. Our Father is very tired; you can leave us now.'

She kept her face quite even but I saw the way her eyes flared and her lips tightened against her snaggled teeth.

'Can we continue our conversation tomorrow?' she asked Adam, and he nodded and smiled. She grasped her thumb, lowered her eyes, and left us.

'Hannah shouldn't worry you,' I said.

'*You* should not keep things from me.'

I scalded my tongue on the hot tea. It was the sedative blend we usually give the novices, excellent for smoothing objections from the mind. Drink too much and you lose all track. It gives a lovely blankness – well, you know that, Dodie. I helped Adam drink his and then he closed his eyes. He looked so done in, so old and finished that my irritation flowed away. I put my head against his chest and he stroked my hair.

'Stella . . .' I began.

He shushed me. 'She's free,' he said, 'she is at one with the Universal Soul, we should rejoice.' But I couldn't think of anything but the awful crunch and the drip, drip, drip, of urine down her leg. I pushed my face against him and, while he smoothed my hair, I wept.

†

After the journey back home, Adam had expressed disappointment at how ordinary Seth was, how lacking in special spirituality. What could I say? Adam was tired and in pain and I think it would have been hard for him to be delighted by any mortal at that point. Did he expect light to be flooding from his son's head, or prophesies spilling from his tongue? Seth *is* just an ordinary boy; very charming I think, very handsome. But he is only flesh and blood.

It was Hannah's decision that Seth and Adam should be kept apart until Seth had been rushed through the Process, after which he could be returned, triumphantly transformed, and revealed to all the Brethren as the son of Adam.

But I wouldn't let her have it all her own way. And one day I pulled myself far enough out of my torpor to go and find Seth, to see for myself how he was faring. I waited till I knew Hannah was occupied, and then I intercepted him on his way out of the dining room after the meal he thought was breakfast.

(Do you realize, Dodie, how we play with time during the Process, so that you might be eating breakfast at bedtime and going for a brief 'night's' sleep – perhaps half an hour – at noon? Warping time and confusing biorhythms is a powerful method of disorientation, and it does no physical harm. It's necessary to break down the personality before building it up again: the drugs and the repetitive meditations, the scant diet, the interruption of normal patterns of behaviour – all part of the Process. On you, of course, it didn't work. On nine people out of ten, it's successful, but, as we say, for every nine sheep there is a goat.)

I took Seth into a side room to be alone with him. I can't describe to you how deeply strange it was for me to be addressing this version of Adam – younger than I'd ever known him. On the journey home I'd been too much in shock to really take him in. He's so like Adam physically but with the trace and flutter of Stella about him too. At first I felt almost shy in his presence, but quickly I became concerned. His pupils were like pinpricks and he was slurring his words – the dosage of narcotic must have been too high – or perhaps it was the combination of drugs; I don't know what concoction Hannah was giving him.

I'd thought I might trump Hannah by sneaking Seth in to see Adam, before she could. *I* wanted to be the one to cause a smile to spread like sunrise over Adam's face. And *I* wanted to be the one to tell Seth that he was Adam's son. *I* wanted to be the one to present him, transformed. He was my nephew, after all, not Hannah's. But once I'd seen him, it was obvious that he couldn't be taken to Adam in that state.

I poured his tea, and watched how he held the cup between his elegant, long-fingered hands – the nails bitten to their beds, just like Stella's – and how the surface of the liquid shivered with the tremble that was going through him.

'How are you, Seth?' I asked.

'Not great,' he said.

'What's wrong?'

'Dunno.' He was swaying a bit, even seated, thoroughly disorientated. Too disorientated.

'Are you enjoying the meditations?'

He nodded and sniffed. The flanges of his nostrils quivered. I wanted to hold him. A tear rolled down his cheek, a huge shiny tear that transfixed me as it crawled through the fuzziness on his jaw and disappeared under his chin. I had to rub away the sensation on my own skin.

'The meditations?' I prompted him. 'Do you have any questions? You can ask me anything.'

'Did Mum want me sent *here*?' he said. 'Did she know what it would be like?' He was having trouble making the words, and then I saw him look at the wall behind me, his eyes flickering back and forth. His lips stretched into a half smile.

'What?' I said, and turned to see what he was focusing on, but there was nothing. When I turned back, I saw that he'd gone shuddery and grey.

'She's there,' he said, extending a finger.

'Who?'

'Mum. Stella.'

I froze and then all the surface of my skin began to creep. It was all I could do not to bolt out of that room and leave him with his vision of Stella. He kept looking at the wall, the smile playing on his lips. His eyes looked gone-out.

It's a hallucination, I told myself. *Stella is not there, she is not there.*

'She's dead,' he said. 'Is she really dead?'

It seemed to me then that I could feel Stella standing behind me, the cold shape of her shadowing my own shape and causing me to shrink, the blood in my veins to turn to ice. I had to tell him yes. How could I lie to him with her shadow on me? And so I said yes and that's when he had a seizure of some sort, or panic attack, I don't know. He stumbled to his feet and began waving his arms and shouting and then he fell, twitching, to the floor. Maybe it was the drugs – they don't suit everyone – or maybe the short rations, maybe the way he'd been allowed very little sleep at all – Hannah's doing, not mine. I would have been kinder, if I'd stayed in control. *I* wouldn't have tried to rush him through.

I ran out into the corridor for help, and there was Hannah – looking for us, no doubt. But I was glad she was there. And once again I let her take him over. I didn't want to be with him if he could make Stella come. Stella saw our mother after death, and now he saw Stella. And what if he saw, if she was able to tell him, how it had occurred? It wasn't my fault, Dodie, I've told you how it happened with Stella, and I swear on my life that every word is true. But Stella after death? She might say anything.

Seth wasn't safe. Even Hannah agreed that we couldn't continue the Process with him, nor allow him to mix with the other Brethren any longer. Perhaps he was not quite stable anyway? As Stella's son that wouldn't be surprising. Or perhaps it was only the effect of the Process so far, of rushing him. To sabotage a personality takes time and patience. But, anyway, it had to stop. And it had to be broken to Adam that Seth was not, could not be, the next Messiah. Neither Hannah nor I could decide how best to do this. We always found a way to distract or stall him when he asked to see Seth – who was in a peace-pod – while we decided how to go on.

And then, one day as I was sitting by Adam's bed, Hannah came bursting in, without even a knock on the door. Her face was flushed with self-importance.

'Adam,' she said, disregarding me.

I don't care what was happening, I don't care how ill he was, she should still have called him Our Father; she should still have paused to grasp her thumb.

'Hannah?' he said.

'I have such news.' She darted a look at me.

I thought she was going to tell him about Seth and I was puzzled by her excitement.

'Go on then,' I said.

'We've had to put Seth in a peace-pod.'

'Martha?' Adam looked to me for confirmation.

'I'm sorry,' was all that I could say.

Adam struggled to sit up, his mouth falling open.

'He's not well,' I said, gently pushing him back against the pillows. 'He's not mentally strong enough, Adam. We've had to stop the Process.'

'But I have good news too!' Hannah crowed, leaning forward, getting between us so that her beaming face was pressed almost into his. 'You have a grandson!'

'*What?*' I said.

'Yes! I was talking to Seth this morning about his family and he told me that your daughter' – emphasising the *your*, of course, to exclude me – 'has a baby son! Stella had made him promise to never mention the child, but *I* got it out of him.'

I felt the tremor of surprise in Adam's hand.

I was thrown into confusion. Joy, surprise – and fury that it was Hannah who'd brought this news. It should have been me. I should have spent less time beside Adam and more time with Seth, talking to him, getting this confidence out of him. This was *my* family, not Hannah's.

And why hadn't Stella told me she had a grandchild? Did she think she couldn't trust me? What did she think I'd do?

Adam closed his eyes, and we waited and watched and held our breaths. You could actually see the shifting flicker of expressions on his face as he switched his allegiance and his hopes from his son to his grandson. He opened his eyes at last and there was a new bright glaze in them. 'I am sorry for my son,' he said. 'But after all, he is Stella's son. He must be well cared for. And we must bring the infant here. This is where he belongs.' He let go of my hand and hauled himself up in the bed. 'I must pray for guidance. I must . . .' But he was too breathless to continue.

'What do we know about the child?' I asked.

'He's called Jake,' Hannah said. 'He's about fifteen months old.'

'*Jacob*,' Adam said, his face relaxing as he exhaled. 'Praise the Lord. *Jacob*.'

'I don't understand why Stella didn't tell me – tell us,' I said. But, of course, I did understand. This was just what she didn't want. She didn't want Adam to get his hands on the child. I thought it odd that she was prepared to give him Seth, yet keep his daughter and his grandson from him. But it turns out that she was wise in this. She was wiser than me.

'Leave me,' Adam said. His voice was faint. 'I must think, I must pray.'

Smiling significantly, Hannah went out.

'Leave me,' Adam repeated.

'But I will pray with you,' I said, 'we'll pray for guidance together.'

He closed his eyes. A small mauve vein throbbed at his temple. He sighed. 'Take me outside,' he said. I didn't think he was well enough to move, but still, I helped him dress and held his arm as we walked a step at a time, outside to the back of the building. There's a gate you can unlock there, that leads you to the edge of a wood where there are hundreds of crows' nests in the trees. It was a blazing October day, and my eyes streamed in the brightness. I settled Adam on a folding chair with a blanket around him and another over his knees. The sun shone through the thin strands of his hair and I could see the greasy shine of his scalp, the capillaries in his cheeks, the pores in the skin behind the sparse straggles of his beard. His eyes were on me and I don't like to think about what *he* saw in such remorseless illumination. The scarlet and yellow leaves at his feet were scattered with black feathers, streaks of white and squirrel bones where the birds had recently feasted.

'Go now,' he said, and closed his eyes. I stood for a few moments, watching, but I could feel him waiting for me to leave, and I obeyed.

I decided that while I was waiting for him, I would go and see Seth for myself, see what he would tell me. I was on my way to him when I was intercepted by Hannah.

'Where's Adam?' she asked, sharply.

'*Our Father* is in contemplation,' I said.

'We must talk, Martha.' Hannah opened the door on to an empty meditation room and more or less shoved me through it. Inside, we stood looking at each other. Though nearing sixty, she was still pretty – not conventionally, with her pointed nose and snaggly teeth, but there was something about her, about the way the lines worked on her cheeks and around her eyes, and she was slim and straight in her robe. I think vital is the word. But there was such slyness there too, such smugness. I wanted to spit in her eye.

'I have sent for Adam's daughter and his grandchild,' she said.

'No.'

'I got Seth to write, inviting her to come.'

'*No.*'

In truth, I hadn't made up my mind about this matter till that moment. But Stella didn't want it. And if it was to be done, *I* should have been consulted first. I clenched my teeth to dam the surge of anger.

'It is too late; the letter has gone. It is in God's hands now,' Hannah said, with a smile that managed to be both pious and triumphant.

'Very well.'

I got to Adam before she could. He was still praying, a dirty feather clutched between his fingers, a leaf lodged in his hair. I stood waiting till he looked at me and indicated his readiness to move. I helped him up and he leant on me as we went back inside, where he consented to let me undress him and put him back to bed.

'Well?' I said, keeping my voice as patient as I could. 'Did Jesus speak?'

'My Grandson, Jacob, is the saviour,' he murmured, 'and we must send for him. The sign is in the name.'

In the rustle of the sheets I clearly heard Stella telling me *no*. Telling me to stop this happening. But how could I stop it now? When I opened my eyes Adam was gazing at me intently and I smoothed out my frown. His lower lids had begun to sag away from his eyes, giving him a bloodhound look.

'Already done,' I said.

'My love,' he said. I sat and stroked his hand, letting my finger slide into the place that was his thumb, such a soft declivity, sweet to touch and warm and live and throbbing with a secret pulse.

I had to face the truth then. He was dying. He was an old, deluded animal, dragging himself through his last few weeks or even days. I had to be practical; I had to plan. I had to think of myself and of the future. I had to think of Seth and of you, Dodie; and now I had to think of Jake. When Adam went, what then? What would be left for me? Once he was gone, I would be leaving Soul-Life; that much at least was clear.

I would find a doctor and get myself checked over – the breathlessness and the pains in my chest were worrying me, but, of course, even to think this within Soul-Life was blasphemy. I decided I'd buy you a house to make up for the loss of Lexicon Avenue – the profit from which had of course, been absorbed into the Soul-Life bank. I did allow myself to dream that one day we might be a family and live together. All I ever really wanted was a family.

Obadiah had taught me enough about the internet and about the financial side of things for me to be able to divert money into a fund of my own – I'd started it back when Adam first became ill. Why shouldn't I be recompensed? I'd worked all my life for Soul-Life and now my love, and that life, was dying. What was I to do?

†

We awaited your arrival. Adam was nervous, agitated, anxious to see his grandson, and so, of course, was I. No one could settle while we waited for you to make your decision and then your journey. I was determined it should be me who would welcome you, not Hannah. At last the day arrived. My heart had been fluttering in my chest since early in the morning, but it was afternoon, and I was sitting with Adam, reading from the Bible, when Hannah charged in.

'She's at the gate,' she said. 'But she hasn't brought the child.'

'No child?' Adam struggled to a sitting position. The stress brought on the pain in my own chest but I would let nothing stop me. I hardly cared about Jake just then, I so much wanted to see you. Would you remember me? You were such a little dot when I gave you back to Stella. But still, I hoped you might look into my face and remember something, perhaps just the sensation of being cared for and loved.

I got up and dropped the Bible. 'I'll go,' I said.

'What shall we do?' Hannah said. 'Adam, what shall we do?'

'Wait. We must pray.'

'But she's here!' I said. 'I must go.'

'Wait.' He gestured to each of us to kneel as he mumbled a prayer.

I couldn't pray; my mind was spinning. You were waiting at the gate. What if you went away? From between my lashes I looked at Hannah to see that she wasn't praying either, but watching me.

'Martha, you go and greet Dorcas,' Adam said, and I couldn't prevent a little dart of victory towards Hannah. 'All is not lost. We must persuade her to bring the child.' He closed his eyes again and frowned. It was as if he was having trouble tuning into a channel. 'You must not tell her you are Stella's sister,' he said.

'But –'

'Think what Stella might have told her about you and me!' He opened his eyes and smiled. 'Telling her might scare her away and then I'll never see my grandson. Welcome her in the parlour.'

'And put sleeping drops in her tea,' Hannah said.

'But she'll be tired anyway,' I argued.

'It will ensure docility,' Adam said.

The parlour was where we often greeted visitors. Adam didn't like the unchosen within Soul-Life itself. The parlour was bugged, all conversations recorded, because there were those who threatened our existence. And if a person seemed to be a dangerous influence; then the parlour was as far in as they got.

'I'd better go,' I said. 'The poor girl is waiting.'

'You must keep her here and remember, you are nothing to her, just Martha,' Adam reminded me as I hurried off. My brain felt as if it was bulging against my skull, and my heart was pounding. I felt so dizzy I had to stop and lean on the wall to steady my breath before I came out to greet you. And there you were. You were fidgeting outside the gate and I could barely breathe in your proximity when I came close: your hair so dark and glossy and gloriously thick like Adam's once was; your eyes that intense bottle-glass blue; the fresh rosiness of your skin and the shape of your face, so much like Stella's. So familiar to me and yet so much yourself.

Almost the first words you said: 'I'm bursting for the loo,' and when you said that, so natural, so English, so like yourself, I could have swooned with love. To sit with you in the parlour; to breathe you in; to watch the expressions on your face, to touch you – I can't tell you what joy these simple things gave me. I had to fight against the impulse to tell you who I was; to tell you that for nearly three years I brought you up as if you were my own.

Of course you wanted, and expected, to see Seth – and right away. What were we to do? There was no question of letting you see him then. But if we hadn't at least allowed you to speak to him on the phone, you might have left, or gone to the police perhaps. So Hannah was with Seth each time you spoke, helping him with his responses. In truth, I think she had him drugged so much he hardly knew where he was or what he was saying.

Over those first few days it was agony for me, to see you disappointed over and over again, and to have to be the one to disappoint you. But you see, Dodie, there was no other way to ensure we could get Jake – and the thought of Jake was the only thread of hope keeping Adam alive. And I do admit that I was longing to see him too: Adam's grandson, my great-nephew, my blood.

But each time you weren't allowed to see Seth, it got harder to persuade you to stay. You *were* more goat than sheep. The idea, at first, was to smooth you through the Process so that you brought Jake to Soul-Life of your own free will. If you had been more malleable, more persuadable, we might have revealed that Adam was your true father; that Jake must come and be the saviour – but you never went far enough below the surface to be safe. You proved yourself truly Stella's daughter in *that* way. A bad influence on the other Brethren, a dissenting voice.

†

From the day of your arrival, any pretence of politeness between Hannah and me was shattered, except in front of others. Your presence broke the surface of the water like a newly fallen branch we must all flow round. Adam lay in wait of news of you, or tuned in when you were in the truth-pod – the room with the ripped sofa, wired for him to listen in. When Rod phoned, Hannah spoke to him, or I did. He rang more often than we told you, for your own peace of mind. I won his trust in our conversations and he told me all about your troubles.

'You're too smothering,' I told you, after Rod had confided that to me. Your face crumpled and something inside *me* buckled too. *Smothering.* Is that how I'd loved *you* as a child? Is it possible to exceed the decent limits of love? Has that been my mistake with Adam; to have loved him no matter what? Has my whole life been a mistake?

I would have spent more time with you but I wasn't well; the pesky cramping in my chest sent me away from you from time to time. And I wanted to be with Adam. Always, I was torn. I was sitting beside Adam as he slept, pondering these questions, when Hannah came into the room. She'd taken to walking in, no knock even, the concept of privacy forgotten.

'Shhh,' I said, 'he's sleeping.'

'No,' Adam said, opening his eyes.

'She's sabotaging the plan,' Hannah said.

'I am not.'

'Telling her she can go. Telling her not to bring Jacob here.'

'No,' I said, 'you are too simplistic. Have you never heard of reverse psychology?'

Hannah frowned from Adam to me.

'She's clever,' he said, meaning me, I think.

'I tell her she can go – and then she stays. I tell her she needs time away from the baby – then she wants all the more to be with him,' I said.

Hannah sat on the other side of the bed; Adam lay between us, his face turning from one to the other, a beat behind the rhythm of our conversation. Who did she think she was, sitting on *our* bed like that?

'If he comes –'

'When,' chipped in Hannah.

'What is the plan?' I pressed on.

'I'll bless little Jacob,' Adam said. 'Our Lamb of God. I'll baptize him. He will be the Saviour of Soul-Life.'

'You won't be able to *keep* him here,' I said. 'Not against Dodie's will.'

'No?' Hannah said. I caught the tip of her index finger surreptitiously stroking Adam's arm.

'And anyway,' I said, 'how would we get him here? If she goes home to fetch him, she'll never come back. I have to battle for every moment that she stays.'

'Yes,' Hannah said. 'But I've been talking to Rod again. I told him Dodie might not make it back in time for him to go on his trip and he was furious.' She smiled, and leant in to Adam as if to exclude me from the conversation. 'How about we offer to pay for his flight to bring Jacob here before he goes off?'

Adam blinked, smiled. 'Yes, my love,' he said.

My love. He didn't know which of us was which any more. His vision foggy; his mind foggy. My breath was coming fast, that rising pressure in my chest again.

'Are you not well?' Hannah said. 'Look at her colour, Adam, she needs to rest.'

'Yes,' I said, 'I'll rest here.' And in front of her I slipped off my robe and climbed into bed next to Adam and I knew that wasn't what she'd meant; I saw the darkening of her face. Adam shifted. He was in pain of course, and so much worse than mine. I held my breath, praying that he wouldn't tell me to get out in front of her, but he didn't and I laid my head against his shoulder and closed my eyes till I heard the door click shut.

'Jesus wants a sacrifice,' Adam said, waking me some time later from my doze. 'A Festival of the Lamb.'

I hauled myself up to look at his tired face. He lifted the lids of his eyes, so watery now, as if he was on the edge of weeping all the time. He winced as I shifted.

'You're not well enough,' I said gently.

'Jesus has spoken unto me,' he wheezed.

I laid my hand across his forehead, like a mother. I stroked his cheek. 'I really don't think you're up to it, my love.'

'One more lamb,' he said. 'Ask Isaac to procure a lamb.'

I dreaded the Festival of the Lamb. I had always thought it a cruel and ludicrous pantomime – those thoughts, suppressed for so long, sprung up toughly now. I never could bear to watch Adam slice the razor edge of the knife through the wool and skin. I could never bear that he could bear to do it.

'Perhaps. But you're hardly well enough to stand,' I pointed out.

'The Lord will provide me with the strength,' he said. The thought of the festival already seemed to have energized him. His breathing changed and he began to fumble at my breasts. 'Soft,' he said, 'so soft.' He took my hand and pushed it down under the quilt.

'Hey,' I said.

'Please,' he said, and rolled his eyes up. We had not made love for such an age I didn't know if either of us was even capable. But by the time I was lying back down beside him, the impulse had gone. He wept a little and we lay together skin on skin and slept.

†

Obadiah rarely came to our room. It had been months since Adam had even pretended to have anything to do with the mechanics of running Soul-Life – and in fact it had always been Obadiah's operation in the financial sense. He had a genius for making money – or once he had. Whether it was age that was catching up with him or whether it had always been inevitable that the IRS would catch up with us, I don't know. He said the global economy had gone into meltdown and whether that was truth or excuse, I neither know nor care.

I'd just left you, Dodie, after one of our conversations, and was hurrying back to Adam, worried by your attitude, wanting to talk to Adam, praying that Hannah wouldn't be with him, when I met Obadiah in the corridor, outside the door to our room.

He was walking with his characteristic deep stoop – the result of years bent over paperwork and in front of a computer screen.

'Oh hello, Martha.' He smiled when he saw me.

'I imagine Adam's asleep,' I said.

'Can you check?' Obadiah said. 'He needs to know –'

'No,' I said. 'He doesn't need to know anything.'

'But –'

'*Listen*. He hasn't got long, Obadiah, please don't upset him.'

'But Hannah said –'

'Hannah said what?'

He shrank into himself, all the grey hair and whiskers and long trailing eyebrows, you could hardly see his features any more. I'd known him as a youngish man, or a tall and virile guy at least, and now look. It made me angry to see time and age so cruelly demonstrated.

'Hannah doesn't understand how ill he is,' I said. 'Not even in his right mind half the time. What's the point of making him think it's all going to collapse? He'll just die bitterly.'

The whiskers stirred as his lips pursed. 'Sure,' he said, after a moment. 'Maybe I'll just put my head round and say hi.'

'Yes,' I said. 'Thanks. Wait there.'

I went into the room. Adam was alone and asleep. The Bible lay on his chest, his finger trapped between its pages. I let Obadiah see.

'Later?' I said. I closed the door on Adam and we stood outside the door, suddenly awkward.

Obadiah took my hand in his.

'What will you do?' he asked.

I looked at him, puzzled, though I knew what he meant.

'Once Adam dies?' he said.

Although I am over fifty, I still feel like a child with Obadiah. Older than Adam even, he's the oldest member of Soul-Life. I looked at the floor. The circumstances had never been so openly acknowledged. The sense that things were spinning out of control, that we were hurtling towards dissolution. It struck me for a horrible instant, that maybe Hannah had been right; Adam should have been told the entire state of things, to have had the chance, while still capable of deciding, how the end should come. But it was too late now.

'When he's gone, I'll go too,' I said.

He grabbed my hand and squeezed. 'Not *you*, Martha. You're too young.'

'No, not *that*,' I said. '*Leave*. Leave Soul-Life behind.'

Those words hung in the air between us, simple but momentous, and tears flooded down our cheeks. We stood and cried, staring at each other aghast, as the truth presented itself, cruel and stark and unavoidable.

†

The following day Obadiah sought me out to give me an envelope, which he made me promise not to open until after. After *what*, there was no need for him to say. I couldn't wait, though, and as soon as I was alone I opened it. It took me a few moments to understand that the document I was looking at represented the transfer of the ownership of a house in Florida from Obadiah to me. Ten years ago, it seemed, he'd bought it for himself. *Ten years ago.* A house by the ocean.

And then I understood that I'd not been fooling Obadiah with my innocent questions about how the banking system worked. He'd actually been helping me in my embezzlement of Soul-Life funds, and had been doing the same himself. How many others of us had been doing that?

A house, though. My own house. I went straight to the admin block where Obadiah was gazing at a screen, the mouse scrolling over columns, aimlessly, it seemed to me.

'I opened it,' I said, 'and thank you.'

His eyes didn't leave the screen, though the cursor jerked wildly among the columns.

'But why don't *you* keep it and go there yourself?'

'At my age?' he said, and smiled and shrugged his bent old shoulders. 'You should go soon,' he added. 'It's only a matter of time till the law gets in. And that'll be the end. We are preparing for the end.'

'Come with me then,' I said.

'Years ago, if you'd said that. . .' His eyes lingered for a moment on my face, slid down my body and I shivered as if stroked by a feather. I looked down at the floor, blood throbbing in my face. It had never occurred to me that Obadiah had thought of me like that.

'But *still*, come,' I said. 'I'll look after you.'

'It's too late,' he repeated, with a sad and puckered smile.

†

In a coincidence, which confirmed for Adam that the Lord's will was being done, Rod and Jake arrived at Soul-Life during the Festival of the Lamb. I was busy all day helping Adam and didn't know till later that they were there. It was the first occasion that Adam had been out of bed for days, and I had to help him walk onto the platform. It was amazing that he found the strength to speak, to slaughter the lamb, to bless the Brethren with the blood. You looked so pale and shaken, Dodie, as he smeared you with the blood. I longed to take you aside and reassure you that everything would be all right, but it was Adam who needed me most then. After the ceremony he was in a state of near collapse. I took him back to our room and helped him from his robes. I washed his hands and feet and got him settled in his bed. I lay beside him, listening to the rasping of his breath.

Every atom of energy in him had been spent, but Hannah had told him that Jake had arrived and he was happy, he murmured, and Jesus was happy; a lamb for a lamb.

'The sacrifice,' he said, 'has brought Jacob to the fold.' He struggled to find the breath to speak and I was sure he'd die that night. Though I wanted to come and find you, I couldn't leave him to die alone. Couldn't bear to leave a vacancy for Hannah to fill. All night I lay and listened to the rattling of his breath; it sounded far away, like marbles rolling down pipes deep under the ground. I got up only to use the bathroom, to moisten his lips with water, to drink water myself.

Next morning his will once more overcame the weakness of his flesh and once more he struggled back. He indicated that he wished to sit up and I helped him. I freshened him with a flannel, cut up a melon so he could suck the sweet flesh. Now that he was awake, I thought I'd leave him for a short time and come and find you and Rod and Jake. I wanted to be the one to bring Jake to Adam, to see the joy in his face, a final gift for him from me this time; not from Hannah.

But before I'd even left the room, Hannah came in with Jake in her arms. The fury that struck me was like a bolt of lightning, fusing me to the floor and it was a full minute before I was able to think, to speak, to act.

'Adam,' she said. 'Your grandson.' She spoke with such pride you'd think she'd personally conjured him into existence. You should have seen the gloating expression on her face.

I looked away. My teeth ground together so hard I felt a corner give, a speck of sharpness on my tongue. I picked it off and pressed it between my fingers, hard and jagged. *Let it go*, I thought, *let it go*, and I hummed silently until I regained control enough to turn and look at Jake.

What a bonny child he is, dark and rosy, and with your blue eyes, wide and round with wonder. Adam was holding out his weak and stringy arms.

'Come to me,' Adam said and muttered something else. *Suffer little children*, I think. But Jake was too big, too real and live and kicking for Adam's arms. And the weight of the child on his abdomen was excruciating, you could see. I quickly snatched Jake up.

'Say hello to Grandad,' I said. He wriggled to be put down. His legs pedalled in the air; he wanted, as children do, just to run. To be out of the fetid atmosphere, no doubt. He wanted his mum.

'Where's Dodie?' I asked.

'Meditating,' Hannah said.

I looked at her sharply. 'Really?'

'Shall I take him?' she asked Adam, and he nodded his head. Hannah lifted him out of my arms and carried him away. My fingers went to a damp dribbly patch on my shoulder and I smiled. That burst of young life into the room had altered the composition of the air. Adam smiled at me.

'We must have another ceremony,' he said. 'We must praise the Lord. He has not forsaken me. He moves in mysterious ways. This is the greatest gift of all.'

'You must rest,' I said.

He met my eyes. '*Another* ceremony,' he insisted. 'I will speak to Hannah.'

'You can speak to *me*,' I said. But he did not.

†

Hannah inveigled her way in, of course, whenever I was out of the room, and encouraged Adam in his nonsense. Cruel,

I thought it. Together they planned another Festival of the Lamb. It was unheard of to have two so close together. The idea was ridiculous and amateurish. In his right mind, Adam would never have considered it. You only had to look at him to know he'd never stand again, never have the strength to slaughter and to bless. And there were no preparations, no lamb, no word had gone out among the twitchy Brethren, no cakes had been baked. I couldn't take it seriously.

I didn't like to leave Adam for Hannah to get to, so I couldn't come and find you as I should have done. When Adam was safely asleep I did try to go and see Seth, but the codes to the peace-pods had been changed without my knowledge. It was as if the sand was sliding away under my feet. I'd always known the codes. Of course, it was Hannah's work. But I didn't guess that you were also locked up.

I found Jake being petted by a posse of frustrated grannies – Bethel and Kezia among them. They echoed Hannah, saying you were in a final meditation. Of course, Hannah would have told them that, and why should they have questioned it? But I should have questioned it. I *should* have thought harder. I should have insisted on seeing you – and Seth. My blood. But with Adam and Hannah and all, my mind was flayed to rags.

Adam was so weak he could hardly speak now, or the words he said were cloudy and edgeless. When he woke up, I sat on the bed, telling him stories about our past; reminding him of the ferry to Bawdsey, the mud, the herons – and weeping sometimes at the memory of my little sister. I massaged those parts of his body that were not too painful to be touched. He loved to have his feet stroked, his toes pulled, and moaned in pleasure when I did that for him. I lay beside him to sleep, sniffing his skin, from which rose a peculiar smell, mud and undergrowth and something chemical that reminded me of how a newborn infant smells. I expect it's the smell of death. I mumbled love into his skin and wished for him to die, now, with only me beside him, but he didn't die and whenever he emerged into consciousness he talked of sacrifice. They were the ramblings of a dying man and so I humoured him.

'The Lord's last task for me on earth,' he said, and mumbled Hannah's name and I felt myself stiffen.

'Do you think you're strong enough to stand, to speak, to do the blessing?' I said sharply.

'Just us,' he said, 'a sacrifice here, just us,' and he looked at me with eyes gone pearly and I felt he was looking not at me, but Hannah, there was no differentiation any more.

I took a breath and closed my eyes to hum away the whoosh of pain, and he tried to join me but his sound, once so strong, was stuttery. He couldn't get enough breath to make a prolonged vibration, and my heart softened and I sang to him instead:

You seem to be a bird
With feathers and a beak
You seem to be absurd
You seem a little freaky
But though you cannot speak
You bring the word
You bring the word
You bring the word.

And weakly he tapped his fingers on the sheet. We dozed together for a while, his thumbless hand in mine.

There was the sound of a helicopter overhead. They had been circling for a few days, that stuttering sound, swooping low, with cameras maybe. People tried to get in, but we didn't let them. The phones had been unplugged in the office. The end was coming for us all. There was a sense of bustle, of movement through all the place, of bewilderment, but I was so taken up with Adam, with planning what I'd do as soon as he had gone, that I hardly registered the larger situation.

'It's me,' I whispered to Adam, 'it's me, Martha. It's your wife.' He opened his eyes once more to look at me, and this time he knew me. A sliver of him was waving to me from somewhere very far away, and then he closed his eyes again.

I stayed there for a while, watching the painful rise and fall of his chest, then I stood up and stretched. I wanted to move and fill my lungs with fresh air, to feel the energy in my body. I already looked forward to more life after this – and after all, I had a family now. A family I must support. I was full of restless energy but didn't want to leave the room. What if he died alone, or worse, what if Hannah snuck in and he took his last breath with her instead of me?

I walked around the room that has been ours for more than thirty years. Knowing I was soon to leave, I saw it as a stranger would. Our robes on the clothes rack, the stupid blankness of the masks gathering shadows of dust. A spider had nested in the eye of one of them, a clot of cottony thread with something dark inside it, moving. The curtains, once white and floaty, were yellowed and brittle. It was early afternoon and the sky was the colour of cream; condensation streamed down the inside of the glass. Adam's breath struggled from his mouth and he groaned painfully in his sleep.

In the closet was my bag, and in the bag were Obadiah's house deeds and keys, my old driving licence and my passport, both in the name of Melanie (a name that sent a sparkle through me, the memory of youth), and my bank details. Nothing else. When my husband died there would be nothing for me there. Neither the house nor the money would save me from grief, but they would provide what I needed to exist.

I indulged in the dream: you, me, Seth and Jake together in Obadiah's ocean-side house in Florida. Seth could go to school and you could work, if you wished, go back to teaching, or anything else you liked, and I'd be there to babysit. We'd be happy. We'd be a proper family.

I opened the door of Adam's closet. On the floor was the lacquered box in which we kept the sacrificial knife, razor sharp so as not to cause the lambs more suffering than necessary. The box rested slantwise on the galvanized bucket used to catch the sacred blood. I was about to shut the door when I caught sight of something else there, hidden in the bucket, just a little poking corner. I knelt to explore and pulled out a plastic bag containing something small and soft. Inside the bag there was folded tissue and inside the tissue a small, white cotton gown, like a christening gown. In the bucket, by the knife. My heart began to rush.

A final sacrifice, Adam had said.

No.

Surely, a symbolic sacrifice? Surely that was all that was meant: to sacrifice Jake's life on earth to the Lord, rather than his life itself. A baptism, no more than that. Hannah had said nothing to me, and Adam had only mentioned it in his confused ramblings. The small and private ceremony was planned by Hannah, and I wasn't included. Surely he could not, my Adam *could* not, contemplate a human sacrifice. His own grandson. And yet, he wasn't in his right mind. He wasn't my Adam any more. The disease was in his brain – and so was Hannah.

But surely even *Hannah* could not?

I don't know. I don't think so, now. No, no, she could not. But in my panic, at the time, that's what I thought.

Sweat from my hands dampened the gown. Hands trembling, I refolded and replaced it. I took my bag, a plan forming. I would find you, Seth and Jake, and together we'd leave. I had to get your baby out of there. I went to Adam and gave him a last kiss on his slack mouth. He murmured something and I couldn't tell if it was my name or another. I didn't stay to listen to any more.

Within the corridors of Soul-Life there was movement; unrest. The police would be in soon, Obadiah said; they were getting warrants to impound the computers and he'd been working night and day to try and straighten out, or wipe, the records. But most of the Brethren didn't know how near the end we were.

†

I couldn't find you, Dodie. I looked into all the rooms but couldn't see you. Again I tried the peace-pods. I had to get Seth out. I had to find you. And I had to find Jake.

At first I couldn't find any of you. It was all slipping away from me; in all the long white corridors I was the one who was lost, turning corners, trying doors, losing my breath among the hammering of my heart. But at last I opened the door of a small and seldom-used communing room to find Jake with Daniel. My ears were ringing with the tension. I blinked and held my thumb.

'Where is Dodie?' I asked.

'Not sure,' he said, refusing to meet my eyes. 'I just babysit.'

Jake was playing with some plastic beakers.

'Ask Hannah,' he added, with a flick of slyness. 'Here Jake, put it on top.'

They were building a tower. Jake held the beaker carefully in his chubby fingers, sticking his tongue out as he concentrated on the balance.

'That's right!' Daniel said and clapped his hands. Jake laughed and clapped his own.

'I'll take the child now,' I said. 'You can go to meditation.'

'Oh, but Hannah told me –' he began, but I ignored him and stooped to pick Jake up. I settled him on my hip, a proper fleshy hip, unlike Hannah's scrawn. Jake waved his hands in frustration at the tower, and his bottom lip turned down.

'I must speak to Hannah,' Daniel said, defiant now.

'Come along,' I said, and it seemed I still had enough authority that he must obey. We walked together down into the central corridor – and then he bolted.

'Daniel!' I called.

'I'll find Hannah,' he said, over his shoulder.

'*Daniel!*' I shouted, but he was gone.

I had to think fast. He would go to Hannah, and she would come and take Jake and lock me up. That's what fled through my mind then. She knew the numbers and I didn't. That's when I guessed you were in a peace-pod too.

I went to the office to ask Obadiah for help, but even he didn't know the codes. He wasn't in on the plan and didn't believe me when I told him about the sacrifice. Little Jake was fascinated by his beard, and kept trying to snatch at it.

'I have to go,' I said, trying to flatten the panic out of my voice. '*Now*, I have to go.'

He looked at me with a gentle, weary expression and then he nodded. 'It's all over here.' He ruffled Jake's hair. 'Take him somewhere safe.'

'The house in Florida,' I said. 'Please send Dodie and Seth.'

'Don't worry.'

'And give them money.'

'Don't worry.'

He looked so sad, so done in. I hesitated. 'Why don't you come?' I asked, but he shook his head.

'God Bless.' He pulled me towards him to print a hairy kiss on my forehead. And then he reached for the phone to call a cab.

I had to go like that, without you, without Jake. You see that Dodie? I didn't dare to stay a moment longer. I said a last goodbye to Obadiah, and then, clutching Jake, I ran.

DODIE

1

The air fizzes with particles in the light that's always on. There's no change in it, no fluctuation, no dark, no day, no night. The particles are all there is to watch; they dance in the commotion caused by her breath.

The feeling of hunger is interesting. Actually, she's hardly hungry any more. There's a tap and she can drink as much as she likes. Every time she thinks it's time for breakfast or lunch or dinner she clamps her mouth round the tap and glugs till her stomach is full. It must be at least two days and nights she's been here, she calculates, but not as many as five.

She sleeps, she wakes, she sleeps. In sleep the dreams are more vivid than anything that happens when she's awake. Mostly it's a half sleep, a doze, which is almost cosy. For some reason, 'Bohemian Rhapsody' goes round in her head, looping and rising and falling to a whisper of *Be-elzebub* and how did that get there? And it won't stop; the particles in her brain must be stuck in a loop or a holding pattern. *Nothing really matters, nothing really matters.*

There's no sound outside: no footsteps or voices or birdsong or drainpipes. Only the sounds from inside and they are deafening. *Easy come, easy go*. And then the door opens and Seth seems to be there.

Seth?

He's as vivid as a dream and as interesting: thick eyebrows, deep blue eyes, a smattering of dark young whiskers. And the darling straightness of his nose. He fidgets about in the way he's always had, never able to keep still for five minutes. It used to drive Stella crazy.

It really *is* Seth. His face is his face, at the top of a crumpled lilac robe. The crumples are shadowed grey and blue and there are stains, soup stains, tea stains. The particles in the air have gone berserk with the opening of the door.

'Thank *God*. Dodie.' It's his voice and he leans down. The warmth of his cheek shocks her properly awake, pushes her up to sitting.

'Where's Jake?' she says, and letting in that name fills her with a hot wash of fear. The room wobbles and spins and her focus shifts, there's a smell of something familiar but she can't think what it is.

'Get up,' Seth says. 'We've got to get out of here, now.'

'What's happened?'

'*Now*.'

'I can't.' She tries to stand but her legs are weak. 'Jake?' she says again.

'Come on.'

'Daniel took him,' she says.

'Daniel?'

And then she recognizes the smell of burning and a soundless scream comes from her mouth. Seth pulls her to her feet and rushes her along the corridor.

'Where is he? Where's Hannah? She made Daniel take him.'

'What? We're going to him.'

'Are we?' Dodie's legs stop working, and she crouches, faintness fizzing and sparkling in her ears and eyes.

'Not now,' Seth pleads. 'Come on.'

'But *Jake*?' She's bitten her tongue and the sharp iron taste wakes her. A small reservoir of energy gets into gear, going to Jake, going to him, going to him.

'Where?' she says again, but Seth is concentrating on finding his way through the corridors; maybe they're lost, like rats in a maze, coming to a dead end or a locked door, but it's all different now; there are doors that are open where once they were all shut, doors gaping onto rooms, and in one Dodie sees three people sleeping on the floor, neatly, face up, hands folded on their chests and she thinks she recognizes some of the faces. Her feet stop. *What?*

Seth drags her on and he is stronger and she lets herself be whisked along like a ghost of herself just above the surface of the ground. They go to a room she's never been inside before, with filing cabinets and computers and a plastic smell. An old man is sitting with his head in his hands. On the desk in front of him, there's a pile of pills beside a glass of water. He raises his hairy grey face when they come in.

'Ah, good,' he says. He gives Seth a thick brown envelope. 'Now scram.'

'I can't,' Dodie says. 'My little boy . . .'

'You're going to him,' the man says. 'No time, no time.'

Dodie's head goes into a swoon but her legs still work and so does her ability to obey orders. Outside a car is waiting, engine revving. There is smoke in the air, looming blackly from somewhere at the back of the building. There's the heavy thwack, thwack of a helicopter, its belly a fat glassy shine above her. Seth opens the car, shoves her in the back seat and slams the door.

2

Rebecca's in the driving seat, revving the engine.
'Rebecca?' Dodie says. 'How? *You?*'

'It's Bex,' Rebecca says, and, 'Shhh, let me concentrate. Haven't driven for frigging yonks.' She manoeuvres the car through the open gates, out onto the road and puts her foot down.

Seth reaches back to give Dodie a banana. She holds it for a moment before peeling back the skin and filling her mouth with the dense sweet flesh. Her salivary glands start to pump again and it hurts, like small explosions in her cheeks; she swallows a big lump and it forces down her throat like rape. Nausea clamps her stomach almost shut but at the same time she feels the sugar immediately getting into her blood, a distinct tracery through her body as it branches, miraculous how fast it spreads. She eats another bite and then another and then her throat closes and her stomach feels like it will split.

There is the sound of sirens. 'Fuck, that was close,' Rebecca says.

'What's happening?'

'It's all gone tits up,' Rebecca explains. 'The police are arresting everyone who hasn't scarpered or . . .'

Died, Dodie thinks. The banana threatens to come back up again; she swallows hard, hardens her eyes.

'Your clothes are there, better change and we'll chuck the robes away.'

'Why are they arresting people?' Dodie says.

'We don't know,' Seth says. His voice sounds very young and gruff. She would hug him if she could reach. There's a tangled pile on the back seat. Rebecca, or Bex, Dodie notices, is wearing a denim jacket and specs.

'You're wearing glasses,' Dodie says.

'Not allowed to in there,' Rebecca says, 'so I was blind as a frigging bat.'

'Not allowed?' Now Dodie comes to think of it, she'd not seen anyone wearing glasses at Soul-Life. She imagines glasses with a mask and gives a soggy giggle.

'It's fantastic to see straight again,' Rebecca says. 'I can't think straight when I can't see.'

The saliva is still pumping stupidly in Dodie's mouth. She swallows it; watches the low suburban sprawl flow past the windows.

She takes a deep breath. Her heart is swinging like a pendulum, hurting each time it strikes her ribs. 'Do you know where Jake is?' she dares to ask.

'Florida,'

'*Florida?*'

'Martha took him,' Seth says. 'I've got the address and everything and money to get us there – from Obadiah. I've got our passports and thousands of dollars.' He holds out a wad of money.

'Martha took him?' Dodie says. Her stomach is cramping. 'No, it was Daniel – it was *Hannah*.' In the sound of a siren she hears Jake's cry as he was snatched from her arms.

'Obadiah said it was Martha,' Seth says.

Dodie's mind scrambles. Was Martha in league with them, then? But no, no.

'*Why*? Why would Martha take him?' A bus overtakes them, sending up a sluice of water. '*Florida?*' she says again. Adrenalin fizzes through her, yet there's nothing she can do but sit here, sit still, in this car.

Rebecca looks back over her shoulder. 'Better change before we get to the airport. The police are searching.'

'For what? I don't understand,' Dodie says weakly. 'What I saw, did I see bodies? I thought –'

'Later,' Rebecca says. 'Let me concentrate; never driven on the right before.'

'But there were *bodies*.'

There is no response. It's starting to rain and Rebecca fumbles about to find the wipers. Dodie watches them swish to and fro and to and fro. She looks at her brother's shoulder, leans forward and pokes his arm. 'Why wouldn't you see me when I came all this way?' she demands.

Seth twists his neck to look at her, his expression puzzled, dazed, as if he's just waking up. 'Don't know,' he says. 'Don't remember. I . . . Hannah was telling me . . . no . . . it's all fuzzy. I went kind of ballistic when we got there and someone gave me a jab and then . . .' He bites a knuckle, as if that will help him think. 'I remember you on the phone and she said I mustn't worry you.'

'Worry me?'

His brow is furrowed with the effort of remembering. He looks older. In just these few weeks – and yet he looks like a baby too. Her baby brother. She sees how bitten the nails are, the specks of blood around the cuticles.

'Hannah said you were ill again,' he continues. 'She told me to humour you, she said and I . . . oh, I can't remember. And I kept seeing Mum. . . *I kept seeing her*, Dodie.'

'What do you mean?' Goosebumps riffle over Dodie's skin and she hugs her arms.

'Like a ghost,' he says.

'Maybe a dream?' Rebecca suggests.

Seth shakes his head, almost angrily. 'No.'

He turns back to look out of the windscreen, and Dodie takes in his fine, familiar profile, his fluffy stubble, his filthy ears. Another police vehicle screams towards them in the opposite direction, siren warping as it passes.

'Fuck,' Rebecca says.

'Yeah, fuck,' Seth agrees and Dodie feels her face split in an empty, automatic grin.

'Anyway,' Seth says after a moment. 'They put me in a peace-pod, like in solitary, for *weeks* it felt like.'

'Pea pod?'

'Peace-pod, like you were in.'

'Cell,' she says, and no one contradicts her.

'Seth,' she says and leans forward to touch the reality of his shoulder. 'It's all right.' He catches her hand and squeezes it tight. Their eyes meet, and snag, and look away again.

It's cold. She reaches for the clothes, the jeans, the sweater, the leather jacket; she shoves Seth's clothes to him and they shift and wriggle in their seats as they struggle to dress. She has to undo her seatbelt and sit sideways to get into her jeans. They are stiff and alien, so much too big around her waist that she doubts they're really hers – but yes, there is that bleach mark, and in the pocket the New York transport map she shoved there, it seems like years ago. The watch has gone though, those clever little numerals that Rod did.

'Did you see my watch?' she says.

Rebecca shakes her head. 'I just had to, like, grab what I could quick.'

'Doesn't matter,' Dodie says. And it doesn't. Some things she can let go. Just things. They throw the robes out of the car window and see them swirl away like lilac spooks.

The wipers are making Dodie sleepy now. To and fro – *going to Jake, going to Jake* – clearing a space that is only a space for a split second before the raindrops slant, gelid, halfway to being sleet. It's winter after all. 'What's the date?' she says.

'Dunno,' Seth says.

'Must be nearly Christmas,' Rebecca guesses. She looks over her shoulder. 'You OK?'

Dodie opens her mouth on a logjam of too much to say, but where to start? It's impossible, and she shuts it again, swallows hard.

'We'll get there,' Rebecca says, 'we'll get a flight and then we can fill you in – on as much as we know.'

'You coming with us?' Seth asks her.

'You joking?' Rebecca says. 'I've always fancied Florida.'

'Me too.' He gives a weak little laugh, and begins to gnaw what's left of his thumbnail.

Dodie closes her eyes and goes into the thought of Jake, willing him to be safe. She saw him for such a brief time; held him, inhaled him and then he was snatched away. Still, in her hands is the sensation of him, his weight on her lap. And she can still feel Hannah's hands on her back, pushing. *Were* they in it together, Hannah and Martha? In what, though? Why would Martha take him and leave her behind? Poor Jake, he'll be so confused. Why would Martha want him? But it's no good, there's no sense to be had and her mind stalls. She lets the wipers lull her into a shallow kind of trance.

3

The airport swarms with uniforms and the long black snouts of guns. It's Christmas here, Santa ringing a hand bell, the ground wet from boots and dripping umbrellas. The three of them buy tickets for the first flight to Tampa and go to a café. Dodie and Seth sit down while Rebecca orders them each a cheese sandwich with a sticky heap of coleslaw and a mountain of crisps. She brings back three giant milkshakes: one pink, one yellow, one brown. The cheese has a waxy, personal taste and the sandwich is so gigantic Dodie can do no more than nibble the edge, but she sucks the milkshake, strawberry, in long, smooth, glugs, feeling her stomach stretch and bulge against her ribs. Seth finishes his sandwich and reaches for the rest of Dodie's.

'You must be starving too,' she says. 'I think my stomach's shrunk.'

'I had plenty of food,' he says.

'While you were locked up?'

'Yeah.'

'I had none,' she says. They stare at each other.

'Nobody brought you *anything*?' Rebecca says. 'For how long?'

'Who put you in?' asks Seth.

'Hannah.'

'But Hannah's cool,' Seth says.

'*Cool?*' Dodie chokes on a crumb in her throat, and Seth whacks her on her back, till tears fly from eyes. '*Cool?*' she says again, when she can speak.

'She was OK with me. She was like, motherly?' he says.

Dodie inhales sharply and hides her face in her hands. *Motherly!* A surge of laughter comes up her throat like sick. She counts to ten, finds the phrase *Let it go*, in her mind, tips her head back to see a twizzle of tawdry tinsel. *You'd better be good, you'd better not cry,* pumps from some vast speakers, and she bleats out another laugh.

'What?' Seth says.

Rebecca pulls a face at her and takes a final gurgling slurp of milkshake. Seth munches loudly in a way that would make Stella scream. *Stella.* Dodie pushes away the milkshake.

'Mum?' Seth says. Is he reading her mind now? His hand, all salty from the crisps, clamps hers. 'Did she, I mean . . .' He clears his throat. 'Did she . . . I mean was it, like, *suicide*?' This last word sticks in his mouth, but Dodie hears it. She nods.

'That's what she said. Her head was all like . . .' He twists his head to one side and she shudders, her innards turning hot and liquid.

'Did *you* find her, Dode?' he whispers.

Their eyes meet for a flinch of a second.

'Come on guys,' Rebecca says, grabbing his arm, 'we can do this on board. We'd better buy some stuff – it'd look sus going through security with nothing.'

They follow Rebecca into a shop where she buys bags and books and gum and tampons and tissues so that they can look like normal passengers. Dodie puts her passport in the pocket of her new, tacky flags-of-the-world bag. Seth unwraps a stick of gum and puts it in his mouth.

They remove shoes and coats to go through security; put the brand new bags full of brand new stuff in the trays. Dodie retrieves her jacket gladly when it comes through the X-ray machine; it's hers, a part of her, and the parts are hardly holding together now. In the pocket there's a tissue, a pound, a bus ticket, her lipstick and a Lego pig.

The flight is ready to board and they go straight on. It's only half full, so they could spread out, but the three of them cram together in a row, Dodie in the middle.

They watch obediently as the air steward performs the safety procedure routine. The take-off flattens them back against their seats and the plane tilts into the rain and cloud of the winter afternoon. Rebecca has her eyes shut, specs clutched in her hand. Her freckles swarm against her skin, gone milky pale. She opens her eyes and catches Dodie's look, puts her glasses back on.

'Did you know *he* died too?' Rebecca says.

'Who?'

'Our Father.'

'No. When?'

'A couple of days ago. He was really sick, but, of course, no doctors.'

'Like John,' Dodie says and Rebecca nods. A quiver passes between them. 'So he's dead, then.' Dodie digests this for a moment, can't make it matter. What was he to her?

'That's when it all started to, like, fall apart,' Rebecca says. 'Helicopters, police and that. Fights. Actual shouting in the corridors, and no one telling us anything. I was shit scared, I can tell you.'

'I didn't hear a thing.'

'Nor did I,' Seth says.

Dodie notices that his hands are trembling as he savages the skin around his thumbnail. She catches his hand and pulls it away from his mouth. And he starts to bite his lip instead. 'Calm down,' she says, as much to herself as to him. She squeezes his bony knee. 'It's OK, we just get to Jake and after that we can talk and it'll all be OK.'

They are quiet for a while. Seth chews gum. Rebecca takes her glasses off and shuts her eyes. The pilot tells them how high up they are and what the temperature is in Florida.

'Why did Martha take Jake?' Dodie says, reaching across Seth to touch Rebecca's arm. 'She's nice isn't she?' she pleads. 'She wouldn't do him any harm?'

'Yeah,' Rebecca says. 'Martha's OK.'

'Maybe she was trying to keep him safe?' Seth says. 'She *is* his auntie, I guess. Great aunt?'

Dodie stares. 'Great *what*?' she says.

'Well she's Mum's sister so –'

'*What?*' Either the plane has hit some turbulence, or it's her stomach plummeting.

'Didn't you know?' he says.

'What? *What?*' On the screen the plane noses clumsily down the east coast of the continent. 'What?' she says again. 'Martha is Stella's *sister*?' She's silent for a moment, her mind scrambling. 'But she never said. Why wouldn't she say? Are you sure?'

'Yeah. She came with Our Father to pick me up from Sheffield. Mum said she was my aunt.' The way Seth's chewing his gum is starting to drive Dodie mad. She puts her hands up to her eyes, cups the warm dark, feels the tickle of her lashes on her palms as she pictures Martha's face. But it's nothing like Stella's.

'Are you sure?' she says again. 'Why didn't she tell me then?'

He shrugs. 'It was the night I was meant to be babysitting,' he says, adding, 'Sorry about that.'

Dodie snorts.

He tells her about the night he left, the shock of strangers in the house, the rush of it all, no time to pack, even.

'Why did you agree to go, then?' she asks.

Puzzled expressions chase across his face. 'Mum said . . . School . . .'

'Were you being bullied again?'

He swallows hard, ignores the question, and rattles through the story: the hotel, the first-class flight. He tells her about the films and the on-board food and then his voice trails off as he gets into his arrival at Soul-Life. 'I was totally freaked,' he says. 'I didn't know it was going to be a churchy thing, I thought it would be like a house and . . .' His fingers go to his lips as if trying to retrieve something slippery from his memory.

'The day you left, do you remember what time it was?' Dodie asks. 'Was Stella wearing the red dress?'

Seth nods. 'That *weird* red dress. After school.'

'I must have just missed you,' Dodie says weakly, her mind going back to that dark, wet afternoon. It seems like years ago. She sees Stella's reaching hand, glittering with rain.

Seth shrugs and stretches the gum between his lips, sticks his tongue through the grey skin of it.

'Will you spit that out, *please*?' Dodie says. Funny how you can long for someone till your bones ache, and then be irritated so quickly by their habits. She gives him a tissue.

'Sorry I couldn't let you know,' he says. 'I tried but I didn't really get a chance. I lost my phone –'

'Doesn't matter,' Dodie says. 'It's OK now.' She folds the tissue, puts it in her bag and attempts a reassuring smile. Something's coming back to her and she needs to concentrate. It's something Stella told her once: how she had an older sister, not Martha, that wasn't the name but it did begin with M – Marjorie or Melody or something? And this sister couldn't have a child of her own and had tried to steal her, to steal Dodie herself when she was a baby, that's what Stella had said: *steal*. Her own sister had tried to steal her child. Could Martha be that sister?

'*Jake*!' she says, a shock jolting through her. 'Why did Martha take him away when I was locked up? Why was I locked up?' Her voice rises and she takes deep breaths. Has Martha stolen Jake? The air feels thick in the cabin, made of plastic, hardening in her lungs.

'Shhh,' Rebecca says.

'I didn't even know Jake was there,' Seth says. 'Until Obadiah said –'

'Who?'

'The old man. He was, like, Our Father's right-hand man kind of thing,' Rebecca says.

'He was the one who told me Martha had taken Jake,' Seth says. 'When the fire started he made Hannah unlock the peace-pods – and we had to get out of there fast.'

The steward is there with a trolley. 'Coffee? Soda? Beer?' Dodie shakes her head and the others ignore him. He shrugs theatrically, rolls his eyes and clanks off down the aisle.

'Everyone was going ape-shit,' Rebecca says, and then catching Dodie's expression, adds, 'Martha *will* look after him.'

Dodie moans. 'But what if . . . ?' But she cannot even bear to name her fears.

'We've got the address and instructions,' Seth says. He pats her knee and tries to sound reassuring. 'It'll be cool.'

He takes an envelope out of his pocket and she grabs it. The instructions have been downloaded from Google and printed out. It tells them to hire a car at Tampa and gives directions to an address on the highway towards St Petersburg.

'Oh God, Oh God.' Dodie rocks in her seat trying to urge the plane forward; the flight is three hours, three whole hours and then there is the getting to the house and who knows how long that could take? *Tried to steal you when I was ill. Tried to turn you against me.* It was something like that that Stella said, and Dodie had taken it as some comfort that Stella hadn't let her be stolen. Taken it as evidence that she wanted her. But later she'd decided it was a lie. Stella *was* a liar. She gets a sudden image of the toes, the empty, dangling hands. Her head throbs and her mouth fills with sticky water as if she's about to vomit.

'Hey, try and relax,' Rebecca says. She takes Dodie's hand. 'Try humming.'

'No,' Dodie says, 'not that. And . . .' she suddenly remembers those bodies behind the open doors. 'People were *dead*,' she says.

Rebecca looks out of the window. Raindrops flee across the scratchy glass like sperm racing to their destination, the plane slumps and wallops through a patch of turbulence and the seat belt sign pings on.

'Yeah,' Rebecca sighs. 'After word got round about Our Father dying and Martha pissing off, it all, like, blew up, fell apart and helicopters everywhere, and I don't know. I don't know what was going on. Some people ran off and some, like, freaked out at the thought of being out in the big bad world and wanted to follow Our Father. There were these pills.' She stops and shudders. 'It was like a kind of virus spreading and people topping themselves all over.'

Dodie shuts her eyes and swallows sickly, thinking of the looming pall of smoke, picturing the pills beside the old man. Obadiah.

'I'd already decided to leave,' Rebecca says, 'but it was hard, it wasn't like you could just walk out, was it? It wasn't just *you* made me want to leave, before you came I was starting to think, like, this isn't me, though they hardly give you room to think. I never knew you were in a peace-pod,' she adds. 'I didn't even know they existed. I thought you'd legged it after John died. *Lucky cow*, I thought. If I'd known what was going on . . .'

'In-flight store – want anything?' says the attendant. His trolley is packed with perfume and toys. 'Pantyhose on special,' he adds. 'Nice line in lingerie.'

They all shake their heads and he tosses his head as he flounces on up the aisle.

'I'm watching a movie.' Rebecca puts her earphones on.

Rod! The thought of him shoots through Dodie like an arrow. She should try his mobile, you never know – but she hasn't got a phone any more. She holds the plastic pig tight in her fist and it's wet with sweat.

Seth's asleep, mouth hanging open and Rebecca's pretending to be lost in whatever's on the screen. Dodie puts on her own earphones and watches a news channel: all terrorism and flooding and freakish storms and fires. You could think Our Father right, you could think it was all rushing toward an end, but there's sport too, of course, and then an old episode of *Frasier*, which actually makes her lift the corners of her mouth and forget for a few seconds at a time where she's heading and the reason why.

The three-hour flight seems to take six but at last the pressure changes, the pilot thanks them for travelling with him, wishes them a safe onward journey. They get out of the airport in the hot golden glue of late afternoon. The nearer she gets to Jake, the tighter a screw turns in her guts. Has Martha stolen him? No. That's sick talk, Stella talk. Don't think like that. Picture him instead. She knows his eyes are blue and his wispy hair is dark and that he has fading stork marks at the nape of his neck but she can't picture him all together, only one detail at a time, and nothing will do but to hold him in her arms. The air is humid and flower-scented and she scuffs her feet on some waxy petals on the concrete while she and Seth wait for Rebecca to rent the car.

'Do you think he's all right?' she asks Seth, and he says yes, of course, and it's a comfort to hear that, though she knows he's got no more idea than she has. 'Why would she do that?' she pleads, unable to stop herself. 'Why would she take him? Why would she steal him and leave me locked up? What if she's not there?'

'Shut up,' Seth says. 'I don't know, right?' She's startled to see tears wobbling in his eyes. It makes her see that this is happening to him too. He loves Jake too. Think of his shock. Plunged so suddenly into this, this panic.

'Sorry,' she mutters. She takes off her jacket and jumper and gets a sour whiff of sweat from her armpits. Taxis churn and hoot and planes take off and land and the air charges about in the wake of all the movement, all the burning fuel, hellish despite the efforts of the stiff and waxy flowers.

4

Air conditioning makes the car icy inside. Shivering now, Dodie sits up front beside Rebecca, the directions on her lap. Rebecca clamps a bottle of Coke between her thighs and takes an occasional swig as she negotiates them out of the airport and on to the low highway where the ocean gleams through the haze. They do not speak except to work out the way. The road is terrifying with all the metal bullets shooting along and the fumes of heat and petrol shimmering the insubstantial world outside the windows. It takes less than an hour till they find the intersection and leave the freeway.

'Well done,' Dodie says. The snout of the pig is indented into the palm of her hand. Her skin has tightened with the cold of the air-conditioning. They find the boulevard without trouble and start to count the houses but the numbers aren't sequential. It's a long, rich road, houses set back from the street, behind trees, no two identical. Some are mock Tudor, or castle-like, and some are modernist boxes of glass and steel.

It takes three trips along the road till they find the house, one of the starkly modern ones. In front of it a bush is studded with pink blossoms big as human hearts. Rebecca pulls the car onto the empty drive. When they step outside they're met by a wave of heat, and the sound and smell of the ocean. A bird chips away regularly as if counting out the seconds. They get to the door and ring the bell but there's no answer and the house is still.

'Sure this is the one?' Dodie says, although it clearly is.

Seth has a pee in the bushes. 'Sorry,' he says, looking over his shoulder, 'can't wait.'

It's like a film set with all the shining from the polished steel, the glass, the sea and the glossy leaves.

'We'll get him,' Rebecca says. She hammers on the door. 'Oi!' she shouts. 'Anyone in there? Martha?'

'What if it's a trick?' Dodie says. 'We should phone the police.'

'Not yet,' Rebecca says.

'But what if . . . what if . . .' No, no, no, don't go there, don't think like that. She sinks down on the wooden step.

Seth squeezes down the side of the property. He comes back with petals in his hair.

'I'll climb over and go round the back,' he says. 'Might be able to get in.'

Dodie rattles and hammers at the door, searches under shrubs and stones for a key. And then the door opens and Seth is there, grinning, though his face is so pale that the grin is ghastly.

'Back door was unlocked,' he says. 'There's steps down to the beach. No sign of anyone though.'

Dodie swallows. She's almost reluctant now to step in. Better maybe to stay here in this spot and never know. A bright green insect climbs the door frame, opens its leafy wings and zips away. Rebecca steps inside and Dodie follows. It's sparsely luxurious with so much white and wood and – she catches her breath – a childish scribble on the wall. A wax crayon. A little shoe. And then Jake, all alone, sitting in a vast white room among a drift of loose screwed-up and scribbled-on pages.

'Anything?' Rebecca calls from upstairs.

Dodie holds herself back a moment and makes her voice come out smoothly.

'Yes,' she calls, her voice an octave too high. 'He's here. Jakey . . .'

'Mumma.' He drops his crayon, pushes himself up on his feet and comes towards her, dribble running down his chin.

'Hi sweetheart,' she says.

Rebecca and Seth are there.

'Thank fuck for that!' Seth shouts. His fist flies into the air.

'Come on Jake,' Dodie says. She scoops him off his feet and buries her nose in his soapy clean neck.

He giggles. 'Mumma,' he says again, patting her.

'Mumma's here,' she says.

'Dink,' Jake says.

Dodie carries him back into the kitchen. There's an empty feeder cup on the floor. She fills it with water and he glugs it back, the whole cupful in one noisy go. She fills it again and he drinks half.

'Oh, he's so *cute*,' Rebecca says.

'Can I?' Seth holds out his arms. Dodie is reluctant to let go but she hands him over.

'Watcha, mate,' he says, but Jake struggles to get down. He waddles about sprinkling water from his cup on the silver-flecked floor tiles.

'So where the fucking hell is Martha?' Rebecca says.

Dodie spots half a cup of coffee on the counter. It's still warm. 'Martha?' she calls, but they already know she's not in the house. 'She must only just have left,' she says.

Jake trots through into the wide, glass-fronted sun lounge. Dodie peers through the window, but can't see Martha, or anyone, on the beach. It's starting to get dark, the sun swelling scarlet as it dips closer to the sea.

Rebecca kneels on the floor to gather the scattered pages. 'She's written tons,' she says. 'Jake's ruined some of it. Here, this looks like it's the start. It's for you.' She hands Dodie a splattery tattered page.

Written for Dodie, it says.

Stella and Me.

In May 1974, when I was sixteen, and Stella thirteen, our mother died of drink. Dad was in Saudi with his brand new family. We nearly had to go and live in Peebles with Aunt Regina, but we convinced the social worker not to

'It's about Mum,' Dodie tells Seth.

'Let's see.' He takes the page from her and Dodie stoops to pick up another:

I don't know how long till we found Stella. We'd gone miles I think. We'd gone way past the places where it was safe and easy to walk. She was in the mud.

Seth picks up some random pages and reads, frowning. Dodie gives up. She'll read it later. The words make her eyes sting and she presses her fingers to her temples.

'Martha is my aunt,' she mutters. 'Doesn't make sense.'

'*The dream was convenient, just as Stella said. It was expedient,*' reads Seth.

'What does that mean?' Rebecca says.

Seth shakes his head and lets the papers flutter to the ground, then grabs Dodie and hugs her hard. She still finds it odd that her little brother is taller than she is; his chin rests on top of her head.

'We'll be OK,' he says, that touching scrape in his voice, that fledgling manliness, 'won't we?'

'Up?' Jake tries to squeeze in between them, arms outstretched. Seth swings him into the air and he shrieks with joy.

'Yeah, we'll be all right,' she says.

'So what about your boyfriend?' Rebecca says. 'Where's he?'

Dodie blinks and sighs. Yes, she'll have to think about Rod. 'He went travelling,' she says, 'but I could try him. He should know where we are. Seen a phone?'

They hunt about and find it and she sits, feet curled under her on the sofa – which is white, but grubbed with dirty little hand prints – keys in the number and waits. Rebecca brings her a glass of water. Jake stands beside her, gnawing on a biscuit. His fingers flex against her knee the way they did when he was tiny and breastfeeding, a kind of kneading. She tries Rod's mobile and gets the message: *Sorry, but this phone is not currently in use.* She finds international directory enquiries and rings his mother's number. Jeannie answers quickly, in her neat, clipped voice:

'Jean Stewart speaking.'

Dodie's mouth has gone so dry she has to take a sip of water before she can speak.

'Hello there?' Jeannie says.

'It's Dodie.'

Jeannie takes a breath. 'Dodie, well hello there, dear.' The voice warms. 'And how are you?'

'I'm fine,' Dodie says. She smiles wryly at Rebecca.

'Are you still in America?'

'Yeah, me and Jake.'

'I am glad you rang,' Jeannie says. 'I'm so sorry.'

'Sorry?'

'I do hope we can stay in touch? I hope you'll let me continue to see my grandson?'

'Er. . .' Dodie begins, and then she understands. 'Yes,' she says, falsely bright, 'of course.'

'It's been such fun getting to know the wee fellow.'

'I'll bring him to visit,' Dodie says.

'I am sorry about my son, dear; ashamed of him to tell you the truth. And I don't know about this new lassie. He's just, oh I don't know, he's got no sticking power. No sense of responsibility.'

'No.'

'I gave him a piece of my mind, you know. I said, *When are you going to grow up and be a man?*'

'It's OK,' Dodie says, quickly. 'Talk to you again soon.' She cuts off the call.

So. That's that, then. Rod has really left her for someone else. Inside her chest there's a sharp sensation, like the give of the final filament of fraying rope, and then she drops. But she doesn't drop far. After everything she's been through, this doesn't seem that much. She goes to stand with her face to the ocean. The glass is smeared with a blossomy frieze of handprints at Jake's height. The red-stained waves silently heave and flop. Someone is walking a dog in the distance. There's a tree in the sand, a whole tree, washed up as driftwood, silvery in the dusk.

Seth has found the remote and is flicking through the channels on a vast flat-screen TV; each hopping blurt and blare of sound makes Dodie jump. Jake gawps at the screen. 'Let's find a cartoon,' Seth says.

'Rod's left me,' Dodie says, as she turns. She scoops up Jake and holds him, warm and solid in her arms.

'Shit,' Seth says.

'No, it's OK,' she says. 'Honest.'

'Sure?' Rebecca says.

'Yeah?' Seth waits to be reassured by her smile, and goes back to the TV.

Dodie's stomach growls. Her jeans are falling off her wonderfully, there's space between her thighs. She'll have to go shopping for new clothes. Skinny, at last. Will she be able to stay like that? She hitches Jake onto her hip and he snuggles his face against her neck.

'We must eat,' she says.

'Can we send out for pizza?' Seth asks.

'Sounds good.'

'I could handle a drink – like a *drink*, drink.' Rebecca puts the gathered manuscript on a shelf out of Jake's reach.

Dodie wanders round the house, murmuring nonsense to Jake, who submits to her nuzzling his neck and inhaling his smell, giggling at the tickle of her breath. The massive fridge, she finds, is full of cheese and cake, wine and cream and dozens of pots of organic infant food – though Jake's been on normal food for ages. She takes a bottle of wine and carries it through, just as Seth shouts: 'Dodie! Holy shit! Look!'

The screen is filled with Our Father's face. Dodie puts Jake down and sinks onto the sofa to watch a helicopter-eye view of flames and fire-fighters. An excited newscaster, wind flapping her hair, talks into her microphone: 'Tragedy strikes in upstate New York. The religious cult known as the Church of Soul-Life disintegrates after the death of leader Alan Robertson. Many of the followers appear to have entered into a suicide pact. This community has recently been the subject of an IRS crackdown as well as numerous lawsuits from families who claim their kids have been brainwashed into abandoning their families . . .'

Speechlessly they sit and watch. A picture of Obadiah – the financial mastermind, they call him – and then there's Daniel, along with Hannah, being led away by a policewoman. Daniel's head is bowed, but Hannah smiles at the camera, blinks and holds her thumb.

Now the screen is filled with a picture of Martha, taken years ago when her hair was still brown. 'This woman, Martha Woods, also known as Melanie Anna Woods, is wanted by the authorities to be questioned on several counts.'

'Turn it off,' Dodie says.

'What?' Seth is gripped, leaning towards the screen.

'*Please*,' Dodie says.

'But I want to watch.'

'Me too,' Rebecca sloshes wine into glasses.

'I'll be outside then,' Dodie says. She steps out, shuts the door against the news, humming to try and block her own scrambling thoughts. She carries Jake down the wooden steps onto the beach. The darkening sea roars, though it isn't rough. Jake squeals and struggles to be let down. As soon as his feet touch the ground, he's off, sand puffing up behind his feet. Dodie removes her boots and socks, leaves them by the steps and follows Jake, relishing the emptiness of the beach and the cool sensation of shifting sand under her soles, between her toes. And then she catches sight of a woman standing at the edge of the sea. The waves sweep over the woman's feet and run away again, surf hissing. She appears to have seen Dodie, but stands frozen, except for the flapping of her skirt. And then, tentatively, she raises her hand.

Dodie will go and say hello, say what else, she doesn't know. But first she takes a deep lungful of fresh salty air and tips back her head to see, floating high above her in the inky sky, a single star.

Acknowledgements

With thanks for their help to Bill Hamilton, Andrew Greig, Shirley Henderson and all at Tindal Street Press.

About the Author

© Andrew Greig

Lesley Glaister was born in Northamptonshire and grew up in Suffolk, moving to Sheffield where she took a degree with the Open University. She was 'discovered' by the novelist Hilary Mantel when she attended a course given by the Arvon Foundation in 1989. Her first novel *Honour Thy Father* won the Somerset Maugham Award and a Betty Trask Award.

Twelve novels later, Lesley Glaister lives with her husband between Sheffield, Edinburgh and Orkney. She has three sons and teaches Creative Writing at Sheffield Hallam University.